RULERS OF THE CITY

"Mr. Fleming has beautifully portrayed two exemplars of diametrically opposed but all too familiar personality types working toward the same political goal . . . Explosive . . . touches close to the bone of modern society."
—*Parade of Books*

"Frank; no pulled punches; fine entertainment."
—*Publishers Weekly*

"Expert novel by a writer who knows his politics, his sociology, his history, and the people he's selected to dramatize his story."
—*Boston Herald American*

"While Fleming is a first-rate storyteller, his greatest talent is the depth of character portrayal."
—*Huntington Herald-Advertiser*

"The author maintains a furious pace and yet manages to keep one guessing what his true viewpoint is until the touching climax . . . an intellectual exercise in law and morality, with a good story and believable characters."
—*Library Journal*

"Most any American city . . . could use a Thomas Fleming, or at the least, their rulers should read his book."
—John V. Lindsay,
New York Times Book Review

Other Books by Thomas Fleming

A Passionate Girl
Liberty Tavern

Published by
WARNER BOOKS

ATTENTION: SCHOOLS AND CORPORATIONS

WARNER books are available at quantity discounts with bulk purchase for educational, business, or sales promotional use. For information, please write to: SPECIAL SALES DEPARTMENT, WARNER BOOKS, 75 ROCKEFELLER PLAZA, NEW YORK, N.Y. 10019

**ARE THERE WARNER BOOKS
YOU WANT BUT CANNOT FIND IN YOUR LOCAL STORES?**

You can get any WARNER BOOKS title in print. Simply send title and retail price, plus 50¢ per order and 20¢ per copy to cover mailing and handling costs for each book desired. New York State and California residents add applicable sales tax. Enclose check or money order only, no cash please, to: WARNER BOOKS, P.O. BOX 690, NEW YORK, N.Y. 10019

Rulers of the City

Thomas Fleming

WARNER BOOKS

A Warner Communications Company

All of the characters in this book are fictitious,
and any resemblance to actual persons
is purely coincidental.

WARNER BOOKS EDITION

Copyright © 1977 by Thomas Fleming
All rights reserved.

ISBN: 0-446-82612-X

This Warner Books Edition is published by arrangement with
Doubleday & Company, Inc.
245 Park Avenue, New York, NY 10017.

Cover design by Gene Light

Cover art by Elaine Duillo

Warner Books, Inc., 75 Rockefeller Plaza, New York, N.Y. 10019

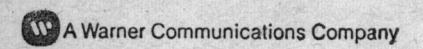

A Warner Communications Company

First Printing: April, 1980

10 9 8 7 6 5 4 3 2 1

William Carlos Williams, *Paterson.* Copyright 1949 by
William Carlos Williams. Reprinted by permission of
New Directions Publishing Corporation.

From "Looking into History" in *Things of This World,* ©
1956 by Richard Wilbur. Reprinted by permission of
Harcourt Brace Jovanovich, Inc.

For Malcolm Reiss

What manner of man the ruler of the city is, such also are they that dwell therein.

                     Ecclesiasticus

The dead give no command
And shall not find their voice
Till they be mustered by
Some present fatal choice.

      Richard Wilbur
      Looking into History

What end but love, that stares death in the eye?
A city, a marriage—that stares death
in the eye

            William Carlos Williams
            Paterson

Rulers of the City

1

The bright beating bell of a distant ambulance penetrated the murmurous silence of Paula Stapleton O'Connor's bedroom. She sat up with a violent start and swung her legs off the bed. Was it time to dress for dinner? She was shocked by how easily the hot air registers had lured her into the past. First into those briefly happy childhood days when those lugubrious sighs had been the sea, and the house was a great ship under sail, carrying her across an immense ocean to a land where everyone smiled and Santa Claus was President. Older, at ten or twelve, the sound had become the house breathing. Bowood was a monster complacently digesting another generation of Stapletons. The dead of other decades prowled the halls, wondering in bewildered unvoices where their lives had gone. Grief was noiseless here. It was devoured by the Aubusson rugs, the Chippendale double chests with their multiple brass mouths, the accusing faces of the ancestral portraits on the walls.

Terror. Adolescent terror, wished away, willed away by years of adult effort, by words like maturity, sobriety. Now she was those words. She was those ruinous admirable words. Why was she trembling at an ambulance bell? Such a common city sound. She had heard it a thousand times. It echoed down her nerves every time she looked up at the Medical Center, a cluster of white towers on the city's dominant hill.

As a mature woman, she had long since accepted the city's pain. It was far more inescapable than the smog that pervaded the air, the ugliness that oozed from the downtown blocks of decaying tenements. Smog could be eliminated by air conditioners, dehumidifiers, electrostatic purifiers, ugliness could be eluded by the classic grace of Bowood's curving walnut balustrade, by dishes of exquisite Meissen blue, by the scrolled shells and capricious curves of trays and bowls and braziers made by the great silversmiths of the eighteenth century, by handpainted wallpaper alive with rococo designs or Chinese scenes, by the library's glistening rows of leather-bound gold-titled books. But none of these possessions eliminated the city's pain, or made it more bearable. If anything, they sharpened the intensity with which the pain probed her nerves and spirit. With the pain came sadness, a sense of the city as a huge unmanageable invalid which not even the most charismatic physician could heal.

Paula drew the purple drapes on the two tall rectangular front windows of her bedroom-sitting room. A gray January twilight confronted her. The old oaks on both sides of Bowood's crescent drive raised their stripped limbs like prisoners begging mercy from a heartless judge. At the gate a burly black policeman stood outside his sentry box, stamping his feet and beating his arms against his sides. Like a horse, Paula thought. For an uneasy moment she wondered whether she would have made the same comparison if the policeman were white. Probably. There was something horselike about policemen, the way they stood for empty hours staring dully. But beneath the stolid endurance of boredom there was dangerous strength.

Out on the Parkway cars whipped past in the gloom. A black limousine slowed abruptly and swung to a stop beside the sentry box. Between the glaring headlights Paula could see the familiar license place: CITY-1. As if on cue, the streetlights came on, casting a frosty glow on the car's black metal skin. The policeman raised his arm in a half-wave, half-salute, and pressed a button inside the door of his sentry box. The gold-tipped wrought-iron gate at the apex of the drive swung open. In her mind Paula heard the big car crunching the gray gravel beneath its whitewalled tires. Why did the sound mean power, pride? The mystery of associations.

The limousine stopped in front of the door and Jake got out. He was hatless, as usual. His brown hair, which he wore in shaggy contemporary style, rippled in the wind as he turned to speak to someone still in the back seat. He was about to say something witty. Paula felt warmth stir deep in her body. For a moment she was inside the car, the recipient of His Honor's joke. She was smiling up at him, testifying love, anticipating delight.

A face appeared in the door of the car. It had the frantic eyes and desperately grinning mouth of a fifth-rate comedian. Eddie McKenna, chairman of the city's Democratic Party. Why did her husband spend so much time with this man? She understood the necessity of having someone like him, an easily controlled nonentity, to handle the petty details, the greedy little conflicts of local politics. But most of these trivial quarrels could be settled on the telephone. She saw no reason why the Mayor had to pretend to enjoy the company of this boring spokesman for politics as usual. It was bad enough that he was coming to the dinner tonight. She must double-check to make sure he was seated as far away from her as possible. Paula stalked away from the window to add this item to a list of directives and reminders for her scatterbrained Irish butler.

From the hall, faint shrieks and shouts penetrated her bedroom's walnut double doors. The children were running to greet their father. Paula started to join them. But she withdrew her hand from the filigreed bronze handle, and waited behind the closed door like one of those ghosts she had once imagined lurking everywhere in Bowood. Would she get a greeting without running childishly to give one? The Mayor's striding steps passed her door and vanished with a slam. His Honor was not in a wife-greeting mood. Just as well, Paula decided. His wife was not in a husband-greeting mood.

The twilight had deepened to a charcoal gray. Paula closed the draperies and began to dress for dinner. It was a very important dinner. It might be the most important dinner of the year 1976. Why did that make her think about Mother? Paula wondered. She reached deftly over her shoulder and zipped up the back of her dark blue velvet hostess gown. Forty years ago in this same room her mother would have had two, perhaps three maids helping her dress. Her daughter was contented— no—she preferred to dress herself.

Much more than forty years separated her and Mother. There was an historical chasm between them now. Paula had made a choice that enabled her to cross the chasm, like an explorer on one of those rickety bamboo bridges out of the pages of the *National Geographic*. She could still see those symbolic heroes of her youth in their pith helmets and tropical shorts, surrounded by barebreasted Filipinos or Nepalese in casual loincloths, all grinning into the camera while the chasm yawned beneath their feet. What had Jake called it? *Wasp pornography,* looking up at the decades of bound volumes on the shelves of Bowood's library. She had laughed. It had been easy to laugh about their different pasts in those days.

Reaching for her perfume, Paula's fingers strayed against the small plastic cylinder of tranquilizers on her William and Mary dressing table. The cylinder spun drunkenly into the hand-carved teak jewelry box and bounced onto the rug. Off popped the top and the tiny red pills scattered across the yellow sails of a Persian ship. With an exasperated sigh she knelt and put them back into the bottle one by one, wishing again that her doctor had never prescribed them. He had been so casual, murmuring that he wasn't surprised . . . occasional attacks of nerves—highly strung people . . . at a time like this. Paula had accepted the pills and resisted taking them. In the two weeks that the cylinder had stood like a warning signal on her dressing table she had used only four—when she awoke in the middle of the night and found sleep eluding her. Did she resist their chemical calm because they reminded her of Mother's "nerve medicine"? She had crossed the chasm without that kind of help. She did not need it now. The snap of the plastic cap as she replaced it was an exclamation point.

But it did not prevent a swift, sad montage of scenes from the past. Thin, homely little Paula knocking on the always closed bedroom door, hearing Mother's querulous "Who is it?" latent with hysteria. The silent dinners, Father glowering at his end of the table, Mother dropping spoons and knives, knocking over her water glass, leaping up at last to flee the room and escape her husband's accusing eyes. A fragment of a conversation overheard—Mother crying out, "When I think of the life we could have had!" Father's reply, choked, furious. "The real world—the real world is where a man has to live—" Mother's last days, doctors and nurses coming and going in and out the door of this bedroom. The closed bronze coffin with its single wreath of yellow roses in the ballroom downstairs.

College had been Paula's salvation. For the first time she found a place where she could criticize Father's futile clinging to past glory, lost power. For the first time she found an alternative to breeding horses or collecting Early American silver or fighting the bulldozers to preserve Greek Revival mansions. But this alternative had been complicated, its value intensified by the deep thrust of emotion Paula had felt in response to those passionate words, *the real world.* She would learn from her father's defeats, she had told herself with a dangerous combination of Stapleton pride and wounded longing. She would master the real world. That was part—a very small part, Paula hastily assured herself—of the reason she was here in Bowood, dressing to stand beside her husband and greet the very important people who were coming to dinner.

It was easy to embrace that image of marital partnership. But it failed to suppress that other voice, which seemed to whisper mockingly from the walls of the room, Mother's cry of despair—*When I think of the life we could have had—*

Paula sat down in a Chippendale wing chair with a country landscape in two-hundred-year-old needlework on its back. From a mahogany tilt-top table inlaid with delft tiles she picked up a remote-control switch and turned on the television set. A small Sony sat on a japanned lowboy from Boston, circa 1734. Beside it a pendulum clock in an elaborately carved walnut case told her it was 6 P.M. It was time for a half-hour summary of what had made January 15, 1976, memorable.

First came the usual collection of bad news from around the world. The British pound was still tottering. There were rumors of revolution in Spain and Italy; Israel and Syria were eyeing each other ominously; the Philippine civil war continued to grow. The came a swatch of non-news from Washington about the economy, the jockeying of Democratic candidates for the presidency, and other forms of political infighting endemic to the nation's capital. Finally came the local news. The spaniel-faced announcer faded from the screen to be replaced by the new City Hall. With its cantilevered roof, its soaring aluminum tower, its four-story-high glass walls surrounding the inner courtyard, it was a symbol of the city's will to change. Paula was proud of it. She had helped to build it. She had found the architect. She had defended his conception against know-nothings from the city's North and South slopes and against patronizing academics from the state university.

The camera cut from City Hall's gleaming facade to a human face. It belonged to Tony Perotta, head of the Italian American Alliance. A squashed nose flared between two inflated cheeks. A thick upper lip was curled in clownish rage. To Paula, it was a loathsome face. There was no clean line where bone met flesh, no architecture. Only the accidental shape of the potato or turnip. The camera froze it on the screen while the announcer's bland voice informed the viewers that tension between pro- and anti-busing forces was mounting as the city prepared to implement a federal court order to desegregate its schools.

"Anti-busing spokesmen bitterly criticized Mayor O'Connor for persuading the Board of Education to abandon plans to appeal the court order. They claim appeals would have given the city another two years of racial and ethnic peace."

Tony Perotta began talking into a hand-held microphone while behind him a chorus of voices screamed "NEVER." "Duh Mayuh don't represent duh people in dis city no more. He's turned intuh uh paid clerk uh duh rich, uh errand boy for his wife and huh sports-car liberal friends and relatives out dere in duh suburbs. Dey try tuh bus one Italian kid offa duh South Slope uh dis city, an blood is gonna run in duh streets. An he kun f'get all about bein' a senatuh."

"Similar sentiments were expressed by Mrs. Kitty Kosciusko, head of the newly formed multi-ethnic coalition, RIP, which stands for Restore Independence to the People."

Kitty Kosciusko was a six-foot-one earth mother who wore a babushka out of the previous century and one of her husband's cast-off checked mackinaws. She leaned toward the mircrophone as if she was going to take a bite out of it. "We are gonna RIP the Mayor to shreds politically and literally, if that is what it takes to make him realize that this here is the United States of America, where a majority rules."

Behind them, members of RIP unleashed a football cheer. "LETTERRRRRRRRR RIP."

The cameras panned across the plaza to the black protestors who were singing "We Shall Overcome." Paula's eyes misted. A fat, big-busted black woman wearing a shiny broad-brimmed hat began explaining why she was there. "Before they was so many Negro people in this city, my boys went to school with white boys and they turned out to be good students. One a them's a deteckive on the po-lice force, the other's a teachuh. They both good boys."

Next came City Councilman Adam Turner. Well over six feet, he added several inches with a magnificent Afro. His narrow, bony face, particularly the wide vivid mouth, had a remarkable ability to project emotion. "Once and for all the white people of this city have got to understand that the plantation system is dead. You can't keep the blacks down in the slave quarters no longer. Our children are gonna grow up free. After four hundred years they gonna be free—"

The camera abandoned Adam in mid-sentence.

"There was a scuffle between members of the city's tactical patrol and protestors from the Malcolm X Ujamaa," the announcer said.

A half dozen brawny tactical cops wearing white helmets and plexiglass vizors stood over the prostrate body of a black wearing a striped robe. They picked him up and hustled him to a nearby patrol car. Paula felt nausea mingle with anger in her body. Lately she had had a half dozen tense arguments with her husband about the club-swinging proclivities of the tactical patrol. He had stubbornly refused to talk to his police commissioner about it.

"Inside City Hall, Mayor O'Connor emerged from an afternoon-long conference with Kevin McGuire, the president of the Board of Education, to announce a one-week postponement of the busing program. He said there was no intention of attempting to evade the federal court order. The city needed the extra time to guarantee the safety of the children."

The cameras wafted a half million viewers inside City Hall. The Mayor sat behind his desk. It was not his real desk, but an exact replica in the fully equipped television newsroom which Paula Stapleton O'Connor had donated to City Hall when the City Council had declined to spend the taxpayers' money to improve Mayor O'Connor's image. The inadequate lights which the TV newsmen used when interviewing him in the old City Hall had distorted his craggy face. At times his forehead had acquired a truculent, Neanderthal cast. At other times he had looked weak. Shadows had accumulated beneath his eyes, his mouth seemed slack. Now the strong chin, the attractive bone structure of the high, typically squared Irish cheeks were defined. The real man—or as much of the real man as a camera could show—was there.

"I am convinced that ninety-nine per cent of the people in this city will obey the law. The members of the Board of Education will obey the law. I will obey the law. Judge Stapleton has been patient. I trust he will be patient for another week so that no child will be in danger, no child will miss even a day of school because his transfer has not been completely processed. As I have said more than once, I am not a believer in forced busing. But I am a believer in law and order. I care about every child in this city, black and white."

At first, Paula was not sure which of these sentences made her more uneasy. Was it the knowledge that the words about the reason for a week's delay were a lie? The buses were ready to roll. The children were all transferred. The police were ready with a half dozen contingency plans. The real purpose of the delay was to make one last attempt to persuade Judge Paul Stapleton to back down. Those words, *I am not a believer in forced busing,* were also a lie, carefully programmed to conform to the findings of pollsters who had been probing the voters of the state for the last three months. This was what Mayor O'Connor had to say, if he hoped to reach the U. S. Senate.

For a moment Paula wished she was part of the faceless multitude sitting patiently before this magic box like true believers in a vast cathedral. But she had eaten of the tree of the knowledge of good and evil. She had become one of those who understand the necessities of power. It was too late for simple faith.

If he did not win this bid for the Senate, it might also be too late for Mayor O'Connor. Fourteen years was a long time to hold one political job. The Mayor was no longer a promising young man. Only his physical vitality, his aura of energy saved him from becoming an old pol. Before the bicentennial year was over he would celebrate his fiftieth birthday. America in its perpetual fascination with youth had very little sympathy for the middle-aged.

Paula recoiled from these painful thoughts. It may have been too late for simple faith. But it was not too late for deeper, more personal faith. It was unthinkable that the man to whom she had pledged her love and her faith, might fail. The political turmoil of the preceding decade had denied him the recognition—and higher office—he deserved. But now his time had come. He would master this crisis and reap his just reward at last.

The reporters began asking questions.

"Does this delay mean you expect serious trouble, Your Honor?"

The Mayor shook his head. "It means we're determined to avoid it."

"If we have violence on Boston's scale, how do you think it will affect your chances for the Senate?"

The Mayor frowned. Indignation suffused his face. "How many times do I have to answer that question? I'm not running for the Senate. Even if I had the party's nomination, I would not let the consideration of any higher office influence my performance of this job."

Another lie? Paula wondered. No, only an expert half truth, the kind of statement that politicians are forced to make. It was necessary to mask ambition, lest it arouse the latent envy of those faceless judges, the voters. Or worse, gave the Tony Perottas a target at which to spew their hate. Astride the half truth, Paula asked herself which way her wishes faced. Did she want those last brave words about influence to be true or false? She did not know. Only in recent months had she realized how desperately she wanted her husband to escape this city, how much she wanted to escape it.

Downstairs in City Hall's inner courtyard, television newsmen began interviewing other politicians. First came Democratic City Chairman Eddie McKenna. Giving him precedence was annoying enough. He proceeded to preen himself before the camera, and talk in a solemn, statesmanlike tone. "I'm only a spokesman for the rank and file of the Democratic Party in this city. But I share their opinion that forced busing is a violation of the constitutional rights of parents and children. Nobody voted for this thing. It's being imposed by an arrogant federal judiciary and a coalition of smug suburban and university liberals. The black kids in this city don't need it. They're gettin' good educations in their own neighborhood schools. The Mayor won't say this because he's tryin' to be fair to everyone in this mess. I feel sorry for him. I just hope the black citizens of this city realize even sympathetic whites can be pushed only so far."

Paula was breathless with rage. For fifty years McKenna's kind had ravaged the city morally and financially. Why didn't he slink in shame? Or at least cringe enough to disqualify himself as a spokesman? Was he convinced that when it came to a crunch the solidarity of his own kind would mean more to the Mayor than words like trust and care? Never, never, Paula told herself fiercely, as the television interviewers asked Dominick Montefiore, the president of the City Council, for his opinion and he denounced busing in his dignified, vaguely clerical way.

Paula tried to see past these little men to her memories of the Mayor at his best. She told herself that the man who spoke to her and the rest of the city was the same man she had admired from the moment she had seen him at a political rally eighteen years ago, projecting the same combination of energy and purpose, realism and idealism. O'CONNOR—THE MAN WHO CAN GET THE RIGHT THINGS DONE. That had been the slogan of the first campaign. Paula had believed it, with a fervor that burned deep into her nerves and flesh. She had backed her belief with twenty million Stapleton dollars and all the power of hidden and not so hidden persuasion possessed by the Stapleton name.

The telephone rang. Paula turned off the television's sound. Terence Mahoney, Bowood's butler, informed Mrs. O'Connor in his picturesque brogue that there was a man calling with a message from Ray Grimes, the head of Community Projects, Inc., the city's anti-poverty agency. Paula told him to transfer the call to her private line.

"Mrs. O'Connor?" said a sepulchral voice. Paula recognized it immediately. She pressed the receiver against her ear to stop her hand's trembling. "Mrs. O'Connor? It's your friend. I wanted you to know that we've taken a vote. It was unanimous. The Mayor is condemned to die. If you continue to support him with your dirty money, you will also be condemned."

Paula pressed a button on the table beside the telephone. It activated a tape recorder in the basement. Forcing calm into her voice, she began a conversation which might give the police a better chance to identify this man, who had already called four or five times.

"You don't sound like my husband's enemy. The way you talk about him—you sound like an old friend."

"I am."

"Why do you want to kill him?"

"Because he's become a stench—a moral stench—in the city's nostrils. We are not going to let him escape the judgment of this city to spend the rest of his days in the sanctimonious sanctuary of the U. S. Senate."

Paula slammed down the receiver. The television cameras had returned to the Mayor's office. With the sound off, he sat behind his desk, mouthing voiceless words. It was worse than a parody. It was closer to a nightmare. Did she really know what this man believed as he sat there effortlessly lying to the people? Was that Celtic curve of the upper lip subtly mocking her? Once she had been certain that he believed what she believed about everything that was important to her. Now? With a gasp of anguish, Paula turned off the set. As the image of her husband faded, she spoke to him and to that sepulchral voice on the telephone.

"It's not true. It's not true."

2

In his bedroom, Mayor O'Connor was sitting in another Chippendale wing chair covered with brilliant flowers in historic needlepoint. A scotch and soda fizzed on the piecrust walnut tea table beside him. From a contoured black box beside his bed, a murky voice ordered a police car to investigate a disturbance in the First Ward. In his left hand the Mayor held a small book, bound in an old-fashioned piebald leather cover. In his right hand he held a magnifying glass which enabled him to decipher the tiny handwritten words on the faded paper.

There are two distinct ways to serve as mayor of a modern city. The first—at a glance the most tempting—is to place one's self at the very center of your city's life, with dramatic words and gestures. To hold out to the multitudes the hope that you possess almost magical powers. Suffice to say that most heroes, in both myth and reality, die violent deaths. We are simply men, after all. Finite creatures with finite minds, often fearfully finite. Unless the hero acquires an army of fellow heroes, all equally brilliant, fearless, and uncorruptible, the heroic approach to governing a modern city (or for that matter a modern state or nation) is doomed. The heroic style excites hopes and aspirations that cannot be satisfied. We live in a mass society, where there must needs be millions of small, a few dozen thousand mediums, and a handful of large. This situation virtually guarantees that the end product of the heroic style will be rage, frustration, and the destruction, politically—sometimes literally—of the hero.

The second style makes no claim to ameliorate every misery, resolve every grief, right every wrong in the city. Instead it seeks to instill confidence in the social engine, so that these inevitable pangs will be borne as the price of progress. This is the philosophy of the modern industrialist. He tells us that we are the children of a new age. The steel mill has no precedent, the locomotive is without ancestry, the telegraph centers on no heritage. We must bow to these new gods and temporarily endure the pain they inflict on us, to create a golden future for our children's children. Personally I am a skeptic about this future. I even have a sneaking sympathy for those romantics who wail so eloquently over an irrecoverable past. But the facts are against them. So I have adopted the businessman's style to run this city. It has worked tolerably well thus far to keep the forces of chaos—I mean the Irish and our other foreign effluvia—in check. It grieves me that this has become the primary task of the Mayor of an American city in this year of our Lord, 1870. But the Irish with their absurd pretentions and all too visible greed give us no alternative.

The Mayor paused to rest his eyes. The police dispatcher's voice suddenly acquired an urgent tone. "TEN THIRTEEN TEN THIRTEEN CORNER KEMBLE AND TALBOT STREETS. TEN THIRTEEN." Ten thirteen meant a policeman in trouble, menaced by a gang of teen-agers or a pair of stickup men. Kemble and Talbot streets were in the center of the Congo, as the cops called the black ghetto. Most 1013s happened there. They might be happening all over the city next week.

Mayor O'Connor put the journal aside for a swallow of scotch and soda. The self-confidence of this long dead Mayor was unnerving. It bristled at him from each precisely written word. Mayor O'Connor had never been an avid reader of history or biography. Like most Americans of his generation, he had identified culture with literature and had acquired a respectable knowledge of English, Irish, and American poetry and fiction. His historical information consisted of a few scattered dates and a very general picture of what had happened in the United States and Europe over the past two hundred years.

The Mayor looked around his bedroom. No sign of chaos here, in spite of the presence of foreign effluvia. The mahogany Chippendale bookcase, the rosewood Philadelphia highboy exuded the serenity of old money, old authority. The Mayor admired the chaste lines, the rich wood of these antiques. Almost in spite of himself he had become moderately well informed about New York chest-on-chests and Newport roundabout chairs.

On the paneled wall behind Mayor O'Connor were a half dozen framed photographs that would have caused the author of the journal he was reading to goggle with disbelief. One was a picture of the Mayor's father, Ben O'Connor, a stocky, strong-jawed man, standing in a hall surrounded by hundreds of paper bags—Christmas baskets distributed annually by the previous generation of city fathers to the poor. In a nearby frame, a bigger, more arrogant-looking man with a fur collar on his expensive overcoat was in the process of throwing out the first ball on opening day. Ben O'Connor stood beside him looking strangely pensive. There was a picture of Ben O'Connor in a World War I lieutenant's uniform with a high tight collar and a wide Sam Browne belt. In a news photo Ben stood on a shaky-looking street corner platform making a speech to the citizens of the Thirteenth Ward. Another crowded picture caught Ben leading 4,000 voters of the Thirteenth Ward into Bayshore Park for their annual picnic. Finally, there was a picture of the tall baseball thrower leading the St. Patrick's Day parade. Ben O'Connor and several other dignitaries were in the rank behind him, with broad bands of green ribbon across their chests. The Mayor called this gallery his Irish Corner.

"Jake."

The Mayor greeted his wife with a smile as she paused in the doorway. His eyes went to her dark brown hair, which she was wearing in a Grecian style, with small hanging curls on either side of her narrow face. It was amazing how different this woman could look, depending on her hair style, her dress, and above all, her mood.

"I like the hair," he said. "It's regal."

A frown, followed by an almost imperceptible shake of the head. She was not interested in compliments. She simply could not believe that she was no longer plain Paula Stapleton, that she had become a formidably attractive woman. Not beautiful, but striking, with those wide gray eyes above the high delicate cheekbones, the mobile, sensitive mouth that communicated her mood so infallibly.

"He—he just called again."

"Who?"

"The man who threatened to kill you."

"What did he say?"

"It doesn't matter. He sounded . . . dangerous."

"Did you tape him?"

"Yes."

"Maybe I can recognize his voice."

"How can you be—so calm about it?"

"Come on, come on," he said. "Haven't I given you a lecture on the Irish approach to this sort of thing? Fatalism. It's the only philosophy."

"It didn't work for the Kennedys."

"Who says it's going to work? If it happens, that's the time to cry."

"You'd better get dressed," Paula said. "They're starting to arrive downstairs."

"Okay, sweethaht, atcha service."

Throwing aside his dressing gown, the Mayor stood for a moment in his undershirt and pants. "On second thought maybe I'll make thuh scene informal like."

He snapped his suspenders at her. Paula frowned. She used to be amused when her husband played lowbrow, adopting the standard accent of the North Slope bars. Now the Mayor suspected that she was not sure when he was kidding.

"The Institute's business office called today. They said you forgot to pay your brother's bill again."

"Goddamn it," the Mayor said.

It was the second or third time in the last year that he had missed this monthly payment. A good index of how little enthusiasm he had for paying it. Each month he was supposed to write a check for $3,500 to the Brompton Institute to pay the nurses and psychiatrists who were theoretically curing his brother Paul. That was $500 more than the city paid Mayor O'Connor each month. The Mayor was not particularly fond of his brother, a dropout priest who had wandered around the city for several years embarrassing him by preaching radical sermons on street corners. He had been inclined to put him in a state mental hospital. But Paula had insisted they could afford Brompton, the best private psychiatric hospital in the state. It never occurred to her that the Mayor disliked seeing his entire salary committed to this apparently endless act of brotherly love, leaving him dependent on his wife's income. Money as an emotional reality barely existed for her. They had a joint checking account in which her money and his money supposedly blended.

"I wrote out the check. All you have to do is sign it."

"Maybe we ought to offer them a lump sum for a lifetime commitment."

She shook her head. "He's getting better. I have faith in Dr. Kane."

The Mayor grunted skeptically. He had no faith in Dr. Kane or anything else, these days. He even suspected that Paul knew exactly how much he was annoying his brother by sitting it out in the Brompton Institute at $3,500 a month. What better way to remind old Jake each month that when it came to paying for something really expensive, he was a middle-class schnook and a rich wife was a necessity.

Paula fingered the leather cover of the book on the tea table. "What's this you're reading?"

"The memoirs of your great-granduncle, Mayor Mortimer Kemble."

"That old scoundrel? Where did you find them? I don't remember them being listed in the family archives."

"Our new city historian found them in the basement of the library. Mortimer doesn't think much of the Irish. He calls them foreign effluvia."

Paula's nod was clearly an emphatic agreement. "But he sold his soul to them. He turned Democrat to get elected."

"Hey. Careful what you say about Democrats. Sometimes I think you're still a Republican at heart."

"I was a Democrat ten years before I married you."

"I was one for thirty-six years."

"Pooh. To be converted is better than being born into something. It means you gave it some thought. But old Mortimer wasn't converted. At least from what I know about him. He was just ambitious. I never heard the family speak of him with anything but contempt. As far as they're concerned, he was a pariah. He sold his soul."

The Mayor listened to this pronouncement and felt tension stiffening his lips. His wife simply had no idea how arrogant she could sound. He had just been informed: (A) That he was an inferior Democrat; (B) That he was wasting his time reading Mortimer Kemble's journal; (C) The family—that collection of snobs who shared the Stapleton name and money—had placed its stamp of approval on this judgment; (D) In those declaratory words, *he sold his soul*, the Mayor heard the implication that Jake O'Connor might do the same thing.

"I'll let you know what I think after I read his journal," he said.

"I watched WPLO," Paula said. "They had about fifteen minutes of coverage downtown."

"How did they play it?"

"It was the lead story."

"Did they give Adam Turner his usual five minutes?"

"No. He was interrupted by the tactical patrol beating up one of the demonstrators."

"Black?"

"Of course."

The Mayor heard the uneasiness in his voice and wished it was not there. He did not want another argument about the tactical patrol. "I'll find out exactly what happened," he said.

"I still feel it was a mistake—this delay."

"That's what your Uncle Paul thinks too. I hear he's ready to find me in contempt of court."

"He's not my uncle—when he's sitting on that bench. He's a federal judge who's taken an oath—"

"I know, I know. I just get the feeling he enjoys making life difficult for me."

"He's not the sort of man who appreciates—political maneuvers," Paula said.

Her hesitation before the word political made him angry.

"I had a feeling I'd regret it the day I backed him for the nomination."

"Why? He was certainly the most qualified man for the job." A pause, and she went to the heart of what he was implying. "In Boston, the judge's name is Garrity. He's been just as tough."

"Maybe that's the answer. Uncle Paul couldn't let a Mick outdo him."

He smiled up at her, hoping it looked spontaneous. Her response was a wan flicker of the lips. It was not a good omen. The Mayor picked up the telephone and called the kitchen. "Send up another scotch and soda," he said.

The frown on Paula's forehead said everything. There was no need for a temperance lecture.

"I'll wait for you in my room," she said.

"Okay. I want to watch WTGM."

The Mayor was knotting his tie when a conspiratorial knock summoned him to the bedroom door. Terence Mahoney's morose face confronted him above the fizzing glass on the silver tray.

"How's the guest list shaping up?"

Mahoney wrinkled his snub nose. "The niggers are here."

"Mahoney," said the Mayor, taking his drink. "You're a prejudiced son of a bitch."

"And who isn't?"

The Mayor took a long swallow. It always tasted best when the soda was first mixed—before the ice started to melt. He loved the bite of the scotch in his throat. "How's the IRA doing, Mahoney?"

"They machine-gunned a Prod bus last week. Killed ten of the orange bastards."

"How much money have you sent them so far?"

"A good thousand, Your Honor."

"What would you do about the IRA if you were Mayor of Belfast, Mahoney?"

"Sure I couldn't be, Your Honor. I'm Catholic."

"I know what I'd do," the Mayor said.

"What, Your Honor?"

"Put you in jail."

"Ahh, Your Honor's always jokin'."

Mahoney departed, his prejudices intact. Paula had hired him. Three years ago, she had developed a phobia against blacks doing "menial" jobs. The Mayor had told her she was silly. But Paula had been adamant. They suffered through a series of white cooks and butlers, ranging from a Swede who drank a quart of gin a day to a Slav who was clearly insane and cursed to herself while she stirred their soup. About eight months ago, Paula had discovered Mahoney and his wife Hannah, who was a very good cook. They were only in the country a year. The Mayor had remarked that it was a good thing he was not sensitive about the Irish doing menial jobs. Paula had frowned and hired them anyway.

The Mayor sipped his drink and decided to redo his tie. This fondness for getting ahead of the party with a few preliminary belts invariably created a frown on his wife's forehead. Should he give it up? he asked himself in the mirror. What was the point? Almost everything he said or did these days created frowns on Mrs. Stapleton-O'Connor's aristocratic brow.

The Mayor glanced at the porcelain-encased Directoire clock above the fireplace. Six-thirty, time for the local TV news on station WTGM. He switched on the round twenty-first-century television set dangling from the ceiling at the foot of his four-poster bed. An earnest young man with the face of a clothing store dummy told the listening millions that there was only one way to be sure that their cars would start tomorrow morning—by using the motor oil that he was selling. Then came a housewife who orgiastically caressed a box of cleanser, and described how it had changed her life by eliminating grease from her sink. The Mayor watched, wondering if anyone else noticed that people on black-and-white television had mouths without tongues or gums. There was nothing behind all those smiling teeth. They were robots, artifacts.

Anchor man Jack Murphy, with his wispy mustache and vaguely wounded manner, began talking about the cold wave that was gripping the city. For thirty days the temperature had not risen above ten degrees. WTGM was the city's conservative television station. Instead of playing the busing crisis as number one, they were trying to get their viewers involved with other worries. They were not admirers of Mayor O'Connor and his administration. Murphy dolefully reported the shocking number of tenant complaints about lack of heat, the destruction of another family by fumes from a faulty gas heater, the record number of fires fought by the fire department in the course of the day, in which ten firemen and a dozen tenants were injured. The understrength fire department—Mayor O'Connor had slashed their budget by 10 per cent—was one of WTGM's running feuds with City Hall.

The camera glanced briefly at the new City Hall's facade. In the dull black and white of the electronic eye, the glass walls of the first four floors were invisible and the building seemed to gawk on its spindly outer columns like something made from an Erector Set. Excelsior! cried the soaring aluminum tower to a city that did not know the meaning of the word. Once the Mayor had gazed on that tower with pride. He had defended the radical architecture with passion. Now he found himself preferring the old City Hall, with its decaying green copper dome above the two stubby soot-encrusted wings. *Ugly but real,* he thought. *Ugly but real.*

"Meanwhile, pro- and anti-busing factions demonstrated downtown," announcer Murphy's voice-over said.

The station's interviewers concentrated on moderate whites. Tony Perotta and Kitty Kosciusko were allowed only thirty seconds of grammatical incoherence. City Council President Dominick Montefiore, looking and sounding more than ever like Pius XII, pursued circumlocutions about the rights of all the people, the safety of the city's children and the sanctity of the neighborhood school. Bony Esther Kilpatrick, member of the Board of Education and a staunch Catholic with all her children in parochial schools, insisted that racism had nothing to do with her opposition to busing. It was the cost that appalled her. Twenty million dollars. Think of how many new schools we could build with that money! Esther's family owned a contracting company. Beefy Kevin McGuire, president of the Board of Education, who had run against the Mayor as an antibusing candidate in 1975, wondered how a politician who did not represent a majority of the voters could be effective. McGuire had turned the mayorality election into a three-way race which Jake O'Connor had won with a limping 44 per cent of the vote.

"Up yours with a split ticket," the Mayor muttered.

Next came Councilman Adam Turner. The Mayor felt visceral dislike run through his body like a jolt of some powerful drug. The son of a bitch stood there in a camel's hair coat backed by a hallelujah chorus from the welfare rolls calling the city a plantation. Turner's Afro made him look like something out of a Tarzan movie. Did he think he was going to change any minds on the North or South slopes? The Mayor felt savage pleasure when Turner's harangue was interrupted to cover the scuffle between the tactical patrol and the black demonstrators.

Party Chairman Eddie McKenna repeated almost word for word the statement he had rehearsed with the Mayor before leaving City Hall. Good old Eddie, the Mayor thought, remembering the skinny hustling hero-worshipping manager of the football and basketball teams, always hungry for a pat on the back from Jake O'Connor. Eddie believed every word of what he was saying. But if Jake O'Connor had told him to say the exact opposite, to go down there and say black is beautiful and kiss Adam Turner's thick lips, Eddie would have done that too. Eddie was loyal.

Jack Murphy began reporting Mayor O'Connor's decision to delay busing for a week.

"The Mayor conferred with spokesmen from the protesting groups. After the demonstrators dispersed, he issued the following statement."

Mayor O'Connor saw a twelve-inch version of himself staring at him. His right hand reached out for a moment and toyed with the tip of a fountain pen, one of a group standing erect in metal holders on the front of his desk. All the pens had another name engraved in gold on their marble bases: *Benjamin F. O'Connor*. It was invisible to the average viewer, but the Mayor knew the name was there, knew the pens had belonged to his father, one of the many mementos he had received during his forty years in politics. It had been the fashion in the old days to send gifts to newly elected officials, and what was more practical, more visible, than a desk set? Now on election day, the Mayor thought ruefully, they sent you death threats.

No jokes. A year ago, he would have taken a modest pride in this semi-witticism. But now the Mayor admonished himself for the twenty-ninth or thirtieth time that week: *No jokes. It's too important.* For some time the Mayor had been watching himself on television with mounting anxiety. In the easy years of his first term he had seldom bothered to look at all. Only when Paula had begun to criticize his TV image, and hired voice and drama coaches to improve his performance, had he started watching himself. Even then it had been a purely technical interest, a desire to check his timing, to make sure he was obeying the injunction to speak at half his normal pace, to examine certain gestures to see if they were convincing.

Now the Mayor watched for symptoms of betrayal. Was there a hint of a tremor in the twelve-inch mayor's reassuring voice, a flicker of panic distorting those confident blue eyes, any sign that revealed his inner uncertainty? Fourteen years in City Hall, fourteen years that included the collapse of the New Frontier and the Great Society, the failure of Washington's wars against North Vietnam and Poverty, Stagflation and Watergate, fourteen years climaxed by this ultimate upheaval over forced busing, had profoundly, invisibly changed the Mayor.

Gone was the decisive energetic optimist he had tried to project—and believe in—during his first two terms. Now he saw that figure as part fool and part the product of his wife's wish. Faith in the people, envisioning a bright future did not come naturally to him. When the chaos of the sixties sent alienation racing like a virus through the electorate, he had instinctively withdrawn from the madness and insisted that Vietnam, student riots, black power, had nothing to do with running a city. If they disturbed the peace, or threatened the safety of his streets, he dealt with them. But he refused to get involved with them as political issues. This made him an instant outsider in the state's Democratic Party, where young activists from the universities and suburbs seized control. Now, after a series of disastrous defeats, the pros, his people, were back in charge. But it was late, very late, for the Mayor to become a bright new face. Instead, he was an "urban statesman," according to the flacks his wife had hired to beat the media drums for his Senate campaign. Worst of all, Paula believed it. Embroiled in making him into a national figure, she did not even seem to notice her husband's lurching loss of inner direction.

So Mayor O'Connor studied the twelve-inch mayor on the curving screen while he tensely assured the voters that he was acting to guarantee the safety of the city's children and remained thoroughly dedicated to obeying the law. The interviewer asked him if there was any chance of modifying Judge Stapleton's plan? The twelve-inch mayor shook his head. Determination suffused his tiny features. He closed his right fist and socked his left hand with it. Judge Stapleton was not likely to change his mind unless dramatic new facts were presented to him. Were there any dramatic new facts? The twelve-inch mayor looked owlish. That depended on what Judge Stapleton thought of these facts. Would His Honor be willing to tell the citizens something about these facts? That would be unwise, unprofessional, possibly unethical, intoned the twelve-inch mayor. The city had a case for delay, substantial delay. But the argument would be presented to Judge Stapleton in the proper manner, by the city's attorneys. Was His Honor personally hopeful that a delay would be granted? Wouldn't it help his campaign for the Senate? The twelve-inch mayor was indignant. There was no campaign for the Senate. Sock went the right fist into the left hand. He was not thinking about any other job. He was going to do this job and do it right. He cared too much about this city to do it any other way.

The watcher-mayor switched off the sound and asked himself to rate the twelve-inch mayor's performance. As image, it was at least three stars, the watcher-mayor decided, while boxes of soap suds cavorted around the screen. As reality, it barely rated a single star. He was lying all the way about his approach to Judge Stapleton and its relation to his hopes of becoming a United States senator. But the Mayor had been lying to the public since the age of six, when he used to answer his father's telephone during the Depression. *I'm sorry the Commissioner isn't home,* he would say to the desperate job seeker while Ben O'Connor sat a foot away reading the newspaper.

The distance between the truth and what he said on television did not disturb the Mayor in the least. But this did not mean that he was a cynic who saw politics as a meaningless con game. On the contrary, Mayor O'Connor also studied the twelve-inch mayor for signs of sincerity. The hand reaching out to touch Ben O'Connor's pen was one of these signs. The Mayor found it reassuring. But it was flawed by a fatal ambiguity. He both wanted and feared the connection that reaching hand implied. He still liked it—but he had also begun to loathe it.

Why? He did not know. These days, he did not

know the answers to a lot of questions he found himself asking. Most of the time he felt like an explorer moving through a labyrinthine jungle that he had once known with the instinctive confidence of an animal. Old trails had vanished, exotic new growths confused him, dangerous new beasts menaced him wherever he turned. At other times he felt like an actor who was trying to perform while an unseen director diabolically changed the scenery, the costumes, the rest of the cast, without consulting him.

Out of control, that was the essence of it. Too much of his life was out of control.

Maybe old Mortimer Kemble had the answer. The Mayor flipped open the diary of his 1870 predecessor to a random page.

Today there was a cave-in at an excavation in front of City Hall. Two Irish laborers were killed. By the time I reached the scene, they had been dug out and lay white and stark on the ground near where they had been working, ten or fifteen feet below the level of the street. Around them were a few men and I suppose fifteen or twenty Irish women, wives, kinfolk, or friends who had gotten word of the accident. The men were listless and inert enough. But not so the women. They were "keening"—a wild unearthly cry, half shriek and half song, wailing like a chorus of daylight banshees, clapping their hands and gesticulating passionately. Now and then one of them would throw herself down on one of the corpses, or wipe some trace of defilement from the face of the dead man with her apron, then resume her lament. It was an uncanny sound, quite new to me.

Our Celtic fellow citizens are almost as remote from us in temperament and constitution as the Chinese.

That was definitely not the answer. The Mayor switched off the television set and finished his scotch and soda. He inserted the solid gold cuff links, each a miniature of the old City Hall, which his wife had given him for Christmas ten years ago. He could feel the scotch seeping through his brain, blurring the memory of Tony Perotta and Kitty Kosciusko. In another sixty seconds he would be ready to go downstairs and exchange small and large talk with his guests.

Like most Puritans, his wife simply did not understand the value of alcohol. To Puritans, a drink was an indulgence, a letting go that they secretly condemned, even when they enjoyed it. They had even less appreciation for alcohol as a time machine. The Mayor smiled at himself in the mirror and straightened his tie. An Irish time machine, not the H.G. Wells English version. This one did not catapult you into the past or future. It drew a silken curtain around you, making the past a little less grisly, the future less ominous. It freed you to make jokes, to say and do daring things, to ignore collapsing political careers and wifely frowns, to face life steadily and see it whole. Or hole, which was the way it looked lately.

The Mayor drained the dregs of his drink—more ice water than scotch. The service in this dump was terrible. There should be a man assigned to him to keep his drinks fresh. He must talk to his hostess, Mrs. Stapleton-O'Connor, about that. He must talk to her about several things.

Turning to the image in the mirror once more, the Mayor checked his tie and pondered the man he saw there, so different in so many ways from the man on the television screen. Was he more—or less—trustworthy, this fellow with the swelling neck and the puffy eyes, looking vaguely like a prince who was turning into a frog? The twelve-inch mayor on television had mastered the art of winning admiration. But this fellow somehow stirred one's sympathy. The Mayor sighed. Both men were probably dangerous.

Stepping into the hall, he listened for a moment to the murmur of voices, the clink of glasses, the bursts of laughter below him. He took a long slow breath. The old time machine was working beautifully. Everything was going to go great. The Mayor walked down the hall and knocked on the door of his wife's bedroom. Paula opened it and smiled at him. He smiled back. The smiles said they both realized it was time to stifle the personal emotions that threatened them. Downstairs were ten very important people.

"Ready, sweethaht?" the Mayor asked.

"You betcha, boss," Paula said.

His Honor the Mayor and his rich charming wife were going to work.

3

"Okay, so we couldn't get Judge Stapleton to go along. Lemmy ask you this. Why couldn't we get you guys to go along?"

Eddie McKenna flung this question like a brick at the two black men opposite him—Councilman Adam Turner and the Reverend Quentin P. Brown, Jr.

Paula Stapleton clutched her wine glass and let her eyes wander to the Lowestoft porcelain pieces on the sideboard. She was trying to escape a mounting sense of disaster. Her husband, the Mayor, was doing nothing about it. He was letting Eddie McKenna dominate the conversation. They seldom invited Eddie to Bowood. When he came, the Mayor usually managed to keep him inconspicuous, parking him below the salt with some other local pol of his mental caliber. Tonight the Mayor had rearranged Paula's seating list and promoted Eddie to his right hand. He was turning this dinner, planned as a rally of key O'Connor supporters in the city and state, into a racial brawl. Eddie had ignored the wine and continued to down scotches and soda throughout the shrimps remoulade, the consommé, and the ragout of beef Normandie. Instead of trying to slow him down, the Mayor had matched him drink for drink. An Irish—or was it masculine?—habit that Paula utterly failed to appreciate.

Not that the scotch affected in the least Jake's self-control. Over the shrimp he had made a crisp speech, citing pledges of support from ex-governors and legislative leaders and polls proving the weakness of the Republican incumbent, who had supported Nixon with passionate sincerity until the sludge of the awful truth finally spewed from Watergate. Paula felt sorry for the incumbent. She had gone to school with his sister, who lived in the fashionable Society Heights section of the city. The sister had told Paula how her not too bright brother had been lied to by Nixon and his gang. But personal sympathy did not translate into political sympathy. The incumbent was a bespattered sitting duck and the Democratic politician who got the party's Senate nomination was a guaranteed winner in November. With an intensity that was almost embarrassing, Paula wanted that politician to be Jake O'Connor.

Paula had listened with approval as Jake summarized their key issues—a Marshall Plan for the cities, a National Shoreline Policy, and massive reform of Medicaid and Welfare. He looked and sounded like a man who could think and act not only for a city but a nation. The orchestration of statements and public appearances would begin with the announcement of his candidacy at the city's annual St. Patrick's Society dinner on March 17. The campaign would be managed by Tynan & Pope, professionals who had won sixteen of their last seventeen contests. Everyone had put down their forks to say warm admiring things. If it had been a formal banquet, they would have applauded.

But that momentary enthusiasm had somehow yielded to apathy. No one seemed interested in asking pertinent questions about the Marshall Plan for the cities or any other issue. They seemed to prefer gossip about the sex lives of the various presidential candidates, the possible impact of New York City's bankruptcy, the plight of the state's Republican Governor, who was locked in combat with a recalcitrant legislature over the budget. Watching her husband, Paula had seen pleasure fade into unease, and then into boredom. It was his worst flaw as a politician, and perhaps as a man—this sensitivity that read rejection into the slightest failure to dominate an audience. This reading was usually followed by a to-hell-with-them withdrawal into a less charming self. Like all politicians, he had several selves.

Tonight he had allowed Eddie McKenna to lure him into his Son of the Old Ward Boss act. Throughout the main course, Eddie and the Mayor regaled their end of the table with tales of the outrageous political tactics of the machine that had run the city for the first twenty-five years of their lives. Eddie told how his father was asked by the Big Man, as they called the machine's boss, to take a heavy suitcase to New York and give it to a clerk at a brokerage house. The suitcase was returned, many pounds lighter. Eddie's father had asked the Boss what was in it. "Money, you stupid bastard," he was told. The Mayor told about the time that his father was busy stuffing ballots and accidentally threw into one box the purse of the Republican woman poll watcher. It took her three weeks and a court order to get it back. Another time, an overenthusiastic district leader in Ben O'Connor's thirteenth Ward had arranged for a Democratic landslide of 708 to 1—forgetting that there were two Republican poll watchers, who presumably voted for their ticket. The Mayor and Eddie and a few other people at the table thought this was very funny. Paula found it hard to force a smile.

As they finished their vanilla mousse, McKenna had given these crooks of yesteryear a sentimental eulogy. They may have looted the city and left it with a reputation that made it a national synonym for municipal corruption, but they were good politicians. They knew how to work with all kinds of people. They knew when to fight and when to go along.

Why, Eddie had asked Jake in a voice so loud it stopped conversation all around the table, why wouldn't Judge Stapleton go along with the man who put him on the bench? Jake had told him that Judge Stapleton was more interested in going along with the Supreme Court. McKenna had ignored the ironic use of the phrase and turned on the blacks with drunken truculence.

To Paula's relief, Councilman Adam Turner ignored McKenna's tone. "I think we're already going along,"

Turner said. "We've accepted the Mayor's explanation of why he has to say he's against busing. We're still supporting him for the Senate. I think that's going along with a capital G."

"That's not what I mean and you damn well know it, Adam," McKenna said. "If you're really backing this guy, why didn't you let the whole thing sit on a desk somewhere until we got him elected?"

"I don't run the NAACP," Adam Turner said.

"No, but the pastor here does. Didn't his daddy found the local chapter?"

"That's true," said the Reverend Brown. "But that doesn't mean I can tell them what to do. The money and the orders come from national headquarters."

"Do you really expect us to drop a lawsuit we've worked on for five years, just when we're about to win it?" Adam Turner asked.

"I'm not telling you to drop it. Just lose it for twelve months. You owe this guy that much," McKenna said, putting his hand on Jake's arm. "He's done more for you than any other mayor in the history of this city. More than any other white mayor in the country."

"There's no point in getting sore about it now, Eddie," Jake said. "We decided last year—not to fight this thing."

Paula knew that he had been about to say "go along with this thing." In the context, the words were too painful. When he hesitated and chose the other expression, he looked down the table at her. An almost imperceptible change of expression flickered across his face—an undercurrent of anger and regret.

"The polls say we'll survive, Eddie, if we keep our heads," Jake said.

McKenna glared at rotund Sam Tucker, the man who had done the polling. Tucker practically shriveled into his hound's-tooth jacket. He did not like quarrels.

"I don't give a goddamn what the polls say, Jake. This busing thing will ruin you. We've been pussyfooting around it all night. It's time someone said it."

Paula looked uneasily at the red-haired man sitting on her left. He had a lopsided face. From the left he

42

looked as bland and innocent as a choirboy. From the right he was as crafty and complex as a Vatican Cardinal. As State chairman of the Democratic Party, Bernard Bannon always tried to have his picture taken from the left side. But he was not averse to letting friends and associates see him from the right side. Born and raised in the city, he had moved to the southern part of the state after the war and utilized the skills he had inherited from his politician father to build a formidable county organization. He had been chosen last year to reunite the fractured state party. Shrewdness as well as sentiment inclined him to back Jake O'Connor as his first major candidate. Bernie needed a politician who had stayed out of the quarrels of the Vietnam years. Above all, Bernie needed a winner, and that was why Paula was looking anxiously at him. But Bernie had long since mastered the basic lesson of a party chairman: never commit yourself. Catching Paula's eyes on him, he shook his head and smiled, as if to say, "Eddie's some character."

The expression on the face of the man sitting beside Bernie Bannon did nothing to improve Paula's morale. Ted Finsterman looked like he was ready to say at any moment: "A plague on both your houses." Tall and balding, with a deadpan astringent wit, Finsterman had been an important member of earlier O'Connor administrations. He had been the head of Community Projects, Inc., the agency that Paula and a team of Harvard-based consultants had persuaded the Mayor to create to bring new politics to the city's neighborhoods. The son of a wealthy downstate industrialist, Ted had met the Mayor in law school. Three years ago he had abruptly resigned and retreated to the Bahamas with his wife and children. Jake had lured him north in the hope of persuading him to become chairman of his Senate campaign.

Everyone else was busy brushing nonexistent crumbs off his or her lap. Joel and Gloria Chasen, sitting opposite Finsterman, were exchanging coded husband-wife glances. Gloria's maiden name was Teitlebaum. She was the heiress to one of the largest textile fortunes in America. Lean and intense, Gloria had spent a lot of money financing liberal candidates around the state in the last ten years. Gloria did the political thinking for handsome, vacuous Joe, whom the Mayor had appointed to numerous boards and commissions. Gloria was obviously unhappy with Eddie McKenna's performance. The rest of them—the labor leaders and the state legislators, the Mayor of the state's third largest city, the Republican bank president who backed Mayor O'Connor to keep Paula Stapleton's trust funds fructifying in his coffers, were either neutral or in agreement with Eddie McKenna. Only one man, sitting on Paula's right, answered the city chairman.

"What's the difference whether busing is something that has happened in Boston or is happening right here?" Ray Grimes said. "It's an issue and both candidates will have to deal with it. I wouldn't be surprised if it will be to Jake's advantage. He'll have had practical experience with it."

"You might as well say concentration camps are an issue and it helps if you're Adolph Eichmann," McKenna snarled.

"Really, Eddie, now you're being ridiculous."

Paula felt angry pleasure throb in her throat. It was about time someone shut up McKenna. Ray Grimes was the perfect man to do it. He was the city's liberal spokesman. He was also the current head of Community Projects, Inc., which put him in constant touch with the neighborhoods. What did McKenna and his cronies, clubhouse hacks all, know about the people in the streets?

Paula and Ray were old friends. They had trudged the downtown streets as fellow social workers in the midfifties. She had admired the religious dedication Ray had brought from his Catholic education to the daily struggle with the city's maladjusted and discontented. She had supported him with money and endorsements when he became an activist politician during the turmoil of the sixties, and ran for Congress on a platform that called for an immediate end to the war in Vietnam, sweeping integration of unions, and equal rights for women. The uptown wards, where a liberal constituency clustered around St. Francis College and the burgeoning branch of the state university, had not been strong enough to overcome the hard-hat hostility of the North Slope.

Ray Grimes had been Paula's first encounter with a type of Irish Catholic that she had heretofore only read about—the idealist who believed as she did that the world could be saved if enough people cared. She had brought Ray into the O'Connor administration as deputy director of Community Projects, Inc., and backed him strongly for the director's job when Ted Finsterman resigned.

"I'm inclined to agree with Ray," Gloria Chasen said, serving notice that the liberals in the O'Connor coalition were sticking together.

So do I, Paula wanted to add with ferocity. But she was the Mayor's wife. She had to play the neutral nodding hostess.

"I hope this doesn't mean your people are going to sit on their hands, Eddie," Joel Chasen said. "You've done too much of that in the last few years."

"My people don't sit on their hands, they get on their feet and head for the polls when they see a candidate that speaks their language," Eddie McKenna said, glowering down the table at Ray Grimes. "There isn't a man in the state who can do that better than Jake O'Connor. Aside from that, he's one of my oldest friends. He's got my support no matter what happens. But I think we ought to face the truth about our problems."

"He's got the black vote. That's what we're here to prove," Adam Turner said.

McKenna shook his head. "I don't think you guys can deliver the black vote to a white man. You don't know the meaning of the word organization. You think you can get people out to vote with a speech."

"We did pretty well for the Mayor last election," Adam Turner said.

"I call winning with forty-four per cent of the vote pretty bad," McKenna snapped. "Sure, the ones who came out voted for him all right. But in some of your wards the turnout was barely fifty per cent. We're going up against a guy who can and will spend money like

45

Rockefeller. That forty-four per cent win and now this goddamn busing crisis guarantees that Congressman Dwight Slocum will go for the nomination. He's sitting out there in the suburbs rubbing his hands right now. He doesn't need your votes. He doesn't want them. Don't you people read the papers? The Democrats in New York just elected three people to the state Board of Regents pledged to fight busing to the death. Your own guy down in Mississippi, Charles Evers, said it all in two sentences the other day. 'The era of civil rights is over. This is the era of politics.'"

"Is there any reason why we have to sit here and listen to this, Your Honor?" Adam Turner asked.

"No reason at all. We're serving coffee in the library," Jake said.

Everyone filed out, but Mayor O'Connor did not follow them. "I'll see you in five minutes," he said. "There are a couple of things I want to discuss with Eddie and Bernie."

Paula did not believe him and neither did anyone else, she was certain. Staying behind with McKenna and Bannon suggested that he half agreed with the city chairman's diatribe. In the library, Paula struggled to make conversation while her unease mounted. Ray Grimes unintentionally added to her distress by asking her if she knew whether Congressman Dwight Slocum was considering a run for the Senate. She told him, with an abruptness that sounded like a rebuke, that she had no idea what Congressman Slocum was going to do. Gloria Chasen said she did not trust Slocum. Paula said nothing. Some of these people probably knew that Paula Stapleton and Dwight Slocum had once been engaged. She saw no reason why she should reveal her private feelings about Mr. Slocum.

Ray Grimes began assuring everyone in oratorical tones that Eddie McKenna was wrong. The black vote was not only pledged to Mayor O'Connor—it would swing the state's liberals behind him, in spite of his pragmatic stand on busing. The era of civil rights was not over, it would never be over for people who cared about this country. Ted Finsterman wondered aloud if such people ought to be declared an endangered species.

Jake finally appeared alone. The state chairman had taken the city chairman home, he announced with a smile. Adam Turner and the Reverend Quentin P. Brown, Jr., put down their coffee cups and said good night. Was it a vote of confidence or a gesture of hostility? Within ten minutes, everyone except Ray Grimes, Sam Tucker, and Ted Finsterman had followed them into the darkness. Paula collapsed into a Philadelphia armchair. Jake went to the bar for another drink. He asked Ray Grimes if he wanted one. Ray shook his head. He rarely took more than a single drink, and that was usually Dubonnet. Tucker and Finsterman said they would have brandies. Tucker lit one of the small black cigars that he had begun smoking. Paula handed him an ashtray. Tucker smiled nervously at her. He sensed her disapproval. He was uneasy about offending his biggest client even in small accidental ways.

"Whatin God's name is wrong with McKenna?" Ray Grimes said.

"Couldn't you stop him somehow?" Paula said.

"In vino veritas," the Mayor said. "That's especially true for sentimental Irishmen."

"Sentiment doesn't give him a license to wreck your campaign," Ray Grimes said.

"He was trying to save it."

"With friends like him—"

"He's exactly the kind of friend I like to have around, Ray. He talks from the gut. And the more I think about it, the more I think—he's right."

As Jake hesitated before that last shocking word, he had glanced at Paula. What had she seen in his eyes? Some of the defiance that was in his voice. But also a subtle plea.

"Jake," Ray Grimes said. "That's ridiculous."

"Is it? Let's do a little scenario writing. I'm the guy who says he's against busing, but he can handle it, he can be fair to both sides. Slocum says he's against busing too and nobody can handle it. Suddenly all our whites start imitating Boston's South End. I've got to go to the Governor on my hands and knees and ask for the National Guard. Who's ahead? Who's got the egg on his face?"

"It won't happen, Jake. Everything I get from my neighborhood people tells me it won't happen."

"Everything I get from *my* neighborhood people— the cops—tells me it will. That's what I'm trucking over to Judge Stapleton tomorrow. A small library of police intelligence reports that predict everything from riots to arson to assassination."

"It won't change the old boy's mind, Jake. You must know that," Ray Grimes said.

The Mayor went over to the bar and refilled his glass. "Let's try another scenario. Everybody in the state is watching us. None of them wants busing. They know we don't want it. They're wondering if we can beat the rap or at least delay it. Suddenly, for reasons best left unsaid for the moment, Judge Stapleton cancels his plan and tells the Board of Education to come up with another alternative. We've got a year to breathe. Who looks like the hero?"

"Do you want to look like that kind of hero, Jake?" Ray Grimes said.

"I don't want to look like a jerk, Ray. That's what you made me look like in the last election. That's why we only got forty-four per cent of the vote."

In vino veritas, Paula thought, staring at the drink in her husband's hand. But was it the truth or more of the same morbid defeatism that Eddie McKenna had just preached to them, mixed with more of the same unfair recrimination? At the beginning of the last mayoralty campaign, Ray had been one of several advisors who had persuaded Jake to abandon an appeal against Judge Stapleton's ruling that the city's schools were de facto and hence illegally segregated. An appeal would have damaged Mayor O'Connor's special relationship with the blacks, Ray had argued. Everyone knew an appeal would only delay the inevitable. The idiots at the Board of Education had made transcripts of their meetings at which they discussed how to rig school districts and block transfers to keep blacks out of white schools.

"I'm not the only one who thought that way," Ray Grimes said, looking straight at Paula.

"I know," the Mayor said. "But most of the others admit we made a mistake."

Paula was distressed to see Jake publicly displaying his dislike of Ray Grimes. He had appointed him head of the CPI only because she had wanted him—and because he had lost interest in the agency, once the federal funds stopped flowing. Jake had disliked Ray from the moment he had met him. It went beyond politics. It was visceral. Jake and Ray were opposites, like the Mayor and his priest brother, Paul, even though they shared the same Irish American heritage. It was a mystery, a disturbing mystery, Paula had decided. But at least it confirmed her opinion that ethnic differences were largely nonsense. People differed on deeper, more important levels of the personality.

"What's the point in second-guessing me," Ray Grimes said with justifiable bitterness. "They'd desegregated Denver without much trouble. Dropping the appeal seemed the right thing to do, morally and politically. How did anyone know that Boston would explode, and create an anti-busing candidate here?"

"I predicted it," Sam Tucker said. "Jake had me run a poll on it. Don't you remember?"

"It was all so hypothetical. I thought—I still think—we had a right to ignore it," Ray Grimes said.

"So do I," Paula said.

"What do you think, Ted?" the Mayor said.

"I'm out of it, Jake," Finsterman replied. "You might as well ask the bartender at Papa's Reef, where I do my drinking these days."

Jake looked discouraged. He needed an ally. Paula could see from the expression on Sam Tucker's face that he was ready to abandon the battle. Miss Moneybags had spoken. Ordinarily she would have disliked Sam's reaction. But she found herself liking it now. She was glad she was able to upset the balance of this argument.

49

It was grossly unfair to criticize Ray Grimes for the near disaster of the last election. He had worked himself to the point of nervous exhaustion to pull them through to victory.

"Maybe the whole thing is academic," Paula said.

Jake glared at her, his face suffused with shocking anger. Instinctively she retreated. "Jake," she said, struggling to reprove but not rebuke him. "You thought it was a good decision when we made it. How many times have I heard you criticize hindsight specialists?"

"Sure," he replied. "But you and Ray still think it was a good decision. That's what worries me, Paula."

"It was the *right* decision, Mayor," Ray Grimes said.

Jake looked at him with vivid dislike on his face. "It was like hell," he snarled. "It was the wrong decision. It was a mistake. If we sit here and let the Judge steamroller us, we're making the same mistake all over again. We know what we're up against now."

"Jake—don't get rattled by a couple of loudmouths," Ray Grimes said.

"I get rattled by anybody who can take fifty thousand votes away from me. I've had Sam run a few polls downstate to see where we'll be if RIP and people like Kevin McGuire pin a pro-busing label on me, no matter what I say. Tell them the good news, Sam."

"It would cost him anywhere from twenty-five to thirty-five per cent of the normally Democratic vote," Tucker said, nervously eyeing Paula. "And twenty per cent of the independents."

"As I see it, we've got one chance to pull this out," Jake said. He turned to Paula with a complex expression on his face. It was hard and wary and vulnerable at the same time. "We've got to ask the Judge to back down."

"He's not a back down type. There are moral issues —" Ray Grimes began.

"I don't mean back down completely. I don't expect him or any other federal judge to buck the Supreme Court. I mean throw out the NAACP plan on the basis of the police reports, or any other goddamn reason he or we can find. Call for a new plan. It would give us a year. And we only need nine months to walk away with this election."

"A man who's won three Distinguished Service Crosses in two wars isn't going to get scared by police reports predicting riots on the North Slope," Paula said.

"I know that," Jake said. "There's only one thing that will make him do it. A personal appeal."

"Who's going to make it?"

"You, Paula."

He was looking at her with intense emotion on his face. Even as she tried to read it, she was reacting, speaking involuntary words.

"Jake! No!"

Paula heard the reproach in her voice, and wished she could somehow combine it with sympathy. But it was impossible.

"It wouldn't work," Ray Grimes said.

"How do we know until we try it?" Jake said. "Tomorrow night, we're going out to his birthday party. It would be a perfect time to ask him."

"What—what would I say?" Paula asked.

"That you want it. That you never wanted anything as much in your life. That if you don't get it I'm through. Everything we've worked for and sweated over for fourteen years is going down the drain."

"I—I couldn't do it, Jake. Ray's right. It wouldn't work. And—it would hurt him, hurt him terribly."

The expression on her husband's face made words superfluous. *But it's all right if I'm hurt.* That was what he was thinking. What else could he think? For a moment, Paula almost changed her mind. *I'll do it.* The words were on her lips.

But they were silenced by the way Jake raised his drink to his sullen mouth to drain it in one long obliterating swallow. "Okay," he said. "Okay."

He got up and walked to the bar for another drink. Paula watched his footsteps. There was no sign of a stagger or a stumble. Yet it must be his sixth or seventh scotch of the night. "Okay," he said again as he flung the ice in his glass. "We'll do it your way, folks. We'll re-enact the Charge of the Light Brigade. We'll make Sir Galahad and Sir Lancelot look like moral cowards. We'll do the right thing, and after it's over, I'll retire to Papa's Reef with Finsterman here and live on martinis."

"You could do a lot worse, Jake," Ted Finsterman said.

"Jake," Ray Grimes said. "You've had too much of that stuff. It's giving you the Irish glooms. Things aren't that bad. You've still got the blacks, no matter what fools like McKenna say to them. The white ethnics have got to stick with you. They've got no place else to go. What could they expect to get from Slocum? The polls show you ahead by three to two in every congressional district in the state. There's no reason to assume extremists like RIP or McGuire can pin any kind of label on you."

"You've cheered me up no end. Good night, Ray."

Ray Grimes sighed. He gave Paula a wry, sympathetic smile. "Good night, Paula. It was a delicious dinner."

"I'm for the sack too," Sam Tucker said. "Can you give me a ride, Ray?"

Tucker obviously had no desire to get caught in a cross fire between the Mayor and his wife. A true pollster, he liked to know which side was going to win before he got into a fight.

"You'll feel better about this in the morning, Jake," Ray Grimes said.

"I said good night, Ray."

Terence Mahoney appeared in the library doorway carrying a tray. "Mahoney," Paula said, "Mr. Grimes and Mr. Tucker are leaving. Would you get their coats?"

"Certainly, madam."

No one spoke until they heard the front door close. Mahoney returned with his tray and briskly removed the coffee cups. Paula studied Ted Finsterman's face. It was impossible to read it. There was neither approval nor disapproval on it. Only a kind of serene blankness. Was this what three years in the islands gave a person? Cool empty serenity, delicious martinis followed by a gourmet dinner followed by nights of placid sleep? No, cool had always been Finsterman's style. He never let anyone know what he was thinking until he spoke. His impenetrability made Paula wary. She was afraid the Mayor would begin the argument again. If Finsterman chose to join it, he would be a much more dangerous ally than Sam Tucker.

"I'm exhausted," she said. "Good night, Ted. I hope you'll change your mind and join the campaign."

"It sounds more like a civil war," he said.

"Wait up for me, will you?" Jake said. "We'll have a nightcap."

Paula hesitated. In other years, victorious years, a nightcap in the bedroom had been a ritual after a successful dinner or rally. They would clink glasses, celebrating how well the evening had gone. Then they would make happy, triumphant love. Now there was nothing to celebrate. What she had heard tonight made her wary of his love. But she could not refuse him in front of Ted Finsterman.

"All right," she said.

4

"I just don't see any point in it, Jake. Why are you killing youself? You've given this lousy town more years of your life and a lot better government than it deserves. You and Paula have all the money you could possibly want. Why don't you bag the whole thing and come down to Dominion Cay with us?"

"I told you, Ted, I don't like to fish."

"The fishing is incidental. It's the exposure to—purity. Nature before the city got to it. Sea, sand, sky. It gives you a chance to get back to the roots of your self. And incidentally amputate yourself from this rotten country."

Ted Finsterman had written this stuff to the Mayor in letters of Hemingwayesque prose. There were lyrical descriptions of dueling sailfish to the death, diving along barracuda-haunted reefs, walking empty beaches in the dawn. The Mayor had responded with long reports of the latest lunacies in City Hall, written in deadpan third-person prose and signed "J. Gatsby." It continued a friendly feud they had conducted since they met in law school and argued over who was the best American writer. Finsterman was a Hemingway man. The Mayor favored F. Scott Fitzgerald. The Mayor ignored the remark about the country, which carried the argument beyond prose or life-styles. He was as dismayed as Finsterman by the political and moral aberrations of the previous decade. But he rejected his friend's fondness for seeing Götterdämmerung around the corner.

"I just don't speak the language, Ted," he said. "That's for you Hemingway types."

"Seriously, Jake, what the hell is the point of it all? The goddamn city is ungovernable. Will the Senate be any better? You know what Truman said about it. The first day you wonder how you got there. Six months later you wonder how the rest of them got there."

"Maybe I'm used to an imperfect world, Ted. Maybe I was just born to run."

"That's my point, Jake. No one's born to do anything. If you've got the freedom to choose."

"I've always thought that freedom stuff was overrated. You'll never get anyone on the North or South Slope to agree with it."

"I'm not talking about them. Leave them to their quiet—or noisy—desperation. They're all infected, Jake, the whites and the blacks, by the great American aberration, getting yours. There's no law that says you've got to spend your life trying to referee them."

When he put together his first administration, the Mayor had seen people like Ted Finsterman as prime assets. Wealthy enough to have no worries about money, yet committed in an intellectual way to making government work for all the people. Paula had known a dozen and the Mayor had collected half that many on his own. Most had been disappointing. Either they had been dopes like Joel Chasen or they had no staying power and quit in six months or they trended upward to state and federal service, where there was more status and power. The others, the middle-class lawyers and businessmen, the ones you had to watch, did not stay much longer. They left to pursue the big buck the moment they saw it gleaming on the horizon. You could not blame them.

Then there were the few good ones whom he had been able to excite and persuade, the Ted Finstermans. But too many of their generation had been infected by Hemingway at an early age. They yearned for the symbolic encounter, the challenge that tested them. They wanted to fight hard, hit cleanly, win decisively. Instead, they found themselves wrestling in the daily mud with an amorphous adversary who aroused more pity than fear.

It was like Vietnam, a war in which Americans were psychologically crippled. The Mayor sometimes wondered if the country had been ruined by a yearning for simplicity engendered by writers like Hemingway, Twain, Thoreau.

In recent years, the Mayor had almost given up on getting so-called good people into government. He had turned to the clubhouses for more and more of his appointments, and backed them with sophisticated largely faceless experts from the universities. More and more, the image of playing with a pick-up team obtruded itself. Yet they were not playing in the little league. Governing the biggest city in the state needed constant care, enormous energy.

Did he secretly agree with Finsterman?—the city was ungovernable—or was not worth governing? Was that the real reason he was running for the Senate? The Mayor rejected the idea. He knew that Paula had given up on the place. He had watched his wife's enthusiasm dwindle, year by year, as he continued to fail to produce the miracle cure that she apparently thought she had administered to the body politic when he won his first election. He had tried in a hundred ways to tell her that this was a delusion. He knew it would take at least a decade, without any guarantee of success, to wean the city from the old politics. He never promised to redeem the goddamn place. Was that what Finsterman wanted too?

"I never have become—I guess you'd say reconciled—to losing you, Ted. I thought we worked well together. We got some things done and had a pretty good time."

"I'll never have a better one, Jake. But—when you ran for governor I started thinking about moving on."

Those words aroused both anger and guilt in the Mayor. He did not like to think about his ruinous run for the governorship. He found himself thinking about others who had left the city government after that wasted, mistaken effort. Had the fugitives gotten a signal from him that released their alienation—a signal that said he no longer thought the job was worth doing? Or was it simply the standard American reaction to anyone who gets loser stamped on him? He tried to conceal his uneasiness with a brutal question.

"Isn't it a little boring, Ted? I mean, to paraphrase a certain politician, if you've caught one fish, you've caught them all."

"It is a little," Finsterman said with a grimace. "That's why I'd enjoy your company."

"I'd enjoy yours a lot more up here. I need help, Ted. You saw Grimes in action tonight. The guy's an asshole. But he's got a following in the uptown wards. Would you consider taking your old job for nine months, if I canned him? Anybody else I put in there would have to be a combination of Mahatma Gandhi and Martin Luther King to keep people like Gloria Chasen happy."

And my beloved wife, the Mayor mentally added.

Finsterman shook his head. "I agree that he's an asshole. But I'm used up for that assignment, Jake."

"The Senate thing could be a hell of a brawl if Slocum runs. Wouldn't you like to take on that arrogant bastard?"

"The way I heard it tonight, Dwight isn't going to run unless he's got it locked up. And he won't have it locked up unless everything comes apart here. In other words, either you don't need me—or I won't be able to do you any good—nobody will."

Ted, the governorship didn't count. That was idiocy perpetrated by my wife. This is the one I want, because if I don't get it I'm through. I can't last much longer in City Hall. There are too many people gunning for me. I need your help, Ted.

The words were on the Mayor's lips. But he could not say them. They would expose him to the ultimate defeat, the one that led to sympathy, commiseration, the consolations of weakness. He could not permit that to happen. He had been trained in a stoic tradition, as classic in its own tough way as the creed of the professional soldier or Indian warrior. It was his father's code: Take it as it comes. If the pain becomes unbearable, have a drink, have several drinks.

"At least do this, Ted. Stick around town for a

week or two, until we get this busing thing on the road. You've still got a lot of friends in the neighborhoods."

"Jake, I wish I could. But I promised an old friend I'd go looking for marlin off Manzanillo."

The Mayor watched Finsterman stroll into the night. Maybe the whole thing was a course in spiritual growth, he thought moodily. He was being taught humility. A virtue that did not come easily to a politician.

The Mayor turned the huge old brass key in the front door and paused in the gleaming center hall to study the portrait of Kemble Stapleton. He was the family's Revolutionary War hero, killed by the British after having performed countless feats of daring. Pride bristled from every square inch of that narrow face. The eyes seemed to glare with angry disapproval on the herd of ordinary mortals he had had the misfortune to lead. Or was he gazing into the future, frowning as only Stapletons can frown at the foibles and failures of the "foreign effluvia" who would desecrate his country? His resemblance to Paula was extraordinary. She had the same thin-lipped sensitive mouth and high delicate cheekbones, and a feminine version of that flaring aristocratic nose.

Beside Kemble Stapleton was a John Trumbull painting of his fleshier cousin, Hugh, the Continental congressman. Even before the Revolution, his ships had traded American wheat and whale oil, timber and tobacco in Europe and the West Indies, and brought back teas, spices, silks, and slaves to be sold at whacking profits. A few feet away was a Copley portrait of Hugh's son, Malcolm, who had financed the state's first railroads and for two decades monopolized transportation in the state. Malcolm's son had built the city's first factories, just in time for the Civil War to make him a millionaire.

The Mayor went into the library. He tucked a silver ice bucket under his left arm. He seized a Waterford crystal decanter of scotch with his right hand and looked up at the 1668 portrait of Charles Stapleton, the "Proprietor" and founder of the line, gazing from his preeminent position above the huge marble fireplace. Behind the Proprietor, a vast estate had been carved out of the wilderness. In the distance, tiny figures could be seen toiling in the fields. The artist, an accurate observer, had carefully painted each of these toilers black. An interesting detail, the Mayor thought as he mounted the curving staircase to the second floor.

As he reached the head of the stairs, a door opened farther down the hall and a little girl with silvery blond hair flowing down the back of her blue nightgown darted into the hall.

"Good night, Daddy," said the Mayor's four-year-old daughter, Dolores. She blew him a kiss.

"Hey," he said, "that's no kiss. I want a real one."

She raced down the hall. He dropped to his knees. She flung her arms around his neck and gave him a loud wet kiss on the mouth.

"That's more like it," he said, patting her on the rump. "Now go to bed and stay there. Your mother—"

"Her mother is very angry with her already." Paula stood in her bedroom doorway. "At this rate, she will get no dessert for a week."

"Did you hear that?" the Mayor said. "Get going."

"Okay, grouchy," Dolores said, hurling the defiant word at her mother. She gave him another kiss and scampered back to her bedroom. Paula gave an exasperated sigh. During cocktails, Dolores had burst into the library crying that she was not going to bed until she gave Daddy a kiss. The Mayor had not only proceeded to kiss her, but had hoisted her onto his hip, dismissed her agitated nurse, and carried her around with him for twenty minutes, forcing the guests to fuss over her. He knew it would produce reproaches from Paula, but he could not resist showing her off. She was such an incredibly beautiful kid.

"Really, Jake," Paula said, "you will just have to stop spoiling that child."

"Oh, she's okay. She just loves a party," the Mayor said.

He almost added: *like her namesake*. But that was

a potential wound. More wounds, especially at this time of night, were to be avoided. He had inflicted enough of them for one evening. But the Mayor could not avoid seeing Dolores' namesake with a mocking smile on her exquisite face, asking him the question she always asked these days: *Why are you trying to run away from the city now, Jake? You could have left with me twenty years ago. But you said no. Are you glad you said no, Jake?*

A stupid question. A question that Dolores Talbot was no longer capable of asking. Any more than that supremely kissable mouth was capable of smiling. There were worms in that mouth. The lips had withered to a ridge of bone. The once silken skin, if there was any left, resembled one of those Egyptian mummies he had seen a few years ago in the British Museum. Dolores Talbot was dead and by the time she died he no longer loved her.

None of these admonitions had any effect on the smiling face asking the question in the white inner space of the Mayor's mind, while his wife's face frowned from her doorway.

He followed Paula into her bedroom and put the scotch decanter and the ice bucket on her dresser. "What'll it be?" he said. "Single or double?"

He did not like the sound of his own voice. It had a throaty thick-tongued timbre. He was close to getting loaded.

Paula sat down in her favorite wing chair. "I don't think I'll have anything. I wish I could have said yes downstairs, Jake, I really do. But getting me drunk won't change my mind."

He was astonished. For a moment he wondered if she was reading signals on his face or in his eyes that betrayed an intention he did not know. "I'm not trying to change your mind. Can't I want to have a drink with my wife without—?"

Want. He could see the word scrape her nerves. Deep in her Puritan soul, Miss Stapleton did not approve of wanting. Only giving. Giving was good, wanting was bad. But a good stiff drink freed Miss Stapleton from this ancestral bag. It freed her to want quite a few things. It made her a veritable wanton. And that was what the Mayor needed right now. A half hour or so with a wanton wife, who would treat him like a winner even if he was on his way to being a loser.

He was drunk, horny drunk, the best kind. It would help him hold it and hold it and hold it until she was biting him and whispering come come come and there was nothing between them not even skin and he was in her an unpuritanical mile and his tongue was tasting parts of her that made her whisper don't yes don't and then he would come and there would be peace, the deep throb of letting go and still holding on and she would belong to him for a while in a deep sure way that he found more and more important.

The importance troubled him. The liquor allowed him to conceal both the importance and the uneasiness. He was still amazed by how much he enjoyed her physically. On their honeymoon her shyness had aroused a protective gentleness that he never knew he possessed. When she began shedding her inhibitions, he found himself proud of her at first, as if she was his creation. Then came the startling desire to see and caress that long lithe body, to fondle those small snub breasts, to kiss that pulsing aristocratic neck. For a few months the sexual initiative had shifted; she had had the power. He had been uncomfortable; then subtly opposed. He had pretended a coolness that he did not really feel. He thought she had accepted it as the ordinary decline of ardor—with him retaining the privilege of displaying it when the moment or the mood was right. Too late he saw that she regarded the decline as inevitable for another reason. Plain Paula Stapleton had no hope of expecting anything else. Now they were best when liquor allowed them to escape her lowered expectations and his need to mask his desire.

After it, perhaps a little mind changing? No, he told himself, no. There had to be some place politics could not reach. Some place that politics could not spoil.

"I'm sorry," Paula said. "I really am."

For a moment the Mayor found himself paralyzed by the plaintive honesty on her face. She had such good intentions, it was hard not to be touched, not to find himself agreeing with all sorts of ideas, based on nothing more substantial than her good intentions. How could he tell her that she was dangerous, that her good intentions were destroying him?

"What I'm trying to do—and say is—let's leave the politics downstairs."

"Easier said than done."

"I know."

"Jake—"

She still did not believe him. Another warning, another lecture was on her lips.

"I give you my word I'm not trying to change your mind. Not about politics, anyway."

"All right. I'll have a light—very light—one."

He talked as he mixed the drink. "I've had my say. I knew it was a long shot before I opened my mouth. But in this business, if you don't follow your instincts—or at least talk about them—you wind up with a hole in your stomach. Now I'm ready to do it the hard way. And I'll give it everything I've got."

"Jake—isn't it more important that it's—the right way?"

He found it difficult to conceal his irritation. He thrust the scotch and soda at her. "Paula," he said. "How many times have I told you that in politics there are usually a half dozen right ways. The trick is to pick the right one at the right time."

"I admit that's usually true. But in some situations—where the moral issue is clear-cut—there is only one right way."

The Mayor sat down in the wing chair opposite her. He let his head rest on the curved, padded back for a moment. *You are beat,* he thought, *in more ways than one.*

"I didn't come up here to argue. I want to help the blacks just as much as you do. But I can't see what moral obligation has to do with it. It's a political problem and the more I think about it, the more complicated it gets. I'm beginning to wonder how much the government can do to help anybody."

"I agree. All we can do is create an atmosphere in which they help themselves. But a government can do negative things—it has done dreadfully negative things —that prevent people from helping themselves."

She was on the edge of her chair now, elbows on her knees, both hands clutching her drink, which had now become a meaningless object, not a libation to old times, good times, to memories of nights when scotch persuaded her to stroll out of the bathroom with her nightgown slung impudently over her shoulder.

"When you talk about delaying busing, I wonder if you really understand the dynamics of the situation we're trying to create."

Dynamics. That's a Ray Grimes word. I see dynamite. He sees dynamics.

"Confronting one's hostility is a necessary first step in conflict resolution. That's why it's necessary to give busing an aura of inevitability."

Bullshit, Ray Grimes bullshit. The last time we confronted our hostility we had a civil war.

"As long as you hold out the hope of winning, the whites will never face their hostility."

How about blacks? When do they face their hostility?

The Mayor drained his drink. Was it a bad sign to have so many unspoken thoughts between him and his wife? Maybe not. He had told himself sixteen years ago that it would never be the ideal marriage. After Dolores Talbot, not to mention twenty-one or -two previous years in a household where father and mother rarely had a civil word for each other, he did not consider himself a candidate for an ideal marriage. Maybe that was why it surprised him so much to discover how close his marriage was to ideal for the first six or seven years. They had balanced each other, temperamentally, sexually, yes, even politically, they were a nice blend of opposites—the swinging Irishman and the shy Wasp, her cool dignity and his earthy instincts, her money and his energy.

He would give it one more try. "You are only convincing me that husbands and wives shouldn't talk politics after midnight. Especially opinionated husbands and wives like us."

Paula smiled halfheartedly. "You're probably right."

Wow. There was real enthusiasm, Your Honor.

"But this goes beyond politics, doesn't it?"

"I suppose so."

"Jake, it's so important."

"I know that." His harsh tone produced a kind of stain that momentarily distorted her face. "But I don't think it can be settled with conflict resolution techniques. Only time will settle it. That's what I'm trying to do. Buy the city time. And incidentally get myself elected to the Senate. The two aren't necessarily in conflict."

"What if the time isn't for sale?"

"Jesus Christ, are you determined to have an argument about this now?"

Another wrong move on the marital checkerboard. Paula assumed her Queen Elizabeth I pose, both hands gripping the arms of her wing chair, her back braced, her chin slightly tilted.

"There is a difference between a discussion and an argument."

Not on this subject.

"Look. I've had a hell of a day and I'd like to relax and go to bed with my wife, not my political advisor."

He instantly hated those maudlin words. Was he feeling that sorry for himself? The unnerving answer was: maybe.

Groping for self-respect, the Mayor picked up the decanter of scotch and the ice bucket. "But what the hell," he said. "Maybe a couple of more belts will have the same effect."

Before he could even turn toward the door, Paula sprang from her chair and raced across the room to throw her arms around him. "I'm sorry," she said. "I just—I just care."

"I know," the Mayor said, giving her a rough squeeze. "That's what I like about you. But believe it or not, sweethaht, you can care too much. I mean—you've got to know when to turn it off and coast a little."

"Do you really think so, boss?"

"Would I lie to you?"

She tilted her chin, challenging him, but not seriously.

"Take some advice from a middle-aged pro. Think sexy. It'll get you a lot farther than thinking politics. That's the secret of my success."

"I'll take that advice, Your Honor. Give me ten minutes."

In his bedroom, the Mayor poured himself a light scotch and a splash of soda. He sipped it, and began undressing. Another crisis surmounted. The question is, Your Honor, how many more surmountings have you got left before you say the hell with the whole thing?

In another moment he was under the hot beating water of the stall shower, letting it cleanse away everything, inside and out, the doubt and the frustration that seemed to travel like a poison through his whole body by the end of the day. If he could also wash away the temptation to substitute anger for thought or pity for politics. Letting the water run symbolically through his mind as well as down his body, the traitor body that could no longer absorb six or seven scotches in a night, and produce a springy step and a natural smile the next morning.

The Mayor shut off the shower, stepped out, and toweled his big bulky torso. He frowned at what he saw in the full-length mirror on the back of the door. There was too much suet gathering around his waist. He stretched his neck to see if his halfhearted diet had done any damage to a recent portent of a double chin.

Suddenly he was flung upward and outward ten thousand incandescent miles into space and yet never moved from the paralyzing confrontation with the naked man in the mirror. He was face to face with the essentials. What did he conclude from that sagging belly and suety neck? What did he see?

He saw a man who had squandered himself. Year after year he had dipped into his assets, the ruggedly handsome face, the rakish smile, the athletic grace. All these gifts, even the intelligence in the bold blue eyes, had been converted into foreign currency; other people's thoughts, other people's wishes. Where was he going now? Where else but to sell off a few more ergs of his dwindling assets to his wife, the head buyer?

Buyer. Maybe that was the best description of his marriage. She was the buyer in every way, from the liquid scratch of the pen on the sky blue checkbook to the intangible, so much more dangerous insistence that her principles were synonymous with God, eternal truth, the Constitution, and the Gettysburg Address, while he, the hustling Mick, had no principles and therefore no alternative but to obey her. There was nothing he possessed, between the cash in her hand and the principles in her head, that she could not buy.

A knock on the door. Paula's tense voice. "Are you all right?"

"Yes," said the Mayor. He had no idea how long he had been staring at himself in the mirror. "Yes. I'm all right."

What did one more lie mean now?

"I'm falling asleep. Are you coming?"

Oh yes, coming, Mother. Coming right away, just as fast as my little bandy legs can carry me. Jesus. The Mayor raised his clenched fist as if there was a knife in it and smashed it against the glib, too knowing face of the salesman in the mirror. The glass splintered in a hundred different directions. Exploding lines raced out like hysterical cries in search of a listener.

There was blood dripping from his murderous hand. Paula flung open the bathroom door. "Jake—"

The Mayor looked from his wife's frightened face to his bleeding hand. "I—I don't know what happened. I slipped and—"

"How many more drinks have you had since I went in to take my bath?"

The perfect out, the easy explanation. It explained everything so beautifully. The Mick was reverting to type. He was turning out to be the drunken slob that all the Stapletons expected him to become.

"What difference does it make?" he said, putting his hand under the cold water faucet. "Just let me get a Band-Aid on this thing and—"

She opened the medicine cabinet, took out a box of Band-Aids, and handed it to him. He reached for it, missed, and the tin box hit the marble floor with a clank. A half dozen Band-Aids spewed out. As he knelt to pick them up, she said, "I've tried to tell you in a nice way—but I'm afraid you don't listen to anything until it's said in an unpleasant way. You're drinking too much. I don't like it."

Someone must be directing this scenario, the Mayor thought. How else did he get down here on one knee, like the original suppliant?

"I'm not drinking too much," he said. "You have an absolutely ridiculous idea of how much liquor a man can handle. There's a hell of a difference between my capacity and Ray Grimes's."

He stood up and struggled to put a Band-Aid on the jagged cut across the heel of his right hand. It was impossible to do with his left hand. He finally had to let her do it. It made him feel like a small boy who had defied mother and now needed her help. He looked into her unsmiling face and saw nothing there but disapproval. *Love me, Love Ray Grimes. Is that the latest edict from on high?* Behind the sarcasm he heard another voice, or voiceless wish, wanting to tell her what he had just seen in the mirror. But he could not do it. He could not add another humiliation to the evening's list.

Pain from the cut throbbed dully up his arm. Blood was beginning to seep from beneath the Band-Aid. "Maybe I'd better call your secretary for another appointment," he said.

"I think it would be the sensible thing to do," she said. "Good night."

The Mayor looked in the mirror to find out what the salesman was thinking. A wandering ear, a disconnected mouth, a berserk eye stared back at him. The man in the glass was gone. Only pieces of him were left.

5

Paula Stapleton O'Connor flung cold water against her aching eyes and wearily ran a brush through the ruins of her Grecian hairdo. She had heard four bongs on the grandfather clock in the center hall before she went to sleep. With a groan, she tried to avoid a serious look in the mirror. Sleeplessness dehydrated her skin, until it was stretched across her face like a ghastly mask made of third-rate rubber. That was not the only reason to avoid a confrontation with herself. She did not want to see the accusation in her eyes. How could she have so persistently ignored what her husband had been trying to say to her last night? Had politics really infested her soul to the point where she took them to bed with her?

For a moment, stepping out of her nightgown, Paula thought wistfully about the early years of their marriage. From the first time they had touched each other seriously, above all, the first time she had given herself to him, with the trade winds sighing outside their cottage at Caneel Bay, they had been surprised by the delight they found in each other's bodies. All the things she had dreaded—his condescension at finding her a virgin at thirty-three, the inevitable comparisons he would make with some of his earlier conquests, above all with Dolores Talbot, that dead yet somehow imperishable rival—none of these goblins had turned out to be real. For a while nothing outside themselves was real. They had seemed to swallow each other like competing winds. The rest of the world had no more than accidental existence, it was something to be ignored with a frown or a smile. His hand on her thigh, her breast, her lips against his mouth, those were the things that sent tremors through her universe. There had been something almost dangerous in the way she had wanted him. And he had wanted her. Unless he was one of the world's best actors, his wanting had been real, his pleasure with her . . .

The sudden kiss . . . *How's the ex-puritan tonight?*

Where had it gone? It had slipped away, like perfume from an unstoppered bottle. At least, it had seemed that way at first. The jokes had dwindled, then ceased. Next the offhand caresses. They had both become more serious in a strange, somehow threatening, way. There was no one moment Paula could indict, it was not something that was over, finished. It was still happening, and she and Jake were both in the middle of it and that made it difficult to analyze, much less control.

Yet—standing before his smiling photograph on her dresser, Paula remembered the long hard thrust of him in her, the delight her fingers found in exploring the pulsing muscles of his back, the harsh maleness of his cheek in the morning. She still loved him. But it was a different love, more consultable, somehow (sadly) more fragile than the love she had felt in Caneel Bay. It was even more fragile than the admiration that had preceded this love, when she had backed his political promise with her money and exhausting, eighteen-hour working days. Then everything had been wish, possibility, future. Now so much seemed regret, reality, past.

But she still loved him. What else explained this drained body, these gritty eyes, the numbing sense of near catastrophe?

There was a knock on the door. "Everyone is ready for breakfast, Mrs. O'Connor," said Flora Mackey, the children's nurse.

"I'll be down in a moment."

Swiftly, she stepped into a pair of plain white pants, snapped on a bra, shrugged into a slip, and chose one of a half dozen lacy peignoirs in her dressing room closet. Why did her husband keep giving her such sexy things? Was he trying to get a message through her neuroses?

She shook her head. She must stop calling herself neurotic. She was trying to be honest. Ruthlessly honest. The problem was deciding when ruthlessness became fanaticism, and honesty a hardening of the heart. Strange how those old biblical phrases from her girlhood stayed with her.

She confronted herself once more in the mirror, noting with an inner tremor the frown lines on her forehead. Another, more ominous line crept from the right corner of her mouth toward the too narrow jaw. No one had ever used words like beautiful or lovely to describe Paula. She had had to cultivate other qualities. She had taken seriously the principles preached by Talbot Stapleton, the rector of Grace Episcopal Church. While those others, the lucky ones, strode carelessly past preachments and principles, serenely confident of their beauty or their strength.

No regrets about that, Paula. Beauty was transient. It could be smashed against a car windshield, the way Dolores Talbot had died. At best, it faded into middle age. Masculine strength could be corrupted, and it too seemed to dwindle in middle age's grip, as choices narrowed and decisions became irrevocable. But those old-fashioned phrases that had enriched her life seemed more meaningful than ever. It *was* a terrible thing to harden the heart. It *was* still important to believe that all men were brothers. Above all was the belief in the power and responsibility of the elect, the saving remnant, as Talbot Stapleton used to call them. *You only have I known of all the nations of the earth, therefore I will punish you for all your iniquities.* Yes, that is the awesome, even terrifying responsibility of the elect. They must bear the burden, they must choose.

She still believed all that, Paula thought sadly. But she did not really believe in the stern-but-loving God who had inspired it. When was the last time she had said a genuine prayer? Gloomily, Paula blamed this last unanswerable question on the Catholic church which she attended with her husband. Whose faith would not wither, listening to those atrocious sermons? But it was unfair to blame Jake. He did not believe in the sermons or anything else the Church professed. He went to Mass for purely political reasons. She at least retained a faith in—what? Some caring intelligence. But for a long time praying to God seemed much less important than action, effort, to make Christ's teaching about justice and love a reality here in this city, this country.

Down the curving, polished oak staircase Paula went to the breakfast room. Jake was already there, looking tired. His craggy face was lumpy and drained in the gray morning light. For a moment Paula felt pleased. She hastily reproached herself for such a mean reaction and sat down at the table, forcing a smile and a pleasant "Good morning" to her lips.

"You look like you didn't sleep very well either," she said.

She was trying to tell him she was sorry, but she was afraid it somehow sounded as if she were glad. "I was reading old Mortimer Kemble's diary," he said. "It got better and better."

So much for sympathy, Paula thought. He doesn't need it or want it. As for getting any from him . . .

Her ten-year-old son, Kemble, took a Rye Krisp from the filigree silver basket in the center of the table and cracked it on top of his father's head. Four-year-old Dolores shrieked with glee. Jake continued to eat his grapefruit, pretending not to notice as the crumbs dribbled down his neck.

"*Please,*" Paula said. "How many times do I have to tell you I can't *stand* that game. It's so *vulgar* to play with food."

"You mean to say I don't get a chance to even the score?" Jake said.

"We have to vacuum the whole room every time you play that game," Paula said.

"Okay," the Mayor said. "But you can bet your life I'm going to get some revenge before I go to work."

"The Indian burn. Give him the Indian burn," Dolores screamed.

"Dolores, don't yell. It's not polite. Especially at the table."

"Quiet, or I'll give *you* the Indian burn," the Mayor said to his daughter. "You were egging him on all the way. How am I going to run this city when I shake my head to say no and a lot of cracker crumbs fly all over the place?"

"They'll say you're a crumby mayor," Kemble said cheerfully.

"I hope no one calls him that," Paula said, smiling to make it clear that she understood the joke.

Dolores giggled. "He *is* a crumby mayor."

She was her father's daughter. Almost as disturbing was the startling perfection of her face. Her classic good looks were obviously derived from his handsome profile. So was the blond hair, according to the Mayor. His hair had been snowy white at her age, he said, grandly—or was it tactfully?—dismissing blond hair that had belonged to another Dolores in the Talbot branch of the Stapleton family tree.

For a painful moment Paula wondered if she had made a mistake, naming her daughter after her dead rival. It had been easy to do; even Jake had not been especially startled by it. Dolores had, after all, been her cousin, and Mrs. Talbot was still alive, grieving for her spoiled darling. Privately Paula had seen it as a gesture of humility, a way of implicitly acknowledging that Dolores was still alive in Jake's memory. Now she realized there had also been a subtle self-interest in the idea. Paula had assumed her daughter would resemble her. It had been pleasing to imagine her husband bestowing that special name on her gawky, homely childhood self. Instead, Nature, God—someone or something with a nasty sense of humor—had produced this beautiful little creature who reminded him—and her—of dead Dolores more and more every day.

Kemble, in an ironic switch of the genes, resembled Paula. He was a thin, excitable boy with wide Stapleton gray eyes and a narrow Stapleton chin. But his antics at the table demonstrated that he had inherited his share of O'Connor waywardness.

None of these thoughts prepared Paula for what came next.

"You should hear what the black kids call Daddy," Kemble said. "Motherfucker."

"Kemble! That is a vile, disgusting, insulting word," Paula cried. "How dare you use it at this table in front of your sister?"

"What does it mean, Mommy?" Dolores asked.

Kemble's eyes filled with tears. Paula realized that he did not know what it meant either. "It means something very bad. Something that nice people just don't say. Never say. It's a bad word," she said, floundering into complete confusion.

She darted a frantic look toward her husband, but His Honor was finishing his grapefruit. As usual leaving her with the impossible jobs.

Her bitterness shocked her, and she was on the point of reproaching herself, when His Honor looked up from his grapefruit and *smiled*. No, not smiled, grinned. He was laughing at her, silently, mockingly saying: *You were the one who insisted on him going to that school*. Perhaps, worse, perhaps even trying to tell her that he didn't care, that it didn't matter in the least that his son was learning such obscenities. He had heard them all and survived in his Irish gutter.

A blaze of anger, wildly out of proportion and utterly uncontrollable, raced through Paula's mind and body while she listened to her husband trying to dissipate some of the confusion she had just sown in her son's mind.

"Don't worry about what it means for the time being," Jake said. "You'll find out in a couple of years. You'll think it's dumb, I guarantee you."

He shoved aside his grapefruit and drank his coffee in one long swallow. She *must* speak to him about that habit, Paula thought. He didn't drink it that way in public, thank God. But it was not the best example in the world to give his children.

"Gotta get to work," the Mayor said. "Gotta feed the birdbrains."

"What about the buttonheads?" Dolores asked.

"And the screwballs," Kemble said halfheartedly, still not recovered from his mother's rebuke.

"I'll work on them tomorrow," the Mayor said.

"They're not all birdbrains, buttonheads, and screwballs," Paula said.

"That's right," the Mayor said. "Some of them are pinheads."

Kemble hastily finished his breakfast and followed his father into the hall. He was bused downtown each day to PS 19, a magnet school in the First Ward. The school was brand new. They were teaching French, Spanish, and Latin, the latest version of the new math. The pupil-teacher ratio was the lowest in the city. Every classroom was crammed with audiovisual equipment. The city had built four of these schools in the last three years in a final attempt to forestall forced busing by persuading white parents to send their children downtown voluntarily. Kemble's school was still 90 per cent black. The others were about the same discouraging ratio.

Dolores abandoned her breakfast to pursue Kemble and her father into the hall. Paula heard her demanding a kiss, then some chatter about revenge from Kemble. There was a delighted squeal of pain from Kemble. "Do it to me, too," Dolores demanded.

She scampered back into the dining room to show her mother the red mark on her arm where her father had given her an Indian burn. It was a sadistic game that Paula disliked on principle. But the children loved it.

Dolores went back to spooning cornflakes into her cupid's bow mouth, then stopped and said with a sigh: "Daddy is fun."

"Kemble. Aren't you going to kiss me good-by?" Paula called.

"Wow," Kemble said, running back with his books under one arm. "He really gave me an Indian burn. You should see it."

"I don't want to see it. I don't like it. I hope you learn a lot today."

Kemble made a face. "Yeah." He slouched off to meet his school bus. He had no enthusiasm for his magnet school. He had already had some unfortunate collisions with his black schoolmates.

"Why should anybody want to shoot Daddy?" Dolores asked, her spoon poised over her cereal.

Paula was raising her coffee cup to her lips. Her arm froze. "No one wants to shoot Daddy."

"Dorothy's boyfriend does. I heard him tell her. He used that word Barney used."

"Kemble. Call your brother Kemble. You've never even seen Dorothy's boyfriend. You're making this up."

"No, I'm not. I listened on the telephone. On the ex-tension in your room. I listen there lots of times, when I'm supposed to be taking a nap."

"That's a *very* naughty thing to do."

"I know," said Dolores, giving her mother a shattering smile, "but it's fun."

"What—what did you hear Dorothy say?"

"She said she loved him. Just like on television. Then he said, 'You've got to help us get that——,' that bad word Barney used."

"Good morning, Mrs. O'Connor."

Paula whirled to stare up at the earnest black face of her secretary, Dorothy Washington. The coffee cup jerked loose from her frozen fingers, and hot brown liquid cascaded into her lap. Cries of alarm from Dorothy, nurse Mackey, Hannah the cook, emergency application of towels, napkins, washcloths. All in vain. Her peignoir was hopelessly stained. Paula sat there, rubbing mechanically at it, thinking, stained, stained, stained. By what, Paula?

She looked in bewilderment from her daughter to Mackey to Dorothy's black face. Her mother's cry echoed down her nerves. *When I think of the life we could have had.*

6

Sleeplessness and a hangover added to the sense of unreality that surrounded Mayor O'Connor like an envelope of smog as he entered his office. He paused in the doorway to let his eyes enjoy his secretary's lustrous black hair and creamy white skin.

"Good morning, Your Honor," Helen Ganey said.

A beautiful girl, but she was too religious for her own and anyone else's good. She was always saying novenas and lighting candles for him. The upheaval of Vatican II that had transformed millions of Catholics from true believers to Mass-skipping skeptics had missed Helen completely. Her piety reminded the Mayor of his mother. She even looked a little like Katherine O'Connor. But the Mayor was able to tolerate Helen's holiness because she never tried to inflict it on him. It also made seduction impossible. An important requirement for a politician's secretary.

Helen was reading the Garden Square *Journal*. "What's new in the people's bible?" the Mayor asked.

Helen grimaced. "They've got a story on your dinner party last night."

"Who wrote it?"

"Dennis Mulligan."

The *Journal* was owned by a family of Neanderthal Republicans who never missed a chance to make the Mayor and his appointees look corrupt or silly. They had been fighting Irish control of City Hall for sixty years and they saw no reason to change their attitude for

Mayor O'Connor. At the start of the first term, Paula had been confident that she could persuade them to support him. "Only if I change my name to Stapleton," he had told her.

The Mayor had tried to blunt the paper's hostility by wooing the reporters and editors. This was an even more frustrating experience. After months of off-the-record talks, informal breakfasts, and late-night drinks, he would get a good man on his side—a month before he quit to double his money on the Los Angeles *Times* or the Milwaukee *Journal*. Only the second-raters seemed to stay.

At the head of this list was Dennis Mulligan. His father had been a spear carrier in the old organization—a precinct worker who never got near any real money or power. This made Dennis Mulligan envy—perhaps even hate—Jake O'Connor, whose father had not only gotten very close to both these presumably marvelous goals, but he, the hustling son, had apparently reached them. Mulligan knew where to look for dirt. His employers loved him for his ability to ferret out petty scandals—cops and firemen retiring on phony disability pensions, contractors with brothers-in-law in the Water Department, welfare chiselers.

But a glance at the front page told the Mayor this was not one of Dennis Mulligan's typical excursions. Someone had leaked him the whole story of last night's dinner, down to the expensive menu. He had put it all into his column, "Around City Hall."

> The O'Connor for Senator bandwagon stripped a gear, lost a wheel and broke an axle at Bowood last night. Worse, its hero lost his head in the wreck. All the king's men may not be able to put it—or him—together again. O'Connor backers from the mountains to the sea were summoned to this feast, which began with shrimp remoulade and ended with vanilla mousse, to be reassured that the city's busing crisis, largely created by the Mayor's ineptitude, would have no effect on his candidacy. His dutiful black servants, Adam Turner and the

Reverend Quentin P. Brown, Jr., were on hand to pledge their support on election day, no matter what the Mayor said against busing to hold the white ethnics in line. But dissension erupted between the white and black sides of the table. Before the feast was over, the faithful were snarling at each other like Protestants and Catholics in Belfast. The Mayor's solution to this crisis was more scotch all around. This only made the conflagration blaze higher. Eddie McKenna, the token leader of the city's Democrats, left without saying goodnight to anyone. By that time, according to the insider who told your reporter this tale of woe, the Mayor was not *able* to say goodnight to anyone. He had had too much of his own solution. . . .

Slowly, methodically, the Mayor crumpled Dennis Mulligan into a ball and stuffed him into the wastebasket. As he completed this satisfying symbolic act, the six telephones on his desk began to flash. Down the hall twenty-five-year-old Charlie LoBello, his appointments secretary, was fending off the callers. The Mayor would spend the afternoon returning the calls. Mornings were reserved for meeting people face to face.

In previous administrations, the Mayor had begun the day by spending a raucous half hour with Happy Burns. An ex-union organizer with a mug's face and an accent to match it, Happy had helped the Mayor negotiate the intricate jungle of the city's politics after the collapse of the old machine. In the middle of the race for governor, which he had urged the Mayor to duck, Happy had come home at 3 A.M. as usual, lay down on his bed, and astonished his wife by complaining that he was tired. He never got up. It made the Mayor feel a little more lonely in City Hall.

He had tried replacing Happy with another man his age. The Mayor realized when it did not work that he would never be able to find that special blend of shrewd advice and emotional rapport that he had gotten from Happy. He had been just old enough to function as a kind of semi-father, without a father's complications.

He had been smart enough to keep his advice to a minimum, and never to challenge the Mayor when he had made up his mind. With Happy's replacements—there had been several—the Mayor soon realized that he no longer wanted paternal advice. He had dumped the last replacement for twenty-three-year-old Charlie LoBello, just out of the Marine Corps with a Medal of Honor from Vietnam. Charlie regarded the Mayor with affectionate awe. He was practically prehistoric. He had fought Kamikazes off Okinawa with Charlie's father.

Pursuing the same new generation philosophy, the Mayor had hired the son of another old friend as his press secretary. Dave O'Brien was even more inclined to view Mayor O'Connor as legendary. His father, George, had been one of the Mayor's drinking partners in his wild late teens and early twenties. Nostalgia had quadrupled the Mayor's capacity for liquor and women in the stories George O'Brien told.

Dennis Mulligan called these appointments "the aging Mayor's youth movement." With his habitual unsympathy, neither Mulligan nor anyone else noticed that it left the Mayor isolated. Ted Finsterman and Happy Burns had been the nucleus of his inner City Hall circle, with others aboard largely as temporary favorites. This isolation left him exposed to forays from various members of his administration, who sensed a vacuum—and from his wife. The Mayor bore these power plays patiently. In some ways he liked them. But he did not like and he was sure that he never would like the way he was now deprived of his standard defense in his disagreements with his wife. No longer could he blame Finsterman or Happy Burns for the rejection of her latest attempt to turn the town into the biblical City on a Hill. Now he had to admit that he was the abominable no man.

The intercom on his desk buzzed. "Police Commissioner Tarentino is here, Your Honor," Helen Ganey said.

"I'm ready."

With his wavy, well-barbered gray hair, his Roman nose and determined jaw, Victor Tarentino looked ready to play the leading role in one of those Italian pictures about the doomed love of a middle-aged Florentine and a sex-starved American spinster. But the Mayor had long since learned that this image, like so many other things in his life, was deceptive. The Mayor was sure that Commissioner Tarentino had never touched another woman since he married shapely Della O'Connell the day after he was discharged from the U.S. Army in 1945. If Tarentino had his way, there would be no theaters showing *Deep Throat,* which had just returned to one of the city's so-called adult movie houses for the fifth time with the approval of the local judiciary. There would be no whores shoving pussy in the faces of visiting salesmen on almost every corner in the uptown business district, thanks to the open-mindedness of those same black-robed guardians of everyone's rights. There would have been no demonstrations against the war in Vietnam on the steps of City Hall. There would be no school buses to protect with meticulous contingency plans.

But Commissioner Tarentino never permitted his disapproval of these things to interfere with the performance of his department. His detectives had arrested a half dozen right-wing super Catholics, who had been phoning bomb scares into the porno theaters. His plainclothesmen never entrapped a prostitute, which was more than the Civil Liberties Union could say for the police departments of New York, Chicago, and Los Angeles. The anti-Vietnam marchers had been shielded from hard-hat bricks and bottles by a phalanx of tactical patrolmen. The school buses would get the same scrupulous protection, no matter what the color of their passengers.

Commissioner Tarentino was a professional cop. But that was not the chief reason for the scowl he normally wore on his pallid handsome face. Tarentino knew that he was also a symbol of a new order of things—the first Italian to head the city's police force, which was still 50 per cent Irish. The Mayor had deliberately chosen him to announce to the city—and to the Irish themselves—that the era of Celtic political domination was over. The Mayor had finessed this move by ordering Tarentino to make war on his own kind. In the power vacuum left by the collapse of the old machine, one of the state's Mafia families had reached for control of the city's multimillion-dollar gambling habit, and everything else that they could grab, from unions to corporations. With patient investigation, courageous informers, and a wizard's ingenuity at planting mikes and tapping phones, Tarentino had smashed them. Don Carmine Biaggi himself and two of his capos were in jail.

But it had been a costly victory. The Biaggis had retaliated with sophisticated hatred. Several of the state's congressmen suddenly became vocal defenders of the right to privacy. Stories were leaked to Dennis Mulligan alleging that Mayor O'Connor was tapping the phones of half the officials in his administration. Soon gullible liberals were deploring Tarentino's "fascist tendencies." When the Mayor ran for governor five years ago, the Biaggis had reportedly spent a half million to help beat him. Tony Perotta and his Italian American Alliance were financed by Don Carmine, who continued to reign from his prison cell. The family still flourished in a half dozen nearby small cities.

"Hello, Jake."

Commissioner Tarentino's muscular hand came at him across the desk. Mayor O'Connor seized it and met the squeeze with a muscular response of his own. *Shake hands like a man,* the first lesson he had learned from his father. The cut on the heel of his hand sent flickers of pain up his arm.

"I see you just read it."

"Mulligan?" the Mayor asked, glancing into the wastebasket.

"You've been trusting a lot of wrong people, Jake. Who's the leak?"

"It could have been any one of them. Maybe even Bernie Bannon. Nothing would surprise me anymore."

Tarentino shook his head. "It's somebody closer. Somebody who wants you up against the wall right here."

"Adam Turner?"

"Let me put a tap on him, Jake."

"Out of the question, Vic. Jesus Christ, haven't you heard of a little mess called Watergate?"

"A bunch of amateurs from California. I guarantee you the boogie'll never know a thing about it, if we broadcast him for a year."

But you'll know. Tarentino's success with the mob had made him arrogant. He had never used it against the Mayor. But it created a thin wedge of distrust between them.

The Mayor shook his head.

"Jake. Didn't we tap the whole Biaggi family, right up to Don Carmine? And they never knew it, until we moved on them. With all their so-called bug experts."

"That was law enforcement, Vic."

"You got to play as rough as the other guys are playing. What would Benny do?"

The Mayor twisted in his chair like a man trying to avoid a blow. This invocation of his father was a ritual. Ben O'Connor had gotten young Victor Tarentino onto the cops. His uncle, Lou Tarentino, had been a close friend for decades. This meant Benny had moved heaven, earth, and half of City Hall to make Vic the youngest sergeant on the force.

"Vic," the Mayor said, "you know I think Benny was a hell of a guy. But he was a ward leader. He never sat in this seat. He never had to think about running the whole goddamned city. And he never had a glimmer of running for the Senate. He went along with the organization. Are you saying we ought to start playing it their way, one hand in the till and the other around a nightstick?"

"Of course not. Jesus Christ, haven't I given you the cleanest police department in the history of this lousy town? But I want to see you go all the way, Jake. If that means getting rough, I'm ready to do it. I owe it to you."

"You don't owe me a goddamn thing except a good day's work—and I've been getting that for nine years."

Commissioner Tarentino shook his head. Neither compliments nor insults were going to stop him. "Listen to me, Jake. You've got to start thinking for yourself. You've been letting too many other people do it for you."

"Bullshit," the Mayor said. He swiveled away from Commissioner Tarentino to stare out the huge oblong window behind him. Once this same view from his office in the old City Hall had been nothing but grubby gray. Now fountains played on a broad plaza. Four gleaming white buildings, designed by some of the nation's best architects, soared into the winter sky. Beneath the ground there was parking for a thousand cars and a half-mile arcade lined with weather-free shops, steam heated in winter, air-conditioned in the summer. He had created this plaza, those shops, those soaring buildings.

Paula had suggested a new City Hall as a symbol of change. He had vetoed the idea. It smacked too much of the ego trip, of building a palace for himself and his friends. A visit to Montreal for an international conference of mayors had changed his mind. After a tour of the Place Ville Marie, he came home willing to accept the new City Hall as part of a skyscraper complex that would give the city a new focus, a new pride. Paula had blanched at the cost and argued in favor of putting the money into people not buildings. A half dozen of his early supporters denounced him for his "edifice complex," but he still believed he had made the right decision. The buildings spoke to another generation, to men and women who needed pride more than paternalism.

Unfortunately, at the southern end of the plaza there were two huge empty lots where the poverty money and the private investments had dried up in the recession. Visible across their acres of rubble and dirt were the downtown wards. When they began building the plaza, a third of those wards were still white, mostly Poles and Slovaks. In the next five years they had abandoned their flats and houses in totally unexpected numbers, ignoring frantic efforts by the CPI and other city agencies to steady them, leaving the plaza an island in a black sea. A white island that was rapidly becoming a white elephant.

The Mayor sighed. The change had made downtown a new code word for black. It had added geography to the city's racial division. It had made him the Mayor of two cities.

Suddenly the Mayor was back thirty years, standing beside his father on a rickety street corner platform in one of those downtown wards. "You are my people," his father had said. Something deep in the Mayor had responded to those words even at sixteen, although he had looked down at the heterogeneous faces with more curiosity than concern.

But caring, simple caring, the Mayor told himself, was no longer enough.

True, but at the same time he could not bear losing it. Why? Wasn't it inevitable? What did that old kind of caring have to do with pollsters' charts and issue-oriented politics? Staring out at the buildings and the empty lots, while Victor Tarentino's face and voice accused him, the Mayor realized that underneath the fear of loss was another fear, another question. Had the caring ever existed? Was this gleaming downtown plaza one more attempt to evade the missing emotion, the felt responsibility? Was it ultimately what he envied rather than disliked in his wife —her emotional commitment, however erratic it tended to become? The Mayor sat there at his window, letting the questions gnaw at his nerves.

"Okay," Tarentino said. "I just thought somebody ought to say it to you. I didn't expect you to like it. We trucked all those intelligence reports over to the Judge yesterday afternoon. You still don't think they'll change his mind?"

The Mayor shook his head. "Not a chance."

"What's the next move? The Judge may not believe those reports, but I do. The North Slope is gonna blow, Jake. And when we get to the South Slope next fall—I don't want to think about it."

"We don't have any more moves."

"What about your wife—I mean Paula—can't she get to this guy?"

Paula and Victor Tarentino were not very friendly. She tended to listen to liberals, such as Ray Grimes, who had a pathological dislike of Tarentino's hard-nosed style. Recently she had told a reporter that the tactical patrol force, the elite riot control unit that the Commissioner had developed during the turbulent late 1960s, was a symbol of police brutality and ought to be disbanded. The Mayor pondered the possibility of telling Tarentino that he had asked his wife to approach Judge Stapleton and she had refused. This was one of the few details of last night's meeting that the leaker had not told Dennis Mulligan. The Mayor decided to lie. *Never tell anyone too much.* That was the only piece of advice his father had given the Mayor when he was elected.

"I wouldn't ask her, Vic."

"She'd probably say no."

The Mayor saw no need to answer that one. Tarentino was ready to change the subject too. "I'm worried about these death threats. I'd like you to have a twenty-four-hour-a-day bodyguard from now on."

"Jesus Christ, Vic. What for?"

"To keep you alive."

As a police commissioner who tried to double as a political advisor, Tarentino had one weakness. He always feared and predicted the worst. He was right only about half the time. The Mayor found himself remembering the last time he had been right.

When the black ghettos had erupted in the late 1960s, this was one of the few cities that did not burn. Mayor O'Connor had gotten most of the press clippings for it. His walk down Division Street into the heart of an incipient 1970 riot had been embellished and exaggerated by every newspaper in the state, until they had him taking on 60,000 foaming-mad blacks armed with nothing but his Boy Scout honor badges. Pure flackery, of course. Commissioner Tarentino had had squad cars with shotguns jutting from their windows on every side street. In a scenario as carefully worked out as D-Day, Tarentino and his cops played the heavies, and the Mayor was the nice guy who was trying to save the ghetto from the law's harsh vengeance. It was a brilliant adaptation of an old police interrogation routine. It had worked because even the drunkest black rioter knew that Tarentino's cops were ready to pull those triggers.

Most newspapers had praised the performance as an

act of racial statesmanship and physical courage. Rah. Rah. Mayor O'Connor had become an instant national figure, a gubernatorial, even a presidential prospect. With the superficiality of the mass media, the reporters went on to another story, and never bothered to note that the Mayor had suffered dangerous political wounds.

While he was persuading his black brothers not to burn down the city, they were exuberantly liberating some three million dollars worth of jewelry, liquor, television sets, suits, sweaters, and shoes from the local merchants. From that day, Mayor O'Connor had lost control of the city's racial politics. From that day began the Board of Education's secret meetings and intricate plots to maintain a segregated school system at almost any cost. From that day, the Mayor ruefully admitted, had begun his own semi-acquiescence in their duplicity, interrupted only by spurts of opposition inspired by his wife.

Did it make any difference? the Mayor wondered. Wouldn't it have happened anyway—this obscene explosion of hate and rage and fear that was tearing the city apart—the moment they began forcing white children onto buses? His wife and her friends had no idea of a school's central role in the life of a neighborhood. They had never experienced the slowly interwoven friendships between students who spent six or eight years together, the subtle links between brothers and sisters, parents and friends that came from years of sharing the same classrooms, teachers, gyms, schoolyards. A private language of teachers' nicknames. *Bonesy, Dynamite Aggie.* A common geography. *They were waiting for me behind Keller's garage, I got away down Timlin's alley into Crotty's yard.* The Mayor knew these things. They were part of his life. But when he tried to explain them to his wife, she dismissed them as sentimental trivia.

The Mayor fingered his flashing telephones. He weighed Tarentino's pessimism against his own fatalism. "Do you have any idea who's making these calls? Paula thinks she got the guy on tape last night."

"She did. I want you to listen to him."

The Commissioner took a small cassette tape recorder out of his brief case and put it on the desk.

In a moment, the Mayor was hearing the sepulchral voice of his self-appointed killer.

"Ring a bell?"

"Play it again."

Tumbling like a man trapped in an Atlantic breaker, the Mayor was swept to the shore of another time. He was in a room lit by a single bare overhead bulb. That same voice was speaking. It was not threatening him with death. It was encouraging other voices, ragged with hysteria and defeat, to accuse Jake O'Connor in his father's name, to lay on his shoulders the thirty years of brutality and corruption that his father had helped to create.

"You know him," Victor Tarentino said, studying the Mayor's face.

The Mayor nodded. "It's Frank Donahue."

"I thought so. This time, let's put that prick away, Jake."

The Mayor shook his head. "He's harmless, Vic."

"He wasn't harmless six years ago."

"You can't put a guy in jail for handing out anarchist literature. Not in this country, anyway. They did it up in Buffalo and it stank for the next ten years."

"He was yelling fire in a crowded theater. Only a miracle saved us from another riot. I still don't understand what happened."

The reluctant confession of a past mistake gave the Mayor the leverage he needed to say no to Tarentino. After the 1970 riot, Tarentino had talked the Mayor into spending a half million dollars on special weaponry. In spite of agitators such as Frank Donahue, rioting had abruptly gone out of fashion, and the gadgetry slowly turned to junk in the police warehouse.

"It's a statute offense to threaten anyone's life over the telephone. We can put him away for five years," Tarentino said.

"I don't want to make a martyr out of him, Vic. He's still got a few screwballs who listen to him."

"What about the bodyguard?"

"I'm afraid it's no on that one too, Vic. If Donahue's our only worry, I think I'll survive. He's always been all talk and no action. But the main reason is the city's mood. If it ever got out—it would make me look like a liar and a coward. I'm telling everybody to keep calm and obey the law—but I've got a hired gun behind me just in case."

"I hope we don't regret it, Jake," Tarentino said.

"If I'm wrong, I'll do the regretting, Vic. Now, take it easy on Frank Donahue. No rough stuff."

"We'll get a microphone into the place. We've got an informant in there. We'll just monitor him."

The Mayor thought about trying to explain his real attitude toward Frank Donahue. He was not sure if he could explain it to himself. When he thought about him, he saw another face with a stubble of beard around the sagging mouth, reading Shakespeare aloud in a dingy living room. Shakespeare blurred, slurred by booze. Dick Donahue, Frank's father, one of the losers, one of the men who had fought the old organization and had been smashed to alcoholic jelly.

Tarentino held out his hand. "Don't worry about it. No one's going to get a shot at you while I'm around. You're going all the way."

The Mayor nodded, and met the Commissioner's bone-crushing squeeze.

"Anytime you get the jitters, just remember who your father was. Nothing scared that bastard. He was one in a barrel."

The Mayor collapsed into his swivel chair and watched his police commissioner stride out the door. It was all so simple in Tarentinoworld. Bug, club, catch, and stash them and don't-lose-your-nerve. If you do, mutter a prayer to Blessed Benny O'Connor. Now he knew why every village in Italy had a local saint. Apotheosis must be an irresistible impulse in the Italian character.

"Councilman Turner to see you."

"Send him in."

The big oak door banged open and Adam Turner strolled into the room. The Mayor felt irritation dim his welcoming smile. Face to face—or head to head— Adam's huge Afro struck him as an esthetic monstrosity

89

and a political disaster. He was wearing a blue denim leisure suit and a yellow turtleneck, both of which also failed to win the Mayor's approval. The Mayor saw Adam's new style as a walking invitation to confrontation politics. Not that Adam looked white in the blue pinstriped suits and short hair on which the Mayor had insisted when he put him on the ticket in 1971. Adam's skin was the color of dark chocolate. His narrow, angular face and thick-lipped mouth were pure African. The Mayor had argued that this reality made the pinstriped suits and neat hair all the more necessary to counter the white backlash he risked to support Adam. Councilmen were elected city-wide, and Adam could not have won without a strong endorsement from Mayor O'Connor.

Two years ago, when the crunch over school integration began, Adam had started changing his style. The business suits had disappeared, his Afro had started to grow. But he had waited until after he was re-elected for another four years to let his new look really flourish.

Adam came toward the Mayor with the casual lope of a distance runner. Adam had been a track star in high school. It was a sport in which the Mayor had never had much interest. He had always played on teams—baseball, football, basketball—on which he had been the star. Adam used to approach the desk in a slower, more tentative walk that suggested mild deference. The Mayor wryly reminded himself that he had not liked that style either. He held out his hand and pressed Adam's pink palm with standard enthusiasm. Compared to Victor Tarentino's, Adam's handshake was a caress. The palm was cold and moist. The only hint that he was not perfectly at ease in the Mayor's office.

The Mayor had thought he was choosing very carefully when he put Adam Turner on his ticket in 1971. The 1970 census had reported the city was now one-quarter black. It was time to give them a voice in City Hall. The Mayor had leaned toward the Reverend Quentin P. Brown, Jr., whose father had been the black leader of Ben O'Connor's old Thirteenth Ward. But Paula and

Ted Finsterman had convinced him that the city needed a younger, more with-it man.

Adam had emerged as a leader during the early stages of the poverty war, when he organized a neighborhood association in Bayshore, at the foot of the city's North Slope. BBV—Bayshore's Black Voice—had impressed the Mayor because it amalgamated the half dozen other black groups in the area into a single organization, and kept them that way. Eddie McKenna's brutal summary of black politics as a surplus of generals and colonels and a shortage of troops was basically correct. It made for frustration and fury in dealing with them. Too often, an agreement with one so-called black spokesman was denounced five minutes later by another one, and neither could muster two hundred votes. The Mayor's instinct had been to build one black into a leader, and deal with him. It was how the old organization had handled the Poles and Italians in his father's day, when the Irish had been the rulers of the city.

Lately, the Mayor had begun to wonder if he had been too successful. Using his city councilman's clout, Adam had applied his Bayshore tactics to the rest of the downtown neighborhoods and organized a caucus of black leaders in and out of the O'Connor administration. For the moment, it was a shaky coalition but its very existence aroused the Mayor's instinctive distrust. Equally disturbing was Adam's growing fondness for talking like a street corner radical. Until recently he had confined his demands to private meetings in the Mayor's office.

The Mayor had assumed that all would be well as long as Adam got his way on a reasonable percentage of things. But the Mayor had soon noticed a difference on the meaning of a reasonable percentage. Adam had begun pushing toward nine out of ten, while the Mayor struggled to hold it to one out of two. This did not particularly upset the Mayor. Everyone pushed to maximize his clout. But he thought there was a lack of gratitude in Adam Turner's case. The Mayor felt that he had responded to the civil rights movement. Blacks had been given a handsome percentage of jobs in the police, fire departments, and other city agencies. He had not always appointed blacks whom Adam recommended. But he did not always appoint the Italians that Dominick Montefiore sponsored, or the Irishmen that Eddie McKenna pushed. He believed in keeping everyone just a little off balance. But Montefiore and McKenna did not go around bad-mouthing the city and talking about a race war. They understood the rules of the political game. Adam either did not understand them or he no longer gave a damn for them.

The Mayor preferred the second explanation. He sometimes thought about bluntly asking Adam for his version, but he always abandoned the impulse at the last moment. Distance, mutual wariness were the now basic elements in his relationship with Adam. The Mayor did not know what to do about it. With other men everything came instinctively. He could say bullshit to Victor Tarentino, trade insults with Eddie McKenna, or put his arm around Dominick Montefiore like a stronger, wiser brother. He would not, could not, do any of these things with this black man. Turner treated him the same way. He was still polite, even deferential, but with an underlying irony in his tone. Almost always, Your Honor, Mr. Mayor, seldom Jake. It left the Mayor feeling constantly uneasy, and this feeling was multiplied now by the larger meaning Adam had suddenly assumed in his life. Councilman Turner's support had become crucial in Jake O'Connor's quest for the U. S. Senate.

"That's a rotten story in the paper this morning, Your Honor," Adam said as he sat down.

"It could have been worse. They could have said we were queer for each other, Adam."

"Seriously, Mr. Mayor. I've got to deny it. I want you to understand that. I'm going to make a statement saying we were at the dinner to guarantee the city's support of the busing program."

"I've already pledged that support, Adam. Won't it sound like you don't believe me?"

"I don't care what it will sound like, Your Honor. I've got to protect myself with my own people."

What about protecting me?

The Mayor did not say it. If Turner had been white, he would have said it. Instead, the Mayor only nodded and lit a cigarette. Why did these people leave him politically helpless? It had something to do with their black skin, with their strange hair. He had no feel for them. He did not know them. He had never sat in their kitchens and eaten their food, as he had done with Polish and Italian friends a hundred times growing up, he had never even known a single black his own age well enough to call him by his first name until he started running for Mayor. He told himself to accept the distance, the strangeness, as fate. But it kept arousing a sullen anger in him.

"I heard there was some other stuff that went on last night after we left. If it's true, I don't like it very much."

"What the hell are you talking about?"

"You got some idea about torpedoing this whole thing. Getting Judge Stapleton to back down. You do that, Your Honor, and you can say good-by to the black vote. I couldn't deliver it, even if I wanted to."

"Who told you this, Adam?"

"I heard it from a couple of people."

"I have no intention of torpedoing anyone or anything. But I have thought about—and we did discuss last night—the possibility of asking for a delay. Maybe of a year. My run for the Senate has nothing to do with it. We need more time to get people ready for this—"

Adam slowly shook his head. "Don't bullshit me, Your Honor."

"I'm telling you the goddamn truth."

Adam sat there looking skeptically at him for a long moment. "It's a sad fact, Your Honor, but I don't trust you very much. If it wasn't for Paula, I wouldn't trust you at all."

And I'm trusting you with my whole goddamn future. How did I get into this bag with this black prick?

"A long time ago, Adam, we said we were building a bridge, you and me—and Paula. I'm still trying to build it."

"So am I, Your Honor. But don't make it too hard for me."

"I can say the same thing. I've doubled the number of blacks on the city payroll. But I'm still the enemy."

"You're not the enemy, Your Honor. But you're not exactly our friend either. I'm speakin' not just for me, but for the black people. I'm the only voice they got around here. I got to think of myself that way, as well as plain Adam Turner. We're grateful for what you've done for us. But we don't trust you. We don't trust any white politician. When we hear you're trying to sink this busing thing behind our backs—when I hear you say just now that you're ready to support a year's delay—it just makes me wonder. Don't you have any idea how that would hit the black community? Don't you realize how much pride and hope black people have put into getting their kids ready for this program? You can't put those things in cold storage for a year. It just reinforces a feeling I've had about you from the start. You don't—"

The Mayor was angry and making very little effort to conceal it. The expression on his face stopped Turner in mid-sentence.

"What?" he said. "What? Let's put everything on the goddamn table for once."

"You don't give a real damn for us. You do the necessary. You put on a good act. But we're just not part of your picture, Your Honor. We're something extra that you work on in your spare time."

"Spare time," the Mayor said. "Jesus Christ, I've given seventy-five percent of my time to you sons of bitches for the last six months. What the hell do you mean, I don't give a damn? I give a damn for everybody in this city. I was born in it and I've spent my life trying to make it a place people want to live in. Not a place people run away from."

"Don't take it personally, Your Honor. I'm just layin' it on the line. I got the feeling we're going to be doing a lot of business together in the next couple of weeks. I thought it might help if we understood each other. I could be wrong about that feeling. I hope I am."

"You are wrong," the Mayor snarled, and realized only after he said it that his tone totally belied his words.

"Okay. Okay," Adam Turner said. "I knew it would make you sore. But I wanted to say it. We got to understand each other, Jake. For the sake of the kids on those buses, if for no other reason."

"I'm just as worried about those kids as you are. What the hell do I have to do to prove it?"

"Nothing, nothing."

From truculence, Turner had descended to something close to cringing. The Mayor was assailed by another spasm of hopelessness. Out of control. His city was out of control, and the reason for it was looking him in the face.

"Keep in touch, Adam," he said. "Close touch."

"Sure."

It was no consolation, but Adam Turner departed looking equally discouraged. The Mayor glanced at the long line of previous mayors staring at him from the walls. *How am I doing, fellows? I know the answer. Barely a passing mark for that one.*

Dominick Montefiore, president of the City Council, was the next visitor. He got to the point immediately. "Jake," he said, "I'm pretty upset about that meeting last night. Why wasn't I invited?"

"It wasn't a local meeting, Dom. It was basically educational, to keep up the confidence of the downstate people."

"Why was Adam Turner there?"

"He was there to convince them that I wouldn't lose the black vote, no matter what I said."

"I still should have been there, Jake."

"Why?"

"Because I would have told them some bad news. You're gonna lose the white vote."

"Why? What have I got to do? Carry a whip and lash every darky I see?"

"Let me be more precise," Dominick said, lighting a cigarette and adjusting his steel-rimmed glasses. He had a remarkable resemblance to Pius XII which inclined the Mayor to make numerous wisecracks behind his back.

But basically he respected Montefiore. He was an honest, if limited, man. They had gone through St. Francis Prep together. They had never been close friends, but they had kept in touch and the Mayor had encouraged Montefiore to go into politics to improve the profits of his family's insurance business. The profits, all strictly legal, had improved spectacularly. Montefiore now lived in one of the largest houses on the Parkway, the city's poshest street.

"I'm speaking for the Italian community when I tell you this, Jake. I hate to do that. I'd like to speak for all of the people of this city. But those are the ones I really know. They want you to tell these black bastards to go to hell, Jake. They want defiance. They're not satisfied with this we-must-obey-the-law act."

"Would you mind explaining to them, Dominick, that I'm an elected official? I have to say things like that. If I don't, I could be held in contempt of court. I can get five years in the slammer."

In his mind, the Mayor cursed Dennis Mulligan and the man who had leaked the story to him. He had planned to work on Montefiore to extract a statement of minimum support of busing from the City Council. Now the momentum was all on Montefiore's side.

The Council president stubbed out his cigarette and wiped his glasses. "I'm so upset about this thing, Jake, I don't know what to do next. I don't sleep. People call me up at two o'clock in the morning and ask me if they should sell their houses. What can I tell them? Who'll buy a house in the city now? These poor bastards are stuck, Jake. They're sitting ducks. What are we doing to them?"

"We're not doing anything to them."

"I mean the country. What's the United States of America doing to people like—like my brother? He owns a truck. One lousy truck. He makes maybe twelve, fifteen thousand a year. He puts it all in the house. Into his family. He's on the road sixteen, twenty hours a day, working his tail off for his wife and kids. He comes home, everybody respects him. If he goes to church on Easter Sunday, he puts ten dollars in the basket. That's a big thing to him. He goes to a social club, shoots pool, people ask his advice. He's a district leader. He gets out a good vote on election day. He doesn't want to leave his neighborhood. His wife is hysterical. She says she'll poison her children before she lets one of them go into a nigger school. She sees her daughters getting raped, her sons castrated. What am I going to say to her?"

"Dominick. Tell her to calm down. Tell her it won't happen."

"She won't listen. Nobody is listening."

"We've got to keep saying it until they listen. Tell her to wait and see how it works on the North Slope. We knew your people were going to be tougher to handle, Dominick. That's why we went for the Irish and the Poles first."

Montefiore's voice became choked with resentment. "You know, Jake, that hurts me. To hear you speak about Italians that way. Without respect. We didn't talk that way before this shit started. We were going someplace. We were making something new in this city. We were all Americans. We were getting out of the goddamned Italian-Irish-Polish bag. We were on our way to something good."

"I know," the Mayor said. "Maybe we can get back to it."

"When? The next century maybe, when we're in wheelchairs?"

He was right, devastatingly right. The words cut through the flesh of the Mayor's effort to soothe and persuade him, momentarily paralyzing him with pain. This had been one of the things he had hoped—even expected—to do for this city—lead them beyond their ethnic tribalism, the narrow world of the ghetto, to a new sense of community. The blacks, with their ferocious insistence on their special identity, had gutted his hope as thoroughly as the Kamikazes had wrecked the carrier *Yorktown*. The dream was dead in the water, a drifting burnt-out hulk.

"Dominick," the Mayor said, "people like us have got to keep calm. We've got to do everything we can to persuade both sides to show some good will. That's why

I'm hoping—and I know this won't be easy—I'm hoping you'll get the Council to pass a resolution asking everyone in the city to co-operate with the busing plan."

"Jake, you want me to commit suicide in public," Montefiore said, "and I'll do it. But only for a good cause. Hari-kari for the fun of it is not my style."

"I'll twist every arm I can for you."

"The answer is *no,* Jake. No. I don't want my windows broken. I don't want threats in the middle of the night. The calls I'm getting are bad enough. 'It's time,' that's all a lot of them say, and hang up."

Ten years ago, at the end of his first four-year term, the Mayor had survived a ferocious challenge from an Italian candidate who had run on the slogan "It's Time." His City Council slate had had exclusively Italian and Polish names. It was an attempt to isolate the Irish, who amounted to no more than 15 per cent of the city's vote. But the Mayor had retained enough Polish and Italian loyalists such as Montefiore to beat back the assault by a hairy 1 per cent. Italian resentment remained a ticking electoral time bomb. Montefiore knew it was why he was president of the City Council.

"The thing we talked about—maybe it ought to be done soon," Montefiore said. "Otherwise I don't see how I can hold my head up on the Slope."

The "thing" was the Mayor's endorsement of Montefiore as his successor, presuming the run for the Senate was a victory. It was an endorsement the Mayor had no intention of giving until he was a certified winner. The moment he gave it, his leverage with Montefiore was gone.

"Maybe you're right, Dom. I'll think about it," he said.

Montefiore departed. The Mayor sat there feeling like he'd just gone three rounds with Muhammad Ali. Sweat glued his undershirt to his back. He flipped on the intercom and told Helen Ganey to stall the next appointment. He strolled down to the other end of his office, which was a cavernous duplicate of the Mayor's office in the original City Hall. He had insisted on the duplication, in spite of protests from Paula and lamentations from the architect. The Mayor stopped before the portrait of Mortimer Kemble. The old boy stared straight ahead, no compromise in his haughty eyes, his brow furrowed, his stubborn chin submerged in Ulysses Grant-style whiskers. Mayor O'Connor walked back to his desk, and took Mortimer's journal out of the top drawer. There were paper clips on a half dozen pages. He flipped to one.

January 17th, 1870. Spent two hours today with McGovern, the Irish leader of the First Ward. A beefy, foul-mouthed Mick, with a greasy neck and egg stains on his green tie. Enough dirt under his fingernails to raise a potato crop. I agreed to give him 20 percent of the jobs in the street cleaning department, in return for his support. Also, I agreed to deal only with him, and have nothing more to do with his chief competitor, Kennelly. He is far more intelligent—and therefore much more dangerous. Divide and conquer.

My fellow native Americans are treating me as a pariah, because of my announced policy of dealing politically with the Irish. Even the few members of my club and the fewer members of the family who are Democrats denounce me. I remain unbothered by their abuse. I candidly admit to myself that I am doing it to further my own career. But I also can see a purpose beyond my personal gain. Someone must work with these people, someone must give them some hope of believing in this country and its promises. If it is not Mortimer Kemble, I fear it will be someone with far worse political principles, someone who will capitalize on the decades of resentment and hatred built up in these people, nay, if you consider their generations of oppression in Ireland, you can say centuries of resentment—and the resultant explosion may tear apart this republic. We must give them a role, however lowly, in the scheme of things.

The Mayor called for his next visitor. In came Kevin McGuire, ex-friend and protégé. Kevin was in his late thirties, about ten years younger than the Mayor. He was the son of an old O'Connor family friend. The Mayor had gotten him appointed special prosecutor to handle the Biaggi family cases. McGuire had become a local hero when he put away the don and his two biggest capos. A first-year law student could have done it with the evidence Tarentino had collected. The Mayor, who had been a very good criminal lawyer before he entered politics, conferred with McGuire continually throuhgout the trials, giving him expert advice and some badly needed encouragement when the desperate Biaggis started making last stand threats against his family. The Mayor had called Don Carmine personally and told him that if one McGuire child was so much as bruised, he would arrange with some cops he knew to feed a dozen or so Biaggis into the city's garbage trucks, head first.

After the big win, McGuire's law practice had zoomed. The Mayor had recommended him to corporations moving into the city. McGuire began wearing tailormade suits and driving a Mercedes. Four years ago, before the integration crisis began, the Mayor had appointed him president of the Board of Education. It was a largely honorary title. A professional superintendent did the educational thinking. But the Board was in charge of creating school districts and had the power to approve all pupil transfer. McGuire had had no trouble going along with a majority of the Board who were determined to keep blacks downtown. Pretty soon it became evident that he was not just going along. He was against integration in any shape or form. Paula had wanted the Mayor to fire him. The Mayor refused, fearing it would destroy his neutral stance on busing. Then came the stunning news that McGuire was running for mayor. Paradoxically, that made it more difficult to fire him, even after he lost. He had gotten 32 percent of the vote, and had elected one of the councilmen on his slate, an Italian named Perella.

Face to face, the Mayor had remained cool but not hostile. He let McGuire talk about the election as an "intellectual difference" that gave the voters a "genuine voice." Now he shook hands and asked Kevin how his wife and kids were doing. He had five boys and three girls. The county Holy Name Society had recently named him Catholic Father of the Year. Kevin said "the brood" were fine and got to the point of his visit.

"Jake," he said, "I'm going to resign."

The Mayor lit a cigarette. "Why, Kevin?"

"As president of the Board of Education, I'm the nominal head of this busing operation." He leaned hard on the word nominal. "I can't live with even that much responsibility for it, Jake."

"Kevin," the Mayor said, "you must be aware of the impact that would have on the city. It would be like a vote of no confidence from the Board."

"That's precisely what I want to do. Register my vote."

The Mayor stubbed out his cigarette. "Listen, you prick," he said. "You wouldn't be sitting there in that four-hundred-dollar suit without me. You'd be chasing ambulances up the North Slope or kissing Don Carmine's ass instead of being the boy that put him away. What do I get for it? A fucking hose job last year. I let you get away with that because I had more important things to do. Now I'm going for a big brass ring, you know what it is, and if you think I'm going to let you fuck me out of it, you need a goddamn brain transplant. I'll ruin you in this town. I'll pass the word that anyone—especially any bank or corporation—who has you for a lawyer would be better off with Dracula."

McGuire's eyes glazed. "I told you, Jake, it's an intellectual—"

"Intellectual horseshit. You tried to walk on my face to get this job. You're a miserable double-crossing piss-pot. But you're going to stay until the end of your five-year term as president of the Board of Education. Unless you want to see if I can deliver on that promise I just made."

"All right. I'll—I'll stick it out. You could have asked me in a nice way, Jake. I might have reconsidered."

"Get out of here before I throw you out."

McGuire fled. The Mayor fingered one of his father's pens. What would his wife say if she saw that performance? *Really, Jake, did you have to use such awful language? Couldn't you have reasoned with him?* The Mayor called for a cup of coffee and the next contestant.

Ray Grimes appeared with the coffee in his hand, a smirky smile on his bland butterball face. His paunch bounced inside his tailored blue jeans, his blond hair flopped over his ears. In spite of the mod style, the Mayor saw the grammar school goody-goody who squealed to Sister on smokers in the bathroom and evolved into the college intellectual who was big in the sodality and worried about the meaning of meaning and how to reform the Catholic Church. It even annoyed the Mayor that Grimes now had a lower opinion of the Holy Roman Church than he did. It was part of the gospel among the university liberals for whom Grimes spoke. The Mayor never bad-mouthed the Church with these people, who considered Catholic and moron synonymous.

With phony jollity, Grimes handed the coffee to the Mayor and asked him how he was feeling this morning.

"Never better."

"I don't know how you do it. If I drank as much scotch as you did last night, I'd be in bed for a week."

The Mayor knew he looked no better than he felt. This patent insincerity did not increase his fondness for Grimes. He listened while the CPI director reported on his progress in relocating the eighteen hundred families being displaced by the Harborside housing development, and his lack of progress with the Italian community in negotiating for the right of way of a projected South Shore expressway. The Mayor nodded glumly and told him to concentrate on relocating the Harborside families, all of whom were black. "When we open that project, I don't want anyone living in a shanty out on the meadows, claiming it's all my fault."

He told Grimes to forget about the Italians. He would try a little personal diplomacy on them. Grimes asked him what he had in mind and the Mayor shrugged. "Maybe I'll just get the buses to run on time."

Grimes missed the reference to Mussolini and gingerly asked the Mayor if he had read Mulligan's story. The

Mayor nodded curtly. The question made as much sense as asking him if he was breathing. It was the way someone who thought he was very clever and was actually very inept at intrigue would try to gild his innocence.

"Who do you think leaked it?" the Mayor asked, fussing with some papers on his desk, not even bothering to look at Grimes.

"It could have been almost anyone. But I would think Mulligan's best contact would be someone like Eddie McKenna."

The Mayor shook his head. "Eddie's loyal."

"But he's got a big mouth."

"He knows when to keep it shut. Which is more than I can say for you, Ray. I don't want you to make a single statement on this busing thing before you clear it with me. You can say what you damn please to me in this office or up at Bowood. But in public, I want complete agreement from everyone on our approach to this mess."

"You're the boss."

"The leader, Ray. Just the leader."

The Mayor had had misgivings about making Grimes the head of Community Projects, Inc. The anti-poverty agency touched too many sensitive parts of the city's daily life. Legal aid to the poor, slum clearance, creating neighborhood associations, small business loans, were part of its broad mandate. As an outsider, Ted Finsterman had had no interest in empire building, and he was personally loyal to the Mayor. Grimes lacked both these virtues. His allegiance was to the pie-in-the-sky principles he had spouted during his disastrous run for Congress. If he had any personal loyalty, it was to Paula, who he knew had played a large part in persuading the Mayor that he needed a "liberal presence" in the upper levels of his administration.

When Grimes became CPI director, he began whirling around the city making announcements that normally came from City Hall. New programs—modern dance in the schoolyards and Shakespeare in the parks—new policies—organizing rent strikes against lackadaisical landlords—appeared in the newspapers before anyone in the Mayor's office heard about them. The Mayor had called Grimes downtown for a little talk. He had expected a two-hour shouting match. Instead, it was more like five minutes with a punching bag. Grimes whined a little and collapsed. It did not improve the Mayor's opinion of him.

But the Mayor soon realized it was an illusory victory. He did not have time to give serious thought to every proposal that came from an agency as diverse as the CPI. Although he ostentatiously got the Mayor's approval, Grimes went on doing pretty much what he pleased. When the Mayor did veto him, Ray did not have to shout or curse. He could win with his whining style because he had a collaborator that no one else in the O'Connor administration possessed: the Mayor's wife.

CPI had been the one city agency in which Paula felt she had a right to "meddle." She had helped the Mayor develop it and she had used her Uncle Paul's excellent contacts in Washington to get it gobs of federal money. She had gone along with the Mayor's "even-handed" approach, which spent roughly equal amounts of money in white and black neighborhoods. As long as federal funds were plentiful, this formula seemed to satisfy everyone. But now the agency was dependent on city taxes for most of its money. Ignoring the political implications of this fact, Grimes, with Paula's help, had persuaded the Mayor to switch CPI to a "greatest need" approach and spend most of its money downtown. Some of its recent programs, such as group therapy for unwed mothers, had drawn fierce fire from the City Council. Grimes had to go. But firing him would bring on a brawl with his uptown supporters—and with Paula—that the Mayor preferred to delay as long as possible.

Eddie McKenna was next. He pranced into the office whirling a shillelagh. "Jakie, me boy," he said, "are you holdin' your own? If you are, let it go. It's a mortal sin, don't you know."

Thirty years ago, Eddie's talent for this kind of humor had kept the senior class at St. Francis Prep in convulsions. Now the Mayor tolerated it for sentimental reasons. He also tolerated Eddie's rediscovery of his Irish heritage. In the early years of his administration, the Mayor had carefully avoided references to his ethnic background. Part of it was personal. He had never had much enthusiasm for American Irish culture with its emphasis on Joyce Kilmer's third-rate poetry and songs like "Mother Machree." Another reason was political. He had been serious about trying to build a political order that minimized ethnic differences. But the upsurge of black consciousness had, as Dominick Montefiore reminded him, wrecked this particular dream. He even found himself subtly encouraging the resurgence of ethnic pride among the Italians, the Poles, the Slovaks, the Irish, although his deepest instincts told him it was neither good for the city nor the country. All this made it easy for him to manufacture a smile at Eddie McKenna's prep school humor and pause to admire the shillelagh which Eddie claimed was straight from the old sod. He planned to flourish it on St. Patrick's Day, as grand marshal of the city's parade.

After bestowing some epithets on Dennis Mulligan and the Garden Square *Journal,* Eddie sat down and asked the expected question.

"How did it go last night?"

"She said no."

"So we're stuck."

"It looks that way."

The Mayor found himself regretting that he had ever agreed to let McKenna stage his scenario at the dinner. Eddie had poured out all his premonitions coming home in the limousine earlier in the day. The dire words had crystallized the Mayor's random thoughts about Paula and Judge Stapleton. But bringing Eddie into the plan forced the Mayor to tell more about his marriage than he cared to reveal to anyone.

"Jake," McKenna said. "I talked to our mutual friend and esteemed state chairman Bernie B. for a long time last night. He's nervous as hell. You know the spot he's in. He can't afford to lose this election."

"I'll talk to him," the Mayor said.

"It won't do any good, Jake. There's only one thing that will do any good. You've got to wait a week or two and when the shit starts to hit the fan around here, you've got to go on television and make a goddamn speech saying you think busing stinks and the people who are for it stink even more than the idea."

"There goes the black vote."

"Let it go. They don't amount to twenty per cent statewide. And they don't vote. They won't give you ten per cent."

"I still can't see it, Eddie. They've got a following. This is a liberal state."

"Not any more. No state's a liberal state. Liberalism, whatever the fuck it meant, is a dirty word. Except in a few rarefied circles."

The Mayor lit a cigarette. He was not used to getting lectures from Eddie McKenna. The Mayor had made Eddie the nominal head of the Democratic Party in the city with the understanding that Jake O'Connor was the real chairman. But over the years, Eddie had accrued a certain amount of power. Crises economic and politcal had absorbed a tremendous amount of the Mayor's time. He had let Eddie handle the party machinery. How well he handled it was seldom crucial. Party allegiance was a fading phenomenon. But it was by no means an extinct habit. A party leader could still influence a hundred or a hundred and fifty thousand votes in the city.

"I'm going to go after the Judge myself tonight, Eddie. It's the old bastard's birthday. I'm going to put him in a corner and go after him."

"Jake. I can hear it in your voice. I can see it on your face. You know it won't work."

"Jesus Christ, Eddie, let's not panic until we have to panic."

"Then it's too late. Jake, we've been friends a long time. I've never said a goddamn thing to you about Paula. But I'm like a lot of people. I never thought it was a good idea. I was always afraid something like this was going to happen. She'd start telling you what to do, when you could least afford to do it."

"She's not telling me a goddamn thing, Eddie."

"Okay. Let's put it in the negative. You can't tell her what to do. It amounts to the same thing. I'm not telling you to get divorced, Jake. I don't know anything about that side of it. But maybe you ought to get—financially independent."

"How do I do that?"

"It can be arranged. I got a call last week from a guy in Chicago. He threw a lot of zeros at me, six or seven of them—if we open this town up again. Get rid of virtuous Victor Tarentino and open things up. That's all they want."

"Why should I do that now, Eddie? Why should I ruin a winning act?"

"Because it may not be a winning act anymore. Because—it would make a lot of people more enthusiastic about this campaign, Jake. Including me. I could use a few of those zeros. I'm not greedy, Jake, but a hundred grand would go a long way toward letting me sleep better at night."

Suddenly the Mayor was back four years. He was in the kitchen of his boyhood home, having a drink with his father. *The town's too tight, Jake, open it up a little. A few card games. A little dice. People are going to do it anyway. This way you keep track of it.* Eddie McKenna had been sitting on the other side of the table. But O'Connor and Eddie's father had been good friends. Eddie's wife, Marie, was the daughter of the Thirteenth Ward's bookmaker, who would have died rich if he had not kept betting until he was senile. The Mayor had seen hope and not a little hunger on Eddie's face. He had also seen another face, not present at that kitchen table, a woman's face. He had made promises to that face, promises that forced him to shake his head and curtly tell the old ward boss that he was an anachronism. The almost forgotten revulsion of his adolescence against the casual corruption of the old regime had added a cutting contempt to his voice. Ben O'Connor had never mentioned it again. Six months later he was dead. The incident lay like a stain on the image of his father in the Mayor's memory. He found himself wondering if Eddie McKenna had been responsible for planting that idea in the old man's mind. The suspicion added unnecessary harshness to the Mayor's voice.

"Out of the question, Eddie. I don't even want to hear you mention it again."

"Jake, these guys aren't connected to the Biaggi family. I can understand why you'd never mess with them. They're not interested in our political—"

"Bullshit. The answer is no, Eddie. No."

"Jake, I'm not your goddamn puppet. I've gone along with you and you've gone along with me on a lot of things."

For a moment the Mayor almost told Eddie he was fantasizing a political career he had never possessed. But there was some truth in the words. One of the reasons the Mayor liked McKenna and had worked well with him was Eddie's fondness for the intricacies of city politics. They had spent more than a few hours in this office, analyzing and arguing about the web of loyalties and grudges, neighborhood clout and ethnic pride involved in appointing a city judge or a deputy commissioner of sanitation. His wife thought the Mayor spent too much time worrying about such things. She was probably right. But the Mayor enjoyed it. He liked to pick up the telephone and personally deliver the good news to the new judge or deputy commissioner. He even liked soothing the ruffled feathers of the losers. Besides, if he let Eddie McKenna handle such things, the Mayor knew that he might wake up some morning and find Eddie not only telling him what to do, but why he had to do it.

Instead, he was still the man in charge and Eddie's challenge could be heard without anger or panic. "I wouldn't want a puppet in your job, Eddie, I want a friend like you, who's got the guts to argue with me. But didn't we agree fourteen years ago that there was only one way to play it? Two guys with Irish names from this city can't afford to let a dirty nickel even get near them."

"I got to live, Jake. I married young, you know. I got two kids in college and another two ready to go. I got no complaints about city business. I get as much, probably more, than a lot of guys. But it's murder making a profit these days. Labor costs, the price of everything's out of sight. You can't pick up a little extra on a job like the old days. The quality control boys are on your back every second."

The Mayor nodded glumly. He had seen this coming for a long time. Eddie was a lousy businessman. His father, stumpy, pot-bellied Brendan McKenna, had probably not been much better. But he had been one of the old organization's favorite contractors. Eddie had taken over the company when the old man died in 1960. The Mayor had done his best, within the limits of the law, to push work his way. But he could not deliver the guaranteed annual income that old Brendan had enjoyed from the city or let him get away with the padded payrolls and other gimmicks that enabled him to be the worst horseplayer in the state and still live like a Stapleton.

"I'm sorry as hell to hear this, Eddie. But the answer isn't hot money from Chicago. Maybe you ought to hire a couple of those quality control guys. Get tougher with the unions. Just because you need their votes on election day they don't have a license to loaf on your time."

Eddie McKenna sat there looking like he'd just backed the wrong horse with the company's assets.

"Eddie," the Mayor said. "We've come a long way playing it straight. Let's not quit in the last quarter."

"I used to buy that, Jake. But now I wonder. Maybe whatever the old crowd stole, they had it coming to them. The Wasps stole twice as much before we got here. And shafted us in the bargain."

"That isn't the whole story, Eddie. Even if it was true, it wouldn't excuse anything you or I did. I don't believe that anyone's got the right to break the law because his grandfather got a raw deal."

Eddie McKenna had to struggle to get his answer out of his throat. He gasped for breath like an asthmatic. Finally, the words were there, words the Mayor sensed Eddie had wanted to say for months, perhaps years.

"We don't think the same way anymore, Jake. It

doesn't mean anything to you that I'm pressed for dough. You don't worry about those kinds of things anymore."

"Eddie, if you really need dough I can arrange for you to borrow it."

"That's the quick way to go out of business, Jake. You must know that."

"I don't know that, Eddie. I'm no businessman. The only job I know is the one I'm doing now. I don't know enough law any more to defend a traffic violation. Maybe that's why I want to do this job right."

"Okay." Eddie fiddled with his shillelagh. "Think about that speech, Jake. Maybe you can make it and still keep Paula on the team. You got to say it. That's honest to God, Jake. For all the years we've been friends. You got to say it."

Eddie McKenna departed, trailing his shillelagh behind him. The Mayor slumped in his chair while the lights ran up and down and across the plastic buttons on the telephones with science fiction speed. He could feel defeatism seeping through his veins like a polluted tide. He fought it by putting through a call to Judge Paul Stapleton. He could not get past his clerk. He knew him, a smooth, extremely polite young man named Pignatowski, with an NYU Law School degree. "Tell the Judge I'd like to have a private talk with him some time today in his chambers."

"I'll see what I can do, Your Honor."

The Mayor knew what he would see: nothing.

The last visitor of the morning was Simon Burke. The Mayor had hired this walking blimp for purely sentimental reasons. His father had been one of Ben O'Connor's best committeemen in the old Thirteenth Ward. Burke had stumbled into City Hall just off a bender, hands shaking, lips twitching, maybe a little suicidal. The Mayor had made him city historian, a job that the City Council had recently created to assist the Bicentennial Committee. It only paid $6,000 a year and had been intended as a stipend for one of the professional historians at the city's branch of the state university.

Gratitude had energized Simon's spherical flab. He had plunged into the sub-basements of the main library and discovered vaults full of memorabilia from the previous century. It was the sort of material that the city's Bicentennial Committee should have found. The Mayor had left the bicentennial planning to Paula, and she had allowed Ray Grimes to capture it. They were in the process of creating an agenda that featured street theater, jazz concerts, ethnic cooking—everything but the history of the city and the country. The Mayor had hacked $50,000 out of the Bicentennial Committee's budget and told Simon to create an exhibit that would tell the story of the city's past.

As usual, Simon's tie was askew. Two buttons were missing on the cheap shirt that strained across his paunch. The shine of poverty glistened on his blue serge suit. He was a pathetic example of the Catholic intellectual gone to seed. He had been a high school classmate of the Mayor's brother, Paul. After college, Simon had tried to make a living writing Catholic magazine articles and books. Then he had run a tax-deductible hospice in New York, Holyrood House, where Catholic intellectuals gathered to discuss nothing in particular. When that collapsed, he had bluffed his way onto the English faculty of the state university, using (he confided to the Mayor) a forged Ph.D.

"I'm happy to report that the bicentennial exhibit is making excellent progress, Your Honor," Simon said. "But before I go another step, I have an idea to discuss with you."

How, Simon asked, was he supposed to describe the thirty years in which the city had been ruled by the old machine? They were both extremely well acquainted with how that machine had operated. He was prepared, even inclined, to tell the truth about it. To use the newspaper headlines announcing the latest probe by the state legislature of yet another massive vote fraud, to blow up the pictures of the Big Man's cops defying state troopers trying to impound suspected ballot boxes, to display the Big Man and his assembled warriors on St. Patrick's Day, receiving the Archbishop's blessing from the reviewing stand.

"Put it in," the Mayor said. "Don't leave out a

thing. There's no reason for me to be ashamed of it. Or for you."

"But I am. I always have been, Your Honor. If I may ask a personal question, why doesn't it bother you?"

Looking at Simon Burke's bloated cheeks, the sad pursed mouth, the vaguely pained eyes, the Mayor saw his brother Paul. Walking wounded. Another Catholic literalist who broke his skull trying to figure out how to obey God and love a father who was a crook. In Simon's case, a crook on a small scale. Which was why he still half functioned as a human being. In Paul's case, a crook on a large scale, which was why a staring zombie sat in his mental hospital room calling himself the ghost of Father Paul O'Connor.

"It's hard to explain, Simon," the Mayor said. "I—I spent some time with my father. I—I connected with him. I saw it from his point of view."

"Is that possible?"

They were in the hospital. The Jewish specialist in circulatory diseases was rending his garments, screaming that he had never had a patient like him. He bribed the nurses to smuggle him cigarettes, whiskey. Now he was discharging himself to fight a political campaign. Walking out on that leg, with gangrene still infecting his foot. How could he stand the pain? How could he risk his life for a few thousand votes? Ben O'Connor ignored him. He put on his pants. He put on his shirt. He put on one shoe. He put a slipper on the corrupted foot.

They had limped down the corridor together, his father's arm around his shoulder, his arm beneath it around the thick torso and under the other arm, making them one grotesque thing, a three-legged animal joined by Ben O'Connor's will. He could still feel the dead weight of that sagging body, he could still hear the gasp of pain each time his father put too much weight on that rotting leg. He could still smell the pale sweat of Ben O'Connor's deodorized hospital flesh, a smell he still associated with losing, dying. Yet it was a kind of victory toward which they were walking, a victory that was also a defeat. Down the corridor they went with the nurses wishing him good luck and crying like they were his daughters into the May sunshine and the waiting limousine. How could he explain it to someone who had never done it?

"It's possible, Simon. That's all I can tell you. Maybe I was lucky."

Or was it unlucky? Was that the worst, not the best thing that ever happened to him? Was that arm still pinning him to this gangrenous city, was the dead weight of that body still on his shoulders?

"I was hoping—I might even say I was sure that you would tell me to play the history straight, Your Honor. I am not a complete ignoramus about politics. There were some good things about the old machine. They gave people a sense of hierarchy, group solidarity."

"Caring," the Mayor said.

"Yes, even that, I suppose."

"Suppose, hell, Simon. It was the main thing."

"I bow to your superior knowledge. But what I am suggesting—is this. What about making a virtue of necessity? Creating a study of how a ward worked. Naturally we would take the Thirteenth. Is it our fault that the leader's name was O'Connor? We would show the good things—the Christmas baskets, the outings, getting jobs, doing small favors, helping people cope."

"Not bad," the Mayor said.

"I will need your help, Your Honor. Did your father leave any—any papers, pictures, that sort of thing?"

"He left a few things. They're around Bowood somewhere."

"Could I go through them?"

"I'll do it with you. To tell you the truth, I've never done more than glance at them. When the old man died I was sort of—fed up with him. He was getting a little loose in the head. He was starting to give me all kinds of bad advice."

Simon Burke looked owlish. Was he catching a whiff of guilt in that admission? Were there things in Ben O'Connor's papers that the Mayor did not want the public to see? He was probably right on both counts.

"Call me in a day or two, when things calm down a little. We'll make a date."

"Whatever you say, Your Honor."

Simon Burke departed murmuring thank you. He was the wrong close for a bad morning. Maybe it was better not to think about the past, the Mayor told himself. Better to forget the day he had half carried, half walked that bulky man out of the hospital to the last political battle of his life, a hopeless battle to which his son had given only half of himself, knowing the cause was lost and deserved to be lost, even if the winners, the pseudo-reformers were more corrupt and infinitely more inept, confidently telling himself that when his time came he would have a better cause and a better way to win it. Where has that confidence gone, Your Honor?

The telephone twinkled only feebly now, as if communication with earth had been cut off by a power failure in this ill-fated space capsule. In another moment, Charles LoBello would step through the small door midway down the office and shamble toward him like a good-natured grizzly making mournful rumbling sounds. He would drop the morning's sheaf of calls on his desk and groan: "Jesus, what an afternoon you got."

The Mayor buzzed Helen Ganey. "Did Judge Stapleton call?"

"No, Your Honor. I even said a prayer to St. Jude—for you, but—no call."

So much for the saint of impossible causes. The Mayor looked out the window. Beyond the gleaming plaza he saw the gray and brown mass of the city on its long low hill above the river. He thought about Frank Donahue's threatening voice on the telephone. Maybe he was a seed planted by his father in those tired houses and scarred streets. A seed the son had subtly cultivated in his own way. Maybe in the end nothing happened that did not somehow even scores, convert losers into winners, even if it was only for a brief breathless moment. Maybe the winner, especially if he was Irish, secretly wanted it to happen.

What mystical crap.

7

Paula Stapleton O'Connor sat in a William and Mary banister-back chair fingering the ram's horn arms as she stared abstractedly out the window of the upstairs study. Above the spiked tips of Bowood's massive iron fence, her eyes moved down a lane of trees to a broad sweep of sunlit park. Once the park had belonged to the Stapleton family. Now it was George Washington County Park, proof that capitalists, from one generation to the next, could be persuaded to abandon exploitation for benevolence. Paula's eyes swung back and pondered Dorothy Washington's morose black face.

"What does your new boyfriend do?"

"Nothing much. He can't get a job. He's got a record."

In a painfully polite way, Paula was trying to find out something about the man Dolores may have overheard on the telephone. Paula did not want to tell the Mayor about it. Dorothy had an unfortunate tendency to get involved with ex-convicts, most of them political extremists. Her previous boyfriend had joined the Black Panthers and breathed threats to burn down the city. Police Commissioner Tarentino had tried to get Dorothy fired because of him.

Paula looked out the window again, defeated by the silent plea in Dorothy's eyes. She was the only member of her family with a job. Her father—at least the man she thought was her father—was in prison serving a twenty-five-year sentence for armed robbery. Beneath the passivity that seemed to permeate Dorothy's character, there was a blind groping for this man's love. What else explained her attraction for the same kind of men?

Paula picked up her copy of the Garden Square *Journal*. The leaked story of last night's dinner leered up at her from Dennis Mulligan's column, "Around City Hall." *You've got to help us get that* ———. Could Dorothy be part of a plot to destroy Jake politically? Perhaps this man was working for the Mafia, who would pay thousands, perhaps even millions, to get the Mayor out of politics. What better way than to plant a spy or a concealed microphone in Bowood?

This was too important to be defeated by the plea in Dorothy's eyes. "Dorothy," she said. "I don't want to interfere in your personal life. But we've received some very upsetting phone calls from a man who says he wants to kill the Mayor. Does—Andrew Barton—Andrew 77X he calls himself—ever talk that way?"

"Sometimes. But only when he's—he's kind of drunk, you know. When he comes from that place he hangs out."

"What place?"

"A store. He hangs out there. Lot of people hang out there. I try to get him to stop. That place is full of bad people. Winos and junkies and crazy people. They all talk that way. About revolutions and killin' the Mayor, the governor, the President. It don't mean nothin' Mrs. O'Connor. I'm tryin' to make him see it don't. If he could get a job and get away from that place—"

In her body, if not in her mind, Paula felt revulsion mingle with despair. Was there any hope of helping these people? Yes, she told herself, yes. Wasn't Dorothy, with her willingness to tell her these things, with her steady improvement at typing and shorthand, her pride in her work, wasn't she proof that they were ready to strive, ready to accept help that did not demean, humiliate? Now was not the time to falter before the ugliness that still threatened to engulf them.

"Councilman Turner and Commissioner Grimes are coming to lunch. I'll speak to them. Maybe they can do something. But, Dorothy, will you promise me something? If this man—Andrew 77X—or any of his friends—if you think they might—really hurt the Mayor, would you tell me?"

Dorothy nodded morosely. "Yes," she said.

From her tone of voice, it was hard to tell whether she resented becoming an informer or thought the promise was futile.

A frantic knock on the study door. It burst open before Paula could answer it. Flora Mackey, the children's nurse, came puffing into the room. Her veined eyes rolled in her powdered cheeks. "Oh, Mrs. O'Connor," she said. "They're bringing him home again with a nosebleed or a concussion or God knows what."

"Did they call you?" Paula said.

"No. I just saw him from the nursery window. They left him at the gate, just like the last time. They don't even have the decency to bring him up the drive."

"Finish those letters I gave you, Dorothy," Paula said, and rushed down the stairs into the freezing air without bothering to put on a coat. The policeman on duty was coming up the drive with his arm around Kemble. A trickle of blood ran from his small nose across his trembling lips. The policeman was giving him some lower-class advice.

"Listen, Barney, next time tell'm t'fight one at a time. Tell'm they're a buncha no good yella—"

"I'll take him. Thank you."

She could not remember the policeman's name. He was Irish. They all looked alike to her, with their standardized television faces.

"Oh sure, Mrs. O'Connuh," he said. "He's okay. Just shook up. He says about six of'm jumped him in the baatroom." He bashed Kemble on the back. "Tell'm to fight one at a time, Barney. Give'm the old left hook like I showed you. Then the right cross. Got it, Barney?"

"His name is Kemble," Paula said.

The cop looked baffled. "The Mayuh calls'm Barney."

Paula shivered, forced a frozen smile, and turned her back on him. "What happened, dear?" she asked, drawing her son to her as they walked toward the door.

"They beat me up again. Those same kids," Kemble said, a sob rising in his throat.

"Did you do anything, did you say anything?"

"No. I didn't say anything the last time either. They just hate me, Mom. They call me white ass."

As she took off his coat in the center hall, a drop of blood fell from his nose onto the parquet floor. Dorothy Washington appeared on the stairs, looking anxious. "Is he all right?"

"Yes. Yes. He's fine, Dorothy. Fine, thank you."

"Mom," Kemble said as she hung his coat in the hall closet, "I don't want to go back to that school. Do I have to?"

"Of course you have to," Paula said. "We'll talk it over and see why this nasty thing keeps happening. We'll find a way to stop it."

"There's no way you can stop it, Mommy," Kemble screamed. "They just hate me. I won't go back."

He turned and ran up the stairs.

"Kemble," Paula called. But he kept on running till she heard his door slam at the far end of the hall.

"Oh, where is he, where is my sweet boy?"

Flora Mackey came waddling down the stairs. Paula braced herself for a barrage of unwanted advice.

"Madam, you will simply have to have the boy escorted around that school by a policeman."

"I'm afraid that's out of the question."

"Then what are we to do? Is the poor little lad to live in terror? Three nightmares in the past month, I told you, madam. All about the same thing. Them."

"I know. I'll talk to Mayor O'Connor. I'll see if we can—decide something."

"It is no longer can, Mrs. O'Connor, it is must."

"Yes. Yes. Would you go up, Mrs. Mackey, and make sure he gets some lunch?"

Dolores appeared at the head of the stairs. "What's Barney crying about, Mommy?" she asked.

"He had a fight with some boys."

"The niggers?"

"Where did you learn that word?" Paula glared at Mackey. "Have you been letting her use it? You know the strict instructions I gave you—"

"Madam, I swear," Mackey said. "It is the first time I have heard it in this house. I hope—I trust—it will be the last."

"It is not a good word," Paula said to Dolores. "It is an insulting word. Dorothy would be very insulted and unhappy if she heard you talking that way. The right word is Negro, or black people."

Paula's indignation washed over her daughter without a trace of emotional impact. "Barney calls them that when no one's listening," she said.

"I will speak to—Kemble. Call your brother Kemble. I don't like Barney."

"Daddy calls him Barney."

Paula took a deep breath. "I know. But don't you think Kemble is a nicer name?"

"No. Barney doesn't like it either. He told me."

For a moment, Paula heard a voice whispering: *How much can you stand?* But she managed to silence it, and say, without rancor: "Well, I think Kemble is a much nicer name."

The bell rang. Mahoney opened the white outer door and Adam Turner strolled into the center hall. His well-pressed blue denim leisure suit somehow enhanced his creamy dark brown skin. He strolled toward her with the grace and confidence of a prince. His Afro was a kind of crown, a visible testament of his royalty. Paula was delighted by his aplomb. She could remember a time when Adam had been awkward and uncertain in her presence.

Beside him was another black man. He wore a flowing African robe trimmed with orange and gold. It was embroidered with mysterious symbols that looked a little like Pennsylvania Dutch hex signs. On his squarish head he wore a shiny black fez with a red tassel. His skin was ebony. His eyes had a hooded jungle look.

"Hey, Boss Lady," Adam said. "How's it going? You know Gowon."

"Of course," Paula said. She had given Gowon

Soyinka a lot of money to operate a ujamaa, a center for African culture, in Bayshore. For a while, it seemed to flourish. There were over 200 black youngsters learning Swahili and doing African dances, singing African songs. But it had dwindled away in the last two years, leaving only a few devotees.

"Where's Ray?"

Adam jerked his thumb over his shoulder. Through the door held open by a shivering Mahoney, Paula could see Ray Grimes in the rear of his limousine, talking on a white telephone. He was always trying to cram an extra minute of work into his day.

"Is the soup gettin' cold?" Adam asked.

"Oh no, you're early," Paula said. "We're still trying to catch the chicken out back."

Adam roared with laughter. Gowon Soyinka managed to achieve a smile. "Boss Lady," Adam said, "you is too much."

Paula was proud of her ability to relax with Adam Turner. But she never heard him lapse into black English without a twinge of regret. She knew too much about the effort her grandfather's generation had made to teach the Irish and their fellow immigrants the rudiments of grammar. Black English was now the gospel of the city's educators, as well as politicians like Adam, college graduates who had decided it was cool to sound like street people. For the ninth or tenth time, Paula told herself she would learn to like it, some day.

Ray Grimes got off the telephone and trotted up the steps to join them. Smiling warmly, he kissed Paula on the cheek. He had to bounce up on his toes to do it. "I told Gowon to order one of these for me," he said, fingering the African robe. "I've got a couple. But I haven't seen anything quite this striking."

"It's a ceremonial robe of a chief of the Tiv," Gowon said.

"The what?" Adam said as Paula led them into the hall. "The TV? Them cats worship a television set?"

"The Tiv is one of the great African tribes," Soyinka said.

"How good is their football team? Could they beat Grambling?"

"You are a walking example of our need for African culture," Soyinka said.

"I've told you before, Gowon, I haven't got time. And I get more pride out of knowin' how to read the city budget."

Gowon Soyinka wore the mournful look of a prophet unhonored in his own country.

"Before we get down to business," Paula said, "I'd like some advice with a personal problem."

She told them about Dorothy Washington's boyfriend, Andrew 77X Barton, omitting the possibility that he may have threatened the Mayor's life. "He's something of an extremist. Dorothy says he spends his time at some store where there's a lot of wild talk."

Gowon Soyinka nodded. "I know the place. Belongs to a cat named Donahue. White."

"Dorothy didn't mention him."

"He's real strange," Gowon said. "Some people think he's got the evil eye."

"For Chirst's sake, Gowon, can the jungle superstition," Adam said. "You ain't got nobody here you can scare with that stuff."

"You tell Dorothy to send Andy to see me. I'm sure we can find a meaningful job for him," Ray Grimes said.

"I'd be so grateful, Ray."

Mahoney took their drink orders, scotches and sodas for Adam and Soyinka, dry sherry for her and Dubonnet for Ray Grimes. She listened while Adam explained why they had asked for this lunch date. The busing program was running short of funds at a critical point. Gowon Soyinka's Malcolm X Ujamaa was serving as a training center for the adult escorts. They had imported a staff of twenty, all with experience in places such as Boston, Denver, and Detroit.

"We've been on the phone for money all day yesterday and most of last night. There just ain't any around. The NAACP national headquarters is broke. They're havin' trouble meetin' their payrolls. The Jews are givin' all their shekels to Israel. The big foundations ain't interested in a city like this. Pourin' money down a hole, they say. So—"

"How much do you need?" Paula asked.

What a businesslike voice. As matter-of-fact as the money that gave her the power to ask that question. If they only knew how little interest she really had in it, how inept she was at handling it. If they ever knew that it was Dorothy Washington who balanced her checkbook each month. If they ever knew that her husband was even more uninterested and possibly more inept with money. The little secrets of the rich and powerful.

"Twenty thousand dollars."

Paula nodded stiffly. "All right," she said.

Giving money always embarrassed her. She wanted to get it over with as quickly as possible. She summoned Dorothy Washington and told her to get the foundation checkbook. She funneled income from one of her larger trust funds into this instrument of tax-deductible benevolence. Swiftly Paula wrote out the magic words and numbers on the sky blue check and handed it to Adam.

"Thanks, Boss Lady," Adam said.

"That calls for another drink," Gowon Soyinka said.

"Help yourself," Paula said. Mahoney was in the dining room, getting ready to serve lunch.

Gowon came back from the bar with a very dark brown scotch. The sight made Paula uneasy. "We have to understand one thing. Where you got the money—is absolutely confidential."

"Of course," Ray Grimes said.

"No reason to mention it to a soul," Adam Turner said.

"Personally I don't feel the slightest need to keep it a secret. But from a political point of view I think Jake—would want it."

Adam smiled. There was more than a hint of sarcasm in the leftward droop of his mouth. "We read the papers, Boss Lady."

"Believe me, he's still on your side. As much as I am."

Gowon Soyinka was deep into his dark brown scotch. He did not seem to be listening. Adam clapped him on the thigh. "We believe, don't we, Gowon?"

Gowon managed a nod. But he seemed busy believing something else, something dark and distant, in an Africa he had never seen. Paula was relieved when Mahoney arrived to announce lunch.

Over the consommé, Ray Grimes took charge of the conversation. "I'm sure Adam is sincere in what he said about believing. But he's also been candid enough to tell me that Jake's stand on busing has aroused a lot of bad feelings."

"Is that true?" Paula asked.

"Let me put it this way, Boss Lady," Adam said. "Black people think it's old-fashioned politics. And we thought the Mayor stood for something new. Something better."

"He did—he—does."

"We want to believe that, too. But there ain't no built-in reason for us to trust him, any more than there is to trust any other white politician. It's distrust he's working with, four hundred years of distrust. But he don't seem to understand it. Maybe you can explain it to him."

"I'll try."

"I don't think he can get away with this neutral high-wire act. Black voters are just sitting there waiting for him to make one wrong move, one move that proves the black man was right all along, he can't be trusted. The thing I can't figure out is why you let him do it, Boss Lady."

Ray Grimes picked at his filet of sole. Had he put Adam up to this denunciation? No, that was an unworthy thought. Adam was talking to her as a personal friend, not just the Mayor's wife. Her face flushing, Paula tried to explain that she did not control her husband's political decisions.

"The polls show such strong feelings—white feelings—it seemed the only realistic thing to do," Paula said.

"How about trying to change those white feelings?"

123

Adam asked in a low sad voice. "Not many politicians around that could do it. But the Mayor—with his name—and his background. They might listen. Instead, he's giving the game away to morons like Kitty Kosciusko and Tony Perotta."

Paula could feel the words sinking into her flesh, with the pain that so often accompanies harsh truths. Regret gripped her throat like a brutal hand.

"But I keep forgetting the city isn't really important to the Mayor anymore," Adam said. "The city's just one corner of the senatorial checkerboard. We're playin' for the whole state, maybe for the country now."

"That's *not* true. The city is still as—as important as it ever was," Paula said.

It was a lie. How sad that admission made her feel. Sad and ashamed.

"I want to see him get there," Adam said. "Because I really do believe he's still on our side. But let me level with you, Boss Lady. I believe that because you're by his side."

"What—what do you think I should do?"

For a moment she had a nervous glimpse of herself asking this question too often, waiting humbly for the answers from her father, her uncle, her husband, Ray Grimes. She did not like it. But was it her fault? She seemed destined to spend her life repairing damage done by men, ignoring the damage her humble servant act was doing to her. Was that a woman's fate?

"You've got to persuade him to make a series of gestures, Paula," Ray Grimes said. "Gestures of solidarity with the black community."

Paula glanced at Gowon Soyinka. He was briskly devouring the last of his filet of sole. Beside the plate stood another dark brown scotch which he had persuaded Mahoney to deliver. He was deep in his African world. Politics was not his thing. He was just a figurehead, window dressing. The power was emanating from these other two men, and she was caught in its vise.

Suddenly Paula saw a door open between Ray Grimes and Adam Turner, a door framed by their demanding mouths and accusing eyes. Jake stood in the doorway, shafts of sunlight playing on his face. She walked effortlessly into his arms and for a moment she was alone with him on the island where they had spent their honeymoon. Black faces smiled each morning on the surprising discovery of their love. She heard their dark gusty laughter, their carefree music. Travel brochure love, Hollywood love, yet it was real, and these insistent eyes and sullen mouths of her friends, beside the brooding black strangeness of Gowon Soyinka, were destroying that love, ripping it out of her bleeding body like priests in some primitive rite.

Paula struggled to control her panic as Mahoney poured more wine. But the terror rose through her body into her throat, as remorselessly as the Pouilly-Fuissé rose in the glass. For the first time she experienced a total loathing for politics, public life. A voice within her cried out wordlessly for the right, the chance to think about her husband in a secluded place. There was something obscene about this confession of their differences to people who did not know or really care about them as husband and wife.

That was not entirely true. Ray Grimes cared. He was a true friend. So was Adam. But the intensity of his caring for his people confused their personal relationship.

"We got to get the Mayor into the streets," Adam said. "That's my recipe for holdin' the black vote. It's probably too late to get him reversed on busing. But he can still make some positive moves. How about a tour of Bayshore?"

"A perfect choice," Ray Grimes said. "It's part of his father's old ward. It'll be a staging area for kids being bused up the North Slope."

"We could work in a visit to that lousy high school. Make people see why busin' is needed."

"At the same time," Ray said, "we've got to give black people—especially the women—a chance to ventilate. Would you chair a rap session on busing in Bayshore the same day?"

"I ought to talk to Jake first—"

"You've got to make black people feel you're listening, Paula," Ray said. Adam nodded agreement.

Paula surrendered. She could not say no to these people. "All right," she said. "I'll talk to Jake. About Bayshore. Maybe I can even get him to modify his position on busing—to say some things that would reassure the black community."

"That would be the impossible dream come true," Ray Grimes said.

A half hour later, watching Ray Grimes's limousine glide out the front gate into the flow of traffic on the Parkway, Paula was swept by anxiety. She retreated to her bedroom and took from the bottom drawer of a walnut highboy a scrapbook of the O'Connor adminstration. There were the headlines of the first victory. O'CONNOR WINS BY 26,000 VOTES. PLEDGES "NEW APPROACH" TO CREATE "NEW FUTURE." Details of that campaign came surging into her mind. It had been an exhausting but exhilarating experience. She had pushed doorbells in Society Heights, the wealthy uptown neighborhood where prim Paula Stapleton had once attended parties. When the man or lady of the house frigidly informed her that they had no intention of voting for O'Connor, she would smile graciously and say: "May I speak to your servants, then?" Often they shut the door in her face. Politely, of course. After all, she was Paula Stapleton. A few of them actually slammed it. It had made great newspaper copy.

There was a picture of her and the Mayor rolling a huge plastic ball full of petitions up the front steps of City Hall to browbeat the City Council into creating Community Projects, Inc. On the next page they stood side by side beaming at the first rehabilitated street on the South Slope. Rehabilitated, in spite of the fact that most of the poverty money was still stuck in the bureaucratic machinery in Washington. The Mayor had persuaded the Italian residents to spend their mattress money on improving the exterior of their houses, promising them that the city would match the individual homeowner dollar for dollar. Neither Paula nore Ted Finsterman, the first head of CPI, had ever heard of mattress money.

It was good to remember how much they depended on the Mayor's inherited knowledge of the city in those days. Ted Finsterman had dolefully declared they would need six months to analyze the ethnic and economic composition of the city's wards, before they could even begin to plan any rehabilitation. The Mayor had canceled his appointments and spent the next day dictating a ward-by-ward descriptive analysis that was so staggering in its thoroughness, so perceptive in its subtle differences between neighborhoods and parishes and school districts, that Ted Finsterman swore all it needed was some footnotes to get the Mayor a doctoral degree from Yale.

"Where did you learn all this, Jake?" Paula had asked.

"I didn't learn it. I inhaled it," the Mayor had said.

Was the beginning of that tendency toward arrogance that she found so irritating? Or was the irritation really envy, a desire to compete with him on every level, envy rooted in the undeniable fact that she could never achieve this intuitive, seemingly effortless knowledge of all levels of the city's life? It wasn't fair, Paula thought, sullenly yielding to resentment. She had served her time in the city's less lovely neighborhoods, but always as the outsider, the earnest do-gooder. She had never had a chance to stand at a bar and inhale their sweaty solidarity.

It was as much a woman's as a rich girl's fate, and she began wondering if her dissatisfaction with her role in the O'Connor administration had something to do with her sex. How often did the Mayor tell her in a hundred unspoken ways that his politics were remorselessly male? He was willing to elect a token woman here, appoint one a token chairperson there, but the decision making was 100 per cent male. Not surprising, really. In the Irish American world from which the Mayor had come, women were conveniences to be left at home while scores were settled and fates decreed in bars and clubhouses and hotel rooms where sex—except for reflex verbal obscenities—was nonexistent.

Stop, Paula, stop, she told herself. She had reached

for this scrapbook to restore, or at least remember, the good feelings, the proud memories. Turning another page, she winced at the memory that was both proud and sad. FOUR-DAY MARATHON WINS NEW AID FROM LEGISLATURE. Four days at the state capital in which no one had had more than an hour or two of broken sleep sprawled on a couch or in a chair. The Mayor and his aides had come home semi-triumphant with only half of the money they had hoped to win but with enough to match the federal grants and make the anti-poverty program possible. When her husband walked in—no, stumbled in—the door of their apartment at the end of that ordeal, she wondered for the first time about politics as a way of life. He was a staring zombie who could only mutter, "Drink—get me a drink." There was a two- or three-day beard on his cheeks. He looked like a fugitive from a secret police interrogation.

That was only the first of a dozen more marathon neogtiations to surmount other crises—threatened strikes by the garbage men, the policemen, the firemen. Whether it was the dock strike, the hospitals' strike, the newspaper strike, there was a final call from strikers and mediators and the public for the Mayor's intervention. What was it she had cried one morning when he came home at 6 A.M., not quite as zombie-like as after the budget negotiations but so tired he could barely talk above a whisper? "They're killing you. I'm not going to let them do it!" She had flung herself into his arms, totally a wife, abandoning her Stapleton dreams of political power. He had kidded her in the tough-talk style she had once found so amusing. *Ah, jus' give's a little squeeze, babe. I'll be reddy for anudder round wit t'bastuds.* They had laughed and made love in the dawn.

Where had they lost that defiant camaraderie, that heady sense of *us*, the two of them against the rest of the city, the state, the world? How had it dwindled into today's tense querulous partnership? Paula turned another page and saw a large part of the answer. The faded headlines from the Garden Square *Journal* leered up at her. O'CONNOR LOSES GOVERNORSHIP BID BY 200,000 VOTES. The stain, the pain of that defeat had been the beginning of the end of *us*. It was not simply the loss, the blank discovery of his political vulnerability, it was Jake's reaction to it. He had gotten drunk in a way she had never seen before. A moderate amount of liquor had often made them freer, closer, more spontaneous. That night Jake had used liquor as a private anesthetic, a retreat from pain—and from her.

She had walked into his bedroom in her nightgown to offer him the taste of her tears, the comfort of her arms, her lips, the consolation of her caring. She had been prepared to say strong proud things about her unshaken faith in him. She found him sitting in the wing chair in his Irish corner beneath the pictures of his father and the old boss, a dark brown scotch in his hand. His head had come up, his eyes had leveled on her like two gun barrels. "Are you satisfied now?" he had snarled. "Are you satisfied? I made the big try and got my brains beaten in. What I told you would happen."

She had been too astonished and too hurt to answer him. Even now, remembering it with more fear and pity than anger, she could not accept the accusation in those words. Running for governor had not been her idea. It was a decision they had made together. They knew the risk of a primary fight with an incumbent Democratic governor. But it had been worth taking. They had jointly decided it was worth taking. Jake had just gotten state and national publicity as a racial peacemaker. Private polls had shown them winning by a narrow but by no means recklessly thin margin. She *had* urged him to make the race; the governor was an old-politics hack with an administration scarred by a half dozen scandals. But he was a potent vote-getter outside the city and he had turned the Mayor's past against him in a smear campaign that accused him of trying to restore the city's political dominance over the rest of the state—a dominance which he predicted would be a prelude to massive corruption. He portrayed the Mayor as the leader of an army of unemployed clubhouse hacks from the old machine, ready to loot the State House in the gaudy style of their predecessors.

Jake's response to this crude tactic had been fatally

ambiguous. He had refused to denounce the politics of the old machine, to pour on it the scorn that Paula believed it thoroughly deserved. He had limited himself to a pro forma repudiation of corruption and "accentuated the positive"—talked about his accomplishments as mayor. But the downstate voters were not especially interested in the art of rehabilitating city neighborhoods. Two thirds of the electorate were suburbanites, and they did not think the city was worth rehabilitating. The result was political disaster.

She had stalked out of his bedroom that night, refusing on principle to argue with him when he was drunk. The next morning he had apologized. Now thinking back on it, she almost wished they had had the argument. It might have been healthier than the undercurrent of distrust and resentment that had begun to flow between them that night. A few months later the first rumblings of the school integration crisis had added another source of alienation to their lives. Although the Mayor often said they only disagreed on tactics, Paula sensed a far deeper division in their feelings about the blacks. It surfaced in a dozen different ways, from casual remarks to abrupt shifts in policy. She did not know what to do about it. She was entangled in anguished ambiguity —her wish to influence him to do the right thing clashed with her dread of his resentment of that influence.

Paula turned the page of the scrapbook. It was blank. She remembered telling herself at that point that the record was no longer worth keeping. City politics tended to be so repetitious—garbage strikes and school custodian walkouts tended to blur into the same petty crisis. It was a good reason for wanting to see Jake escape from this level of politics, to find loftier challenges which would enlarge his vision and his character. At times Paula felt the city was a kind of Lilliput which had lashed Jake O'Connor to its littered streets and was diabolically shrinking him to its own mean proportions. But there was, alas, a side of her husband's character that co-operated in this bizarre, wholly unexpected process. She remembered his sullen response to her refusal to plead with Judge Stapleton on his behalf and found a sudden anger of her own responding to it. It was not only immature, it was grossly unjust, this habit of blaming his political misfortunes on her. Whatever was happening between them, it was not entirely her fault. No, not her fault by a very long shot. Nor would the trouble end if she gave up her side of the argument, became the simpleminded yes-saying all-supporting wife. If there were changes to be made, His Honor ought to make a few of them. Now was not the time to give up the fight. On the contrary, even if he ended up hating her, she would continue to assert the ideals and goals that brought her—and supposedly him—into politics in the first place. She heard herself promising Adam Turner and vowed that it was also a promise to herself. She would speak out even if it meant—

But she prayed it would not mean—

Why was she sitting here weeping?

8

Rolling home from City Hall in the warm womby back seat of his limousine, Mayor O'Connor struggled to lift his morale by sheer willpower. The wheels were turning smoothly in most parts of the city government's machinery. There was no danger of bankruptcy, the specter that haunted a half dozen other cities in the country. The youngsters with the public administration degrees from Harvard, the outsiders whom the reporters called "The Brain Busters" because the newsmen had trouble following their computer jargon, had done their jobs well. A get-tough policy had stabilized the welfare rolls. Fourteen years of honest government had persuaded corporations to move back to the city to take advantage of its excellent transportation mix. He could be—he should be —proud of this record. Would it be destroyed by this explosion of irrational emotion he saw coming toward them?

If it happens, it happens, he told himself with gloomy fatalism. He could not do anything about it— any more than his father could have stopped the old machine from self-destructing twenty-five years ago. It was not his fault. It was not Paula's fault. There was no point in nagging himself or his wife for the part they had played in putting Judge Stapleton on the federal bench. Nine years ago, blithely enjoying his re-election for a second time, sitting in the old City Hall with the state's power brokers, the labor barons, the big givers, the party chairman, hastening to shake his hand and consult him, it had sweetened the taste of the triumph to nominate Paul Stapleton. A mayor named O'Connor backing a superwasp for the juiciest piece of federal patronage in the state. The newspapers had published cartoons of old Irish bosses spinning in their graves. It had convinced more than one skeptic that a new era in city and state politics really had begun. It had bolstered his appeal to the independent voter, the new god of the pollsters and professional campaign managers.

But he had found that it made no difference to Judge Stapleton. The son of a bitch never even thanked him for his support. When the integration crisis began, the Judge had not bothered to consult the Mayor of the city, the man who knew more about its neighborhoods than any other official, a man who could have advised him on how to avoid busing, or keep it to a minimum by resiting new schools and regrouping elementary schools that fed into particular high schools—things he had been unable to persuade the Board of Education to do without a federal court's power. Working together bhind the scenes, the way the Mayor preferred by instinct to work, he and Judge Stapleton could have integrated the city in five years. Instead, they were being ordered to do it in two years. It was a political version of the Charge of the Light Brigade.

What else should he have expected from Judge Stapleton? The old Wasp snob could not bring himself to admit that anyone named O'Connor might give him some worthwhile advice. The Judge and the rest of his frosted-over relatives still treated him with barely concealed contempt. At family dinners they cut him out of their conversations, ignored or stared down his modest attempts at humor. They ogled him across rooms and muttered snide remarks.

Wait, wait, the Mayor told himself, trying to control his antipathy. They were not all that bad. A few of them—the Judge's wife, for instance—were human beings. It was the Judge whom he really disliked. He was worse than Paula's father, whose hatred had been undisguised.

The Judge concealed his opinion behind a phony smile. But there was a needle in almost every word he said to Jake O'Connor. The Mayor told himself that he could tolerate a negative opinion. A thick hide was essential to a politician. What he could not forgive was the Judge's role as a superman in Paula's eyes. Too often she had sought his advice, his support, when she had a serious political disagreement with her husband. When the Mayor had wanted to fight for legalized gambling, when he considered starting a workfare program to cool a ferocious media attack on rising welfare costs, Paula had opposed him and thrown "Uncle Paul says" into the argument as if it was a message from Olympus.

"Don't forget we've got a wake stop at Salvia's," the Mayor said to chauffeur Gus Dumbrowski.

"Who croaked?" Gus asked.

"Tony Perotta's mother."

"I didn't know that creep had a mother."

The Salvia Funeral Home loomed up on the corner, at the crest of the South Slope. Suave, well-tailored Peter Salvia greeted the Mayor at the door and escorted him into the inner room, where a weeping Tony Perotta sat beside a four-thousand-dollar copper coffin. The Mayor was pleased to note his flowers were prominently displayed behind the corpse's head. He leaned over the leader of the Italian American Alliance and murmured the usual words of sympathy. Personally, he did not care if Tony died of grief in the next five minutes. The Mayor was there to confuse Tony's followers and continue a cautious attempt to wean Tony from the clutches of the Biaggi family.

"Thanks, Jake," Tony gasped, clutching the Mayor's hand. His grief was obviously genuine. The Mayor knelt for a moment beside the coffin. Mrs. Perotta looked like she weighed about 400 pounds. A white rosary was clutched in her bloodless hands. The funeral director had used the same stage effect for the Mayor's mother twenty years ago. Had he wept at his mother's funeral? the Mayor asked himself. No, not a tear. His brother Paul, the super priest, had gotten all the love and kisses from

Mother. For Jake—and his father—Katherine O'Connor had been someone to cope with—a problem that sometimes caused anger or pain but mostly irritated, like a skin disease.

On his feet, the Mayor turned, patted Tony on the shoulder, and moved swiftly down the room shaking hands with a half dozen Italian politicians. He moved smoothly into the next room, nodding and smiling to familiar faces. At the door, he shook Pete Salvia's hand, and strolled into the night. He reached the curb just as his limousine emerged from the driveway and swung to a stop in front of thfe funeral home.

"Right on the button," the Mayor said, looking at his watch. Gus Dumbrowski always emerged from the parking lot in precisely two minutes. The carefully timed routine enabled the Mayor to make about a thousand wake stops a year. Paula tended to carp at this effort as an anachronism. She disliked anything that suggested the Mayor was imitating the city's previous political generation. The Mayor kept on going to wakes.

Five minutes later, they were slowing to a stop before Bowood's gold-tipped gate. Up the drive they crunched to the big white double doors with the defiant gold eagle above them. The Mayor found himself wishing that Paula and her architectural historians had left the house alone. They had insisted on pulling down the white-pillared portico added by Victorian Stapletons and restoring the house to its severe Federal period lines.

In the center hall Mahoney took his coat and said: "We had a call from the hospital, sir. Your brother's disappeared again."

"Give me the keys to Mrs. O'Connor's car."

The Mayor cursed his way to Paula's red Triumph, parked in Bowood's otherwise empty garage. It had to be ten below zero in the cockpit. He backed out like a TV detective in pursuit of the latest connection and barely gave the black cop at Bowood's gate a wave as he shot past him. After several swift miles on Kennedy Parkway, the Mayor swung right onto the long curving drive down the South Slope into the First Ward's black ghetto. He turned on the heater in the tiny car and thought mordantly about Paul O'Connor. The Mayor knew exactly where he had gone. Paul always went to the same place. It made him suspect that in Paul's scrambled head there was a plan or at least a purpose in always choosing this destination. He was trying to make his powerful, successful brother grovel before the wretched of the earth. He might even be hoping to see the wretched rise up and blast him into oblivion.

One of the candy store's two panes of glass had been replaced by a plywood board on which the words "smashed by the police" were lettered. The Mayor knew the remaining pane of glass was encrusted with dirt and soot. Even in daylight it was impenetrable. The store was a cleft of darkness invading the six-story tenement on the corner. It had been that way when he came here as an uncertain ex-playboy turned semi-idealist trying to make sense out of his father's world.

The Mayor knocked on the glass front door. It took a full minute for Frank Donahue to open it. He had to turn four or five locks. In the half light cast from the back room, Frank looked more spectral than ever, his cheeks hollower, the eyes more remote. The sharp prominent nose was like the beak of a sinister bird. He was not surprised to see the Mayor.

"Hello, Jake," he said. "Paul is here."

"I wish I could charge you with something, Frank. Abduction, or seduction. But there never seems to be a statute that covers your activities."

"I could say the same thing for you, Jake."

He led the Mayor through the store, filled with the sweet smell of cheap candy, to the back room. The familiar round table was still in place. The same whitewashed walls dully reflected the glare of the single overhead bulb. But instead of the coffee that Frank had served twenty-five years ago, there were jugs of wine on the table. Then the drinkers at the table had all been white, except for a single black man. Now they were all black, except for a single white man—the Mayor's brother, Paul.

He was wearing a priest's round white collar like an absurd decoration above a blue and red striped sport shirt. It was typical of the costumes he had worn around the city when he suddenly reappeared, after more than ten years of wandering around America, and began preaching against "the Powergod." The Mayor had been inclined to ignore him, but when Paul's behavior became more and more bizarre—at one point they heard he was celebrating Black Masses on the counter of Frank Donahue's store—Paula had insisted he was mentally ill and needed help. Committing him had brought on a total collapse—a claim that Father Paul was dead, murdered by his brother. Only Paul's ghost spoke now, sending enigmatic poems and gnomic messages from the void.

"Gentlemen," Frank Donahue said. "We have a distinguished visitor."

"His Dishonor, the Mayor," Paul said. "O ye of little faith."

The haunted face had no resemblance to the smug, smiling, well-fed priest the Mayor had known and hated twenty years ago. Paul had started to disintegrate from the moment his mother died. As long as she was around to feed his ego with rapturous praise, he was the original know-it-all cleric, determined to save the world on his terms, no matter how many lives he ruined or hearts he broke in the process. He was the reason why the Mayor loathed the Catholic Church and disdained all other brands of religion. Paul had injected this virus into him. At times he suspected it was a weakness and wished he could achieve his father's tough indifference. Most of the time the Mayor saw his hostility as strength. It had taken strength to fight off Paul and the nuns and priests who had presided over his education and tried to reduce him and everyone else to a nice safe Catholic yes man. Without his father, he never could have done it.

"I came down here to take you back to the hospital, Paul."

"I am not Fakefather Paul. He is dead. I am No One. You can send me wherever you will. You are a

Powergod. Ruler of the City. We bow down before you."

"I wish I could get a few more people to do it," the Mayor said. "Why the hell are you putting me to all this trouble? You always come here. I come and get you. What kind of a game are you playing?"

Paul's face worked. Tears suddenly filled his staring eyes. "The ghost of Fakefather Paul has a message. He wants to tell you. But I cannot—"

"Tell me. I want to hear it."

"He forgives you for killing him. He understands now. It was history. You and he are both in history. And history is—"

Paul looked at Frank Donahue. He seemed afraid of him. "It was only fair that you killed Fakefather Paul. He killed your faith."

"You see how skillfully he can disarm you?" Frank Donahue said to the blacks around the table. "Even this poor slob, who has more reason to hate the great Jake O'Connor than anyone else in the world, tries to forgive him."

Paul closed his eyes, as if he was trying to avoid Frank Donahue's contempt. "I can't hear anymore," he said. "The ghost of Fakefather Paul has gone back to the Isn'tworld."

"You're going back to the Isn'tworld too. And this time I'm going to make sure you don't get out again. But before I go, I want to deal with another matter."

The Mayor studied the hostile black faces on either side of his brother. He decided they were no different from previous denizens of Donahue's back room. They were captives who sat there night after night, spewing the guts of their failed lives into the fetid air, incapable of escaping the empty appreciation with which Frank listened to their stories. Once the Mayor had almost become one of those captives. Once he had almost become hooked on the hatred that lived in this windowless room.

"Let me introduce the other guests, Mayor," Frank Donahue said.

He bestowed a lofty tribute on each man, as if he were the guest of honor at a banquet. The Mayor recognized only the first name. "Bishop McCoy, inheritor of Marcus Garvey's mantle, the Moses who may yet lead his people back to Africa." The Bishop, who was as fat as Simon Burke, had been orating on street corners about the beauties of African emigration for decades. The others were a mélange of inventors who had had their brainchildren stolen by the white corporations, great unappreciated poets, playwrights, philosophers, and a public school teacher who looked like Aunt Jemima in drag.

The last man introduced was sitting closest to Frank Donahue. Ex-con was written all over his flat emotion-drained face and bitter mouth. "Andrew 77X —our Ambassador from the Penal Colony," Frank said. "Of course you know him as Andy Barton."

"I'm afraid I don't," the Mayor said.

"Come, come, Jake. There is no need to lie. We all tell the truth here. Andy Barton, sentenced to five years in jail for something called vote fraud in 1948."

"I didn't read the papers very much in 1948."

"He is one of the many living testimonials to the greatness of the political tradition you represent."

"I represent a different tradition, Frank."

"There is no point in putting on your act here, Jake. We know the man behind it. We know him for what he is. A colossal fraud."

"You're the fraud, Frank. But I haven't got time to debate you. I just want to tell you to stop scaring the bejesus out of my wife with those telephone calls."

"I don't know what you're talking about, Jake."

"Yes you do. I just hope the rest of you don't know anything about it. You can get five years for threatening somebody over the telephone. I'm no friend of Frank's. Not after the way he acted down here during the riot. But I'd like to be the friend of everyone else in this room."

Instinct, crazy instinct, the Mayor mocked himself. He could not resist competing with Frank Donahue for their allegiance. Maybe those people who said that he was a born politician were right. He could not resist fighting for the attention, the approval of an audience. But here it went deeper than attention. It went beyond this immediate circle of lost souls. His response continued a psychological, even a spiritual, contest between him and Frank Donahue—a contest that had begun thirty years ago, when Donahue had returned from World War II and bought this candy store with back pay accumulated from four years as a beach master at landings from North Africa to Iwo Jima.

It was fascinating, amusing, at first. Frank had been one of the most brilliant students in the history of St. Francis Prep, the only challenger to Paul O'Connor's relentless accumulation of medals and first honor cards. Everyone had blamed the retreat to the candy store on shell shock, battle fatigue. Only a few, such as his brother Larry, saw Frank's nihilism. Nothing had become Frank's God. Nothing was what he witnessed with his bland mocking smile. Nothing was what he worshiped with the chorus of losers he collected in his back room.

In the Pacific, Jake O'Connor had seen men die in stupid, meaningless ways. He had heard screams from flooding compartments. He had seen bodies writhing in a sea of blazing oil. He had seen the Kamikazes dropping out of the blue sky like death-bearing insects. He had come home with some of the same spiritual losses. But he had a father who had endured the cauldron of the Argonne, a father who held out a strong hand to him. Frank Donahue had a cerebral ghost for a father, a whiskey voice whispering ironies.

Frank Donahue had tried to loosen the grasp of Ben O'Connor's strong hand. Frank had flung the hatred and loathing of his losers' chorus in Jake O'Connor's face. From his first visit, Jake had sensed the contest. If he could still say yes to his father, in spite of what he heard in this back room about the brutal and the vicious and the mean things that the organization had done to seize and hold its power, he would win and Frank Donahue would lose.

But Jake never thought the contest would continue in Frank's icy soul for the rest of their lives. Once he had made his decision, once he had walked out of that hospital with that limping man's arm around him, for Jake the contest was over. Frank Donahue was irrelevant. The Mayor had been astonished when his brother Paul returned to the city and became one of Frank's denizens. He was even more astonished when Frank surfaced as the ideologist of the American Anarchist Alliance, preaching manic destruction as the answer to the turmoil of the sixties and seventies.

Then the Mayor had accepted the deeper lifelong dimension of the contest. It was part of the reason why he had refused to let Tarentino prosecute or even harass Frank. The basic rule of the contest was unspoken but clearly understood. Jake O'Connor would never use his power. Frank Donahue would never act. He would create an anti-world of hate and loss from which agents of destruction might rise. But a personal act would betray the contemptuous indifference with which Frank surveyed this and all other worlds.

So the Mayor spoke to Frank Donahue's followers. All middle-aged or older now. The fever of the sixties had vanished, and with it, Frank's appeal to the young. He was back to collecting losers.

"I'm in favor of free speech," the Mayor said. "You can say anything you want here or anywhere else in this city. You can bad-mouth me, the President, the Pope, Jesus Christ himself. But when someone starts calling my house telling my wife I'm going to die, that's when I start talking to the cops."

The black, brown, and tan faces around the table remained expressionless. The Mayor realized his appeal had taken a curious wrong turn. He was threatening them. In spite of the invocation of his wife, he was playing the man of power, not the man of understanding, sympathy, friendship that he had tried to be in the opening lines.

The word wife made Father Paul open his eyes. "The Powergod has a wife? Do you curse her like your father cursed his wife? Do you roar and smash tables with your mighty fist?"

"Keep quiet," the Mayor said.

"Let me apologize, Jake," Frank Donahue said. "Those calls have been rather tasteless. They will cease, now that the essential message has been delivered."

"I never thought you'd get so involved, Frank. I thought you were proud of your detachment."

"That was an Irish affectation, Jake. The illusion that the soul has its own satisfactions, and can afford to ignore the body, that heaven is separate from earth. Now that I am part of Africa, Jake, I know that blood is primary. What the heart pumps, what the heart feels, the heart must speak."

"Do you guys believe this nonsense?"

The black faces remained expressionless.

"What about your children, Your Honor?" Father Paul said. "Do you honor thy father's tradition and abuse them because they love their mother? Do you despise their attempts to practice the virtues of faith? Or hope? Do you permit them to believe in God? Or only in you? And of course, in Power."

"Shut up, Paul."

Frank Donahue turned on his high three-legged stool and opened a cupboard in the wall. He struck a match and lit a candle inside the cupboard. The flickering light illuminated a glossy photograph of a young face with a strong resemblance to his own. It had the same hawk nose and gaunt cheeks and intent staring eyes. It was a picture of Larry Donahue, who had been the Mayor's best friend before Larry chose his brother Frank's philosophy as the answer to the corruption of the city's old politics. Beside the picture glistened the black metal of a gun, hanging upside down on a peg.

"Remember what Larry told you the night he died, Jake?" Frank Donahue raised his eyes and recited it like a mocking prayer. "You will marry that lean Protestant bitch and let her play the Stars and Stripes Forever while you run on her money just as far as you can go."

"I remember, Frank. I remember a lot of other things, too," the Mayor said.

"We carry on his work," Frank said. "On behalf of the wretched of the earth, we are committed to fighting the bumbling slaves of the fathergod and his idiot savior son and the phonies like you, Jake, who exploit them. Nothing explains the immense failure of goodness except the conclusion that goodness is a fraud. It is the opposite of goodness—all the things they taught us were wrong—pride, lust, violence, murder—these are the things that cleanse the soul, that create hope. To do good we must first do evil."

"I've heard the speech before, Frank."

Frank Donahue took the pistol off its peg. The gun was a Detective Special with a short ugly snout. Frank fondled the fat bulge behind the barrel.

"Isn't it beautiful, Jake?"

"I've never seen anything uglier, Frank."

"I could shoot you now. I could claim that you walked in unannounced. I have a permit for this gun. I got it by telling your cops I was burglarized five times in the last three months. They didn't even bother to investigate. It's a nice comment on the kind of police protection you give people in the ghetto."

The Mayor stared at the gun, wondering if he could reach it before Frank Donahue's finger tightened on the trigger. Across the table, his brother Paul began to whisper a poem.

> "The ruler of the city
> Sits in a frozen blaze
> His eyes are frozen tenpins
> Deep in a frozen grave.
>
> "His hands are open sesames
> To every frozen door
> But in his heart a horror show
> Makes a frozen roar."

"Let me kill him now, Magister. I'm ready," Andrew 77X Barton growled.

Frank Donahue shook his head. "It would be too easy. It would miss the essential ingredient I insist on Jake's death possessing. I want him to die just when he thinks he's gotten away with it. When he's fooled enough of the people enough of the time to make it to the top. I want to kill him just as he puts his foot on the last triumphant step."

"Frank, if you knew how many things were going wrong in my so-called triumphal climb, you'd throw away that gun. You may never get a chance to use it."

Father Paul continued to whisper his poem.

> "The ruler of the city
> Laughs a frozen laugh
> And walks away from friend and foe
> Into a frozen past.
>
> "On his lips are frozen words
> About a frozen thaw
> All around him frozen smiles
> Echo frozen laws."

"You can twist and turn, Jake," Frank Donahue said. "There is no way for you to avoid what you have become. A symbol of betrayal. A symbol of a man who sold himself, soul and body."

For a moment, hearing those words, seeing his brother writhing and moaning in his chair, sensing the explosive mixture of hatred and fear building in the blacks, the Mayor was ready to believe that Frank Donahue possessed supernatural power. How else could Frank have probed the wound Jake O'Connor had inflicted on himself, the one he saw in all its grisly gangrenous ugliness last night? The Mayor told himself it was exaggeration, a metaphor, he reminded himself that he never had any illusion about that side of his relationship to his wife. What had surprised him, unbalanced him, was the intensity of his personal feeling for her. None of this worked. He found himself lashing out with frenetic sentences.

"I know all about Frank's philosophy of life. I heard that magic phrase from his brother Larry. To do good we must first do evil. I didn't buy it then and I don't buy it now. If you know what happened to Larry— his progress from bribery to blackmail to murder and finally suicide, I can't believe you'd buy it either."

"They know all about Larry," Frank Donahue said.

"Your version. You sat here and watched him destroy himself. That's when I started to despise you, Frank. Nothing I've heard lately has changed my mind."

The Mayor turned to the black faces. "Frank's been sitting here for thirty years waiting for something to happen, something that would include him without any risk on his part."

"I see you are as spiritually obtuse as ever, Jake."

"I don't mean physical risk," the Mayor said. "That's easy to take. Frank did plenty of that during the war. So did I. I'm talking about a moral risk. The risk of trying to do something worthwhile. Trying to build something that will last. Trying to create something—a tradition of government—maybe just good habits—that your children can use."

"Save that stuff for the Kiwanis, Jake. You have governed this city precisely as I predicted you'd govern it. Without a trace of moral vision. Your stance on busing is the final proof."

"I'll defend my moral vision against your brand—or Father Paul's brand—anytime, Frank. I've kept this city alive for the last fourteen years. I've kept it from disintegrating, like Detroit. From burning down, like Newark. If you can compare that to sitting down here, bad-mouthing me and the country, you ought to be keeping Father Paul company in the nuthouse."

"Spoken like a true Powergod," Father Paul said. "But what does your son think? Does he weep for you in the silence of the night? Do you permit him to pray for you? That was what drove Fakefather Paul to the Isn'tworld. He could not get a prayer past Realfather's granite face."

The Mayor ignored his brother and turned his back on Frank Donahue and his gun. He spoke directly to his black chorus. "Here's a proposition for you. Join me instead of shooting me. You know this part of town. You speak the people's language. Help me set up a communications center here, someplace where I can meet neighborhood leaders, street people, men and women who would never come to see me in City Hall. I want to talk to them. I want to convince them that all the whites in this city aren't in RIP."

"You're wasting your breath, Jake," Frank Donahue said.

"If I am, I want to hear it from these people, not you."

"You're wasting your breath all right," Andrew 77X Barton said.

No one else said a word.

Mournfully the Mayor remembered the night he had asked his father to visit Frank Donahue's back room and listen to the losers of that era. He wanted to see how Ben O'Connor faced the hatred and derision they would shower on him. But his father had dismissed the idea with an abrupt shake of his head. A *waste of time,* he had growled. He had been right, of course, and this was more waste—of time, breath, emotion.

A politician could not help these people. They wanted a miracle worker. Maybe he should have talked to them about how little power he really had, how little power any politician in America really had. While Frank Donahue sat with a sneer on his face. But at least, the Mayor thought, as he stared into the impassive refusing faces, at least he might have surprised them. He would not be confronted by this wall of blackness, strangeness, this sense of a world that he could not penetrate.

"I'm sorry," the Mayor said. "I'm sorry for you and maybe I'm even a little sorry for myself."

Paul sighed eerily. "The Powergod pities himself. Fakefather Paul didn't know he had such feelings."

"It's one of his two emotions," Frank Donahue said. "The other is fear. You will see that when—"

The hand with the gun in it moved sideways— the gesture of a man brushing away an insect.

"You haven't got the guts to do it, Frank."

"We'll see, Jake. We'll see."

"Let's go."

The Mayor seized his brother by the arm and dragged him from behind the table into the sweet-smelling front of the store. He knew that he was daring Frank Donahue to shoot him. He also knew that it was a worthless gesture, bravado that would impress no one in the audience. They would cheer the bullet that slammed into his head.

Suddenly he hated them. He hated every one of those black, brown, and tan faces. He shoved Paul into the Triumph and got behind the wheel. He tried to put the key in the ignition and could not do it. His hand was shaking. What was happening to him? *Out of control,* whispered a tiny voice.

Beside him in the darkened car he heard his brother weeping. "Now Fakefather Paul's ghost can tell you. He can say it now. History is not only what Frank says it is, not only the void. It is also words made flesh."

The Mayor finally got the key in the ignition and started the motor. His mind was still in Donahue's back room, confronting those impenetrable black faces.

"Paul prays that you can accept the role assigned to you. The role that he sought in vain. You always beat Paul to everything."

"What role?"

"The suffering servant."

"Shut up," the Mayor said as he slammed the shift into first gear. "For Christ's sake shut up once and for all."

9

Paula paced up and down the glistening center hall while the rosewood grandfather clock bonged eight. CITY-1 purred outside the door. For the third time, she rang for Mahoney.

"The Mayor didn't tell you where he was going? You're *sure?*"

"Quite sure, madam."

Dolores appeared at the top of the staircase. "I won't go to bed till I kiss Daddy," she said, pouting down at her through the balustrade.

"You will go to bed when Mackey tells you. Daddy won't kiss you unless you're in bed."

"Come along, you minx," Mackey said.

Her big hand, visually detached from the rest of her bulky body, seized Dolores and hoisted her back to the second floor. A protesting wail dwindled down the hall.

Headlights, the sound of the Triumph's motor coming up the drive. In a moment, Mahoney was opening the front door and Jake strolled toward her, a gloomy distant look on his face.

"Where in God's name have you been? We're due for dinner at Uncle Paul's right now."

"He'll have to wait," Jake said. "He kept me waiting all day."

"Where did you go? Mahoney said he told you about your brother. And you just got in my car and drove away. I didn't know what to think."

"I'll tell you about it in the car," the Mayor said, trotting up the stairs. "I'll just change my shirt."

"It's black tie," Paula said.

Paula paced for another ten minutes. Mahoney ascended with a scotch and soda. Dolores erupted from her room to bang on her father's door. There was an exchange of strident remarks between Mackey and the Mayor and Paula distinctly heard her husband say, "Get lost." Mackey descended the staircase like an outraged Queen Victoria to announce her resignation. Paula assured her that the Mayor didn't mean it, it was haste, not rudeness or dislike that sharpened his tongue. The Mayor came downstairs in his tuxedo, gave Mackey a glare that belied everything Paula had just said, and growled, "Come on. We can settle this tomorrow."

In the car, Paula begged him to be more reasonable. Mackey would be hard to replace. The Mayor wanted to know why he could not kiss his daughter good night, just because she chose to come in late and was rushing out again. Paula tried to explain that there would be no objection to his kissing her, if he went to her room. The trouble was her flagrant defiance of Mackey, running out of her room after she had been put to bed.

"Since when is it a crime for a kid to get out of bed to kiss her own father?"

"We're trying to teach her obedience, Jake."

"I don't know whether that's such a good idea."

"It's a very good idea for a four-year-old. I see nothing admirable or amusing about a spoiled child. Especially a spoiled girl. I think they turn out to be unhappy women."

Paula could not see her husband's face in the dark. But she was sure it was distorted by sullen reproach. Was it because the remark edged close to a criticism of Dolores' namesake, the quintessential spoiled woman? Perhaps. Even without that presence, they did not agree on what constituted a spoiled child. They agreed even less on the nurse's role in the child-raising process. When Jake had told her that he did not like the idea of a stranger running his children's lives, she had been too astonished to argue, at first. She tried to explain to him that a nurse was the source of discipline, steadiness, regularity in a child's life. Affection, too, when both parents were absorbed in the adult world. "I loved my nurse—almost more than my mother," she had said.

The disapproval that this declaration produced on her husband's face was dismaying. They were suddenly in a very thorny thicket in which his private opinion of her and her private opinion of him became subtle parts of the argument. If he did not approve of the way she had been raised, didn't that imply a certain dislike of her, now? And vice versa? They had both retreated, uneasily sensing for the first time the dangers lurking in their different pasts.

The nurse had been hired—Scottish, of course. Within the year she had quit because Jake refused to regard her as the arbiter of when he could see his son, how late the child could stay up, what he could eat. When Dolores arrived, he became even more unmanageable, and showed no signs of improving. Paula's strategy for keeping Mackey had descended to preventing confrontations between her and Jake—a strategy that had collapsed tonight.

The Mayor pressed a button and shut the window separating them from the night chauffeur, a black man named Jesse Owens.

"What's this Dolores tells me about Barney getting a bloody nose at school today?"

"Some kids—I gather it's a gang—punched him. It happened in the boys' bathroom. The one place where they don't have a monitor."

"That's a great little school you picked out for him."

Paula felt anger burning in her cheeks. "We talked it over, we decided it—together. I really dislike this habit you have of blaming me when things go wrong."

"I do not have any such habit. We did talk it over. I agreed. But you know damn well I didn't have time to give it any real thought. That was your job."

"It's a very good school. It'll be better when there's a decent balance of white and black."

"I wish I could believe that. I'm afraid it will be worse."

"I'm sorry to hear that."

"Why? Can't we be realistic about this mess? Are there articles of faith I have to maintain?"

"No. I just think you're wrong. It will be better. They pick on Kemble because he's one of a tiny minority now. It's just human nature, Jake."

"We had two black kids in my grammar school class. We diddn't pick on them."

"The nuns wouldn't let you."

"The nuns didn't monitor the boys' bathroom either."

Silence for a half mile.

"I swear to God, if he gets roughed up again, I'll take him out of there and send him to some private school like Judson Hall."

"You can't be serious. You'd lose every black vote in the city."

"Paula—doesn't it bother you to see our kids mixed up in this mess?"

"I don't understand why you get so upset about it. Your father was a politician—"

"That's why I want to keep politics out of my kids' lives. I don't want them to grow up hating me and politics."

"You're not going to tell me you grew up that way?"

"You didn't know me when I was growing up. I had to put up with a lot of bullshit. I remember when I was about eight, I knocked a softball into the next yard. I climbed over the fence to get it and the owner gave me hell for ruining his garden. I told him to drop dead, and he said to me, 'Listen, you punk, don't talk to me that way. I pay your old man's salary.' That night, I told my father about it. I was hoping he'd kick hell out of the bastard. Instead, he just got sore in a kind of helpless way. I realized he didn't have an answer to that crack. He was even a little afraid of it."

Paula was touched and saddened by the memory. She had never thought of Ben O'Connor as a vulnerable man.

"When I got a little older," the Mayor continued in

the same brooding voice, "there was always some slob who'd say something like 'How much did your old man steal today?' Generally, I could knock his head against a wall a few times and he'd apologize. But you couldn't do that with the Jesuits. They were always making cracks about crooked politicians while half the class turned around and grinned at me. It didn't make your heart leap up at the sound of the word politics."

"I don't see any connection between that sort of thing and Kemble's troubles."

"I do. He's a bright kid. He knows he's in that school because I'm the Mayor and you're the Mayor's wife. It's not something he chose. As far as I can see, he's going to wind up hating blacks and us in the bargain."

"That's not true. I've explained to him why these—these unpleasant things happen. He understands."

"His head understands. His gut hates them. What do you expect, Paula? Would you like someone who punched you in the mouth for no particular reason?"

"He knows the reason. I've explained it to him."

Silence. A silence that was more dismaying than an angry disagreement. It implied he did not think there was any point in arguing with her. It also declared that there was no hope of changing his mind.

"Did you—find your brother?"

"Yeah. He was at the same place. Donahue's store. I took him to the Medical Center. They'll hold him in the psychiatric ward until the Institute picks him up tomorrow. I'm going to call those turkeys out there and tell them that for thirty-five thousand bucks a year, the least they can do is keep him under lock and key."

"That isn't Dr. Kane's approach. They're trying to create a normal atmosphere."

"A padded cell and bars on the window. That's a normal atmosphere for Paul."

Paula had never met Paul O'Connor. She had heard one of his street corner sermons during his mental collapse and it had shocked and disturbed her. It had been about the meek inheriting the garbage. It had been incredibly obscene. The meek inherited the garbage by having it rammed down their throats and up other body orifices. The politicians were the rammers. His brother, the Mayor, was particularly good at it because he made people smile while he was doing it. The wider their mouths, the more they swallowed without even realizing it.

Instinctively, Paula had sympathized with this babbling, sneering ex-priest. She saw the debris of a man who had tried to preach love and justice to his father's city and found that few listened and fewer cared. She could not comprehend Jake's attitude toward his brother. She had been appalled by his indifference to Paul's street corner rantings, and stunned when he suggested committing him to the state mental hospital, where custodial care was all he could expect. She had been the one who located the Brompton Institute and insisted on paying for Paul's treatment there.

A tax lawyer from her Uncle Paul's firm had suggested that Jake open a separate checking account and pay the bills out of his salary. Since it was more than 10 per cent of his income, it was tax-deductible on their joint return. This perfectly legal maneuver only seemed to make Jake less enthusiastic. It was upsetting to discover this lack of normal affection in the person from whom she expected lifelong love. It made her wonder what Paul had done to inspire such profound antagonism.

"I think we're wasting our money. Or my money, to be more exact."

"It's all our money."

"Sorry. I tend to forget that. Especially after our ritual visit to Stapleton Talbot. When is that scheduled for, this year?"

"April first, I think."

Once a year, she and her husband went to the law offices of Stapleton Talbot to go over the investments of her various trust funds and discuss possible changes in their tax strategy. She had sensed very early in their marriage that this was an ordeal for Jake. He knew nothing about the stock market. He had no investments. So the discussion inevitably revolved around her trust funds, which were all in her name in perpetuity, according to the various wills by which she had inherited them. They put the income from them into a joint checking account, and the liquid investments from her income, something over two million dollars, were held in common. But this hardly mitigated the undeniable fact that they talked about Paula Stapleton's money.

Their tax lawyer, their tax accountant, and their investment banker always directed most of their remarks to Jake. They ignored his first joking attempts to plead ignorance. So did her Uncle Paul, who often sat in on these meetings before he retired from the firm to accept the federal judgeship. They seemed to be implying that if he did not know anything about finance, he had better learn if he was going to be Paula Stapleton's husband. She had been inclined to agree with them. But sixteen years later, he still knew nothing and the visit had become a ritual at which they nodded their heads to whatever the experts suggested, signed their income tax returns, and went home.

"That's one dividend I got out of making Uncle Paul a judge," Jake said. "I don't have to put up with his cracks at those tax talks."

Paula winced at her husband's cutting tone. He must know it hurt her. Paul Stapleton had been the most important man in her life until she met Jake O'Connor. She had tried to explain that her uncle thought his rather blunt, needling remarks were funny. It was his idea of humor. Her husband had simply refused to believe it.

"Can I look forward to coping with the whole clan, down to the second and third cousins, tonight?"

"No. Just the immediate family."

It was unfair, grossly unfair, Paula thought, the way Jake rejected the Stapletons. Not that they were all charming. On the contrary, she was prepared to admit that most of them were bores. But Jake had perversely refused to like any Stapleton. She had stopped accepting invitations to most family parties five or six years ago because she could not stand the way he came home muttering sarcastic comments about riding to hounds or collecting Aubusson rugs. She had expected him to dislike some of the more old-guardish elders. But even they had been exquisitely polite. No one had made a single crack against the Irish or the Democrats, as far as she knew. This made even more unreasonable Jake's determination to take offense at the Stapleton's lifestyles.

They *were* horsey, they did collect Aubussons, eighteenth-century pewter, rare books, Copley paintings. They endowed special collections at libraries and museums, and some of them were fanatic genealogists, active in the Sons and Daughters of the American Revolution. What were they supposed to do? Spend their time getting their pictures into magazines like the tasteless Kennedys? True, the Stapletons drank as much as any comparable group of Irishmen, as Jake was fond of pointing out. But on the whole, they tried to live discreet, moderately constructive lives, enjoying their money without dissipating it or themselves. In Jake's wholesale rejection Paula sensed a partial rejection of her. What would he say, if she told him that? Deny it, of course. It was so easy for him to deny things. Wrapped in his politician's egotistic cocoon, he seemed to have no idea how much louder his actions spoke than his words.

They were rolling through the one-acre zoned suburbs now, Bridgewater, mostly Irish, then Valley Falls, mostly Jewish, the two ethnic groups who had done well enough to escape the city in large numbers.

"I saw an economic survey the other day," the Mayor said. "The Jews and the Irish have the two highest average incomes in the country. Jews are only one hundred and twenty-five dollars ahead of us in this state."

"You're doing pretty well. Maybe it's time you stopped feeling sorry for yourselves."

"I wasn't aware of this character defect."

"It isn't *serious,* dear," she said, patting his hand, "but you do tend to repeat certain stories, like the one about your father being forced to deny his religion to get a job in the Slocum patent medicine factory. And I have heard a lot about the awful wages my grandfather paid your grandfather on the loading platform."

"That medicine factory story meant a lot to my father. It still means something to me. In fact, the more I read Mortimer Kemble's diary, the more it means to me."

"I must read this marvelous book."

"You should. It might cure that tendency to condescension from which you occasionally suffer. Nothing *serious,* but—"

They were beyond Valley Falls now, in rolling country where houses stood on tops of hills or at the bottom of sweeping lawns. Paula did not need daylight to see them. She had spent years of her life out here, if the accumulated visits were added together. In winter she had skated on the numerous small secluded ponds and returned half frozen to drink hot punch before huge crackling fireplaces. In spring and fall she had ridden across the green hills, leaped old stone fences on the back of a galloping horse, exulting in that rare combination of freedom and risk. For her, this landscape was synonymous with happiness.

"Sometimes I still wish we'd moved out here. You could have run for Congress. You might be a senator by now."

"It would have been the worst mistake we ever made."

That had been her first attempt to influence him in a serious way. There had been an almost blind compulsion in his resistance. Why? Was it simply the wariness with which he had regarded her before they were married, when Miss Stapleton was interchangeable with her checkbook? Or was it something deeper, an atavistic impulse to possess City Hall, that pinnacle of power which his father had never attained? She had recently read a book about Jimmy Walker which argued that the greatest moment in his life was the day he was made a sachem of Tammany Hall. Harvard had educated such parochialism out of the Kennedys. But Jake had not gone to Harvard.

She told herself to drop the subject, but she found herself unable to obey her own advice.

"It would have made running for governor so much easier. They wouldn't have been able to use the city against you."

"I might be a has-been, if my voting record didn't measure up to Uncle Paul's execptations."

"He doesn't treat people that way. He wouldn't treat you that way."

"Anyone who runs out here is his boy. Will Congressman Slocum be here tonight?"

"Probably."

"Watch him kiss Uncle Paul's ass. Then tell me if I'm wrong."

"I'll tell you now. In the first place, Dwight Slocum doesn't have to—to kiss anyone's ass. And Uncle Paul is not the sort of man who—who encourages that sort of thing."

"That's not what I heard. Dwight didn't get the nomination out here with his money. He got it by convincing Uncle Paul that he'd been born again. That's when Dwight's money started talking. When he got Uncle's stamp of approval. There's a hell of a lot of lawyers out here in Serenity Acres who don't want to get the state's number one legal eagle sore at them."

"He helped Dwight. I don't deny it. He's helped us too. I don't know where we'd be without him. Who else could have talked my father out of disinheriting me?"

"Paula. My training is in criminal law. I'm no expert on wills. But even a first-year law student knows that your father couldn't have disinherited you. Ninety per cent of the money was left to you in your mother's will. He only controlled it during his lifetime."

"It would have been messy to brawl in open court about it. Aren't you glad we didn't have to tell the whole story in public?"

"That's like asking somebody with a broken leg whether he's glad he doesn't have a ruptured spleen. He'd rather not have either one."

Paula's father had refused to come to their wedding. He never answered Paula's letters or sent gifts to his grandchildren. His final act of hostility should have been no surprise. But it had upset Jake in an odd, unexpectedly intense way. Apparently he had expected—or hoped—that his performance as Mayor would reconcile Malcolm Stapleton. Her father's refusal to change his mind to the day of his lonely death in New York disturbed Jake far more than the attempt at disinheritance, which Judge Stapleton had swiftly smothered. At the time, Paula had been touched by her husband's regret. It had complemented her own feelings, in spite of the heavier burden of personal memory and lost affection she bore. It had drawn them together in a deep, fresh way. But that was eight years ago. Now this reminder of his feelings only irritated her.

"Well, I'm glad Uncle Paul was there to do something about it, no matter what a first-year law student might think."

They rode in silence for the next mile or two. Chauffeur Jesse Owens lowered the window between them and asked for directions. She was glad to have something to occupy her. She turned down one of the jump seats and sat on it, peering up the road, waiting for the headlights to pick up familiar landmarks.

"That big oak. The driveway is about a hundred yards past it. You'll see a boulder on the left now. Just past it—the road." In another minute they were rounding the oval driveway, stopping before the white front door. In the pine-paneled center hall, Jim Fry, her uncle's stumpy Indian orderly in two wars, took their coats. Maria Stapleton, moving with the painful gait of the arthritic, greeted them in the doorway of the living room, a broad smile on her lined, very Spanish face. "We were about to give up on you and sit down, but he wouldn't let us. He just kept saying Paula will be here."

"A crisis in the body politic," Paula said. "I should have called."

"I'm surprised at you, Jake, letting a few votes stand in the way of a good time. You're a disgrace to our ancestors."

"It's what happens when you spend too much time

with these Wasps, Maria," Jake said. "You start to lose your perspective."

"So that's what happened to me."

He gave her a hearty kiss. Paula found herself almost hopeful. In some ways her uncle's marriage had foreshadowed her own. Perhaps, she thought with sudden intuition, influenced it more than she realized. Paul Stapleton had met Maria O'Reilly, born of Spanish and Irish Catholics, when he joined the U. S. Army that pursued Pancho Villa into Mexico in 1916. Once or twice her uncle had hinted about the uproar the marriage had caused in the family.

They followed Maria into the cavernous living room. To make his wife feel at home, Paul Stapleton had added wings to the eighteenth-century Dutch farmhouse in the style of a Mexican hacienda. Massive teakwood beams announced a totally different conception of space and power from the sturdy pine and oak of the modest entrance hall. They descended three steps to the sunken floor crowded with eighteenth-century Spanish colonial furniture. Paul Stapleton was sitting in a huge rectangular armchair talking to someone Paula did not recognize; his back was to the door. Her uncle stood up the moment they entered the room and strode toward her, his arms open, his face aglow. "My one and only daughter has finally arrived," he said.

Paula was shocked by his appearance. There were dark pouches of exhaustion beneath his eyes. Flesh and blood had vanished from his cheeks, giving the patrician face a shriveled corpselike look. Although his back was still straight as a gun barrel, there was an old man's unsteadiness in his stride.

Calling her daughter was a game they had always played. But now it had a sudden rush of deeper meaning. He was the only father she had now. It was disturbing to find herself still wanting, needing him and simultaneously realizing she would soon lose him. She kissed him with almost embarrassing intensity. "Happy birthday," she said.

"A man can't have a happy birthday at eighty."

"Unless he's happy to be having a birthday at all," Jake said.

"That's about it," Paul Stapleton said, holding out his hand. They shook briefly and her uncle said: "How's it going, Your Honor?"

"Miserably, Your Honor. I spent the day waiting for a certain judge to return my call."

Paul Stapleton smiled in a wintry, weary way. "The certain judge will talk to you about that before you go."

"It sounds like I ought to eat, drink, and be merry."

"Look at it this way, Jake. I'm giving you a chance to make history. You can be the city's first Irish Mayor to obey the law."

"All I need is a regular army division to get the rest of the voters to do it."

"That's where leadership comes into the picture, Jake. You haven't given us much lately."

It was said with the same frosty smile on the pale lips. Paula saw anger flash in her husband's eyes. But there was not a trace of rancor in his voice. A small answering smile even played across his lips.

"I'm an old navy man, Judge. We don't go for the frontal assault. Come to think of it, I don't think anybody in the Army does either. That went out with San Juan Hill."

Paul Stapleton's eyes turned cold and hard. He seemed to be looking deep into her husband and not liking what he saw. But he still smiled as he said, "You know what I mean, Jake. But I'm not going to let the goddamn city and its politics spoil my birthday party. It nearly spoiled my life."

He turned to Paula. "Daughter," he said, "I've got a surprise for you. Look who's here."

He seized her arm and led her down the room, leaving Jake to fend for himself. Paula found herself resisting this abrupt separation from her husband, but only for a fleeting emotional moment. She did not physically balk at the firm old hand that propelled her. The negative emotion vanished when she saw the man who was rising to greet her, a smile on his broad face.

"The prodigal has returned for the old geezer's birthday," Paul Stapleton said.

"Dwight," Paula said, "how nice to see you."

"How nice to see you, Paula."

Congressman Dwight Slocum took her hand and brushed his lips against her cheek. He smelled strongly of some expensive shaving lotion. Everything about Dwight was strong, from his wide stubby hands to his barrel chest to his stump-thick neck. He was looking remarkably fit. Pictures she had seen before he surfaced as an instant Congressman two years ago had displayed drooping jowls beneath the square chin, pouches of dissipation in the once flawless cheeks. These had vanished. Except for the thickened waist and neck, this Dwight was a physical twin of the halfback who had carried Princeton to three Ivy League crowns.

"You've gotten younger," she said.

"You've gotten beautiful," he said.

"What a line," Paul Stapleton said. "If only I had learned to lie to women like this fellow. She's not beautiful, Dwight, but she has gotten damned attractive in her late youth."

"Early middle age," Paula said. "You don't have to be gallant. But I don't mind it at all from Congressman Slocum."

Dwight Slocum had been her first love, an absurd romance which he never took seriously. Why should he? Captain of the football team at Lawrenceville and Princeton, he emanated a physical vitality that would have had girls prostrating themselves in his path even if he was not Dwight Slocum, Jr., heir to one of the great fortunes of America. Slocum wealth was in the hundreds of millions. It made Stapleton wealth look picayune. But for reasons hard to fathom, Dwight's life had been aimless and confused. For a few years in his late teens and twenties, Paul Stapleton had struggled to give him some sense of direction and purpose. Even he had been baffled by Dwight's sullen refusal to pursue anything more meaningful than his immediate pleasure. He had quit law school before the end of his first year. Each of his three wives had been trampier than the previous one. He left them as soon as possible to do the only thing that seemed to interest him—hunt rare game in inaccessible places from the Canadian tundra to the headwaters of the Amazon. His abrupt return to enter politics had never been satisfactorily explained to Paula. Her uncle had cryptically told her that Dwight had changed. Apparently he thought—or at least hoped—that Dwight had finally matured.

Congressman Slocum began telling her how he kept his figure. Twice a year he spent ten days at a California retreat called The Golden Door. It was a bargain at a thousand dollars a week. A gourmet cook served fabulous lunches and dinners with a minimum of calories. Baths, massage, exercise, and meditation did the rest.

"It's a mental as well as a physical colonic," Dwight said. "You feel like you've been reborn."

"You look it," Paula said. "How are you enjoying Washington?"

"The House is a bore. It's too big. You have to stay there thirty years to get enough seniority to do anything. But you meet some interesting people."

Dwight began scattering the first names of cabinet members, senators, generals, and columnists. Paula found herself wishing she could match him. Whose names did she have to drop? Eddie McKenna, Dominick Montefiore. The mediocrity of the city's politics never seemed more painful. But if all went well, before this year was over, she would be able to compete with Congressman Slocum. Senator O'Connor and his wife would be in the one-up position.

Dwight suddenly assumed a sympathetic air. He looked down the room and asked: "What's Jake going to do? I really feel for the guy. He had this Senate thing sewed up until—"

"He's still very much in the race."

Paula wondered if Dwight heard the uneasiness in her voice as clearly as she heard it. Did it show in her face? She was never sure how well she concealed her feelings.

"I never thought it made much sense for him to

run for mayor," Dwight said. "Why did you let him do it?"

Paula was momentarily staggered. "I—I don't let him do anything. I mean, I don't run Jake's career."

"Maybe you should," Dwight said.

Friendly old enemies, ex-almost lovers could say these things to each other. Paula forced a smile and turned to Paul Stapleton for support. She was dismayed to see a frown on his pale forehead. "It's none of our business, Paula, especially none of Dwight's business, but he may have a point. I can't believe you approve of the way Jake's handling this busing situation. I couldn't believe it when he called me today, and asked to see me in my chambers. He doesn't seem to realize he's a party to this suit. It's a matter of law, not politics."

What could she say? "He's trying to do the right thing. He's concerned, really concerned for the safety of the city."

Paul Stapleton shook his head. "From where I sit it looks like politics, the worst kind of politics."

"Oh, I don't know," Dwight Slocum said. "I sympathize with Jake. He's in a hell of a spot."

Paul Stapleton glared at Congressman Slocum. "The law is clear. The court has spoken. What else can a public official do?"

"Come on now, Judge," Dwight said, "you know there's a half dozen answers to that question."

"But only one right one."

Sickening, Paula thought, sickening to hear Dwight Slocum, the amoralist supreme, agreeing with her husband's politics. Involuntarily she turned her head to find Jake. If there was some casual way of doing it, she was ready to take the risk of drawing him into this conversation. She wanted him to see how wrong he was about an alliance between Congressman Slocum and Judge Stapleton.

Jake was at the opposite end of the room, smiling into the eyes of Allyn Stapleton, the General's oldest and prettiest granddaughter. Allyn was wearing her red hair in a glistening swath down the back of her white Givenchy pantsuit. She had been living in New York, working for an advertising agency. Her father's death in a plane crash had coincided with the breakup of an unfortunate marriage. She had spent most of the past year on a nearby farm with her mother. Allyn looked as if she had recovered from her griefs—almost too well, Paula thought. From hints dropped at other family gatherings, Paula gathered that Allyn was her generation's spokesperson for a rebellious streak in the Stapleton lineage.

With a smiling lie about the necessity for neutrality, Paula withdrew from the argument between Dwight Slocum and Paul Stapleton and strolled across the room toward her husband. She was intercepted by Agatha Stapleton, her uncle's sister, who looked like his double in a cloud of blue lace. Agatha was the family historian. She was struggling to bring order out of the chaotic family archives. In every generation the Stapletons seemed conscious that they were making history and tried to leave some kind of record—a diary or a journal, a memoir or a collection of letters. But each generation had been too busy coping with its own times to pay much attention to these documents. The bicentennial had spurred Aunt Agatha into action.

She began talking about her latest discovery, a narrative written by Dr. James Kemble, telling the travails of the Revolution in his part of the state. "It isn't a very pretty story, I'm sorry to say. Apathy, disillusion, corruption—my goodness, I wouldn't believe it if I didn't see it on the page in his own handwriting. For the first time we know how Kemble Stapleton really died. It isn't at all like the family tradition. That had him charging some Loyalist fort—"

"Marvelous," Paula murmured, her eyes on Jake and Allyn Stapleton. History had never really interested her. It was almost always either boring or disillusioning. It was better—or at least sufficient—to have a sense of history.

Agatha began telling her how she had obtained the services of a New York historian to edit the manuscript. They were interrupted by Peregrine Stapleton, the family esthete. He was wearing a maroon dinner jacket. Lace ruffles burst from his chest and peeped from beneath his coat cuffs. He had never married. Jake was sure he was gay. If so, Peregrine had been discreet. He lived with Agatha—they were first cousins—in a Victorian mansion in the next township, crammed with memorabilia, antiques, and Peregrine's various collections, which ranged from eighteenth-century crystal to art deco shawls. It included a complete bedroom set which had once belonged to Noel Coward.

"*Paula*, you haven't visited us in a good year. You *must* come see what I picked up at Sotheby's in August—a miniature of Princess Sophia and her sister Princess Amelia, the last two daughters of George III. It completes my collection of Georgian royal family miniatures."

"Wonderful," Paula murmured.

"I hope you've moved Bowood's Meissen china to a safe place. You could store it with us if you'd like."

"Why should I do that?"

"From what I see on television, you may find a mob storming the front gate any day now."

"Now really, Peregrine, that's fantastic."

"I hope so. I'm perfectly willing to let you ridicule me, Paula, as long as I know that china is safe."

Jake had his arm around Allyn Stapleton's waist. He whispered something in her ear. She laughed seductively. Paula reproached herself. It was not seductive. It was just a laugh. She had to stop feeling angry and suspicious every time she saw her husband talking to a beautiful woman.

Maria Stapleton joined them. She smiled in Jake's direction. "It's good to see Allyn laughing again. Your husband is such good company, Paula. It's a shame we don't see him more often."

There was an unspoken combination of confession and regret in those words. Maria was almost saying she was sorry that her husband and Jake did not like each other.

"He looks well," Maria said. "He seems to be bearing up under the strain. But he's young enough. It's killing Paul. I watch him work, work. At his age, it's too much."

For a moment Paula found herself wondering if

Judge Stapleton might welcome the personal appeal that her husband wanted her to make. No, she told herself, looking down the room at his stern solemn face as he lectured Dwight Slocum. If by some miracle he said yes, she would be inflicting her moral weakness on him. She would also betray the trust that Adam Turner placed in her. *I'm on his side because you're by his side.*

Ned Stapleton, the Judge's youngest son, joined them. In his early forties, he was a remarkably close copy of his father, except for his size. He was about six inches shorter than the Judge. He had the same ascetic mouth and intense eyes. "What's Jake going to do, Paula?" he asked. "Will he run for the Senate now? I hear that meeting they—uh—reported in the paper today was really a withdrawal of his candidacy."

"Nothing of the sort, Ned," Paula said. "You should know better than to believe what you hear in politics."

"Dwight told me," Ned said with a brief smile. "Maybe he just wants to hear it."

"That's very possible."

"The people out here—"

Jake joined the conversation. "The people out here aren't a representative sample, Ned. They're a case study in hardening of the political arteries. The cause of the trouble isn't cholesterol. It's cash."

"You sound like Pancho Villa, Jake," Maria said.

"My hero is Alfred E. Smith. Like him, I have a talent for political self-destruction."

Was he drunk? Paula wondered nervously. There was an unnecessary truculence in his voice. Allyn Stapleton arrived with a brimming dark brown glass in each hand. "Here's to double trouble," she said, handing him one.

"Slainte," Jake said. "That's Gaelic for the hell with it."

"When you're in double trouble, drink double scotches," Allyn said. "We've just worked that out as the formula for settling all the problems of our lousy society."

Jim Fry appeared, clanging an old Texas ranch triangle. They trooped into the dining room, which was also decorated in Spanish colonial style with huge silver and bronze plates on the wall. Paul Stapleton sat Paula on his right. Maria did the same with Jake. The Judge's two sons, Ned and George, their wives, and the rest of the company quickly found the places assigned to them. Paul Stapleton raised his wine glass. "To absent friends," he said.

"And to present ones," Maria Stapleton said.

"Did Mark call?" Paula asked.

"No, he sent a card. He always sends a card."

The Judge's second son was a lawyer in New York. He seldom came home. He had apparently had some fundamental disagreement with his father. The oldest son, Randy, the Judge's favorite, had been killed in the crash of a company plane several years ago. Paula wondered, not for the first time, how and where this man found the inner strength to face life so steadily. Maria had aged sadly since Randy's death.

The Judge asked Paula if she did any riding.

"Sometimes I rent a horse at the stables in Washington Park," she said. "But they're closing next month."

"You'll just have to come out here every Sunday."

"I wish I could."

"I wish you would. The older a man gets, the more he values a daughter. She doesn't stand around waiting for the old guy to croak or get senile."

"I can't believe Ned and George are that way."

"Oh, we are, we are. If he says so it's got to be true," George Stapleton said. He looked like his mother and shared her amiable disposition.

"Listen to him," his father said. "He'd be sitting on his duff reading poetry if I wasn't around."

"My ambition," George said, "is to rewrite the U.S. tax code in iambic pentameter."

The expression on Paul Stapleton's face suggested there was an unpleasnat argument just below the surface of this banter. Peregrine began talking to Agatha about the possibility of rioters destroying Bowood. It was obviously something that was very much on both their minds. "What do you think, Paul?"

"I doubt it very much. There may be a little fussing. But it won't get to anything like the French Revolution, if the police and the politicians do their jobs."

"I'm not so sure, Judge," Dwight Slocum said. "The city is an awful lot like Boston."

"Let's ask someone who's really in a position to know," Peregrine said. He turned to Jake. "Your Honor. Some of us think you ought to transfer all of Bowood's antique china, paintings, and the like out here before RIP or their black counterparts get their hands on them. What do you think?"

"Don't worry about it, Peregrine. If they start rioting, we'll just get a court order from the Judge. I'm sure they'll go right home."

Paula felt the needle in the answer as acutely as if it had been aimed at her. Paul Stapleton's mouth tightened.

"Seriously, Jake. There are some very valuable things in that house. Especially valuable to us," Penegrine said.

"They're valuable to me, too," Jake said. "If I thought they were in any real danger I'd get them out of there. But it looks like the heavy fighting will take place on the North Slope. All we've gotten at Bowood are a few death threats."

"Death threats?" gasped Aunt Agatha.

"Oh, sure. We have them with cocktails almost every night."

"Really, Paula, I don't see how you can stay there with the children. What if some maniac threw a bomb?"

"I must confess I've never liked the idea of turning Bowood into the mayor's residence," Peregrine said. "It seemed rather—what shall I say?—utilitarian."

"Would you have preferred demolition?" Jake said. "We couldn't get the state legislature to vote another nickel for it."

"I'm sure we could have gotten someone like Dwight's father to endow the place."

"Why should he do that when he tore down his own house and put up a high-rise apartment?" Dwight asked.

"Slocums don't do those kinds of favors for Stapletons, Peregrine," Paul Stapleton said. "But if you'd come to us, Jake, I think we might have managed to put something together with the help of a few friends."

Paula felt her husband's eyes searching her from the other end of the table. Was he waiting for her to speak and getting angrier by the second because she was hesitating?

"Bowood—making it the mayor's residence—was my idea," she said.

"A good one, I thought," Jake said. "It reminded the city that it has a past. A little history lesson."

It was a lie, but an effective one. Paula felt a throb of deep emotion. He had resisted the idea for months. Something deep in his blood told him it was a mistake. Paula had finally convinced him by paying for a poll which showed 70 per cent of the citizens approving it, once they were shown portraits of mayors' mansions in New York and Boston. But the move had given Dennis Mulligan an opportunity to make endless cracks in the Garden Square *Journal* about the Mayor's aristocratic pretensions. Mulligan, and presumably the public, had gotten tired of this routine about two years ago. To do Jake justice, he had never blamed her for the decision.

"Well," Paul Stapleton said as two Mexican houseboys served thick spicy tortilla soup, "I don't suppose a mob can do much more damage to Bowood than the servants did while I was living there. You couldn't get those Micks to clean anything without breaking it. We finally put all the good stuff down in the cellar."

"I understand they had the same problem in the South before the Civil War, General," Jake said. "Hostility against the system. It comes out one way or another."

That was close to being crude, Paula thought. Her uncle declined to notice it. He continued in the same genial tone. "I remember one time we were kicking a soccer ball around the ballroom on a rainy Sunday. The second footman, a big Mick named O'Toole, got into the game. He booted one that took out a whole french window. Top to bottom."

"I'm sure he was hanged, drawn, and quartered on the spot," Jake said. "I bet his ghost is still haunting the place."

"I doubt it. He got a job on the cops the day after we fired him, and he wound up eating in the kitchen every night, just as if he was still part of the help. Probably took half the icebox home with him, too."

Jake muttered something to Maria Stapleton that made her laugh. Allyn Stapleton, sitting opposite him, laughed too.

"What's that?" Paul Stapleton said. He was a little deaf and hated to admit it.

"He wondered if you took it as a tax deduction," Maria said.

"We didn't have income taxes in those days."

"I'm sure you could have found a way to carry it forward twenty years if you put your mind to it, Dad," George Stapleton said.

Paula was surprised by his acid tone. She knew that Paul Stapleton had made his mark as a tax lawyer, but she did not really understand what was being implied. She was more disturbed by the hostility in her husband's remark and its echo from one of her uncle's sons.

"I'd like to propose a toast," Dwight Slocum said. He raised his glass. "To a man who has given his country far more than it has given him."

"Who had given all of us far more than we've given him," Paula added.

"Hear, hear," said Ned Stapleton.

"That's damn nonsense, Dwight," Paul Stapleton said. "But it's nice of you to say it."

Dwight Slocum began talking polo. Paula could only listen as he delivered opinions on the National Open champions. Paul Stapleton had been a ten-goal player in his day and Dwight had been at the top of this category for years. In her horsey days Paula had followed the sport rather closely. Now she did not recognize a name, and even the teams sounded strange to her. In the center of the table, Peregrine and Agatha began discussing their latest enthusiasm, breeding Afghan hounds. They were losing a fortune on them but they had hopes of a medal at Westminster in a year or two. The conversation turned to sailing and Ned Stapleton told an amusing tale of his adventures aboard the family sloop on last summer's Newport to Bermuda race. By this time they were well into the main course, sliced beef tampiqueña, with traditional fried beans and guacamole, the ground avocados savored by aficionados of Mexican cooking.

"If that Irish cop ate this well, Judge, no wonder you couldn't keep him out of the kitchen," Jake said.

"Who do you have cooking for you at Bowood these days, Paula?" Agatha asked.

"Her name is Hannah Mahoney."

"Good God, an Irish cook," Dwight Slocum said. "That's carrying ethnic chauvinism too far, Jake."

"We never let them get anywhere near the stove in our day," Aunt Agatha said.

"I hired her," Paula said. "She's surprisingly good. She worked as a pastry cook at the Shelbourne in Dublin."

"We usually had a German cook, didn't we, Paul?" Agatha asked.

"German or English."

"We switched to French after World War Two," Dwight Slocum said. "Before that we had blacks. They're rather good cooks."

"The older I get the more I prefer the recipes of the lady of this house," Paul Stapleton said.

"My father was the best cook in our family," Jake said. "My mother couldn't cook to save her life."

There was a pause. Paula sensed embarrassment. Jake seemed to have missed the point. Or was he deliberately ignoring it? That relatively innocuous remark inundated her with a sudden hopelessness. Her husband seemed to go out of his way not to fit in, to take a perverse satisfaction in reminding the Stapletons that they were different.

As the salad was served, Ned Stapleton asked, "Who advised you to take your position on busing, Jake?"

"Nobody. To put it more exactly, I ignored a lot of advice."

"I can understand the reluctance with which people obey it," Peregrine said, "but the law is the law."

"Once and for all, we've got to eradicate racism," Paul Stapleton said. "I saw the results of it in two world wars." He began describing the disastrous performance of segregated black troops in World Wars I and II. He dwelt with special bitterness on his experience in Italy in World War II, where he saw dozens of young white officers die trying to set an example for black men who had no interest in fighting a white man's war.

"I realized then that we'd lost the Civil War. I grew up listening to my grandfather refight all the battles from Bull Run to Chancellorsville to Cold Harbor to Appomattox. I was fifty years old before I realized we'd won the war and lost the peace. That's when I decided we couldn't afford to waste any more time on this thing. I'm glad I've had a chance to do something about it before I die."

"I don't think the real issue is racism, Judge," Jake said. "I think it's power. The race thing gets into it primarily on the verbal level. It would stir up the same kind of turmoil if kids were being bused to assimilate some group that spoke a different language, like the Puerto Ricans. Or if we went back forty years and the Catholics instead of building parochial schools got enough people into the legislature to insist on a religious balance in the public schools. There might have been a law that every school had to be forty per cent Catholic and kids had to be bused all over the city to get this balance."

"Pretty clever, Jake, but racism is a fact," Ned Stapleton said. "We see it on television every night."

"Religious prejudice was a fact back in those days. Do you know what you had to do to work in the Slocum medicine factory?"

"What?" said Dwight.

"Each morning they'd ask you, Catholic or Protestant? If you said Catholic you didn't work that day."

"I don't believe that," Aunt Agatha said.

"My father had to do it every day for a year."

"We will all pause," Dwight Slocum said, "for Jake's rendition of 'Onward, Christian Soldiers.'"

Laughter broke the unpleasant tension. Paula felt like an escapee from a trapped elevator.

"I think racism is much worse than religious prejudice," Allyn Stapleton said. "It goes deeper."

"I'm not so sure that people on the receiving end of either one can see much difference," Jake said.

"Religious prejudice disappears overnight, once people realize how silly it is," Paul Stapleton said. "I saw it happen in the Army."

"I saw it happen in the Navy, too, Judge," Jake said. "But I think it was the end of a long process. The same thing is true for the decline of ethnic prejudice."

"The Mayor's got a point," George Stapleton said. "In the Civil War you didn't see much assimilation in the Army. There were separate regiments for the Irish, the Germans, the native Americans. These things do take time."

"The Supreme Court decided the time was up in nineteen fifty-four," Paul Stapleton said.

"And I applauded like everyone else. But now I think we need a time-out," Jake said.

"The Court doesn't think so, Jake," Ned Stapleton said.

"No kidding. What do you think of the Court's wisdom, Congressman?" Jake said.

For a moment Dwight looked nonplused. He glanced uneasily down the table at Judge Stapleton, and took a sip of his wine. "I sympathize with the spot you're in, Jake. But the Court has provided us with leadership for two hundred years. I think we should trust that leadership."

Jake gave him a disgusted look. "Congressman, we're among friends. Save the oratory for the campaign. Here's what I think the Court should do. Bus every kid in this state and forget all about where the city ends and the suburbs begin—or bus no one."

"Why don't you say this in public, Jake?" Dwight said.

"Because I like to win elections."

"If you can't tell the people what you think, Jake, you're in trouble," Dwight said.

"That is the most asinine statement I ever heard a politician make in my entire life," Jake said.

Maria Stapleton said they would serve coffee and fruit in the living room. Paula felt exhausted. Mentally she had been running around the table inhabiting the skin of every person who spoke. But it had been impossible to stop the chain reaction of misunderstandings. Jake had managed to be both defensive and offensive. He was convinced that the Stapletons were baiting him on Dwight Slocum's behalf. Dwight had decided Jake's hostile question, which he considered unprovoked, gave him carte blanche to be a total hypocrite. Jake's final answer had turned the Judge's icy stare into a glare.

As Paula stood up the whole room churned into an alarming blur. She reached out for a chair, and found Dwight's arm around her waist.

"Are you all right?" he asked.

"I—I think I could use a little fresh air," she said.

Jake was walking out of the room, absorbed in conversation with Maria and Allyn Stapleton. No one else except Paul Stapleton noticed her indisposition.

"Take her out back on the patio, Dwight," the Judge said. "There won't be any wind there. But put on something warm. It's supposed to go down to zero tonight."

She let Dwight keep his arm around her waist and lead her into the downstairs study. One of the houseboys quickly produced their coats and they stepped into the frigid night. The wind howled menacingly over their heads, but the two wings of the house created a protective enclave. The cold was intense but it did not penetrate. Paula took a deep breath and felt immeasurably better.

"Look at that sky," Dwight said.

The winter stars glittered in a vast black canopy. "Makes you nostalgic, doesn't it?" Dwight said. "Remember how we used to lie out in the north pasture flat on our backs in the grass, watching for shooting stars?"

"I remember," Paula said.

"And every time I made a pass you'd slap my face."

"You never made a pass."

"That's right. You had me intimidated from the start. I was sure you'd tell the old boy about it."

Suddenly the cold was gone. They were back in that magical seventeenth summer, alternating between serious arguments about the purpose of life—Dwight saw none—and reckless rides on horseback or in cars with Dwight at the wheel. She had been awed by his strength, his energy, his arrogance. But his cynicism—the strange dark resentment that seemed to bubble from his antagonism toward his father, to poison so much of his attitude toward life—had repelled her. She had swung on that pendulum between attraction and repulsion for a long time.

"Remember when I drove the tin lizzie into the pond?" Dwight asked.

"I'll never forget it."

"It was your idea."

"I never thought you'd do it."

The Ford was a relic that Dwight used to bounce around the farm's pastures and other cross-country terrain. Paula remembered the episode as a kind of high point in her fascination for Dwight's recklessness. It had stunned her when he actually did what she had merely mentioned, without the slightest idea that he would act on it. He had revved the motor up to its top speed, perhaps forty miles an hour, and sent them hurtling off the four-foot bank on the north side of the pond. The old car had gone down like a dignified ship, slowly, methodically.

Paul Stapleton had not been amused. He told Dwight it was a dangerous wasteful act. He insisted on Dwight paying for the car and told him he was no longer welcome at the farm. Later that year, the farm manager had drained off some of the water in the pond and the old car had reappeared, like an exotic creature rising from another time. A sudden freeze had locked it into a bed of ice and it had spent the winter there, looking more and more forlorn.

"What was Jake trying to do in there, put me on the spot?" Dwight asked.

"I don't think so. This busing situation—is a dreadful mess. He's not thinking very clearly about it. No one is."

Paula sensed Dwight was ready to ask several even more embarrassing questions. "I feel much better now. Let's rejoin the party," she said.

In the living room, Maria Stapleton and her daughters-in-law were serving the coffee and passing fruit and nuts. George Stapleton had joined Allyn and Jake in one corner of the room. Ned Stapleton and Peregrine were talking to the Judge. Agatha Stapleton was sitting alone. Dwight gravitated toward the Judge and Paula felt compelled to sit down with Agatha. She began talking about Paula's father, a depressing topic under the best of circumstances. She lamented her failure to reconcile them before his death. She had appointed herself a peacemaker and had made numerous journeys to New York to plead Paula's case, but not even baby pictures of Kemble had any effect on Malcolm Stapleton's resentment.

A peal of laughter from Allyn Stapleton in the corner with Jake. *When was the last time he made you laugh?* Paula asked herself. She tried to console Aunt Agatha for her failure by saying she never expected her to succeed. This made Paula sound like the hard-hearted side of the argument. "Really, Paula, there's no need to be so unforgiving of the dead," Agatha said.

"I forgive him," Paula said. The words were automatic, merely spoken to silence Agatha. Behind them, Paula wanted to ask her how she could forgive a man who nursed such blind violent prejudices against whole groups of people, in particular the Irish who had wrecked his dreams of political power.

"Jake, could I see you for a moment?" Paul Stapleton said. He had left Dwight and Ned and retreated to the far end of the huge room, where the heads of a half dozen animals were mounted. Jake sauntered down to him and they began chatting beneath a huge grizzly, whose jaws were curled in a classic snarl. Paula sensed tension in both men. They stood with their feet apart, like fighters ready to start punching. Jake looked twice as wide as the frail old man he was confronting, and he was a head taller. But Paul Stapleton seemed to be the aggressor. He leaned forward slightly, his jaw outthrust, his face stern.

Agatha was narrating girlhood memories of Paula's father, trying to prove that he was a likeable person before politics soured him. Paula tried to listen but 90 per cent of her mind was with the conversation at the far end of the room, beneath the snarling grizzly.

Suddenly Jake whirled and glared down the room at her. "Paula. Would you come over here, please?"

Even before she reached them, she knew the worst was happening. Anger glowed on both faces. "I'd like you to hear what I'm about to say to this man," Jake said. "I don't want you to get any twisted versions. He's just finished lecturing me about my lack of legal ethics for asking to see him privately."

"Jake," Paul Stapleton said. "Do you know what Judge Garrity did to Mayor Kevin White in Boston when he tried to see him in his chambers? He knocked his head off his shoulders in open court. That's what I could do—what I ought to do tomorrow. But because you're a member of the family—"

"You knock my head off in private," Jake snarled. "Save the sermon for the bar association, Judge. I still say I've got a perfect right to see you in private and ask you to do me a favor. I helped put that gavel in your hand in 1966. You wanted it and I got it for you. Now I'm calling in that favor. That's the code of ethics I learned and I'm not ashamed of it, as long as I'm not asking you to do anything illegal."

"I don't know which I deplore most. Your code of ethics or your arrogance. If I see any more of either one, you'll be in contempt of court."

"Don't worry. I'll be a good little boy from now on. But I want you to know you're not fooling me or a lot of other people. You don't think Jake O'Connor should be a U.S. Senator. That's why you've used your gavel to put him up against the wall and why you're going to keep him there."

Paul Stapleton's shoulders sagged. He looked unutterably weary.

"Don't be ridiculous, Jake. I'm trying to do the right thing—for the city—the country—"

"I'll believe that when your boy Slocum gives up politics to become a missionary in New Guinea."

"If you're trying to accuse me of favoring Dwight Slocum or anyone else in preference to you for the Senate, for once you are absolutely right. I didn't think that way six months ago. But I do now, because your conduct in this busing business has been so irresponsible, crass, and gutless. Everyone knows you'd support busing if you thought you could do it and still get to the Senate—"

Paul Stapleton seemed to exhale these words as much as say them. They came out with relief, release in them, full of a contempt that he had struggled to suppress. Jake matched them with a fury that was careless of everything but a reckless spirit of denial.

"Judge, I wouldn't back court-ordered busing if the goddamn polls said ninety per cent of the people out here in the suburbs loved it. My people hate it. And I'm with my people in the city. I'm doing you the favor of *not* campaigning against the idea. If I did, you'd need a division of paratroopers to get you to that courthouse each day."

"I'd get them. You better understand that. I'll get the paratroopers and I'll get to the courthouse."

Paula felt like a refugee trapped in no man's land by an artillery duel. She did not know what appalled her most, the breach of all pretensions to friendship between her husband and her uncle or the revelation of Jake's real feelings about busing.

"I can't believe you mean anything you've just said, Jake," she whispered.

"I meant every word of it. Get your coat. We're going home."

He walked past the rest of the party without saying good night to any of them except Maria and Allyn Stapleton. Paula followed him in a daze of disbelief and embarrassment. It was obvious that everyone knew what had happened, even if they did not hear everything that had been said. They sympathized with her, of course. But their sympathy was the last thing she wanted. It was inextricably mingled with the I-told-you-sos that they had been waiting to whisper behind her back ever since she married Jake O'Connor.

In the car, Paula angled her body into the extreme left-hand corner of the back seat. She could not help it. She wanted to get as far away from him as possible, yet she wanted to face him. But he would not face her. He lounged casually against the back cushions, his left leg tossed over his right knee. Occasionally he flicked the back of his shoe with his middle finger. Neither of them spoke for at least ten miles. A question pressed in Paula's throat again and again. *How could you?* Should it be said with regret, anger, contempt? No, none of these things, simply a neutral voice. It had to be neutral if anything was to be salvaged.

Then he spoke. "I'm sorry I said it. For your sake. But not for his sake."

She was disarmed. The three-word weapon she had so carefully honed became debris on her tongue.

"Do you really believe he's doing it—trying to ruin you?"

"Of course not. He's an honorable man. He tells himself there's a good reason for everything he does. And there is. If it happens to coincide with eliminating Jake O'Connor as a candidate—and making Dwight Slocum the people's choice—that's very nice."

"Then you admit it isn't a conspiracy. I hope you'll write him a letter tomorrow, apologizing—"

"For what? He had it coming to him. Didn't you *listen* to him, Paula? Didn't you hear him working on me all night? I know you love the guy. You've got a perfect right to do it. But don't see him as some sort of god."

"I don't know what you're even talking about. Working on you."

Jake slouched in his seat until his chin was almost touching his chest. "Forget it," he said.

"He was trying to be helpful, Jake."

"Maybe he was. In his own way." He sighed. "Maybe everybody's intentions are good."

His big hand seized her wrist and drew her across the seat to him. "Let's forget it. It was a bad scene."

The slang of another generation jarred her nerves. She still wanted to be embattled in her corner, facing him, demanding and yet somehow pleading for words that would simultaneously explain and expiate. He had disarmed her with his confession, but this gesture of affection was either insincere or trivialized by his inability to see the awfulness of his performance.

"They—the family—are on your side, Jake. It's just hard for them—to communicate it."

"The next time I'll bring along a translator. Better yet, I won't say a word. I'll let you do all the talking for both of us."

"Don't condescend. I don't like it any more than you do."

His arm around her shoulder loosened. He moved away from her just enough to register anger. "Condescension is what I got all night. Can't you *see* that?"

"No. I did not see one instance of it. It's perverse, Jake, the way you insist on hearing and seeing hostility, snobbery, animosity where they don't exist."

He was silent for a long time. Then he drew a deep breath and exhaled it in a strangely mournful sigh. "Okay," he said, "I'll take your word for it."

Sadness, weariness in those words. Why? Was it her fault? She did not want sadness, weariness. She wanted strength, joy.

Paula suddenly remembered a poem Paul Stapleton had read to her when she was thirteen. It was called *The Portrait of the Good Man*. It had been a favorite of Thomas Jefferson. Her uncle said he had read it to each of his sons and saw no reason why he should not read it to her. Two lines from it rose out of the past. She could hear the proud confident voice reading them. She could see the thin gawky teen-ager listening to the soaring words.

Who to his plighted vows in trust has ever
 firmly stood;

*And though he promised to his loss, he makes
his promise good.*

They began to descend the steep hill that would bring them to the coastal plain and the nearest suburbs. As they rounded a curve, the city appeared in the distance. Radio towers blinked red eyes at them above an immense tangle of lights that sent a ghostly glow into the starry sky. There was something bestial, almost apocalyptic about it. From the heights to the river and the tidal marshes it swelled there on its wedge of rock, a growth as unmanageable, as mysterious as a tumor. It was no more possible for them to live inside its poisoned veins than for a healthy cell to live inside a cancer.

Near the airport they passed the garbage dump. Experts had eliminated the haphazard burning of refuse which used to shroud the western wards in stinking smoke. Huge tractors and plows now ran a landfill operation which had been hailed as a model for cities throughout the nation. But a stench still lingered in the air around the dump. Paula loathed it.

"There it is," Jake said, "the city smell. I remember how it'd hit you here coming up from the shore at the end of the summer. The garbage smoke was so thick on the highway, people would be turning on their headlights. You could hardly breathe."

He liked it. No, he loved it. She could hear, feel, strength, confidence returning to his voice. He lived here. He breathed the polluted air, walked the littered streets without flinching.

And though she promised to her loss, she makes her promise good.

It had been so easy to combine the good man and the good woman at thirteen, to accept the masculine challenge. She was a Stapleton and that was what Stapletons were born to do—accept challenges and win. But now it seemed much more difficult to accept. Instead of pride, elation, she felt sadness seeping into her blood. It was impossible to resist. It was part of the air she was breathing, the gray ugliness that would soon surround her.

At Bowood, the Mayor handed his coat to Mahoney and headed for the library. "How about a nightcap?"

"I've had enough."

"You haven't had any, as far as I could see."

"I drank quite a bit of wine at dinner."

"I'm for a quick one."

He abandoned her in the hall. She trudged up the stairs alone. Mackey appeared in a quilted bathrobe and gave her a long disquisition on how obstreperous Dolores had been before going to sleep. Paula had difficulty stifling a yawn. In her room she undressed quickly and took a hasty shower. In bed she reached for one of the half dozen books on her night table to read herself to sleep. It was a new biography of Benjamin Franklin by a woman named Lopez—a surprisingly intimate study of Old Ben's relationships with his wife and children. It was dismaying but fascinating, this current craze for revealing our great men's private flaws. First one historian claimed Jefferson had a Negro mistress, now we discovered Franklin deserted his wife for the last twenty years of his marriage.

A knock on the door. "Yes?"

Jake came in wearing his pajamas and bathrobe. He had showered. His hair was wet. "What are you reading?" he said.

She told him.

"Sounds good. Maybe I'll read it."

He took the book out of her hand and put it back on the night table. He wanted to make love. She knew why. He wanted to reclaim her. He wanted to reassure himself that nothing had been lost by the blunders of the night. He wanted proof of her forgiveness.

"Jake, it's—"

She was going to say *too soon*. Instead she said: "—late."

"Not for night owls like us."

His hand on her wrist. Just as in the car. Drawing her to him against her will. This time against her visible reluctance. Deep in Paula's body a voice said *no*. She would not let this taking, this possession reach the humbling confusing surrender of the past. She would permit it. That was her duty. But she would not let it reach her essential self, the Paula who said *no*.

It would not be easy. His hand on her breast now, his other hand moving slowly up her thigh. On his lips the faint taste of scotch not quite banished by toothpaste and mouthwash. When his fingers reached her clitoris, warmth, a sweet flow coursed upward making a mockery of her no. She suddenly hated her traitor body. But that was wrong. She was proud of the pleasure she had given this man and received from him. Deny that and she became the other thing she dreaded, the frigid old maid unable to satisfy the man who had had his pick of the city's women, who carried with him like a virus the memory of Dolores Talbot. But behind or beneath this fear was the memory of his flushed angry face, his choked voice flinging those gross accusations at Judge Paul Stapleton while the rest of the Stapletons listened, I-told-you-so satisfaction mingling with shocked disapproval on their faces.

She pushed his hand away. "I'm sorry. I just don't feel like it," she said. It was the first time she had ever done such a thing.

Unreal, she thought. She heard the words and refused to accept responsibility for them. *Unreal.*

She glanced up at him. No more than a flicker of her eyes. He was standing beside the bed. He was not angry. He seemed sad. No, something even more puzzling than sadness. He seemed almost frightened. There was fear—or was it regret?—on his face. For a moment she was glad. She had hurt him as much as he had hurt her. No, she loathed that idea.

"I'm sorry," she said.

"It's okay. I guess I should have gotten the message —earlier."

"I wish we could go away for a month. Even a week."

"We can't. Do you know that old song? We're here because we're here."

"It doesn't make much sense."

"You better start singing it. Maybe it will start to mean something."

He left her with that conundrum. The door to his room slammed. Paula picked up the Franklin book. She stared at the smooth old American face on the cover. She thought of Mrs. Franklin alone for twenty years, without hands to touch her, lips to kiss her. She put the book back on the night table. An echo of the slam of Jake's door seemed to linger in a corner of the bedroom. Paula remembered her mother's words: *When I think of the life we could have had.* But Mother was on the wrong side of the chasm. As the warmth dwindled from her body, Paula was able to decide that she really was sorry. But she was not grief-stricken. Perhaps it was a good thing for him to discover there was a limit to what he could achieve with his confident hands and clever lips.

She turned out the light and waited for sleep. It refused to come. Instead, she saw a stream of disturbing images. The waver in Paul Stapleton's walk. The arrogance on Dwight Slocum's face. The threat in Allyn Stapleton's seductive laugh. After an hour, a surge of anxiety swept over her. Why? There was no reason to be afraid of those images. They told her nothing she did not already know. Again the anxiety struck, a swirling microcosm of dread. For a moment Paula wanted to run to the bed of the man in the next room, to press herself against his big solid body and ask him to make a barricade with his arms and hands against the nameless fear that was assailing her. Was it what he needed and wanted? Or would it be a dangerous surrender, more dangerous than the physical yielding that was the original source of both delight and betrayal? In torment, Paula got up and paced the floor for a half hour. Then the inner voice spoke with finality. No. She took a tranquilizer. In a half hour she was asleep.

10

The intercom on Mayor O'Connor's desk buzzed. "It's two o'clock, Your Honor," Helen Ganey said.

"Okay, okay," the Mayor said.

He was not interested in the time. He was following Mayor Mortimer Kemble through another day in 1870.

Today, I toured the lower wards as part of my campaign for the Irish vote. Ostensibly I was inspecting violations of the health code in their tenements. I came away depressed by the task of governing people who live in such degradation. The gutters and the roadways are lined with filth, and from the dark dingy houses comes up the most sickening stink. Every house is packed to its utmost capacity with brawling, dirty Irish. In some are simply the poor, in others are those whose reputations made the policemen careful in entering them.

The sidewalk is almost gone in many places and the street is full of holes. Some of the tenements are of brick or brownstone, once the homes of the opulent. Others are one and two story shanties flung up by some greedy landlord, not a few of them Irish who preceded their wretched tenants to our shoes by a few years. All are in the same state of dissolution. There is scarcely a building without a bucket shop. Here the vilest and most poisonous compounds are sold as whiskey, gin, rum and brandy. Their effects are visible on every hand. Some of these houses are brothels of the lowest description. Such terrible faces look out upon you as you pass them by! Surely no more hopeless, crime-stained visages are to be seen this side of the home of the damned.

The filfth that is thrown into the street lies there and decays until the kindly heavens pour down a drenching shower and wash it away. As a natural consequence the neighborhood is sickly, and sometimes the infection amounts almost to a plague. There are thirteen thousand tenement houses, fully one-half of them in bad condition, in this section. One small block is said to contain three hundred and eighty-two families. I went into some of these tenements. The stairways are rickety and groan and tremble beneath your tread. The entries are dark and foul. Some of these buildings have secret passages connecting them with others of a similar character. These passages are known only to criminals, and are used by them for their vile purposes. Every room is crowded with people. Sometimes as many as a dozen are packed into a single apartment. Decency and morality soon fade away here. Drunkenness is the general rule. Some of these people never leave their abodes, but remain in them the year round stupefied with liquor, to procure which their wives, husbands or children will beg or steal. Thousands of children are born here every year, and thousands mercifully die in the first few months of infancy. Those who survive rarely see the sun until they are able to crawl out into the streets. Both old and young die at a fearful rate. They inhale disease with every breath.

The exact number of vagrant and destitute children to be found in the First Ward and the two adjacent wards is not known. Some have placed the estimate as high as fifteen thousand, and some higher. They are chiefly of Irish parentage. They do not attend the public schools, for they are too dirty and ragged. A few attend their Catholic schools, where they are taught nothing but superstition, fear, and obedience to a foreign power. The poor little wretches have no friends but the workers of our missions. The missionaries do much for them but they cannot aid all. Indeed they frequently have great difficulty inducing the parents of the children to allow them to attend our public schools. Incredible, these Irish.

They prefer to let their children starve in the streets rather than risk the effects of education and Protestant influence.

At 27 Washington Street we entered the cellar of a building owned by "Butcher Burke," which was the climax of our tour. After we knocked at the door a few minutes, a man, poverty-stricken and dirty in the usual appearance of the Irish, came with a candle to let us in. The room was in a filthy condition, ten by twenty-two and a half feet, with a ceiling of six feet three inches elevation from the floor. A woman wretched and woebegone as the man rose from a filthy bed at the back of the room and bade us welcome in her night clothing, which was scanty.

"And are yees the Lord Mayor himself now? Well, it isn't much we have to show yees, but yees can see it all without any charge at all, at all."

"How much rent do you pay here?" I asked of the man with the candle.

"Is it rint ye mane? Nyah, it's $6 a month, shure, and glad to get it, and if we don't pay it, it's the little time we'll get from Burke, but out on the street wid us, like pigs."

"How do you live?"

"Shure, I put in coal now and thin, whin I can get it to put, and that's not often, God knows, alanna!"

"How much do you earn?"

"Is it earn, d'ye say? Sometimes fifty cents a day, sometimes two dollars a week; and thin it's good times wid me."

"Take up a board from the floor," I said.

The man, who informed us that his name was William McNamara, "from Innis, in the County Clare, siventeen miles beyond Limerick," readily complied, and taking an axe dug up a board without much trouble, as the boards were much decayed. Right underneath we found the top of a brick drain, in a bad state of repair, the fecal matter oozing up with a rank stench. Everyone stooped down to look at this proof of sanitary disregard, and while the entire party were on their knees, looking at the broken drain, two large rats ran across the floor, and nestling in a rather familiar manner between the legs of McNamara for an instant, frisked out of the dreary, dirty room into the luxurious cesspool.

"Are those rats?" I asked McNamara.

"Rats is it? Endade they were, Yer Honor. It's nothin' out of the way here to s~e thim. Shure some of them are as big as cats. And why wouldn't they be— they have no wurrok or nothin' else to do."

The Mayor's private telephone rang. "This is your wife. We're down at the Bayshore Welfare Center. You're a half hour late. . . ."

"My God, Paula, I lost all track of time. I'll be right there."

The Mayor threw Mortimer Kemble's journal back in his desk drawer with a curse. He charged into the outer office. "I'm a half hour late for that tour down in Bayshore," he snapped at Helen Ganey. "Why in hell didn't you buzz me?"

"I did, three times," Helen said, her eyes brimming with tears. "You just kept saying 'five more minutes.'"

"Where's Grimes?"

"He escorted Mrs. O'Connor to that panel she was chairing. The one you wouldn't go to."

The Mayor ran for his limousine, damning his tearful secretary and simultaneously forgiving her. It was his fault. It was another error on the O'Connor scoreboard. That was the only kind of scoring O'Connor seemed able to do lately.

Losing control. That was what it added up to, the Mayor thought as Gus Dumbrowski used the siren to hurtle CITY-1 across the downtown wards to Bayshore. The Mayor studied the gray tenements and wished he was someplace, anyplace else. He was here only because he was losing control of his wife, his life. Maybe they were the same thing.

Once Bayshore had been the best part of the downtown wards. Nestled between the North Slope and a huge bend in the city's river, it might have been prime real estate if builders had been able to use the natural beauty of the river as part of their landscaping. But in the middle of the nineteenth century the railroads had acquired title to the city's waterfront. They sold off some of it to factories, and built terminal sheds, roundhouses, and warehouses on the rest. Pinned between these grimy monuments to industry and the long slope that led to the city's northern heights, Bayshore never became more than lower middle class. Once it had been Irish. His father had grown up here. In those days Bayshore had not been a slum. It had been a step out of the primary slums of the First, Second, and Third wards. Those were the ones Mortimer Kemble had been describing in his journal. In Bayshore the flats had hot water and toilets that worked.

There were no more Irish in Bayshore. They had moved up the two-mile-long slope into one- and two-family houses. More successful fugitives were on the heights or in the suburbs. Bayshore was now 95 per cent black.

For the blacks, as far as the Mayor could see, Bayshore had not been a step anywhere. It was just another place to land, and the neighborhood was becoming a genuine slum. The landlords contributed their share to the decline by abandoning all but the most rudimentary repairs. The crime rate had soared, and the sanitation department put the neighborhood near the bottom of its collection schedule. It was unpleasantly familiar.

Also unpleasantly familiar was the reason the Mayor was making this tour. His wife had talked him into it. She had begun by asking him if he meant what he had told Judge Stapleton about his real opinion of busing. He had avoided admitting anything. He had told her he had just been trying to win the argument. When she insisted on being serious, he admitted it was his real opinion. She had immediately begun trying to change it, even hinting that he ought to do it in public. When he had curtly refused to commit political suicide, she quoted Adam Turner and Ray Grimes to prove that his black support was crumbling. She suggested this tour of Bayshore as a minimum gesture of solidarity.

"I've got a better idea," the Mayor had replied.

"Let's cancel the whole thing and I'll come home for a matinee."

Her answer had been a stonewall stare. It was his first and last attempt to reveal his anxiety about their sexual failure earlier in the week. If he read that stare correctly, there was even a little satisfaction in Ms. Stapleton's frigid posture. Maybe it was all an act, the passion he had thought he was arousing when they made love. It was all part of persuading the Mick to play the game her way and now that he had violated this primary rule, there was no longer any need to perform.

The Mayor had rejected this vicious thought and tried to play the rational statesman. Pacing the library beneath the founding Stapleton's icy stare, he had analyzed her proposition. There might be some value in visiting Bayshore. But only if it was balanced by a visit to an uptown white neighborhood, in the name of racial peace. If he went to Bayshore with her, would she go with him to the Tipperary Square section of the North Slope? They would inspect Buchanan High School, where Commissioner Tarentino expected serious trouble, and Eddie McKenna's wife, Marie, would invite a few hundred local women to a rap session similar to the one Adam Turner was staging in Bayshore.

She had reluctantly agreed, and for a moment the Mayor had been ashamed of himself. What was the point in winning this way with her? He did not really understand what he was doing. He only knew it was better than losing. He could not afford to let any more losing into his bloodstream at the moment. He was already close to becoming toxic.

The Mayor got out of his limousine in front of the Bayshore Welfare Center, unenthusiasm curdling his smile. The weather had turned unusually warm. Bright sunshine and a clear blue sky made it more like September than January. The Mayor kissed his wife and shook hands with Ray Grimes, Adam Turner, and a half dozen local black leaders. Beyond them was a battery of television cameras, flanked by a platoon of radio people with antennas sticking out of their backs like moonmen. Between them were the newspaper and magazine reporters. They were pouring into the city as they had swamped Boston to sneer at the white ethnics, their new hate objects, the replacements for the southern rednecks and the Nixon gang. It gave the Mayor a moment of sour satisfaction to think that his decision to postpone busing for a week was probably costing their employers fifty or a hundred thousand dollars in hotel and bar bills.

The rest of the audience was mostly case workers and clients who had been marched out of the nearby welfare center to create a crowd. The Mayor stood there while Adam Turner welcomed him. Adam said that the Mayor's appearance was a long overdue gesture of concern for Bayshore. He hoped this tour would not only prove to the rest of the city the absolute necessity for busing to get black children out of this rotten environment. He hoped that it also would attract the help that was needed from the city to improve the neighborhood for those who "ain't lucky enough to get off the plantation" for a few hours each day.

Adam was always demanding proof that the white boss cared. He did not seem to realize that people disliked being told that they had to prove they cared.

"That's what Bayshore has become," Adam Turner said. "Another plantation where black people sweat and die. I want somethin' done about it. I want it done now, Mr. Mayor. The people ain't gonna be satisfied with busin'. That's just the beginnin' of the changes that we want to see around here."

"Right on, brother, right on," responded a dozen or so black voices in the crowd. The rest of the audience was silent. Adam was not as popular in Bayshore, as he had been six years ago, when he organized Bayshore's Black Voice. Bayshore had deteriorated steadily, in spite of Adam's voice in City Hall and the city's efforts to stop the slide. Without dictatorial power, a government could not alter the free-enterprise system which permitted landlords to abandon buildings that were losing propositions and merchants to desert stores awash in red ink. Maybe this was not going to be as one-sided as Adam had hoped. The Mayor felt adrenaline begin to flow in his body. "I'm very happy to be here," he said. "This was part of my father's old ward. He grew up here. I'd rather look things over before I respond to Councilman Turner."

Adam seemed disappointed. He had apparently hoped to demolish Simon Legree O'Connor in Round One. The tour began. They climbed up and down flights of sagging stairs and were given demonstrations of rotten banisters collapsing, doors dangling off hinges, radiators dripping icicles. At 167 Jones Street they were shown a sad-eyed, skinny two-year-old girl who had been bitten by a rat.

The Mayor was shaken by the ugly wound in the child's black, tubular arm. He heard himself admitting it was a disgrace to let something like this happen in his city. He vowed to lop heads in the health department if it happened again. But in the street, his sympathy dwindled when Adam began berating the "uptown landlords" who let black children live in such lethal squalor.

The Mayor took some cards from his pocket and shuffled through them. When he noticed that some of the tenements described in Mortimer Kemble's tour of the slums of 1870 were owned by Irish, he had asked the building department to do some research on the present ownership of Bayshore's real estate. The Mayor drew Adam aside, and in a casual tone that none of the reporters could overhear, told him that the owner of 167 Jones Street was a black doctor who practiced medicine only a few blocks away.

Adam said very little until they reached George Washington High School. The principal, a tall, stooped man named Holland, greeted them with the weary voice and sorrowful eyes of a funeral director. They soon saw the reason for Dr. Holland's mournful manner. The place looked battered. Chunks of plaster were missing from the walls, paint was peeling from the ceiling. There were puddles of water on the cafeteria floor. Under the old organization the public schools had starved for decades. The Mayor had tried to change this tradition. The City Council had stubbornly resisted him. The ten new schools he had built were only a fraction of those that needed replacement. Adam Turner pointed to the visible neglect and asked the Mayor if white schools uptown were in the same condition.

"You know as well as I do, Adam," the Mayor said, "it depends on the age of the school. This one was built in 1912."

"But if Bayshore had stayed lily white, would this school be fallin' apart?" Adam sneered. "You've built two schools in white neighborhoods for every one you've given black people."

The Mayor started to point out that whites outnumbered blacks two to one, but the hostility on the faces surrounding him—the reporters, Grimes, Adam and his clique, not to mention his beloved wife—silenced him. Suddenly he could not control the rage that throbbed in his veins as Adam strutted down the hall toward the street.

"Aren't we going to visit any classrooms?" the Mayor asked. "I think the gentlemen of the press would like to tell their readers and viewers a little about the pupils in this school. Let's get a realistic look at that side of the story."

Dr. Holland got nervous. "No one expects a visit, much less—"

"So much the better," the Mayor said, and led them into the first classroom he saw. A plump, round-faced black man was on the teacher's platform, pacing back and forth. He was talking about Thomas Gray's *Elegy Written in a Country Churchyard*. Dr. Holland introduced him as Robert Coleman—"one of our best young teachers." The Mayor shook his hand. Coleman looked familiar. The Mayor paused and let his usually reliable memory make the connection. The last time he had seen this face, it was illuminated by the glaring white light of Frank Donahue's single overhead bulb. The recollection did not make the Mayor feel much warmth for Mr. Coleman. He turned his back on him and smiled at the class. There were only three white faces among the thirty-five or so staring back at him.

The Mayor picked up the textbook and flipped the

pages. Familiar literary names and titles flashed past. Shakespeare, Jonson, Pope. "Anybody got a favorite poem they'd like to discuss?" he asked.

There were squirms and murmurs, but no volunteers. "Do they have a favorite poem, Mr. Coleman?" he asked.

"Well—it's—it's hard to say," Coleman muttered. "Ah, here's one of mine."

> "When lovely Woman stoops to folly
> And finds too late that men betray
> What charm can soothe her melancholy
> What art can wash her guilt away?"

The Mayor looked at his wife and smiled. *Losing control,* a warning voice whispered. *The hell with it,* the Mayor replied. "Who wrote that? Anybody know?"

A pudgy black girl put up her hand. "Oliver Goldsmith," she said.

"Correct," said the Mayor. "Do you know who he was?"

The black girl frowned and fiddled with her glasses. "An English poet, 1728 to 1774."

"English," the Mayor said. "Never. Goldsmith was Irish. As Irish as you could get. Isn't that right, Mr. Coleman?"

"Well," said Robert Coleman, "he's usually classified with the English poets."

"I'm going to demand a revision of the syllabus," the Mayor said. "It's outrageous discrimination. The next thing you know, they'll be telling you that Oscar Wilde, William Butler Yeats and James Joyce were English. Anybody here read those writers yet?"

There were only stares, a few shakes of the head in reply.

"Come on," said the Mayor, "someone must have a favorite poem. How about you?"

He pointed to a thin black boy, with a narrow jaw. He shook his head nervously. The Mayor flipped him the textbook. "Come on. Pick one out and read it for us," he said.

"Stand up," Dr. Holland said in a drill sergeant's voice. "What's your name?"

"Wangombe," muttered the boy.

"Wang what?"

"Wangombe."

"What's your real name?"

"Thomas Madison," said Coleman.

"Pick out a poem," said Dr. Holland.

The boy shook his head, and stared at the book.

"What's the matter with him?" Dr. Holland asked Coleman.

"I'm—I'm afraid he reads far below his grade level, Dr. Holland."

"That's educational jargon," the Mayor said. "I want to *hear* him read."

Dr. Holland picked up the textbook. "Turn to page one forty-three," he said, "and read that poem."

The poem was Walt Whitman's *Pioneers! O Pioneers!*

Wangombe Madison could not get through the first line. The Mayor read the whole stanza for him.

"Come my tan faced children
Follow well in order, get your weapons ready
Have you your pistols? Have you your sharp-
edged axes?
Pioneers! O Pioneers!"

"For we cannot tarry here" was the next line. The word tarry threw Wangombe Madison and he came to another dead stop. The Mayor finished the stanza for him.

"We must march, my darlings, we must
bear the brunt of danger
We the youthful sinewy races, all
the rest of us depend
Pioneers! O Pioneers!"

Looking up, the Mayor found Robert Coleman glaring at him. His angry eyes shocked him into realizing that Adam Turner, Ray Grimes, and Paula Stapleton

O'Connor were not the only spectators of the nasty little drama he was staging. In the doorway, reporters were taking notes. A handheld TV camera whirred. *Losing control* mocked the warning voice. For a moment he was tempted to apologize to Wangombe Madison. But the kid would probably think he was being sarcastic—or a complete hypocrite. It was time to retreat.

Adam Turner and Paula Stapleton O'Connor were looking very angry. Or was it unhappy? The reporters looked baffled. The hell with them. The Mayor told himself that he did not care what anyone thought or felt.

"Do you think that proves busing is a waste of time, Your Honor?" Dennis Mulligan asked in the hall.

"I'm not trying to prove anything. I'm just helping you do your job, Denny. Just giving the people a chance to see the whole picture. Which they'd never get if they waited for you to report it."

Dr. Holland tried to explain that reading was one of "their" worst problems. It was really the fault of the grammar schools, it was terrible the way teachers pushed "them" ahead. By this time they were on the first floor. The Mayor noticed six broken windows in a single corridor overlooking the schoolyard. "When did that happen?" he asked Holland.

"Last night," he said with a sigh. "We've had about a dozen a week, lately."

"Looks like we'll have to put mesh screens in here too. Adam, can you tell me why the kids want to trash the schools, these days?"

"Because the school is part of the plantation system, Mr. Mayor. It's part of the white society's indoctrination and they know it."

"Since when is learning how to read indoctrination?"

"Adam is speaking psychologically," Paula said. "That's the way they *feel.*"

"Will they feel any better when they get indoctrinated uptown and find out white kids can read better than they can?" Dennis Mulligan asked.

"It will make them try harder," Adam said.

"Maybe it will make them give up," Mulligan said.

The Mayor was shaken to realize that he was agreeing with Mulligan. The Garden Square *Journal* was opposed to busing. But it was evident that Mulligan was doing more than following the party line. He lived on the North Slope. One or two of his kids would probably be on the buses next week.

They were outside the school now. Turner and Mulligan squared off. The rest of the reporters formed a circle around them. The Mayor could not resist a certain feeling of satisfaction as he watched Adam become a target. It was also amusing to watch him abandon his black English street style.

"I couldn't read very well when I was in high school. I didn't really learn until I got in the Army and saw all the white boys getting the soft jobs."

"Maybe if you'd spent four years in a white high school, you would have given up by then," Mulligan said.

"The hell I would. I would have gotten mad a lot sooner. I would have realized I was just as smart as those white kids even if I couldn't read."

The Mayor instantly recognized a quote that would haunt Adam Turner. So did Dennis Mulligan. He made some notes on the pad in his hand.

"You don't think it would be better if you stayed in your own neighborhoods and black teachers worked with your kids? Nobody can teach you as well as your own kind. That's the way the Irish did it."

Again, with some discomfort, the Mayor found himself agreeing with Dennis Mulligan. Was blood really so thick? He thought about the slums Mortimer Kemble described in his journal.

Adam Turner was answering Mulligan. "We've got a problem the Irish didn't have." Adam pointed to the back of his dark brown hand. "Skin color."

"You simply cannot compare the prejudice experienced by the Irish with that experienced by the blacks," Paula said.

"Oh?" Dennis Mulligan blinked with pleasure. The Mayor's wife was better copy than Adam Turner. "Oh? Is this an expert opinion, Mrs. O'Connor? The result perhaps of a discussion you've had with your husband?"

"It is my own opinion. No one else's."

"What is your opinion, Your Honor?" Mulligan asked.

"I would say the whole thing is irrelevant, Denny."

He was not about to feed Dennis Mulligan any home run balls. With his ear for gossip, Mulligan probably knew the Mayor's private opinion that parochial schools were the worst mistake the Catholic Church in America ever made. Mulligan had probably heard echoes of the blunt things Mayor O'Connor had said to the Archbishop about how easy it would have been to integrate the public schools, if half the children in the city had not been in parochial schools. But Mayor O'Connor had never said this is public and never would say it.

As they headed back to the welfare center, the Mayor could not get Mortimer Kemble's journal out of his head. There was truth in those pages, truth he wanted to communicate. It was a truth beyond anything his father had told him about the prejudice and discrimination he had met as a boy. By the time his father was born, the Irish had crawled from the gutters of the First Ward. They were almost ready to tackle the slopes.

The Mayor suddenly deserted the group, and wandered down an alley between two flats. It was filled with an unbelievable amount of garbage. Beef bones, chicken carcasses, milk cartons, whiskey bottles, dribbled from split bags. *The gutters and roadways are lined with filth,* old Mortimer Kemble had written. The Mayor asked Adam Turner why there was so much garbage in the alley.

"Because the sanitation department don't pick up the garbage but once in four days. So people figure they might as well throw it out the window. It's a form of protest, Your Honor."

"Baloney."

"What?" Adam said. "What did you say?"

"Baloney. Why don't you admit that poor people always live like pigs, Adam? The Irish were the same way a hundred years ago. I'd like to give you a book I'm reading—"

A waste of time. On Adam's face was an impenetrable shield of distrust and anger. Adam shook his woolly head. He was not interested in reading a book that was supposed to make him feel sorry for the Irish, when their spokesman was riding around in a limousine and eating vanilla mousse at Bowood.

There was a formidable frown on Mrs. Stapleton-O'Connor's forehead. The Mayor responded with an anger that he barely controlled. It was a waste of time talking to them—or her. Nothing was going to make them abandon the politics of pity.

A moment later, as they rounded a corner, a softball whooshed over their heads and landed with a clunk on a car roof. The Mayor stared through a familiar black iron fence into St. Bonaventure's schoolyard. Two or three times a week in his teen-age years he had led his neighborhood team down here to play the local street gang, The Rangers, for a dollar a man. The games had always been close and more than once they had ended in a free-for-all. Now St. Bonaventure's three-story redbrick school had aluminum shutters on all the windows, making it look like a huge blinded animal. The pastor had closed the school when Bayshore's white Catholic population dwindled to the vanishing point. But he still let the neighborhood youngsters use the schoolyard for softball. All the players were black. A kid called to them through the bars: "Hey, get that motha of a ball for me, will ya?"

The Mayor trotted across the street, picked the battered gray ball out of the gutter, and carried it back to him. "Any chance of a ringer getting in the game?" he asked as he handed it through the fence.

"Ringa?" the teen-ager said. "You mean you wanna play?"

I will do almost anything, the Mayor thought, smiling at his wife, rather than go back to the welfare center and listen to Adam Turner make another speech. "I used to play in this schoolyard almost every day."

"Why sho," said the teen-ager, his eyes wide. "If you's who I think you is, you can do anything you wants."

Sixty seconds later the Mayor was at bat, his frowning wife on the first base line, holding his coat, while the photographers snapped pictures. As the Mayor expected, Adam Turner could not resist getting into the act. He volunteered to pitch. The Mayor invited Ray Grimes to umpire. He crouched behind the catcher, edgily complaining that he needed a face mask.

From the infield came excited cries. "Strake the man out. Easy out."

"He can't see nothin'. Put it past him."

Almost the same voices, the same words he had heard when he stood here at seventeen, over thirty years ago. He felt a sudden surge of fraternity with these black kids. If he brought white kids down here, wouldn't they feel the same thing?

The Mayor took Adam's first pitch, which was down around his knees. Grimes called it a strike. The next pitch was waist high and the Mayor swung. Too late, he saw the spin and realized it was a curve. He missed it by a foot. Adam knew something about pitching a softball. The next one would be hard and fast and high, hoping for a box on the front page of the paper: *Turner strikes out Mayor on three pitches*. The Mayor took it and Ray Grimes had to call it a ball. The next pitch would be the curve again. As the ball left Adam Turner's hand the Mayor stepped forward, almost on top of the plate.

For an instant it was all together, the memories of carefree teen-age days, the sweet sound of ball against bat, the sight of the ball rising, rising on a tremendous arc that carried it out of the schoolyard and over the tops of the trees in the street. Everyone stood openmouthed. The Mayor took five dollars out of his pocket and gave it to the catcher. "That's if you can't find the ball."

No one said a word until they returned to the welfare center. In a reception room full of plastic chairs and tables in pink, red, blue, and orange, the Mayor faced the newspaper reporters and their television and radio allies. The Bayshore community leaders clustered around Adam Turner, their black faces impassive.

"I am depressed by what I saw today," the Mayor said. "But I don't think it is as bad as Councilman Turner says it is. Bayshore is not a slum. It is on its way to becoming one. But it can be turned around, if we get together, and make a common effort to stop its decay.

"I think we make a mistake when we categorize everything under easy names, like slum. Let's emphasize the difference between things, instead of reducing everything to one miserable denominator. We can turn Bayshore around by a tougher enforcement of the housing code, by an improvement of city services and—most important—by a sense of community pride. When I was a kid, Bayshore had the best football and baseball teams in the city. They had an annual picnic that was the biggest celebration of the summer. They did things together. They cleaned the sidewalks in front of their houses. They kept their alleys and backyards clean. They respected their schools. They were proud of being Bayshore. Why can't we regain that pride?"

The Mayor began outlining a plan to "twin" Bayshore with an uptown neighborhood, perhaps Tipperary Square. He envisioned rival baseball, football, basketball teams playing in tournaments. He saw block parties. He proposed mutual invitations, conferences between neighborhood leaders to work out other friendly exchanges.

The words went nowhere. The black faces of the local leaders remained utterly blank. Adam Turner scornfully shook his head. For him it was just another attempt to create a phony substitute for busing. Paula continued to frown. Ray Grimes twiddled his thumbs. Later he would tell the Mayor it was a bad, unworkable idea, largely, the Mayor was sure, because he had not thought of it first.

The reporters asked questions. Had he consulted Tipperary Square about this twinning plan? Were they willing? The Mayor had to admit that he had consulted no one. He had only thought of the idea while he was batting in St. Bonaventure's schoolyard. In the last row, Dennis Mulligan took notes, a smirk on his face. A sullen certainty of defeat engulfed the Mayor. With a smile that he was sure was unconvincing, he shook hands with the local black leaders and with Adam Turner and departed.

Paula was waiting for him in the car. He slumped beside her and said: "Pity. That's all they want. Goddamn pity."

"Did you do that on purpose?" Paula asked.

"What?"

"Pick out the dumbest one in the class and ask him to read that poem?"

He noticed she had put up the window between them and Gus Dumbrowski. "I didn't pick him. I could have picked any one of them and gotten the same performance."

"That girl who knew Oliver Goldsmith's dates seemed bright enough. Why didn't you ask her? Wouldn't it help to project a good image—the best possible one—uptown?"

"Even if it isn't true?"

"Since when have you had a passion for telling the truth in public? I thought that was my dumb idea."

Look, I don't know why I did it. I can't explain a lot of things I did down here today. It's part of losing, losing control.

But he could not, he would not take the pity route. He sat there flicking his shoe, saying nothing.

"It was cruel, Jake."

"What about the job Adam Turner was doing on me? That's not cruel?"

"What was he doing?"

"Politically speaking, trying to rub my face in shit. With your help."

They were silent again for another five minutes. The Mayor stared at the back of chauffeur Gus Dumbrowski's thick neck.

"I'm sorry," Paula said. "I must be very obtuse. I had no idea that's what's happening."

"Is that the truth?"

"Yes."

The Mayor sighed. "Okay," he said. "Let's forget the whole thing. Let's try."

Paula nodded briefly. It was obvious to the Mayor that the whole thing was going to be neither forgotten nor forgiven.

11

Paula Stapleton O'Connor kissed her daughter Dolores good night, checked to see if her son Kemble was doing his homework, and blew him a kiss. Down the stairs she went to the waiting limousine, alone. She resented the word and the fact. Her husband had called her from City Hall to tell her that it would be hours before he, Police Commissioner Tarentino, and the Board of Education had solved some last-minute problems in the city's busing plan. They ranged from the sudden resignation of two dozen drivers to the discovery of a garage full of Molotov cocktails on the North Slope. He promised to get there before the meeting ended, although, he added, he didn't really think it was necessary. Paula heard sarcasm in those last words. Or worse, a mean satisfaction. But she had promised to make this appearance in return for his tour of Bayshore. *And though she promised to her loss, she makes her promise good.*

In the car, Paula felt panic clutching at her. Never had she felt so distant, so separate in an inward sense of the word from the people she was about to confront. *The lumpy ones.* It was years since she had used that snob phrase. Where had she heard it for the first time? Sitting in the back of her father's Bentley with her cousin Raymond Snodgrass. Dear faggy Raymond, now the city's chic interior decorator. It was around 1940 and they were waiting for a red light downtown near Principia mills, the Stapleton textile company. A swarm of working-class women came out the gate as the shift changed.

Most of them were middle-aged with bulky bulging shapes. "They're all so lumpy," Raymond had said.

It had become the word of the year. Lumpy described so much about them, the faceless, voiceless thousands who lived in the gray flats and tired apartments, who decorated their walls with portraits of Franklin D. Roosevelt purchased from the local newspaper, who wore shiny hats and dresses with drooping hems, who talked with a peculiar nasal twang and said *ya* for *you* and *nuthin'* for *nothing*. They were the enemies of good taste and good diction, as well as the destroyers of Father's dream of power. With brutish consistency, year after year, they rejected Father's sermons on economy and the earnest, aristocratic Republicans he funded so futilely. They delivered their votes to the Irish bosses, who blithely proceeded to mulct millions from the city's treasury, while Father impotently denounced their crimes.

After Radcliffe had exploded the comfortable assumptions of her class-bound mind and liberated her from Father's narrow politics of creed and greed, Paula saw pathos in their lumpy lives. She had become convinced that they could be saved, that honesty and good taste, perhaps even intellectual achievement, might be possible for their children or their grandchildren, if those who possessed these blessings shared them. How simple it had all seemed when the special interests which Presidents Roosevelt and Truman so regularly denounced were the only obstacles to a better life for all the people. It was enough to be on the side of the laboring masses, the earnest, honest toiling poor. For Paula, it had been exalting, because her conversion had made her one of those fools for Christ's sake, condemned by a chorus of disapproving relatives led by Father. A Stapleton becoming a social worker. Shocking.

Ten years of toiling in the service of this gospel had slowly eroded Paula's faith. Benefits to build gymnasiums and fund summer camps, to get children off the city's sooty streets, endless hours spent visiting railroad flats, sitting on sprung couches, breathing last night's corned beef or spaghetti, none of this exhausting effort really worked. They kept on saying *ya* and *nuthin'*, their dreams still centered on hitting the numbers or the daily double at some distant racetrack or—seventh heaven—the Irish Sweepstakes. Their lives were intricate, incredible tangles of stupidity and personal hatred and frustration and—what shocked her most—self-satisfaction. They were so easily satisfied with their own and their children's achievements. A degree from a third-rate Catholic college made them swell with triumph. Owning their own sagging one- or two-story houses, plus a few thousand dollars in a savings account, this was the boast of a lifetime, to be spoken of with pride bordering on arrogance. More and more, after a decade in the downtown wards, Paula had become depressed, even obsessed by their impenetrability.

There had been some gratifying moments, glimpses of new openness, of change in a few individuals. But what did they matter in the unyielding stupid mass? The net result of her decade of effort had been a kind of social despair, and in this perspective her marriage to Jake O'Connor had been almost an act of desperation. This broad-shouldered, self-assured Irishman had seemed to possess the power to penetrate these people, to speak to their hopes in a way that lifted them above their petty horizons.

CITY-1 rolled down a dark tree-lined street of one- or two-family houses and stopped for an unusual red light. The red was beneath the green. It meant they were entering Tipperary Square. Forty years ago, the city had put a traffic light here with the green on the bottom. It was promptly smashed. After three more smashed lights, they put the green on top. Paula had only one word for this performance, which she had heard her husband describe to the amusement of more than one audience: idiocy. On the right as they rolled across the square stood Buchanan High School, where half the teen-agers on the two-mile-long North Slope went to high school. Commissioner Tarentino was predicting trouble here. RIP had a lot of followers around Tipperary Square. Some would probably be at the meeting tonight.

Earlier in the day, before the Mayor was called

back to City Hall, they had toured Buchanan. Paula had been dismayed (but not, on reflection, surprised) by the lower-class stupidity on many of the students' faces. They had visited a classroom, and the Mayor had asked someone to read a poem. The teacher, a starchy, gray-haired woman, had selected a beefy boy named Michael O'Toole to read *The Tyger* by William Blake. O'Toole had massacred it. Paula could still hear his atrocious accent:

"Tiguh Tiguh burnin' bright
Inna forest offa night."

On the way out, the Mayor had asked the principal how many of last year's graduating class had gone to college. "About eighty," he answered. "Eighty out of seven hundred. This is not a high achiever's school. We try to give them a decent education. That's all."

In the limousine, the Mayor had asked her: "Do you think it's worth twenty million dollars to get Wangombe Madison into the same classroom with Mickey O'Toole?"

She had said yes, and he had dropped the subject. The memory forced Paula to think about the difference between her feeling for someone like the O'Toole boy and the Madison boy. She had *expected* O'Toole's stupidity. It was written on his stolid face. But the Madison boy's face was a blank, an unspoiled possibility and that made his failure heartbreaking. Was that it? She was not completely satisfied with that answer. She could only confess—or at least confront—the difference in her feelings.

Another example of this difference was the anxiety she felt now and her calm confidence during the two hours she had spent with black women at Bayshore's Afro-American Day Care Center earlier in the week. Part of the reason was Adam Turner's presence, and his cool control of the meeting. Not that this meant an antiseptic dialogue. One militant woman had baited her. "Don't you admit every cent you've got is drenched in the sweat and blood of black people?" she had yelled.

How amazed she had been when Paula admitted the accusation was partly true. The Mayor had been infuriated when Paula sent the day care center a check for $5,000 the next day. He had told her that she would have to make a similar donation uptown. She had agreed without an argument.

Marie McKenna, wife of Party Chairman Eddie McKenna, met Paula at the door of the Ninth Ward Democratic Club. Marie was a throwback—or what Jake called a standstill—a woman who repeated the life-style of her mother. This meant she was at least thirty pounds overweight. She wore a blue felt hat that swirled off her head and eventually reached a point. In the swirls were several weary-looking flowers. The hat was from the 1940s. Her blue tweed suit was ageless; it looked as if it were designed for a prison matron. The high pointed heels of her blue pumps were from the 1950s. But they looked new. It always amazed Paula to discover how oblivious the city's neighborhood stores were to changes of style. Marie McKenna had probably bought those shoes yesterday, proudly assured by the shop owner that they were the rage in New York, London, or Paris.

The clubhouse was a two-story brick building with several offices off the central hall. Marie McKenna acted like she owned the place. According to the Mayor, she almost did. Although she pretended to know nothing about politics, both the Mayor and Ray Grimes considered her one of the best politicians in the city. Her husband never made a move without consulting her.

"Paula," she said. "So nice ta see ya."

"I'm delighted to be here," Paula said.

"The girls are waitin' inside. We're just havin' a little coffee and cake. Would ya like ta join us?"

"I'd love some coffee."

"The Mayor couldn't be heah, huh? What's he doin'? I bet he's got another fast move up his sleeve."

"Fast move?" Paula said, disliking Marie McKenna's crafty smile.

"Like springin' that one-week delay. There must be lots more things like that you c'n pull when you're as smart as Jake."

"He has no more tricks. Neither does anyone else. On Monday morning the buses will roll."

Marie McKenna stared unbelievingly at her. "You come here to tell us that? You must be outta your mind."

"I didn't come here to tell you that. I came here to talk to you as one American to another. Just as I've talked to other Americans downtown."

"Oh, sure," Marie McKenna said. "And I bet you're gonna give us five grand, like you give them."

"I'll be happy to donate the same amount of money to any worthwhile charity."

"Well, let me tell you something. Our kids ain't for sale. If you and Jake think y'kin buy our votes, ya crazy."

"Marie—that's a ridiculous idea."

"Don't give me that line, Paula. I been around. I grew up in the Thirteenth Ward. I seen how Benny O'Connuh operated. Bought them boogie votes every election. Just what you're doin', what the Mayuh's doin', scatterin' money around downtown. But our kinda people don't sell their votes. They want sumpthin' more important than money. They want loyalty. Loyalty to yer own kind."

This exchange took place in the center hall, with other women drifting past, staring curiously at them.

"I hope you're not going to conduct the meeting in this frame of mind," Paula said. "If you are, I'm going home right now."

The frightening antipathy that had contorted Marie McKenna's face vanished. She regained control of herself. "Don't worry," she said. "When I chair a meetin' I'm like a judge. I don't take sides with no one. But lemmy warn you. There are people here tonight who're a lot more worked up about this thing than I am. I ain't got no kids of my own gettin' on them buses. Mine are all in good Catlic schools, thank God. It's costin' us a fortune but me an' Eddie think it's worth every cent."

Paula nodded. "Shall we go in?"

They walked into the auditorium. There was a small raised platform at the front of the room. On it stood an American flag furled around a flagstaff and encased in clear plastic. There were about two hundred women in the room. Most of them were younger than Mrs. McKenna. They were not quite as lumpy as their hostess. But they could not be called stylish. Startling numbers of them were wearing housedresses of nondescript brown and blue. Few if any heads showed evidence of a recent visit to a hairdresser. Paula's eyes recoiled from a number of bare beefy arms that might have belonged to longshoremen. All of them stopped consuming their coffee and cake, and stared at Paula with curiously naïve—or were they hostile?—eyes. There was no patter of applause, not even smiles of welcome.

Marie McKenna stepped behind a small table on the right side of the platform and gestured Paula to the lone straight-backed chair in the center, beside a small lectern. All the eyes in the room continued to stare at her. Paula felt they were undressing her and pricing every garment. Marie McKenna signaled for some coffee. A fat woman served Paula a cup from a large tin percolator.

Marie McKenna rapped on the table for attention and said, "Well, girls, our guest a-honuh is here. I'd like to introduce the First Lady of our city, Mrs. Paula O'Connuh. After she says a few words, we'll open the floor t'questions."

Paula stood up, clutching her coffee cup. "I really didn't come here to make a speech," she said. "I thought we'd just have a chat about the things that concern us, as women and fellow citizens. I don't even really see why I should sit up here on the platform. When I talked with black women down in Bayshore earlier this week, I took my chair to the middle of the hall and we formed a big circle. I'm sure that we can do something like that with no trouble here—"

"We're used t' havin' people speak from the platform," Marie McKenna said. "That way everybody can see ya and hear betta."

"Oh—" Paula floundered. "Well—"

She put down her coffee cup and stepped behind the small lectern. She did not like to make speeches.

She clutched both sides of the lectern, and cleared her throat.

"I came here to find out what you wanted to talk about. But I suppose there is one topic that's on everyone's mind—busing. The Mayor is in City Hall working out the final details of our court-ordered plan. We are both terribly hopeful that this can be carried out without any of the violence that has disgraced Boston and other cities. I know it isn't easy for you to accept. I know you have strong feelings on the subject. But try to see the situation from the other side. As if you were black. How would you feel if your children were barred from a chance to get a decent education? If you were told your children weren't good enough to associate with other children, just because of the color of their skins? It would make you angry and sad and desperate, I am sure. This is the way it has been for black Americans for over a hundred years. Before that it was even worse. Most of them were slaves. It was against the law for them to read or write. Now the law says we have to give them an equal chance to share our schools. Americans have always believed in the rule of law. We've had our lapses but that is the ideal toward which we strive. We have to keep striving for it, even if it involves doing things that hurt, or seem to hurt us. It's for the good of the country. Believe me, it's for the good of the whole country."

The silence was total. Paula searched the rows of faces for a glimpse of agreement. They might have been figures from a wax museum.

"As women, we have a special stake in this experiment. Our children are involved. We also have a chance to exercise a special responsibility. We can be agents for peace. Men thrive on conflict. They always see everything in terms of winning and losing a fight. I urge you to try to see beyond the argument, to try to see the whole city as part of a family. Let's act as if members of our family—your family—were quarreling. Let's do what comes naturally. Try to make peace."

Those last words seemed pathetically feeble to Paula. She wondered if they could hear the lack of conviction in her voice. It was rooted in the painful thought of how little peace she had been able to make in her own family. Did these women hear the words as lack of faith in the idea itself, a lip service which would simultaneously sound like condescension?

Marie McKenna advanced to the lectern.

"Ya kin sit down, Mrs. O'Connuh," she said. "We'll open f'questions now."

Paula felt an unsettling loss of control. She wanted to stand here behind her frail shield, clutching it for support. The lectern had become a symbol of her determination to tell these people the truth. She retreated to the single chair on the right side of the platform. As she sat down, she jostled her cup of coffee with her foot. It spilled, creating an embarrassing puddle beneath her chair.

"May Peterson," Marie McKenna said.

A short, very fat woman with an incongruous pageboy haircut stood up in the first row. "Where does your son go to school?"

"Kemble goes to a magnet school downtown, P.S. Nineteen. It's ninety per cent black right now."

"How's he gettin' along?"

"I'll be honest with you," Paula said. "There have been some problems. Just the other day he came home crying. Another boy had punched him in the nose. Boys have been doing that since school was invented. Just because the other boy was black doesn't mean he did it for—racist reasons."

They call me white ass. Was there something in the very nature of politics that turned people into liars? Her husband was cruel about it. *You can't tell them everything,* that was his motto.

"Helen Karpinski, there in the back row," Marie McKenna said.

A tall, thin, very intense-looking woman rose. She was wearing a blue pantsuit that seemed a size too small for her. "What do you think about whacher husband said about busin' costin' twenny million dollars? Why don't we use that money to build schools? Up here we got forty kids to a class when the state law says thirty."

"That's another reason why I'm in favor of busing," Paula said, leaning forward in her chair, trying to meet the accusatory words with a smile. "Because of the Board of Education's policy of refusing to integrate the schools, some white schools are overcrowded. Busing will enable us to reach the right class size all over the city."

"How are the kids gonna learn when half the class is a bunch of ignorant niggers?" cried another voice in the back row not far from Mrs. Karpinski.

"Now, now, let's have a little order here," Marie McKenna said.

"Please don't use that word—I think it's very important to start using the right words in this argument. Black Americans, Afro-Americans."

"They call us honkies," Helen Karpinski said. "My husband's on the cops. Patrols downtown. He gets called a honky bastard every day."

"There are stupid people—I mean angry people, people saying the wrong things—on both sides. But we should set the example, I think."

"Why?" Helen Karpinski said. "My kids don't use the kinda language their kids use. One word, the worst you ever heard in the English language, in their mouths all the time. A word that accuses people of—of rapin' their mothuhs. I don't want my kids goin' to school with people that use that kinda language. I'll take forty, fifty, sixty in a class rather than expose them to that kind of language."

"It is upsetting to hear that word," Paula said. This time she decided to risk telling the truth. "I was very upset when my son Kemble—used it."

The expression on Helen Karpinski's face told Paula she had made a fatal admission. But she struggled gamely through the rest of her answer. "Then I realized he didn't even know what it meant."

"Did you tell him?"

"No. I—his father to be more exact—told him it was a silly word and he should just stop using it."

"Mrs. O'Connuh," Helen Karpinski said. "That ain't the way we raise our children. If one of my kids used that word I'd wash his mouth out with soap every day for a week."

There was a burst of applause from the audience. Paula felt dazed. She stared down at the pool of spilled coffee a few inches away from her left foot. *They are rubbing your face in it. It's your turn and he knew it.*

Now they were standing up without waiting for Marie McKenna to introduce them. "I gotta husband, he drives a cab," said a squat dark woman on the extreme left. It looked alarmingly as if she had a mustache on her upper lip. "For thirty years he's been pushin' that hack. Two days ago he's robbed by one a them. A knife at his throat. He's still so nervous he can't go back t'work. We need more police. Not twenny million bucks worth of integration. This city needs more cops."

"What are you gonna do about drugs?" shrilled a woman in the front row with a voice like a police siren. "They're all on drugs. The cops caught two kids sellin' heroin in Buchanan only last week."

"Doesn't that prove drugs are a white problem as well as a black problem? There are no blacks in Buchanan now."

"There will be next week. Accordin' to what I heard there'll be four or five hundred. What are ya gonna do to control the drugs then? They're all on heroin."

"That's not true," Paula said. "Anyway, parents are the best defense against drugs. We have to talk to our children and convince them that they are being exploited when they use drugs. Exploited by the underworld."

"How can you watch kids twenty-faw hours a day?"

"You can't—"

"The police gotta do it. You should have a cop every ten feet in the halls."

"That would completely destroy all semblance of education—"

"How can ya educate a buncha drug addicts?"

"I'd like ta know somethin'," croaked a hoarse voice from the rear. "How many kids comin' inta Buchanan are from welfare families?"

"I have no idea," Paula said, all her social worker's training infusing reproach into her voice. "Some of them

214

will be. But welfare—being on welfare is not a disgrace. It's a right."

"The right to loaf," barked a voice from the rear.

"Are you in favor of sterilizin' any woman who has more than three kids without a husband?"

"Of course not," Paula said. "That's genocide."

"It ain't genocide if we get a law passed that sez ya gotta do it."

"That's what politics is all about," howled the siren in the first row. "Majority rules."

"That's right," bellowed the wife of the recently robbed cab-driver. "RIP is right. If the majority is against a law, it oughta be changed. If they don't like it, let 'em get out. Go to New Yawk. Or Africuh."

It was impossible, impossible, Paula thought. She could not endure another moment of their stupidity. Should she walk out? That would get into the newspapers. Shout back at them? That might get into the newspapers, too. Perhaps just break down and cry? But was there any pity in these glaring eyes and accusatory mouths?

"Now, ladies. Now, ladies. Calm down," Marie McKenna said. "Before I come in here with Mrs. O'Connuh, she tole me she's be glad to match the gift that she made downtown to them black women to the charity of our choice. That's pretty nice of her. I tole her she wasn't gonna change our minds with her money, but it's still pretty nice of her. Anybody got any ideas about what we should do with it?"

"Let's give itta RIP," someone yelled.

"RIP, RIP," howled the siren.

"I said I would give money to any worthwhile cause," Paula said. "But I don't think RIP is a worthwhile cause."

"Who sez it ain't?" croaked a voice in the back. "Half the women in this room belong to it."

"We ain't gonna let you welsh on a promise," shouted the cab-driver's wife.

A half dozen people were on their feet shouting insults. For a moment, Paula saw herself being beaten, kicked, her clothes ripped, her hair pulled. Marie McKenna was pounding on the lectern with her fist, calling

215

for order and getting nowhere. Suddenly, there was silence. The doors at the back of the room had opened. The Mayor stood there. A gasp swept the room. The shouters sat down.

The Mayor walked up the center aisle. He was calm, smiling, the utter antithesis of the turmoil raging inside Paula. Casually, he kissed her upraised mouth and whispered, "The cavalry has arrived." In the same unhurried fashion, he strolled over and put his arm around Marie McKenna and kissed her on the cheek. "Marie, how are you?" he said. "You get younger every time I see you. It must be those hats. They keep the sun off that beautiful complexion of yours."

He turned to the audience. "I knew you people were going to have a pretty lively discussion. But I didn't expect to hear you outside on the street. For a couple of seconds I wondered if I should call the tactical patrol. But I've got too many friends around here to need protection." Swiftly he scanned the rows of faces. "There's one. Helen Karpinski, a fellow fugitive from the old Thirteenth Ward. How's Bill? Still keeping those trains running on time?"

"He's tryin', Mistuh Mayuh," said Mrs. Karpinski with a silly smile.

It was incredible. He had yet to say a political word, and already the atmosphere of the room had been transformed. The spirit of vengeful aggression had vanished from their faces. They were subdued, like children caught being naughty, cowed by the maleness of him. Paula could not decide whether to be amazed or infuriated by the transformation.

"Helen's one of my old girl friends. I never could understand how she let that Polish Romeo talk her into saying yes. It almost destroyed my faith in my Irish charm."

Helen giggled and half the room joined her. "How's the meeting going?" the Mayor asked Marie McKenna. "I warned Paula you girls were the toughest politicians in town."

"There were some tough questions, Mistuh Mayuh," Marie McKenna said. "But Mrs. O'Connuh answered every one of them. We got kinda excited there at the end because we couldn't agree on what to do with the money she's gonna give us."

"What money?" the Mayor said. "I can't keep up with my wife's generosity. I keep tellin' her I'm gonna take away that checkbook when she's down to her last million."

Marie McKenna explained the disagreement over the gift. "There's a majority in favor of givin' it ta RIP," said the considerably subdued siren in the first row.

"For what? To buy Kitty Kosciusko a new mackinaw? RIP doesn't need any money. They already own a bullhorn. That's all they need to stay in business."

"That's what I say, too," someone cried.

"They're a political organization," the Mayor said. "You watch. In a couple of months they'll be endorsing candidates and running a few of their own, like Kitty's husband, Charlie. I undersrtand he wants to be mayor. That's okay with me. He can have the job any time he wants it. I'm not a mayor anymore. I'm just a servant of the court, obeying orders like everybody else in this city. I don't like it any more than you do. But we're stuck with it, until Congress or the Supreme Court gets us off the hook."

There he was again, Paula thought, almost unable to contain her rage in silence, playing the alternative game, raising their hopes of perpetual segregation. Why didn't he see that was the ruinous flaw in his policy?

"What do you think we should do, Mistuh Mayuh?" Marie McKenna said.

"I think we ought to use it to throw a party—a coupla parties. Maybe one in the spring and one in the fall. We'll take over Van Zandt Park. Here's the point. I want you to invite a hundred couples from Bayshore to be your guests."

"You gonna supply the cops, Mistuh Mayuh?" said a voice in the rear.

"Wait a minute," Jake said, spreading his hands wide. "These hundred couples are gonna be people like yourselves. Working people. No freaked-out junkies, no loudmouth militants. Good steady people trying to make a living and raise their kids, like you. No welfare chiselers."

It was outrageous, sickening, immoral, Paula thought. The language he was using. The idea was also impractical. Black militants would insist on sharing in the selection process. They would denounce him for trying to play image politics with black people.

"We've got a lot of black people like that in this city, and I think it would do you good to meet them. Get a chance to talk to them. I know you're not against them. It's the other ones, the welfare mothers who specialize in illegitimate kids, the muggers, the junkies. The city is trying to help these people. We've got all sorts of special programs to rehabilitate them, to educate them for jobs. Let us worry about them. I want you to help these other black Americans, who are working hard to make it in this country. They want to be accepted by people like you. They want to move a little farther uptown, and find some decent houses."

The word houses produced a nervous reaction. "Oh no. Oh no. We don't want no blockbusters," echoed around the room.

"I don't mean they're going to move in tomorrow," the Mayor said. "There won't be any blockbusting in this city while I'm running it. We've got a standing committee watchdogging it down at City Hall. What I'm asking you to do is help me start building some trust, some conversation between the whites and blacks in this city. It's our best hope of getting rid of busing."

The immoral alternative again, Paula thought. He was lying to them. The whole thing was a foolish, stupid lie.

The Mayor went into more details on his plan. He wanted to set up a permanent community reception committee with a paid part-time executive director and staff. They would arrange for small groups of blacks and whites to get together at coffee klatches and Sunday brunches before the big spring party.

"I don't know whether it'll work, Mistuh Mayuh," Marie McKenna said, "but if you say we can help by tryin' it, ya got my vote. Who else votes in favuh?"

Almost every hand in the room went up. Paula could not believe her eyes. The same people who had been ready to tear her to pieces twenty minutes ago in the name of RIP were now saying they were ready to accept blacks into their homes. The Mayor, her husband, had managed this incredible transformation. But he had done it by saying, promising, all the wrong things.

"I can't tell ya how grateful I am f'this," Jake said.

Fascinating, Paula thought, how he even slipped into their argot. Again, was that good or bad, admirable or abominable? She looked out at the audience and saw on their mesmerized faces no sign of intelligent agreement, thoughtful commitment. They were swallowing what Mayor O'Connor was saying, because Mayor O'Connor was saying it. He could have switched to pig Latin in mid-sentence and no one would have noticed the difference. Another tribute to what Ray Grimes, with not a little irony, called the Mayor's charisma. She had yielded to it herself eighteen years ago when she first saw him on a platform projecting that combination of vigor and intelligence. She had surrendered a lot more than her mind to this charisma.

Did she simply resent the indubitable fact that she had surrendered so much? Or now, with so many more years of history in her mind and body, was she discovering that she disliked charisma politics? That was close to the truth, and it was not a trivial dislike. It was rooted in the knowledge that charisma politics could be dangerously empty, both for the man with the charisma and the electorate.

The Mayor was talking again. "I haven't had much sleep in the last four nights. Neither has Police Commissioner Tarentino or a lot of other people in my administration. The day after tomorrow those buses are going to roll. Some of your kids will be on them. I want to tell you right now they'll be safe. That's what we've been spending our days and nights doing—making sure that every kid on every bus in this city will be safe. Maybe you can live with this thing for a while, if you know that. I hope you can. Let me just add this. We're not going to let this busing crisis destroy the other goals in this administration. We've got programs to make this city a cleaner, healthier, more prosperous place, and we're going to keep working on them, no matter how much overtime we have to put in. Everybody who lives in this city has a stake in it, whether you own property or just breathe the air. But I can't do it without you. I'm depending on you. Don't let me down."

The room rocked with applause. The Mayor kissed Marie McKenna once more, took Paula's hand, and sauntered into the night. Outside, in the crisp cold darkness, Jesse Owens opened the back door of CITY-1. Suddenly the glowing interior of the car became a cushioned trap for Paula. Her husband's arm around her waist propelled her toward some unspeakable humiliation. She almost cried out, NO. For an anguished moment she saw herself running down the silent empty blocks ahead of them, in the harsh futuristic light of the sodium-vapor streetlamps, running past the row houses and the windows full of leering lumpy faces.

"Get in," the Mayor said, puzzled by her sudden resistance to his escorting arm.

Marie McKenna appeared behind them. "That was just great, Jake. But lemmy tell ya one thing. You're gonna have t' deliver on that promise to keep them kids safe. Just let one kid get stabbed by one of them boogies with their knives and ya gonna need the National Guard up here."

"I know it. All we can do is hope, Marie. Thanks for your help."

"Not at all, Jake. We gotta stick together. And thank you, Mrs. O'Connuh. I hope ya didn't mind gettin' roughed up a little in there. It did them good to get some of that steam outta their systems. Betta for them to let it out on you than on Jake."

"You're a great girl, Marie."

Humbly, submissively, Paula got in the car. She felt as if she were in a foreign country, being escorted by a prominent official of the home government. She understood the language the people spoke, in a literal sense. But the nuances, the root feelings behind the words, escaped her. She slumped against the cushions. No crouching in the corner tonight, coiled with anger. The Mayor slammed the door and they rolled south through the silent streets, past the row houses toward Bowood.

He took her hand. "It was pretty rough," he said.

"Yes."

"I could tell from the expression on your face when I walked in. I wish I could have come sooner. But Tarentino couldn't agree with the Community Projects people on anything. I had to be there to arbitrate."

"It's all right—I—I survived."

"The big argument was over Buchanan. Tarentino's undercover cops tell him there's going to be trouble there. He wanted to frisk every student at the door, like they do in South Boston. Grimes and company screamed that this was a violation of everybody's civil rights. I decided they were right."

She sensed that he was telling her this because he knew it was a decision she would approve. It was good to know he wanted her approval. She felt some of the confusion, the weakness that had assailed her as she got into the car, diminish.

"I think it's definitely the right decision. The police role should be held to a minimum."

"Yeah," the Mayor said, without much conviction. "I figured it was a fifty-fifty gamble. Any kid who wants to smuggle a knife into the school will get it past a quick frisk anyway. Or they can take knives out of the cafeteria and turn them into daggers in the machine shop."

Paula almost wept. He had done the right thing for the wrong reason. Why couldn't he see how terribly she wanted his motives to be as good as his decisions? This dismal thought swept her back to the memory of the lies he had just told in the Ninth Ward clubhouse.

"I must confess I didn't completely agree with everything you said to those women just now."

The big arm slipped without warning around her waist and drew her roughly against him. "The hell with it," he said. "Let's make a rule, no more politics after ten o'clock."

She knew he wanted to make love to her. She knew

why. Tonight the power, the confidence was on his side of the car. He had rescued his helpless, hapless, blundering wife from mental, even physical abuse, he had demonstrated his mastery of the lumpy ones. Now he would master her, he would take the reward that he felt he deserved for his performance.

Paula, said another, sadder voice, *stop thinking this way. Stop letting politics infest your mind, invade your blood this way. It can only lead to disaster.* But there was no way to stop it. There was no way to prevent those other words from speaking themselves. No way to prevent anger and contempt and disappointment from surging through her mind and heart. She could no more prevent them than the upside-down traffic light at the corner of Tipperary Square could stop electricity from flowing through its circuits. The feelings came from outside herself, even from outside her husband. Like him, she was ineluctably, perhaps fatally part of the city, another blind force moving on a current of time and emotion toward some dimly foreseen explosion.

But she was also free, free to overcome these feelings, free to give herself to him, as she had in the past, with pleasure, with abandon, with the joyous sense of having found the right man.

No, said the first voice. *Remember your No, Paula. Abandon that and you have abandoned your heritage, perhaps even abandoned him.*

She would let him love her tonight. She would accept the sweet fire his fingers and lips created in her flesh, but she would not let that fire rise to its all-consuming height. Her No would be there, an inner chasm between her and happiness. She would make the sacrifice because the alternative to making it would be unacceptable to so many voices and faces welling out of the past. She had made promises to them too.

When I think of the life we could have had. What about that voice? Paula shook her head. She had never made a promise to that voice. She had never let that pathetic woman penetrate her life. She had promised that other voice, the one that said *the real world is where a man must live.* She had promised that broken fathering voice, and all the other voices that spoke within its huge echo. That was the promise this man sitting beside her was threatening to betray. The other voice—O God, what wat it saying? She would not listen. She would not listen.

12

The Mayor sat in his bedroom-study, waiting for the six-thirty television news to begin. Beside him on the tilt-top table was a confidential report from Police Commissioner Tarentino that estimated there were 20,000 rifles and shotguns oiled and ready on the North Slope, and new weapons being bought at the rate of 500 a day. To avoid thinking about this grisly statistic and the ugliness he expected to see on the TV screen, the Mayor was reading Mortimer Kemble's journal again.

Everyone in the family, including my wife, snorts when I try to tell them that I am proud of being a politician. They sneer when I claim that politics is the grandest of all the arts. Nothing requires more skill or more intelligence, more patience or more effort. True, it is an art that paints with cheap newsprint. Nevertheless, it is an art. We politicians are the most misrepresented, vilified group of individuals in this country. The reporters and the reformers concentrate on our weakness—a love of easy money and a stylish life—and ignore our strengths. They fail to see the role we play in preventing chaos. They ignore the art with which we steer the social engine over the rickety bridges and around the harrowing curves toward that shining city of tomorrow beyond the horizon.

Since no one else gives a particular damn for a politician, he must watch out for himself. This is what I have decided to do. Today I spent an hour discussing the gubernatorial election with the state chairman. An intolerable hick from downstate, who seems to think that Democrats can be elected to statewide offices while safely ignoring the Irish vote. I advised him, if he wished to think that way, to transfer to the Republican Party. I then outlined to him the conditions under which I would run. I insisted on complete control of the party's patronage, and estimated to him succinctly the number of jobs I would be forced to promise the Irish, in return for their support. I then did some mathematical computations for him, and showed him, I think conclusively, that with Irish support and the moderate campaign I plan to run, victory was as certain as anything in this world can be. He professed to be appalled at the thought of bringing the Irish into the state government. He saw the necessity of making some concessions to them here in the city, but thus far the state government had been sacrosanct.

"And that," I told him, "is why the Democrats have lost three gubernatorial elections in a row."

"But is it worth the price?" he quivered.

"They are animals and animals can be disciplined," I assured him. "I intend to exercise the same discipline over them as Governor, that I have exercised as Mayor."

He said that he was not at all sure about my discipline. He pointed to the daring demands some of our city's Irish had been making; claiming the right to unionize, asserting that workmen should earn as much as eight dollars a day. That was Communism, anarchism, or worse.

I told him that I planned to campaign on a platform that called for a better wage for the working man. I told him that working men outnumbered employers 200 to 1, and if we offered them some hope of improvement, they would vote down the line for us.

He warned me against stirring up class conflicts. I told him I would take my chances with that accusation. I was in the fight to win, and I was confident that once I got to the Governor's chair, I could resolve any class conflicts that arose.

Later in the day I saw my two boyos, McGovern

and Kennelly. Not together, of course. I am still following the best of all political maxims, divide and conquer. Each was looking as greasy as ever in spite of the fact that Kennelly was wearing a new shirt. Stolen, no doubt. I said to him, "Kennelly, where did you get that shirt? It hurts my eyes." (It was bright red.)

" 'Tis a birthday present, yer Honor," he said, with a grin that showed more than his usual number of missing teeth.

"What happened to your teeth?"

" 'Tis a bit of a difference we had with the boys from the Fourth Ward at O'Donahue's saloon. They don't fight fair, they don't. Bats, they used."

The moment they remind us of civilized human beings, they recall their origins again.

A knock on the door. It opened and Paula peered into the room. "It's six-thirty. May I watch WTGM with you?"

"That settles it. You are a masochist. You don't see me in there watching WPLO."

"This one can't be any worse. It might even cheer me up."

That would be a novelty.

Looking into his wife's frowning face, the Mayor wanted to shove her in front of the nearest mirror and ask her if she planned to look that way for the rest of their lives. He was tempted to refuse to turn on the television set, to forbid her to think or talk about politics for the next six months.

He wanted to tell her about the conversation he had had with Allyn Stapleton in his office earlier in the day. She had arrived wearing a mink coat and a dark purple dress that clung to every curve. Draping one spectacular leg over another, she announced she wanted some basic training as a politician. She also indicated she was ready for other kinds of exercise with a particular politican she happened to admire. The Mayor had pretended not to get the point. He said that he was surprised that anyone in the kingdom of Stapletonia admired him.

"You're the only one with the guts to talk back to our monarch," she had said.

Pretty astonishing. But a man could not rat on a woman who tried to seduce him, even if he took a somber satisfaction in discovering that he was not very interested in adding Allyn to his schedule. On the other hand, it was depressing. He hated to let it pass by pretending not to get the point. He had been tempted to explain it all very specifically to her. Even though his wife was about as enthusiastic in bed these days as a Barbie doll, he simply did not have time to cope with another complicated woman, especially one as obviously hurt and angry and in search of consolation and revenge as Allyn. Instead, he had called in Charlie LoBello and introduced him as a bigga stronga swingina Italian bachelor who had incidentally won the Medal of Honor in Vietnam and would be very happy to educate her politically if she in turn taught him how to win at backgammon and understand Pynchon and worry about Attica like a sophisticated resident of the great northeast megalopolis.

Two days later, press secretary Dave O'Brien reported that Charlie's equipment was being tested to the limits of its structural endurance. Dave accused the Mayor of favoring the Italians. It was not only unfair, it was a mistake, he insisted, in his pseudo-solemn way. He had a brain, which was a lot more seductive than Charlie's brawn. Dave was about five six and built like a toothpick. The Mayor told him he did not want him to be too tired to use his brain and asked him what else Charlie had done with Allyn. In between orgasms he had discovered she had quite a background in designing exhibits for industrial fairs and conventions. Charlie had sent her down to put some style into Simon Burke's bicentennial show. Simon was no threat in the romance department and Allyn was where no one else in the administration could get at her.

Dave said Charlie had only one complaint. Allyn talked about the Mayor constantly. "My father won't believe that the Jake O'Connor he knew passed her up, Your Honor," Dave said.

The Mayor had found it hard to kid about Allyn. Contrary to his heroic young playboy image, he had never had much appetite for cool uncaring sex. He had changed the subject by telling Dave he wanted him to get to work on the St. Patrick's Day speech. It was the first time he or anyone else except State Chairman Bernie Bannon had given a thought to his Senate candidacy in two weeks. Bernie had been on the phone every other day worrying about what he was hearing downstate.

Maybe, the Mayor thought, pondering his wife's frowning face, his emotions were still operating on the memory of past happiness. Was affection—no, use the real word, love—like money, something a person could bank and draw on to carry him through hard times? Watching Paula flip on the television, her face lined with sleeplessness and gloomy concern, he could only conclude that they were very close to the point where romantic gestures made on either side would start bouncing like rubber checks. It was all one thing, this explosion of racial and ethnic chaos and the steady deterioration of his feelings for this woman. Was it possible to fail on all fronts simultaneously? The television set began supplying an ominous answer.

The images were already familiar to the Mayor. He had seen them from a different angle during the day. Seated beside Commissioner Tarentino in a police helicopter, he had watched the yellow buses crawling up the North Slope and rolling up the east-west expressway that carried most of them to the uptown wards, where the university people and the do-gooders from Society Heights had been working to guarantee them a warm or at least a peaceful reception. Within the panorama of his eye the city was an immense organism, teeming with life, yet simultaneously stricken with blotching, dismaying decay. It was old. Except for his defiant cluster of skyscrapers around City Hall and a few dozen high-rise apartments, practically nothing in the panorama had changed since he stood beside his father on the top floor of the Medical Center twenty-five years ago, looking down on the miles of flat gray and black roofs. He found himself wishing he believed that the yellow buses were a medicine that would cure at least a few of the city's illnesses. But he was a doctor administering a therapy in which he had no faith.

On television, anchorman Jack Murphy began telling him why. "The city began its first day of forced busing with only one major incident. On the North Slope near Buchanan High School two windows in the lead bus were broken by rocks. Otherwise the one hundred and twenty-five black students assigned to that school met with no physical violence. There was some unpleasant verbal violence, however."

The cameras picked up the buses as they rolled into Tipperary Square. Behind police barricades were at least a thousand supporters of RIP. They shouted obscenities and waved Irish and Polish flags. Several held up a series of placards which spelled out CARRY THEM BACK TO OLD VIRGINNY. As the first black students descended from the buses, someone threw a cherry bomb at them. It landed near enough to one black girl to frighten her badly. She cowered back against the side of the bus. A burly adult escort put his arm around her, and she regained her self-control.

When all the blacks were out of the buses, the escorts formed them into an irregular line and they began walking three or four abreast toward the red brick school which sat on a hump of ground behind a tall spiked black iron fence. Kitty Kosciusko appeared on top of a parked car with a bullhorn. She began leading a chant: "GO HOME WHILE YOU CAN. GO HOME WHILE YOU CAN." A rock sailed through the air and smashed another window in an empty school bus. Two tactical patrolmen cut through the crowd, grabbed the rock thrower, and hustled him down a side street to a waiting squad car.

The cameras followed the black youngsters up the steps to the school. There the cameras picked up signs painted in bright yellow on the big metal doors and elsewhere on the building's red-brick exterior. Among the choicer comments were *Everyone should own a nigger. Kill niggers. Niggers suck.*

"We had them painted out by the end of the day," the Mayor said.

"How did they get there in the first place?" Paula asked angrily. "Wasn't the school guarded last night?"

"Only by Board of Education security people."

"You should have had city police."

"We will from now on."

On television, the cameras had followed the black children inside Buchanan. Jack Murphy commented on the tranquility of the classrooms and the speed with which the teachers got down to the business of education. But the day was far from over, he somberly added.

"You can say that again," the Mayor muttered.

The cameras switched to the Buchanan cafeteria. The empty room was a chaos of overturned tables and chairs. Food, plates, cups, saucers were scattered everywhere. The trouble began at lunch, Jack Murphy said. He told how a black girl had thrown a plate of spaghetti at a white girl when she pushed ahead of her in the cashier's line. Before security guards could intervene, more food began flying through the air. By the time the melee ended, it had required twenty-five tactical police to restore order. Most of the white students left the school, and teachers faced almost empty classrooms for the rest of the day. Crowds of teen-agers and some adults gathered outside the school chanting, "Niggers, go home while you can." It was, anchor man Murphy remarked as the cameras roved the decimated classrooms, not a propitious atmosphere for learning. But the real trouble was just beginning.

The camera switched to the crowd outside of the school. Murphy went to work with acid in his voice.

"In spite of the obvious need for re-enforcements, the police department had only twenty-five tactical patrolmen on duty around Buchanan, the same number that were there during the relatively peaceful morning. Police Commissioner Tarentino said this was in line with a low-profile policy laid down by Mayor O'Connor. The Mayor felt that too many police might have a backlash effect on the community. Perhaps Mayor O'Connor is about to start playing games with the police budget and is trying to see how few cops he would need to quell a riot. It never seemed to occur to him that too few police can also encourage disorder. There was no attempt made to interfere with the black students as they left Buchanan for their buses. But the buses were subjected to a barrage of rocks and rotten fruit all the way down the North Slope."

The camera switched to Bayshore, showing the battered buses, with half their side windows smashed, surrounded by hundreds of agitated blacks. There were shots of ambulance attendants applying bandages to bleeding black faces, necks, arms. There were interviews with a half dozen angry black parents who denounced Mayor O'Connor for failing to protect their children. One accused him of being part of a white conspiracy to perpetuate segregation. At least two dozen children and adult escorts riding the buses had been cut by flying glass. But no one was injured seriously, Jack Murphy said. With the battered buses as a backdrop, the newsman ended his report by speaking directly to the city's chief executive, with an ironic play on a slogan from his first campaign.

"Everything isn't jake anymore, Mayor O'Connor. What are you going to do about it?"

"So much for low profile," the Mayor said. "It has now become synonymous with no profile. I can already hear Tarentino lecturing me. He'll want to saturate the Slope with cops tomorrow."

"Can't you go over there tonight and talk to them?"

"What good would it do? I can calm them down while I'm there. But ten minutes after I leave, RIP goes to work and they're crazy all over again."

"Then there's no alternative to the police."

"I could go on television with Adam Turner and appeal for order. That's what Ray Grimes wants me to do."

"Why don't you do it?"

"It will cost me half the white votes in the state. Especially if Adam opens his mouth in his usual style."

"I could talk to Adam."

The Mayor shook his head. "I can't see giving that black son on a bitch equal time with me. He doesn't deserve it."

"Please, Jake, don't use—"

"Jesus Christ. Can't you see I'm just being honest with you? I'm not going to say it on television."

"I don't like you to say it even to me."

"You'd better get used to it."

"What are you going to do?"

"I don't know. I came up here to get away from Tarentino, Grimes, McGuire, and the Board of Education."

And talk it over with you. But that does not mean a thing to you anymore.

"Grimes wants to do more than saturate the area with cops. He wants me to invoke Section Three of the state's Internal Security Law. That gives me the power to disperse any crowd of more than three persons in any section of the city where public order is being threatened. This would cover the whole North Slope. He wants to barricade Tipperary Square and not let anybody into it without an identification card from the Board of Education. He even talked about putting cops inside every house on the access streets to the square. That's police-state tactics. I can't see myself doing those things. If I ever thought I'd have to write an order like that for this city, I never would have taken this goddamn job."

"But you've got the job. And it's necessary."

The Mayor stared in astonishment at his wife. She was as cold, as bloodless as a night stick, a gun barrel. All those ancestors who fought for liberty and the pursuit of the Bill of Rights must be spinning in their graves.

"We're here because we're here," Paula said, a small nasty smile on her face. Or was it just a bitter smile? You can't blame a wife for welcoming a chance to hoist her husband on his own obnoxious petard. This thought did not cool the fury growing in the Mayor's throat. The word sympathy wasn't even in her vocabulary any more.

The telephone rang. The Mayor picked it up. An emotion-charged voice said: "Mayor, you'd better get down here right away."

"Who is this?"

"Adam Turner. We got four or five hundred people in the Malcolm X Ujamaa, and they are mad, Your Honor. They say they want the Man and nobody else but the Man. Grimes tried to talk to them, but they wouldn't listen to a word out of his mouth. They just shouted him down. If they leave here as mad as they are now, I hate to think what might start happening in the streets. There's a hundred or two hundred teen-age kids hanging around outside, just looking for an excuse to raise hell."

"I'll be there in ten minutes."

The Mayor called for his car and then dialed Victor Tarentino's private number at police headquarters. He told the police commissioner where he was going.

"I can't guarantee your safety," Tarentino said.

"That's my problem."

"It's my problem too. Let me send a couple of plainclothesmen with you."

"No."

"Black plainclothesmen?"

"No."

"We've already declared the area in phase one riot stage. There were kids stoning cars on the access roads to the expressway only a half hour ago."

"All the more reason for me to go now."

"Take a walkie-talkie with you. I'll put fifty tacticals in two buses on side streets to the north and south of the place."

"Do you expect me to walk out in front of that crowd with a walkie-talkie in my hand?"

"You can give it to someone offstage."

"No. The minute I show anyone down there that I'm afraid of them, we're through."

"That doesn't make sense, Jake."

"It's the way I feel, Vic. If you're still determined to protect my worthless neck, get one of your undercover people into the hall with a walkie-talkie under his coat. He ought to be able to run outside and sound the alarm before they get the fire high enough to cook me. Unless they've got it going already."

"I'll see what I can do."

The Mayor hung up and confronted his wife's distressed face. She did not like that last remark about cooking him.

"I'll go with you," she said.

"No you won't. One of us has to stay alive to raise those kids."

"You don't really think they'll—"

"I have no idea. I only know what my police commissioner tells me. He thinks it's dangerous enough to give me fifty tactical patrolmen as a bodyguard."

"Nothing will happen if I'm there. I know it."

The Mayor was infuriated by the implication that she was better at dealing with the blacks. He answered her with the most offensive words that he could find.

"They might dislike you even more than they dislike me at this point. Before this is over, I wouldn't be surprised if the blacks hate all you liberals for preaching their children into this meat grinder."

Dismay replaced the frown on Paula's face. "You—liberals? Did you say—you liberals, Jake? Have you really stopped being a liberal?"

"Whoever said I joined in the first place?" the Mayor said. "You make it sound like a religion. I didn't spend twenty-five years getting my head out of one religion to stick it into another one."

"If you're not a liberal, what are you?"

"A politician," the Mayor said.

He stalked out of the room, knowing the answer was worse than meaningless to his wife. He told himself he did not give a damn. In his limousine, he ordered his black driver, Jesse Owens, to imitate his namesake and get them downtown in record time.

"Use the siren as little as possible, Jesse," he said. "But use it. We haven't got time for red lights."

Luck and aggressive lane changing enabled Jesse to get them to Bayshore with only three howls of the siren to go through red lights. It was hard to estimate how many people were milling around on the street in front of the Malcolm X Ujamaa. Most were young and in a feisty mood.

"Hey, look who here. The Man. The Man's here," they yelled, running alongside the car as Jesse slowed to a crawl for the last half block.

"Get yourself and this car out of here, Jesse," the Mayor said.

"How *you* gonna get outta here, then?" Jesse asked. "I don't like the looks a' these assholes."

"It could go one of three ways," the Mayor said. "Either Adam Turner will give me a ride home, or I'll come home in a tactical patrol bus, or in an ambulance."

"I'll stay," Jesse said. "One of those assholes touches this car and I'll break his balls."

Jesse had been an all-state guard in his high school days. He was almost as wide as he was tall.

"That won't do either one of us any good. Take it back to the garage. That's an order."

As the Mayor got out, the teen-agers clustered around him, almost pinning him against the car. "Hey, Mista Mayah," one of them said, "you gonna stop them guys from throwin' rocks at our brothers and sisters?"

"Come on inside. We'll talk about it."

"Why can't we rap right here? We got friends on them buses. We just as interested as them old folks inside."

Jesse pulled away from the curb. The Mayor stood alone. Another half circle formed behind him. But he did not feel he was in any danger.

"I came down here to talk to the people in the ujamaa. They're waiting for me. Why don't you come in with me?"

"No room. They say it's no place for children."

"I'll take ten of you in with me. I'm sure we can get that many in. They can tell the rest of you guys what happened."

"What's gonna happen?"

"I don't know. We're going to talk first. Let it all hang out, you know. And then decide a few things."

"Why you got them tactical patrol buses parked on the next block? You fraid you gonna get yo' ass kicked?"

"I don't know anything about those tactical patrol buses. Maybe they're here because you guys look like trouble."

Quickly he counted ten faces at random from the circle and walked toward the ujamaa. The building had been a movie theater called The Tivoli, at which the Mayor had spent more than one boyhood Saturday afternoon. Instead of posters for the latest Gene Autry movie, there were African tribal shields in the glass cases on either side of the six entrance doors. They went up the three steps and knocked on the center door. Gowon Soyinka opened it. The Mayor knew Gowon as Lester Johnson, an ex-welfare department employee who had been fired for drunkenness. Soyinka's face was shiny with sweat. He was obviously afraid that his ujamaa might go up in smoke in the impending riot and he would have to go back to working for a living.

"You didn't bring no cops with you?" he said.

The Mayor ignored this stupid question. "I promised I'd bring these ten guys inside," he said. "They want to see how things go in here so they can report back to their friends on the street."

"They can come in, if they promise to stay cool," Soyinka said.

"No way you can talk to me like that, you motherfucker," said the tallest boy, who was wearing a big bright orange peaked cap that flopped over his ears.

The Mayor almost laughed, thinking of the money Soyinka had conned out of Paula to help him establish "cultural rapport" with young blacks.

"There ain't no seats. You'll have to stand in the back."

Soyinka opened one of the inner doors which led to the auditorium. The teen-agers stepped inside. The Mayor caught a glimpse of packed rows and heard a voice shouting angrily, with a dozen other voices adding a ragged chorus of commentary. Soyinka led him through another door into a corridor which ran to the rear of the building. There, in a room just off the stage, he found Adam Turner looking worried and Ray Grimes looking tense.

"Jake, I'm so glad you could come," Grimes said. "I tried to handle this for you. I know you said you wanted time to think about—Adam called City Hall first—"

One good thing about dealing with liberals, they were lousy liars, the Mayor thought. Grimes had obviously hoped to get the credit in tomorrow's paper for cooling Bayshore. Stopping riots was one of Mayor O'Connor's acknowledged talents. If Ray Grimes acquired a similar reputation, it was only a small step to claiming superiority in this as well as in other departments of the art of government.

"It would be nice if you let me make up my own mind about this sort of thing, Ray."

"I told him they didn't want no one but the Mayor," Soyinka said.

"They've been hearing reports from the escorts who were on the buses," Adam Turner said. "Each one makes them madder. Why weren't some cops there to stop it, Jake?"

"Ask Ray that question. His crowd were the ones who wanted a low police profile."

"Is that the truth, Ray?"

The Mayor enjoyed watching Grimes squirm. "It was our consensus. There's no doubt about it. But we wouldn't have objected to a lot more police later in the day. When things started turning ugly. Commissioner Tarentino just doesn't have any flexibility."

"Commissioner Tarentino's a cop. He obeys orders. We gave him an order, Ray. Low profile. No cops until, when, and if a real riot started. Stone throwers aren't rioters."

On the stage, a burly young black was giving the audience a highly charged version of what had happened on the North Slope. "They just stood on the corners with rocks in their hands, waiting for us. Not a cop in sight, not one. It was worse than anything I've ever seen, and I've been in Boston and Louisville."

"Who the hell is that guy?" the Mayor asked.

Adam explained. He was one of about twenty veterans of previous busing battles they had hired to train the local adult escorts. The Mayor instinctively resented hearing his city compared to Boston and Louisville. No one had burned or bombed any school buses here. Nor had a white mob chased frantic blacks through the streets like animals.

The audience began chanting: "WE WANT THE MAYOR. WE WANT THE MAYOR." The teen-agers had obviously passed the word that His Honor had arrived.

"Are you ready to go?" Adam Turner asked.

"Sure. Are you coming with me?"

"I'll introduce you, but—"

The Mayor got the message. Adam Turner did not want to identify himself even slightly with Mayor O'Connor tonight.

"Let's go before they start tearin' up the seats," Soyinka said.

Adam's introduction was brief. He told the audience that Mayor O'Connor had "responded to their demand" and was here to answer questions. "First of all," the Mayor said, "I want to tell you I'm sorry. I know you are angry and I want to tell you I'm sorry."

"Are you sorry for being a welsher?" shouted a beefy middle-aged man in the first row. "A double-talking welsher?"

The Mayor felt a flush of anger travel through his body. Nothing more insulting could be said to him. Like his father before him, he took pride in keeping his promises.

A woman in the next row redoubled the insult by making it specific. "That's right. You gave us your word. You promised us our children would be safe. They stepped off them buses covered with blood."

"Now, wait a minute," the Mayor said. "Can't we discuss this calmly? There were twenty-six kids hurt. Out of twenty thousand on those buses today."

A man on the other side of the center aisle stood up. He was dressed in a business suit and wore silver-rimmed glasses. Very middle-class. Most of this audience was middle-class, as far as the Mayor could see from a quick appraisal of their clothing. "My daughter was one of those twenty-six," he shouted. "It took seven stitches to close a cut on her cheek. Even if she was the only one, you're still a double-talking welsher as far as I'm concerned."

"YEAH," roared the crowd. "WELSHAH, DOUBLE-CROSSAH."

A woman leaped up and read word for word the Mayor's pledge to protect the children. "I believed in you," she shouted, "and you let me down. You let all of us down."

"YEAH," roared the crowd. "DOWN, DOWN."

The Mayor found himself struggling for breath. He was engulfed by an overwhelming surge of rage and regret. He never should have come here. He never would have come here if he did not have Paula Stapleton O'Connor for a wife. He was here because she wanted him to play Sir Lancelot to this crowd of primitives. This was her idiotic version of politics. It was not enough to go down fighting the natives with a stiff upper lip. You volunteered for the pot and struck the match to start the fire.

Beside these thoughts and feelings the political part of his mind functioned with appalling clarity. He was a professional. He knew exactly how to handle a berserk crowd. He began talking in a conversational voice, making no attempt to outshout them.

"If all you want to do is insult me, I don't see why you dragged me down here. You could write it all in a letter or send me a tape recording. I came down here to tell you what we're going to do to make sure this doesn't happen again."

"Hey, shut up back there. Shut up," shouted several people in the front rows.

The Mayor kept talking. "I admit that I failed to deliver on my promise. But I didn't welsh on it. I decided it was more important to try to trust people for one day at least. That's the American way to do things. We don't say a man is guilty before he's convicted."

"You had your tactical cops down here fast enough to stop black kids from throwin' rocks at the cars tonight," someone shouted from the back.

"They put another black boy in the hospital," someone else yelled.

"Why wasn't anybody arrested?" cried a female voice. "Not one white person arrested in the whole city."

"We want the National Guard, that's what we want."

"The hell with your cops," roared another man.

The Mayor continued to speak in the same steady measured voice. "In my judgment the situation does not warrant the National Guard. But here's what we're going to do. As of midnight tonight, under powers given to me by state law, I am forbidding more than three persons to gather in the vicinity of Buchanan High School, or at any point along the bus route from Buchanan to Bayshore. The police department will enforce this order without exception. Anyone who disobeys it will be arrested on the spot."

By now the hall was completely quiet. A soft voice in the back, possibly belonging to one of the teen-agers, said, "Right on."

"That's all very encouraging, Mister Mayor," said the man who had called him a welsher. "How about a strong statement condemning the white leaders who encouraged this violence?"

"I see nothing to be gained from a statement like that at this time."

"You mean you're still tryin' to hang on to their goddamn votes, ain't that it? Even though they stone our children."

"I am not trying to hang onto anybody. I'm trying to do a job," the Mayor said. He heard a tremor in his voice and he thought for a moment that the other emotions, the rage and contempt, were breaking through. But the politician remained in control. He pointed into the audience to the woman who had said she believed in him. "I'm not talking about votes. I'm talking about children. I want that woman to believe in me again, when I

240

say her children will be protected. I let her down once. I won't do it again. I came here to ask you for another chance. If I can't produce, I'll get on those buses with you and fight alongside you, if that's what it takes to protect those kids."

"We don't want you, we want the National Guard," a single voice shouted from the center of the room. The man in the first row started all over again with his demand for denunciations of specific white leaders. But they were isolated voices now. He had satisfied them. The cost was high. They had not changed his mind. But they had changed his policy. He had just promised to do for them what he had refused to do for Ray Grimes or for his wife. He was taking the first step toward turning a third of his city into a police state. Beginning tomorrow, the people on the North Slope, the Irish Americans and Polish Americans, his people, would begin to see the police as the enemy. It was unthinkable. Cops with names like Kelly, DeGrazia, Blonsky, the enemy.

The political implications almost disoriented the Mayor. He could hear State Chairman Bernie Bannon on the phone screaming: *Jesus Christ, Jake. Do you think people are gonna elect a goddamn storm trooper to the Senate? Do you call this neutrality?* The Mayor felt like a man who had just stepped into a whirlpool. Those black faces confronting him were a blind implacable vortex sucking him beneath the surface to a nightmare world where everything blurred and voices, gestures were slowed to the bizarre choreography of the dream. Even the rage still pulsing within him was unreal, meaningless to everyone but him.

None of this was visible to the audience. They still heard the politician speaking, wrapping up his extorted promises with reiterated determination. A final thank you for listening and he walked off the stage. There was no applause. Jesus Christ himself couldn't get applause downtown tonight unless he had the foresight to come back black, the Mayor thought, in a vain attempt at consolation.

Adam Turner asked him if he wanted to wait until

the meeting ended. He suspected there would be additional demands they could discuss in private. The Mayor shook his head. He was offstage now and it was not so easy to control his rage. He heard its cold cutting edge in his voice. "I've got a whole city to worry about. I've got to see the police commissioner and work out the details for tomorrow morning. I'll have to call a press conference—"

At which I will tell the white two thirds of the city the shit I am about to shove down their throats. Did Adam get that message from his curt tone? Probably not. Maybe all he heard was the obvious one: *You are not getting any more out of me tonight. Maybe you are not getting any more out of me, period.*

The Mayor asked for a telephone. He called his press secretary, Dave O'Brien, and told him to start rounding up the reporters. He called Tarentino and told him that he had decided to invoke Section Three on the North Slope. "Let's aim at prevention, Vic. Let's break them up before they throw the rocks."

"We'll do out best. But I've got to have permission to use force if necessary."

"You've got it."

"I gather it was a pretty wild meeting. The guy I had in there says he didn't think you were going to make it."

"It wasn't that bad. I cooled them off."

The Mayor did not like the implication that his police commissioner knew this decision had been extorted from him against his will. The Mayor made a policy of avoiding displays of weakness with everyone.

The Mayor called Kevin McGuire, his reluctant president of the Board of Education, and Eddie McKenna, and told them what he was going to do. They were both predictably opposed to it. He asked Eddie to go see McGuire, and talk him into keeping his mouth shut for a few days. McKenna could not have been more surly but he finally agreed to walk two blocks and deliver the message. The Mayor almost lost his temper and told him to forget it. But he was in no position to tangle with

Eddie McKenna or anyone else on the North Slope. He was a suppliant, a role he detested. He swallowed Eddie's snot and did his cursing after he hung up.

Two hours later, the Mayor was back in Bowood, watching himself on television as he told the assembled reporters and the rest of the city that he had "regretfully decided" it was necessary to use his police powers to keep order on the North Slope. He noticed glumly that he did not touch his father's pens. Otherwise he thought he sounded remorseful enough to hold a few votes on the Slope—maybe about 10 per cent.

Paula came into the library as he turned off the TV. She was looking as disconsolate as she looked when he had left her bleating about liberalism. Disapproval still frosted her eyes. "I ate dinner without you," she said.

He said nothing. He had nothing to say to her.

"I—I thought the press conference went well."

"I'm glad to hear that," the Mayor said wryly. "I'm also glad I can't hear what they're saying about me in Tipperary Square."

"How did the meeting with the blacks go?"

"It was fun. They held me over an open fire for a while. After I turned well done they decided to talk instead of eat."

No sign whatsoever of a smile.

"Why do you think I was on television, declaring martial law?"

"That's what they wanted?"

"Hell no. They wanted the National Guard, the Hundred and First Airborne and the Second Marines. I told them they'd get the cops. Why should I keep them happy when I'm making everyone else miserable? I like to be consistent."

Contempt. No question about it; contempt was on her face. "Where would you like your dinner? Hannah can bring it in here on a tray."

"The kitchen's good enough for me."

Paula wheeled and stalked to the door. "I'll tell her to set the dining room table again. I didn't think you'd want to eat in there alone."

"You could join me."

"I've had enough unpleasant conversation for one evening."

"ALL RIGHT, I'LL HAVE IT ON A TRAY IN HERE," he shouted after her. He poured himself a triple scotch and drank it straight. It did no good. The vortex of black faces still swirled around him. Mahoney appeared with a small steak, a green salad, and a baked potato. One of his favorite dinners. He had no desire to eat it. He poured himself another heavy-handed drink.

"That was a job they did on them buses, wasn't it, Your Honor?"

"Yeah."

"Them boyos can throw stones. Maybe that'll teach the nagurs to stay downtown. D'ya think it will?"

The Mayor pondered this question. Was God, or some other supernatural intelligence sending him a message in this brogue? If so, it was closer to a taunt. No wisdom, not even very many brains in your ancestry, Your Honor.

"I'm afraid not, Mahoney. They'll be coming up the Slope again tomorrow."

"Well, I'm afraid thin it's goin' t' get a lot worse before it gets better. From what I hear they'll soon be flingin' more than stones at them buses."

"If they do," the Mayor said, "we'll soon be flingin' a lot of them in jail."

"Sure that's a strange way to win votes, Your Honor. As the sayin' goes, there's a lot more of us than of them."

"Mahoney, anybody who backs the IRA is no expert at winning elections."

The next morning, after a night of broken sleep, the Mayor sat behind his desk in City Hall reading the Garden Square *Journal*. Page one was covered with pictures of bleeding children. Inflammatory statements from RIP were ominously balanced by angry threats from Adam Turner. Dennis Mulligan had a by-lined story down the right-hand side of the page describing the Mayor's appearance at the Malcolm X Ujamaa. Without saying it in so many words, Mulligan described the Mayor's decision to invoke Section Three of the Internal Security Law as a craven surrender. This was not surprising. What irritated the Mayor were the vivid details in Mulligan's story, which could only have come from someone who was on the scene.

Mulligan even knew about the tactical patrol buses. In his story, he parked them in front of the ujamaa. A neat touch. It would disgust black readers and convince whites that the Mayor was a hypocrite when he dismissed their fears of black violence. The Mayor no longer had any doubts that Mulligan was getting information from someone who wanted to destroy Jake O'Connor. Who was it? Ray Grimes was a good possibility. Adam Turner was a better one. Why was either—or both of them—trying to screw him? The weaker Jake O'Connor became—and he would be very, very weak if he became a candidate for the Senate and lost—the more dependent he became on black votes and the liberals whom Ray Grimes claimed to represent.

Ray Grimes, by mordant coincidence, interrupted these thoughts to ask the Mayor if he could see him immediately. He had an "emergency message."

"Come right down."

In five minutes Grimes had descended from his tenth-floor office and was ensconced in the visitor's chair. He twitched uncomfortably, crossed and recrossed his legs two or three times while the Mayor took a call from the Governor, who wanted to know if the Mayor needed help from the National Guard. The Governor was thinking about a grab for the Republican nomination for the Senate and obviously saw the situation as a great opportunity to one-up his future opponent. The Mayor politely refused the offer.

"Do you think that's wise, Jake?" Ray Grimes said. "It wouldn't hurt to have the Guard mobilized—at least on a stand-by basis."

"Ray, from now on let's get one thing straight. If I want your advice, I'll ask for it. Otherwise, don't volunteer it."

The Mayor fingered one of his father's fountain pens. "Did you know the Governor was going to call? Is that why you rushed down here?"

"No," Grimes said. "I have—I have another proposition to discuss."

The Mayor eyed his flickering telephone console. "Let's hear it."

"Adam Turner called a meeting of the black caucus last night. From what I heard, Jake, you're going to lose the black vote—unless you do something drastic."

"I'm doing something drastic. I've declared martial law in a third of my city."

"That's the minimum, Jake. I mean you've got to give them something that will make them feel they have a genuine voice in this city's schools."

"What?"

"An affirmative action hiring program that will raise the number of black teachers in the school system to thirty-eight per cent in the next year. They should have the same percentage of school crossing guards, truant officers, security guards, and custodial staff. It isn't going to be enough, busing them into white schools with all white teachers."

"Did Adam Turner send you in here with this proposition?"

"No. This is my idea. What I think you have to do to hold the black vote."

Ray Grimes blinked earnestly at him, his small mouth pursed, his soft cheeks slightly inflated. He thought he was exuding moral determination. To the Mayor he was a parody of a politician, an abortion of politics as he understood it.

"Tell Adam if he pulls any more moves like this one, he won't even get renominated for the City Council. As for you—if you go to one of those black caucus meetings, you're there as a city official, my representative. You're supposed to project our point of view. Not kiss their goddamn black asses and dump their demands in my lap. From now on you're relieved of that assignment, Ray."

Ray Grimes slid down, down in his chair until he

was almost sitting on his spine. He had obviously thought that the dazed battered survivor of last night's brawl at the Malcolm X Ujamaa would be ready to do anything to placate his erstwhile black supporters. Grimes struggled to his feet and wobbled to the door. As he opened it, the Mayor gave him a parting shot. "One more thing, Ray. Don't get Paula involved in this. I've had it with you trying to outmaneuver me in the bedroom."

For a moment the Mayor thought Grimes was going to answer him. Instead, he ducked out the door. The Mayor sat there, buffeted by regret. Grimes was a part of his past, a part of himself that he had paid a price to reject. The simpleminded do-gooder who saw everything in terms of right and wrong. By now the Mayor knew that life was too complicated to dismiss the appeal of that simplicity by brutally denying its relevance. There were times when it did seem to have enormous relevance, when to do the good thing, to seize the high moral ground, seemed not only comforting but shrewd. But so much of his past, his inherited contempt for reformers like Grimes and pious types like his brother Paul, stood between the Mayor and such a move.

I say unto you, love one another. Was this what he should be telling his city? The Mayor shook his head. It would sound absurd on his politician's lips. He did not believe in its possibility, any more than he believed in a divine mandate emanating from that suffering figure on the cross. For him, love was personal, not universal. He did not believe in abstract brotherhood. For him fraternity emerged from history, from blood. And it did not last. It faded here in America within a generation or two. Even within the circle of the immediate family the ties did not hold. Most of his cousins, the sons and daughters of his father's brother and sister, had fled the city and the state to disappear into America's vast anonymity. Escaping history, blood, faith.

The intercom buzzed. "Police Commissioner Tarentino is here."

Tarentino stalked into the room carrying his black brief case. They exchanged the usual handshake. "All quiet on the North Slope," he said.

"Good."

"They were quiet yesterday morning, too. It's the afternoon we've got to worry about. I'm putting four hundred men on the Slope. But I'm worried about their morale. They don't have much enthusiasm for this job, Jake. A lot of them live in that part of town."

"I know. I hated like hell to give that order, Vic."

"It was the only thing you could do, Jake. I know how you feel. I've got no enthusiasm for this busing bullshit either."

For a moment, hearing those tough words, the Mayor felt vindicated. It was good to hear a friend talking his own language, but doing the job, ignoring his personal feelings. A professional. Why couldn't he explain it to Paula that way? Because calling busing bullshit would be the cue for a half-hour lecture on the black experience. What we owe to them. With the unspoken subtitle, What you owe to me.

The Mayor's next words seemed to flow naturally from these thoughts. "I've got some problems on another front, Vic. Adam Turner."

He told Tarentino about Ray Grimes's proposition. *Never tell anyone too much,* whispered a voice in his head as he talked. He dismissed it. He needed the kind of help Tarentino could give him.

"Maybe it's time to start playing a little hardball with Adam. See what you can get on him to keep him in line."

The Mayor stopped. Those words sickened him. They had been used in this office a hundred, perhaps a thousand times in the days of the old organization. That was how the Big Man maintained his stranglehold on the city for thirty years.

But this was for the good of the city, not just for the good of Jake O'Connor, the Mayor told himself. Adam Turner needed a lesson in practical politics. He had to find out what happened to a man who overreached himself. If he started spouting those demands in the newspapers the city could have a race war on its hands.

Rationalizations, all of them. The Mayor dismissed them and accepted the opposite explanation. It was for the good of Jake O'Connor and no one, nothing else. So what?

"I've got a lot of stuff on that guy already," Tarentino said. "Things that sort of drifted in, you know? I keep them in a top secret personal file. I've got the only key."

The Mayor nodded. He was letting his police commissioner get away with a confession that would have outraged him a year ago. Tarentino had always been too ready to use the police department for political purposes. The Mayor had demurred because it reminded him too much of the old machine. It also made him too dependent on his police commissioner's political advice.

"We've got another problem on the North Slope, Jake. Eddie McKenna just made a deal to run a card game and a numbers wheel with a guy named Collins from Tipperary Square."

"You're sure?"

"Eddie paid the captain of the Tenth Precinct three grand for openers."

The Commissioner's internal investigation unit was one of the best in the country. In the past nine years they had developed almost supernatural skills in detecting corruption in the department. The Mayor had no doubt that the Commissioner was telling him the truth.

"I've been watching that guy for a good year, Jake," Tarentino said. "He's been edging up to this thing. He thinks you're too hassled to do anything about it."

"Let me talk to him before we move, Vic. I'd like to handle it quietly, if possible."

Tarentino nodded. He understood that he was talking to a Senate candidate who would be ruined by even a whiff of the city's old corruption. The Mayor was remembering Eddie's accusing whine—*it doesn't mean anything to you that I'm pressed for dough*. He told himself that Adam Turner and Eddie were part of the same story— each moving in his own way to take advantage of his weakness. That would be Tarentino's explanation. But Turner made the Mayor mad. Eddie made him sad.

The next day Tarentino had the report on Adam Turner hand-delivered to the Mayor's office. It was a typical police document. Like the FBI, Tarentino's informers and undercover people scooped up wholesale amounts of rumors and hearsay information. While he was putting together Bayshore's Black Voice, Adam had had a pretty active sex life. At one point his wife had threatened to divorce him. This and his rise to prominence as the city's black spokesman had apparently calmed him down. But he still paid a lot of afternoon visits to Reta Marshall, the very smooth girl who ran his Bayshore operation for him. More ominous were a number of calls from a major black gambler who boasted that he had Turner in his pocket. Gamblers liked to say that sort of thing. It did not prove much in a court of law. But it would prove a lot to the readers of the Garden Square *Journal*, if it was leaked at the right moment.

The Mayor put the twenty pages in his private file and locked it. He told himself he hoped that he never had to use such garbage. For a week he said nothing to Tarentino about it. Not a word came from Adam Turner and the Mayor finally decided that Grimes was telling the truth for once, the big push had been his idea. No doubt he was hoping to impress Adam and get his support for a run on the Mayor's office.

The deployment of the tactical patrol on the North Slope permitted the buses to roll unmolested by rocks or bottles. But RIP maintained the verbal pressure, stationing the legally permitted three demonstrators on every corner all the way up the Slope to scream insults and obscenities. Inside Buchanan, the white teen-agers, egged on by their parents, were constantly hassling and taunting the blacks. Tarentino kept telling him it would not last, that the Slope would blow as soon as the weather turned warm. He estimated there were another 5,000 rifles and shotguns in the hands of RIP adherents and their friends. Eddie McKenna and Kevin McGuire called with similar warnings. They urged him to withdraw the cops. Eddie put it on the line in the bluntest possible terms. "When the shootin' starts, Jake, I'd hate to see guys we both know, guys we grew up with, gettin' killed." The Mayor told Eddie he was full of shit. He could not imagine anyone on the North Slope, except a handful of punks on parole, who would take a shot at a cop.

During the first week of February, the weather turned mild. As Tarentino predicted, RIP tried to get their people into the streets to block the Buchanan-bound buses. The Mayor went on television the night before the scheduled march and forcefully urged "lovers of peace" to stay home. Only about 400 hard-core Rippers came out and the tactical cops had no trouble dispersing them. RIP retreated to the three-man (or woman) screaming squads on the corners again. The state of siege continued, but the Mayor started to feel cautiously optimistic about his own and the city's chances for survival. Tarentino, his head full of reports from his informers, who earned their money by predicting the worst, remained gloomy. He finally asked the Mayor if he had read the file on Adam Turner.

The Mayor nodded. "It's good insurance, Vic. I'll keep it here, in my private file."

"Insurance, hell. You got enough there to hammer that bastard into doing anything you want. Like agreeing to drop Buchanan out of the busing plan."

The Mayor shook his head. "He's got to make the first move, Vic. Remember, I'm running for the Senate. At least, I think I am."

He had taken a perverse pleasure in avoiding a confrontation with Bernie Bannon about his candidacy. Reports from a half dozen rumor spreaders had Bernie talking confidentially with Dwight Slocum. But the Mayor had no intention of relinquishing the endorsements and promises he had acquired during the past year, above all, Bernie's pledge of personal support. The two weeks of racial peace had emboldened him to make a lunch date with Bernie. For the first time since the dinner at Bowood, he was in a position to deal from semi-strength. Maybe he could finesse the latest polls from Sam Tucker showing a dismal decline in the O'Connor appeal downstate and upstate."

It was happening just as he had predicted. But did his beloved wife even admit that she was wrong? No, she kept on playing Elizabeth Regina up in Bowood. The Virgin Queen, that was what the Mayor had taken to calling his wife these days. It was hard to decide whether she was less interested in his political career or his sex life. As far as he could see, she was prepared to sacrifice both on the altar of racial equality.

Commissioner Tarentino took a familiar cassette recorder out of his brief case. "I don't like what we're hearing from our bug in Frank Donahue's back room."

"For instance."

"I'll play you a few samples."

"Haven't we got more serious things to worry about, Vic?"

"This is serious, Jake."

"It is a good question, Magister," said the deep growling voice. "Who is more guilty, the Mayor or his wife? It is her money that enables him to perpetrate his frauds upon the black people of this city. His father and his friends stole millions from the poor. Her father and her grandfather stole many more millions. The cotton cloth they wove in their mills was drenched in the sweat and blood of black men and women."

"Let them both die," said another voice.

"No," said the growling voice. "We know how weak we are. We know we can only strike once. Even now we do not know which of us Magister shall choose. We shall obey. But until the time comes, we are free to question, to debate. Is that not true, Magister?"

"Of course," said Frank Donahue's thin dry voice.

"I say let them both die. We are strong enough to fire two bullets from the same gun."

"It is not possible, brothers," said Frank Donahue.

The Mayor switched off the tape recorder. "Vic," he said, "I sat in Donahue's back room twenty-five years ago and heard other nuts talk about shooting the Big Man. No one ever did it."

"Twenty-five years ago Jack and Bobby Kennedy were still alive," Tarentino said. "No one had ever heard of the Manson family. My people tell me this could be a combination of the two things."

"I can't believe it."

"We've got an informer in there. The brother of a detective. He teaches English in the public high school in Bayshore."

"How did you get him in there so fast? He was there the night I—"

The Mayor felt sheepish. "I've been meaning to tell you about my visit."

"I've been meaning to give you hell for it."

"Vic. Calm down about this thing. Doesn't it prove they're not going to shoot me? Donahue had a gun in his hand. They let me walk out of there in one piece."

Tarentino shook his head. "You're dealing with a bunch of fanatics. They want to kill you their way. To satisfy their scrambled political and religious ideas."

"What does your informant—this English teacher—think of them?"

"He takes them pretty seriously, as far as I can see from the reports his brother makes to me. But he's not too reliable. We've had a lot of headaches with him. You paid a visit to his English class when you toured Bayshore and you got him sore as hell."

"That was not one of my better days," the Mayor said.

"It might help if you invited him down here and apologized. Don't mention Donahue. It'll impress him if he thinks you don't know anything about what he's doing there."

"I'll see if I can fit him in."

"That won't solve the basic problem. I'll tell you what I recommend. Plant a kilo of heroin in the place and bust them. We'll put them away for a good long time."

"No."

"I know it's rough. But we're in a rough business."

"No."

The Mayor was thinking about Andrew 77X—Andy Barton. He had had Simon Burke check the 1948 newspapers. He confirmed the fact that the old organization had sent Barton away for five years on a phony charge of vote fraud when he began making speeches against him. Bad behavior in prison had doubled his sentence.

"Benny would know how to handle guys like this."

"You've got it wrong, Vic. He wouldn't frame them. He'd get four or five of the biggest guys in the ward, distribute a half dozen blackjacks and clean the place out personally. Do you want me to do that?"

"I could get some people to do it."

"Vic. It isn't necessary. Let them talk."

"Okay."

The police commissioner picked up the tape recorder and pushed a lever. It whirred forward. "There's something else I think you ought to hear. This is Bishop McCoy, the back-to-Africa guy. When he isn't getting drunk on Donahue's wine, he does a lot of drinking with Gowon Soyinka, the cat who runs that ujamaa in Bayshore. Soyinka's on the CPI payroll. He's pretty chummy with Grimes and Adam Turner. Listen."

The growling voice rose from the machine again. But now it was slurred and halting. "So Brother Gowon says to me. What's wrong with you? What you got against Missus O'Connor? She give . . . uh lot of money ta black people. She give twenny thousand dollah to keep the bus escorts on the job. Twenny thousand dollah. That's a lot of bread. Maybe we have misjudged this lady, brothers."

The Commissioner switched off the machine. "Is that true, Jake?" he asked, "Did Paula give Turner and that lush Soyinka twenty grand for those busing escorts?"

The Mayor felt nothing at first. It was like being hit in the head by a fast ball. Only after the shock did the pain begin. He felt his face flushing. Was it shame? What else could it be? Perhaps anger. Perhaps dread. How did dread feel? He should be an expert on it by now. But it seemed to have as many shapes and shades of feeling as the devil.

"I don't know," he said. "But—it's possible."

"Twenty thousand dollars?" the Commissioner said.

Twenty thousand dollars was a lot of money to Victor Tarentino, who had spent half of his life on a patrolman's salary. Even now he probably did not have that much in the bank. The Mayor wondered how he could explain without offending him that twenty thousand dollars was not a lot of money to Paula Stapleton O'Connor. The rich are different, Fitzgerald told Hemingway, and Hemingway replied, "Yes, they have more money." Fitzgerald was right, but not completely right. He said that the rich were different because they possessed and enjoyed early, and this made them soft where we were hard. He was thinking about rich men. Rich women were different in another way. They did not use their money to satisfy their bodies. They used it to fill their souls.

With what? Self-satisfaction? *Be careful, Your Honor, be calm,* the Mayor told himself.

"If that gets out, Jake—and if a guy like Soyinka is blabbing it to a clown like McCoy, it's gonna get out—you better have one hell of a good story to cover it."

The Commissioner put away the tape recorder. "It may not be true. I hope it isn't. It may be twenty dollars, not twenty thousand," he said.

The Mayor found himself fingering one of his father's pens. How would Benny handle this one? At least Tarentino would not give that lecture this time. Benny was irrelevant to this problem. Or was he? Maybe he would jump into his car and roar up to Bowood and smack that dumb broad in the teeth. Maybe that was the way to handle her. It was the one thing he had not tried.

Calm down, the Mayor told himself. *Calm down. She is not a dumb broad. She is your wife. Your intelligent, well-meaning Wasp Queen.*

"Vic," he said. "I really appreciate your coming to me with this now. I'll handle it."

"Good."

Tarentino was avoiding his eyes. The Mayor got the message. He really meant good luck. *Good luck with handling that millionaire bitch you married to simplify your life.* All that money made it so easy to be honest. But now it looks like it will make it easy for you to become the world's biggest, dumbest loser.

"One more thing," Tarentino said. "When you're—uh—talking this over with Paula—tell her Dorothy Washington is hooked up with one of Donahue's family. This guy Andrew 77X. We think he's going to be the hit man if they're serious. Tell her not to fire Dorothy. We've got a nice tap on her phone."

"Is she dangerous?"

Tarentino shook his head. "He's been trying to get a plan of Bowood from her. But she won't give it to him. She's in love with him. And scared shitless of him. But she keeps saying no. So we can play it cool."

The Mayor nodded. He started to tell the Commissioner that there was nothing to worry about, he too was going to play it cool. But he had already made that clear. So he just nodded, realizing at the same time that he had no idea how he would act when he saw his beloved wife. He shoved his finger down hard on the intercom button and held it there until Helen Ganey's voice broke through the buzz.

"Yes, Your Honor?"

"Cancel my lunch with Bernie Bannon."

"Yes, Your Honor."

"And call my car."

13

From her study window Paula Stapleton stared at the gray drizzling February sky. It was less than a month to St. Patrick's Day. Less than a month to the formal announcement that Mayor O'Connor was a candidate for the U. S. Senate. On her desk were the latest reports from pollster Sam Tucker. They were not cheerful reading, in spite of the bright colors—yellow, green, fuchsia—on which they were printed. Voter fondness for Mayor O'Connor had declined as much as 20 per cent outside the city. Inside the city it was worse—a sickening 30 per cent drop.

Copies had been sent to Jake at City Hall. He had not mentioned them. Paula had no desire to bring up bad news. But something should be said or done to counteract the plunge. The memory of his strange passivity, the sullen fatalism that had cost him the governorship, haunted her. His rage the night that he had invoked the Internal Security Law on the North Slope had reawakened the memory of his blind drunken resentment when he had lost the gubernatorial primary. Perhaps his lunch today with Bernie Bannon would galvanize Jake. Sam Tucker thought Bannon still leaned toward him, in spite of the slippage in the polls.

It was strange how little self-confidence there was behind Jake's aura of competence and control. Very seldom was he willing to risk even a minor defeat. Beneath his smiling surface optimism there was a chasm of pessimism. He was always fearing the worst. He could not see that fearing the worst frequently made it happen. Any more than he could see that his absorption by the minutiae of city politics tended to exclude larger ideas, wider horizons.

Dorothy Washington interrupted these troubled thoughts with a dismaying announcement. "Mrs. O'Connor, I'm afraid I got to quit my job."

"Dorothy. Why?"

"It's a personal thing, Mrs. O'Connor."

"Does it have something to do with your boyfriend?"

Dorothy nodded, her doleful expression changing to a stricken look. "Andy wants me to do some things that —I don't want to do. So I'm going to tell him I got fired—"

"What sort of things?"

Dorothy shook her head. "I don't want to talk about it, Mrs. O'Connor. It could get me into a lot of trouble."

"Why don't you talk to the police about it? I'm sure I can arrange it with no trouble. A phone call to the Commissioner."

"No. No, please. I'm scared of Andy. If he thought I—"

There was an appalling silence. "What?" Paula said.

"I think he'd kill me or hurt me real bad."

"But the police—"

"The police can't stop someone like him. He's got power. He's got an evil eye on his side."

"Dorothy. You don't really believe in an evil eye."

"It isn't his. It belongs—to another man. A lot of people believe in him, Mrs. O'Connor."

"Well, I may insist on you talking to the police. I hate to do it, Dorothy, but it may be necessary. I'm going to speak to the Mayor about it. I hope you don't mind."

"I can't stop you."

Would she really talk to the Mayor? She knew what Jake would say. He had wanted to fire Dorothy the last time one of her boyfriends had caused trouble. He had backed his police commissioner, as usual.

Suddenly Jake was in the doorway. There was a

frown on his forehead. His mouth was a dour slash. Paula glanced at her watch. It was twelve-fifteen. "I thought you were having lunch with Bernie Bannon."

"I canceled."

He walked past her and Dorothy to the window. He stood there, glaring down at the empty lawn. "Get out of here, Dorothy. I want to talk to Mrs. O'Connor."

Dorothy closed the green cover of her steno book and fled. Paula stared uncomprehendingly at her husband's saturnine profile. "What in the world is the matter?"

"Let me see your checkbook."

"My checkbook?"

"Do you understand English? Or do you only hear what's mumbled through thick lips with a southern accent? The foundation checkbook."

All Paula could do was stare at him. The words were so atrocious, she was frightened, not angry.

"Why?"

"I'll tell you why after I go through it."

"Unless you tell me why, you won't go through it."

He was facing her now, glaring down at her with unbelievable ferocity on his face. "I'll go through it on my terms if I have to rip this goddamn room apart to find it. Where is it?"

"Are you drunk?"

"I wish I was. After I'm through with you, I think I'll get drunk for the next ten days. Give me that goddamn checkbook."

With trembling hands she opened the top drawer of her desk, pulled out the sky blue checkbook, and handed it to him. He sat down in an easy chair on the other side of the room and began paging through it.

"I have a one o'clock lunch date," she said. "It's that benefit for—"

"Cancel it."

"I will not."

"You will so. DOROTHY," he bellowed.

Dorothy Washington opened the door about halfway, and peered into the room, as if she was afraid she might be hit by a flying object. "Yes, Mister Mayor?"

"Cancel Mrs. O'Connor's lunch date. Say it's at the request of the Mayor. The usual apologies. Terribly sorry, and so forth."

For a moment Dorothy met Paula's eyes. Seeing only bewilderment and fear, she said, "Yes, Mister Mayor," and closed the door.

His Honor continued to go through the checkbook page by page, like an accountant. "Jesus Christ, you give a lot of money away to ridiculous people," he said.

Silence, for another five minutes. Slowly, anger began replacing fear in Paula's mind. Whatever had happened or was happening, she did not like it.

He stopped shuffling the pages. "Ah," he said. He glared at the page. "Here it is."

"Here's what?"

"Twenty thousand goddamn dollars to the Malcolm X Ujamaa."

"How—how do you know about it? It was—they promised me it would be confidential."

"Confidential even from me?"

"I meant to tell you about it. But so many things have happened. First I forgot. Then I thought it would be better—if you didn't know about it."

He stood up. "It would be better if I didn't know about it." He waved the checkbook back and forth. "It would be better if I didn't know about it. I'm your husband, and you give money to people who are destroying me. But it would be better if I didn't know about it."

Who did he remind her of? Senator Joe McCarthy. "I have a list here . . ." There was no real resemblance. This glowering brown-haired charm boy had no resemblance to that swarthy thug, except that they were both Irish.

"The time has come for us to decide who's running this show. The first thing we're going to do is figure out an explanation that you can give to the press when this thing reaches them. Which it inevitably will."

"What kind of explanation?"

"An explanation that will make you look like the dumb stupid bitch that you are."

"I will not make—"

"Don't argue with me. Just listen. For once in your goddamn life, listen to me."

"I will not listen when you talk this way! I'm not used to being treated with contempt."

"You'd better get used to it. Because you deserve it. You deserve every goddamn bit of contempt that I or any other intelligent adult can throw at you. Do you realize how long I've put up with this shit? Has it ever passed through your mind, how much time and effort I've devoted to keeping you happy for the last fourteen years? Or maybe just quiet? Trying to stop you from making a goddamn fool of yourself and me."

It was incredible, the hatred on his face. He almost seemed aware of it, because he kept turning his head away from her to glare out the window, then back again convulsively to fling these murderous words at her, as if he half wanted to conceal it.

Paula stood up and for a moment the room swirled. She willed herself not to faint, not to crumple before this crude onslaught. She would answer it as it deserved to be answered. "Has it ever occurred to *you*, how much resentment I have had to swallow, watching you do your third-rate cynic's act? If you're disgusted, Your Honor, let me assure you the feeling is mutual."

"Don't you think I know that? Do you think I'm blind or just stupid? I remember reading an article by some psychiatrist who said you can't hide anything in the bedroom. I never realized how true that was, until I married you. You're not a woman. You're a goddamn intellectual abstraction. Unless the other intellect for whom you happen to be spreading your legs meets your impossible standards, love is out of the question."

Hot involuntary tears rushed from Paula's eyes. She despised them. She told herself to ignore them. "That isn't true. It never was true. I loved you—I loved you more than I ever loved anyone or anything. And what have you done with it? You've destroyed it, day by day, week by week, month by month, year by year in this stupid city. Charming morons like Eddie McKenna, mediocrities like Dominick Montefiore."

That hurt. He strode up and down in front of the

window, groping for an answer. He did not expect this defiance. He thought she would collapse, weep, beg his towering forgiveness.

"This is really interesting," he said. "Fascinating. To discover the depths of your revulsion for me."

"I have no such feeling. I told you I loved you. I still do but—"

"But little Jake isn't performing the way he was programmed, isn't that it? You really did think, fifteen years ago, that you were buying me, didn't you? What a deal. The quick and easy route to political power, and a nice stud in the bargain. Is that how you saw the package, Miss Stapleton?"

"No. I told you—I told you I loved you."

"You never loved anything. Anything below the neck, anyway. You're all head, Miss Stapleton, and what's up there is so goddamn scrambled it isn't worth discussing. You consented to yield your precious virginity to me for one reason, and only one. You wanted power, you wanted it so badly you'd sell yourself for it. You were the one who was selling, Miss Stapleton, while you told yourself you were buying. Admit it."

"That's not true. That's not true in any way, shape, or form."

"Yes it is. It's the fucking goddamn explicit truth. Admit it."

He was roaring loud enough for every servant in the house to hear him. She turned her head away. She wanted to escape that face, those eyes so full of unspeakable hatred where there should be love, where there had been love, now denied by this primitive rage that was destroying everything, love, hope, all the words that made the future possible.

"Please stop talking to me as if you were in a barroom," she said.

"I will talk to you exactly the way I feel like talking to you. For once you're going to accept me as I really am. Not the intellectual fighter for causes that you tried to construct out of your non-idea of me. But me."

"I have been trying—to accept that person for a long time."

"Accept. You sound just like my brother Paul. That's your idea of love. Mental toleration. But you can't even do that, because you're always lying to yourself, justifying every rotten thing you do in the name of morality or charity or some other goddamn abstraction. Dolores is a good example. You name your daughter after a woman you hated, to prove you didn't hate her and then you treat the kid like a piece of shit."

"I do not treat my daughter like a piece of—shit," Paula said, almost choking on the word. "Do you know why I named her? Do you want to know? Because you've never stopped loving Dolores, I know that. I knew I was beaten in the bedroom game before I started. I wanted to hear you say her name to someone—who I thought would look like me. That's how much I wanted you to love me."

"Oh, perfect, perfect," said the rasping voice, as if she had never confessed this secret humiliation, this scarifying plea for his love. "Paula-the-martyr. Beautiful. That's how you really see yourself. What utter crap. It's the other way around, Miss Stapleton. You are willing to inflict any humiliation on your kids, on me, to satisfy your fucking, miserable Wasp standards. Excelsior. We're all supposed to rip our guts out, climbing that mountain, to the governorship, to the Senate, to schools where blacks beat our brains out while you cheer us on with your slogans. I wasn't a third-rate cynic when I married you. I knew the score, that makes anyone a little cynical. But I really believed that someone like you and your uncle and all the rest of you snobs had something to contribute to this society. To me. I guess I was still, when you get down to it, the immigrant Mick, who thought he was finally being allowed to enter the holy of holies, the inner sanctum of America the Beautiful. I was going to sit at the feet of the elect. And what did I find in this marvelous inner room? Goddamn screwballs wallowing in guilt, like you. Or flint-faced bastards like your old man, who couldn't care less about another human being. Or snobs like the Judge who think the whole world ought to bow down and kiss their goddamn blue-blooded asses, because they've won a couple of medals and had some ancestors on the *Mayflower* or in George Washington's army. That about accounts for your whole family."

"Let me tell you what I found. Will you listen? Will you listen for just one minute?"

"Sure, I'll listen."

"I thought I'd found someone who really cared about this country. About this city. About all the people in it. Someone who could think about people and problems in a new way. Instead I found a fraud. A walking, talking, smiling fraud. Behind his gift for words, that marvelous instant charm, there was nothing. No ideas, no convictions, nothing but a kind of crude instinct for survival on any terms. A cynic who knew every man had his price, because he'd already sold himself to this woman he didn't really love."

"Not true. So help me Christ, not true."

"Let me finish. Sold himself to this woman he didn't really love. In fact, he really despised everything about her, except her open checkbook. Why not, he thought, why not do it the easy way? That was the only thing he'd really learned from his Irish inheritance. Do it the easy way, cut the corners, kid everybody along and hope for the best. And all the time, tell yourself you're a marvelous improvement on your father because you don't steal. You know why? I don't think you've got the guts."

Oh, Paula. Look at those eyes. She had reached him this time. Fury in those eyes. Those clenched fists wanted to smash her face. This was the true primitive striding toward her now, roaring, "Maybe I'll start to steal. Maybe I'll start to fuck everything that's walking in this city. Maybe I'll start to do a lot of things that I've been tempted to do. Not because I want either the money or the broads. I just want to see you reach for your smelling salts, watch you squirm, or at least imagine you squirm, when you go visit the Judge or your starched out aunt or your faggot cousins. I want to do it just because you don't want me to do it. See how much you've screwed up my head?"

He was only a foot away from her now. Any

moment she was sure one of those big fists would smash her face. She welcomed it. She would prefer physical pain instead of more battering annihilating words. But the words kept coming.

"As for me having no ideas, who built City Hall Plaza, who brought industry back into this crummy town, who's built ten new public schools, who ran the Mafia out of here, who's held the goddamn place *together* for the last ten years? You think it's easy, going down there every day and keeping all those animals in their cages? You can call them morons and mediocrities. I've got to keep them happy or they can take me apart. But you don't see anything worth admiring in that. No, it's just my crude instinct for survival. Can't you get it through your fucking head that survival is what this business is all about? What good am I if I don't survive? What can a politician do without any power? What does he do with the rest of his life?"

He spun away and strode back to the window. For a flickering moment she thought she saw why this horror was happening. All he had to do was stop, reach out for her, she would understand. Instead, the words kept coming, colder, harder, more vicious.

"As usual, you've turned the real situation inside out. You're the one with no ideas. We're involved in one of the greatest crises in the history of this city and you don't bother to tell your husband, who happens to be the Mayor, that you're stabbing him in the back, you're undermining his whole political position, you're giving extremists the ammunition they need to burn the city down. You call that thinking?"

"I call it trying to be just, trying to be honest to—our original commitment."

"Oh. That's beautiful. Really beautiful. Our original commitment. Tell me a little more about that, will you please? What was our original commitment? To follow through on the Emancipation Proclamation? Or to make this city a place where people can live with pride and self-respect? For your information, I represent that self-respect. I'm the voice of the people who came out of those goddamn nightmarish slums your great-grandfather and his friends built, I'm the person who can speak for the people who survived that ordeal. But you don't want to listen to me. That would mean you'd have to admit that once upon a time the Stapletons were less than perfect, that in fact they were the biggest bunch of bastards that ever lived, and that includes all the Simon Legrees south of the Mason-Dixon line. You don't want to hear that, do you? You'd rather get rid of me. You keep someone like Dorothy Washington around, even though she's playing games with some nut who wants to kill me. You knew that, didn't you? I can see it on your face. You'd love an opportunity to play the local Jackie Kennedy. Only one thing I can't figure out, who you'll marry. Ray Grimes? Some shithead like that, somebody you could really dominate. On second thought, you wouldn't marry anybody. You'd be so happy to be out of that bedroom scene, you'd play the grief-stricken widow for life."

"Stop it Jake, I don't want anyone to hurt you."

No tears this time. Just pain, or was it genuine hysteria in her voice? She could not stand this brawling much longer. She loathed it. He loved it. He thrived on hatred.

"No, you don't want to hurt me. You just want to turn me into a has-been at forty-nine. That isn't supposed to hurt. Because it's for such a good cause. Getting black kids who lip-read at the fifth grade level into Buchanan High School where they lip-read at the sixth grade level."

"You're so full of hate, Jake. For me. The blacks."

"There you go again with the old switcheroo. Because I don't feel guilty about them, because my guts don't turn to mush every time I see a black face, I hate them. Did it ever occur to you that I've got a sense of history, just as much as you've got a sense of history? You goddamn Wasps think you own this country's history. Well, I've got news for you. You don't own anything but your rotten, stinking money. My history and your history are two different things. Maybe that's the whole story of this marriage. While your grandfather was prancing around this goddamn mansion, my grandfather was living in the basement of a First Ward tenement with no running water and a toilet in the backyard that the whole tenement used, and the shit ran right under his floorboards. You show me any black family in this city that's living the way the Irish lived when they first came here. It's all in your great-granduncle Mortimer's journal. But you haven't read a line of it. You don't want to think about it. You're too busy bleeding over your favorite failures, swallowing their bleats about the debt we owe them. Maybe Charleston, South Carolina, owes them something, but we sure as hell don't. If anyone has any back pay coming to them around here, it's the Irish and the Italians and the Poles."

She was glad that he had talked so long that she had a chance to control her hysteria, and find her anger again. Anger at his insufferable arrogance and ignorance, masquerading as historical knowledge. "You have nothing to expiate?" she said. "You and your kind, as the saying goes. If we are going to treat each other as representatives of ethnic groups, instead of individual human beings, I think you have plenty to expiate. Your grandfather may have only gotten a dollar a day on the loading platform—from what I've heard you say about him in less guarded moments that may have been all he was worth—but your father and his friends did a lot better. They looted this city for thirty years. In fact, your own dear kind were stealing everything they could grab for thirty years before that but your grandfather was too dumb to get any of it. They weren't all living in basement tenements, if what my father has told me has any validity at all."

"Which I doubt."

"That's your privilege. But I notice that you're not denying the thirty years you know about."

"What the hell are you trying to say? My father had exactly forty-six hundred dollars in the bank when he died. If that's looting, then your old man is on a par with Genghis Khan and don't tell me Daddy made his money honestly. He and his father made it by wrecking unions, bribing safety inspectors, sweating women and ten-year-old kids twelve hours a day. Sometimes I hate to think of my kids inheriting your goddamn money. It's got to be tainted. It can't bring them any luck."

"Is that why you want to break up this marriage? I didn't realize you were prey to idiotic superstitions like that."

"I didn't want to break up this marriage. But now that it's happening, so help me Christ, I'm going to get those kids away from you. You're not going to raise them, if I have to take it to the Supreme Court and bribe a thousand witnesses to prove what you really are, a neurotic bitch who gets her kicks out of making other people miserable."

"I won't say names can never hurt me. They can. But at least they prove you're losing this argument."

"I'm not losing it, because I'm not trying to win it. I have nothing to defend. You are the one who has committed the blunder of the year, with your magic checkbook."

Instinctively she pleaded guilty. But she would not admit it. She would not admit anything to this Irish son of a bitch. The tears were coming, the damn tears again. But she was speaking through them. "Do you know what you are? A sadist. A petty, sneaky, cowardly sadist, who never misses and never has missed a chance to hurt me, to laugh at me, to humiliate me in private and before my children and other people, including my own family. Never missed a chance. Because you thought I didn't have the courage to fight back. Because I was a woman and—practically an old maid when you married me. I was supposed to be so damn grateful to get the greatest stud in town. Well, let me tell you, although I haven't slept around and can't speak from experience, you aren't that great, even in the bedroom, Mr. O'Connor. There, like everywhere else, you take yourself for granted and expect someone else to do the work."

Not true, not a word of it. But what did the truth matter now? All she wanted to do was hurt him. Hurt him as much as he had hurt her.

"But that isn't the main point. My real point, my damn point in spite of these tears is this—you can't forgive me because I have fought back, because I haven't bowed down before the myth of Jake the Incomparable O'Connor. And I won't. I never will bow down. If I have nothing else, I have some pride, some confidence in the integrity of my own mind, my own conscience. And I begin to see—I'm afraid I begin to see that I'd better get away from you—far away from you—because you're trying to destroy that, along with everything else. You can't tolerate integrity, Jake."

"You bitch. You believe that, don't you? You're just like your uncle. Inside you've never changed. You're still a goddamn cold-blooded scheming, lying, self-righteous snob."

Paula sat down in a wing chair, half turning away from him. The rage, the pain on his face were too painful to see. She had done it. She had hurt him as much as he had hurt her. Perhaps more. Why didn't she feel exultant? Why this enormous draining sadness? Was it possible that a mere half hour ago she had felt calm and refreshed by her first good night's sleep in a week? It would be her last good sleep for a year, perhaps forever.

"I don't think there's anything more to say."

"No, I guess there isn't."

Was there regret in his voice, the same kind of hopelessness she was feeling? No, just heavy sarcasm. "I'll leave you alone, with your integrity."

The door slammed. There was no longer any reason to fight the tears. She let them fall and fall.

14

"Daddy," Dolores Talbot O'Connor asked, a furrow in her small brow, "when is Mommy coming home for good?"

"Yeah, when?" asked Kemble Stapleton O'Connor, spraying a half dozen cornflakes off his spoon.

"I don't know," the Mayor said. "Ask her when you go to see her this weekend."

"I don't like the farm," Dolores said. "There's nothing out there but a lot of old people."

"I thought you liked the horses," the Mayor said.

"They're fun," Kemble said. "But it's been raining a lot and when we can't ride we're stuck in the house. We can't make any noise. Uncle Paul says he has to concentrate."

"Uncle Paul is a grouch," Dolores said.

"School would be better, if we stayed out there," Kemble said. "We wouldn't have any nig—I mean black kids. But it isn't so bad downtown now."

"Because you've got more white kids?"

"Yeah. And because now the teachers talk about how important it is for white kids and black kids to get along. I mean, if we don't learn to be friends, the whole country is going to be ruined, right?"

"Right," the Mayor said.

Looking into his son's small earnest face, he saw his wife's idealism. Was it such a bad thing, as long as it did not become all or nothing fanaticism? The Mayor was not sure of the answer. He was not sure of very much these days. But he found himself wondering with unexpected intensity what his son would think about him ten years from now. Would he sit in judgment on his pragmatism as he had judged Ben O'Connor? Would Kemble have to struggle with a similar mixture of revulsion and love? And choke on the answer—the half-wish half-truth that there was no other alternative for a realistic man?

"Do you have any black friends yet?"

"A couple. The kid I sit next to is okay."

"No fights any more?"

"A couple of big kids had a fight the other day. But the teachers broke it up. We got together in the auditorium and talked about why it had happened. Then the principal lined up the white kids and the black kids on opposite sides of the auditorium. One by one, half the black kids and half the white kids changed places. Then we shook hands and went back to class."

"That principal sound like she knows how to run a school."

"We like her."

The Mayor finished his coffee, kissed his children, and departed for City Hall. *Three weeks,* he thought as he got into his limousine. Exactly three weeks since the explosion. It was ironic. The city had remained more or less calm, in spite of the sputtering black dynamite downtown and the bubbling white nitroglycerin uptown. An occasional rock had sailed off a North Slope roof to thunk against a school bus or if the thrower was lucky, smash a window. There had been no major violence.

The Mayor took a piece of expensive blue stationery out of his pocket and fingered it indecisively. The initials, PSOC, were engraved at the top in elegantly interwoven script. For three weeks he had been carrying it to City Hall and back to Bowood as if it were a relic. He had received it from a solemn Mahoney when he returned to Bowood on the evening of the brawl. Still seething, he had been ready to renew hostilities. But his opponent had vanished. She had abandoned her sword and buckler. There was nothing to confront but the blue stationery with the scrawled words of mutual defeat.

Dear Jake. I am as appalled by what I said today as by what you said. It seems clear that we no longer love each other—if we ever did. I don't know what to do about it. I am going out to the farm for a few days to think it over.

Paula.

The Mayor stuffed the letter back in his pocket. He had written a half dozen replies and torn them all up. They sounded either too truculent or too apologetic. At one point he contemplated sending her a tape from his dictating machine. A calm, conversational tone. Perhaps even a joke or two. But a few experimental sentences convinced him that there was no point in talking to a machine. The telephone was equally impersonal. If anything was to be salvaged, which the Mayor gloomily doubted, he had to see her face to face.

There would be no point in meeting at the farm. Judge Stapleton would be a frowning presence, in spirit if not in the flesh. He had to see her alone. But was that possible? Would they ever be alone again? History had surrounded them with an army of ghosts and his Irish temper had released them from the subconscious dungeon in which they had been surreptitiously confined.

Every time the Mayor thought about his performance, he was engulfed by despair. He had reverted to type. He had succumbed to atavism. Night after night he lay awake thinking about it, hearing not only his own snarling voice but the roar of his father's verbal assaults on his mother. He heard her screaming hysterics, his brother Paul's tearful pleas. He remembered the night Paul had gotten down on his knees before his father and begged him to stop, as if Ben O'Connor were some enraged deity. It was like trying to persuade a hurricane.

In City Hall, an anxious Simon Burke had persuaded Charlie LoBello to put him first on the morning line. Simon had sent him a half dozen messages in the past three weeks, begging the Mayor to get him that material from his father's papers to dramatize Ben O'Connor's old Thirteenth Ward for the bicentennial exhibit. As the Mayor expected, Simon brought a last frantic request. The Mayor sighed and told him to skip it. The papers were piled on the desk in Bowood's library. But he could not force himself to look through them. He did not know why.

"Maybe it isn't worth remembering, Simon," the Mayor said.

Simon nodded dutifully. Aside from his instinctive obedience to dictums from City Hall, he was inclined to agree with that assessment.

The Mayor asked him how the exhibit was coming along, otherwise.

"It will be spectacular," Simon said. "Miss Stapleton —Allyn—is a tremendously creative person."

"Among other things. She's got Charlie LoBello worn down to his knees. Are you getting any, Simon?"

The pain on Simon's face made the Mayor regret the joke. "I am—aware of her private life, Your Honor."

Three weeks ago, the Mayor would have tried to straighten him out by calling Allyn a cunt and Simon a fool. Now he said: "I'm sorry, Simon. I didn't realize that would hurt."

Simon nodded sadly. "I'll recover eventually. It's not the first time I've fallen in love with someone like her. She's the really hurt one. I wish I could comfort her."

She's the hurt one. The Mayor found himself wondering if those words could also be used to describe his wife. He knew how badly he was hurt. He was an ambulatory wound case, a political, emotional, mental zombie. For the last three weeks he had been sleepwalking through his days and staring away his nights. Was Paula hurt? He almost wanted to believe it. But it was an act of faith that was beyond him.

"If half of what she tells me about the Stapletons is true, I'm glad I'm poor," Simon said.

The Mayor declined to discuss the Stapletons. Simon Burke departed. Next in line were Bernie Bannon and Sam Tucker. Bernie had used Sam to batter down the door. St. Patrick's Day was only two days off. Bernie desperately wanted to stop the Mayor from announcing his candidacy at the city's annual dinner. The Mayor knew what Bannon was going to say. One by one, the labor barons and the county leaders and the state legislators who had guaranteed Jake O'Connor their support were withdrawing behind a barrage of ifs and buts. Most of the ammunition had been supplied by Bernie. He was trying to maneuver the Mayor into a position where he would have to surrender without a primary fight. Bernie would flourish Sam's polls to justify himself and his strategy.

The Mayor struggled to revive, if only for a few minutes, his combative self. He knew that he could not handle Bernie without a fight. Playing the charm boy or the statesman was not going to impress him any more than an appeal to old friendship. The Mayor listened, fiddling with his pens, lighting a cigarette and stubbing it out, while Bernie produced the expected analysis and kiss-off. "Forget about the Senate. A year from now, the governorship will be wide open, Jake. I promise you—"

"You promised me this one, Bernie. Why should I believe you the next time around?"

"Jake—we're trying to be realistic."

"Tell me something, Sam. What would happen if I announced I was forced out of the race because of the busing issue?"

Sam's eyes widened with disbelief. "It would move the blacks and the liberals right out of the party. It would change the whole race."

"You wouldn't do that to me, Jake. You wouldn't do that to an old friend," Bernie Bannon said.

"I'd hate to do it to you, Bernie. But if that's what I've got to threaten you with, to make you stick, maybe we're not so friendly anymore. The way I see it, Bernie, you're like a banker who's loaned a guy a million dollars. He's got you by the balls as much as you've got him."

"Okay, Jake. I'll deal. What do you want for a nice sensible withdrawal? More state aid? A slice of the state payroll? A lot depends on whether we get the governorship next year."

"I don't want to deal, Bernie. I want to play out the hand."

Bannon sighed and shook his head. The Mayor wondered if he caught the hint of a plea in those last words. He was fighting but his heart wasn't in it. Three weeks ago, in this situation, his adrenaline would be pumping at triple speed by now. He would have had Bernie on the ropes, begging him to let him make a public endorsement today.

Did she, did that goddamn woman sitting out there in snob acres, that woman he apparently both loved and hated, have his heart? No, that was unthinkable, she could not walk off with that vital organ. He refused to permit that to happen. A man who ate and slept power all his life would not let anyone steal something that important from him. Especially a woman. That had been what he had been trying to prevent since the start of this ruinous marriage. It meant powerlessness, disaster.

Bernie Bannon was talking tough, sensing he might regain enough momentum to return for a few more rounds tomorrow or the next day. "It looks more and more like the other guys are going to dump our sitting duck and give the nomination to some liberal Republican like the Governor, who never even went sightseeing in Washington while Nixon was there. Can you do this job and run an all-out campaign? That's what it'll take with this monkey you've got on your back. Right, Sam?"

Tucker's head bobbed. He was obviously doing a lot of polling for the Democratic State Committee.

"I can do both jobs," the Mayor said.

The weariness in his voice made the words an instant lie.

"We can't get you on the telephone, we can't see you now, when we call twice a week. What's it going to be like when we need you ten times a day?"

"We'll work it out, Bernie. Once we've got this busing thing under control—"

He had been using the busing crisis as an excuse to stall on everything from union negotiations to judgeships. Behind his neutral stance he had let the busing disputants assail Judge Stapleton with a barrage of motions and countermotions. Some people thought he supported Adam Turner's demand for federal marshals and an FBI investigation of RIP. Others suspected him of backing RIP's suit to silence Adam by court order for making racist speeches. Only his immediate staff knew that His Honor spent most of each day staring dully out the window.

"Paula. We can't get to her either, Jake," Sam Tucker said. "I've called her four times."

"She's got a bad case of nerves, Sam. I sent her out to her uncle's farm for a few days."

Sam Tucker loved political gossip. He left with his nose twitching. Bernie Bannon hoped the St. Patrick's Society speech was going to be a zinger. Did the Mayor have a copy? It might help to circulate it in advance. The Mayor said they were still working on it. That was better than admitting that he had not even read the early drafts Dave O'Brien had put on his desk. Bernie left looking grim. He had only begun to fight.

Next came the man with thom the Mayor spent most of his time these days: Victor Tarentino. He was really running the city. It was only a matter of time before he realized it. He still cleared all his decisions with the Mayor. But each day he came on a little stronger with his suggestions for solving the busing crisis and rescuing the Senate candidacy. Today he wasted no time getting to the point.

"Jake, you've got to go to work on Turner and get him to agree to petition the court to withdraw the buses from Buchanan."

Next came a litany of evidence that the North Slope was very close to an explosion. There had been three more attacks on policemen during the past twenty-four hours. Someone had thrown a garbage can off a roof, smashing the windshield of a patrol car. Another cop had suffered a sprained back when he chased a bunch of teen-agers into the basement of a flat and discovered too late that the steps had been covered with auto grease. More vicious was an attempt to lure two motorcycle cops down a twilit street across which a two-inch-thick wire had been strung at waist level. "An off-duty cop can't even go into a bar on the Slope these days," Tarentino said. "Old friends won't talk to him. It's tearing some of them apart."

They discussed the latest violence between blacks and whites inside Buchanan High School. Yesterday, a sixteen-year-old black boy had been hit on the head with an iron pipe as he emerged from a cloakroom. He was in "guarded" condition at the Medical Center with a fractured skull. The day before, a white girl had suffered a torn retina in a scuffle with a half dozen black girls.

"The pipe is a bad sign, Jake. That's a weapon. We've got to start frisking them at the door."

"Vic, this is a high school, not a penitentiary."

"My informants inside RIP tell me they're just waiting for one incident. One serious incident. They're ready to tear the school apart. I'm not sure I could guarantee the safety of a black kid anywhere on the North Slope."

"I still can't see a frisk, Vic. You can't really search seven hundred kids every morning."

"It's a deterrent, Jake, that's all."

"It's a last resort in my book."

"Paula's still calling the shots?"

"What the hell do you mean by that?"

Tarentino shrugged. "Just a little deduction. Grimes and his fellow fags were against a frisk from the start. They're her spokesmen on most things."

"There are lots of spokesmen in this administration, Vic. But I make the decisions. Because a few local hoods are acting up, I can't see turning every white kid in Buchanan High School against us."

"We've already done that," Tarentino said.

Behind his truculence the Mayor knew that Tarentino was right. His refusal to approve a general frisk was a futile gesture of agreement with his wife. Because it was futile, because his police commissioner recognized it, the Mayor felt rage and self-disgust stir in him. He found it hard to believe what was happening to him. The image of himself as a political athlete moving gracefully through a broken field, with just the right amount of speed and force, deception and determination, was gone. It had been replaced by a more classic image. Old

Sisyphus, trying to push a boulder up a slippery slope, while a chorus of advisors gave him bad advice. Leading the chorus, even in absentia, was Paula Stapleton.

"Where is Paula these days? I was surprised I didn't see her at the Anti-Defamation League luncheon," Commissioner Tarentino said.

"She's staying out at her uncle's farm for a couple of weeks. This situation has really wrung her out."

The Commissioner nodded. He accepted the explanation. Maybe it even reassured him that old Jake had not lost all his political marbles. At least he's gotten his big-mouth liberal wife out of town. No doubt he assumed that the chief reason was to put her beyond the reach of reporters like Mulligan, when and if they broke the story about her twenty-thousand-dollar donation to the busing program. Should he tell Tarentino that story was true? No, let him keep guessing. *Never tell anyone too much.*

"Is everything okay between you and Paula?" the Commissioner asked. "I've heard a few rumors. That butler you've got at Bowood, Mahoney, has a big mouth."

The Mayor shuffled papers on his desk. "I don't want to talk about it, Vic, it's too complicated."

The double oak doors leading to the outer office suddenly burst open. Charlie LoBello came charging at them like a runaway diesel engine. "Commissioner. Police headquarters. May Day at Buchanan."

Phone number five was flashing. The Mayor handed it to Tarentino. He listened, his face expressionless. "How many?" he asked. He listened again. "Send the whole tactical patrol," he said. "Start pulling together another five-hundred-man reserve from the precincts."

He hung up. "A black kid just stabbed a white kid at Buchanan. The white kids have all left the school. The whole goddamn North Slope is in the streets. RIP has got people with bullhorns on every block."

The Mayor saw Marie McKenna shaking her finger at him: *Just let one kid get stabbed by one of them boogies with their knives and you're gonna need the National Guard up here.*

"Can the tacs stop them if they try to storm the building?" the Mayor asked.

"I think so."

"Are you sure? If you've got even a twenty-five per cent doubt, I'll call the Governor and ask for the National Guard right now."

"They can do it. Buchanan's only got four doors and the first-floor windows are too high to climb through."

"What if they've got ladders?"

"They won't get that close to the building. Our plan is to hold the iron fence. It's spiked all around, which makes it damn hard to climb."

"You can do it without guns? Just clubs and tear gas?"

"Yes," Tarentino said.

"Okay," the Mayor said, realizing for the first time that he had his hand on the telephone. "How do we get those black kids out of that school?"

"A lot depends on the size of the crowd. We'd better go down to my office, where we've got some decent communications."

They raced through the City Hall's huge glass-walled lobby into the March sunshine. A reporter saw them and yelled, "Hey, what's going on?" They ignored him and reached the curb as the Mayor's limousine braked to a stop. A three-minute ride with the siren howling and they were at the door of the barrel-roofed fieldstone police headquarters. In the Commissioner's office they made radio contact with the man in command at Buchanan, a lieutenant named Mike Reardon.

"We're inside the buildin', Commissioner," Reardon said. "There's gotta be four thousand people out there. They'd swamp us if we stayed at the fence. We can hold the stairways, I think. But I'm worried about fire bombs through the first-floor windows."

"Any sign of the tactical patrol?"

"Not yet. I'm glad to hear they're on their way. But I think we're gonna need the Hunnert and First Airborne to get these kids outta here."

"We'll get them if we need them, Mike," the Mayor said. "This is Jake O'Connor. Where are the kids?"

"In the auditorium, Mayor. They're okay. We got the one who stabbed the Finch kid. He says it was self-defense. We found a pair of brass knuckles in the Finch kid's pocket."

"How is he?"

"We're keepin' him quiet. Waitin' for the ambulance. He ain't bleedin' too much. But it's a stomach cut. He could be in bad shape inside."

Tarentino got the tactical patrol buses on the radio and learned they were being forced to inch up the North Slope. People were blocking the street with trash cans, old cars, even their bodies, refusing to move until the lead bus almost rolled over them. The Commissioner called the Medical Center and found that an ambulance had just been dispatched to Buchanan. Studying his map of the city, he told the hospital to order the driver to come downtown and take the westernmost street up the North Slope. He got back on the radio to the tactical patrol buses and told them to go down a side street, wait for the ambulance, and follow it to Buchanan. It worked. In ten minutes a relieved Lieutenant Reardon was reporting that the ambulance and six buses were pulling into Tipperary Square. The wounded teen-ager was carried to the ambulance, which went clanging back to the Medical Center. Beefy Joe McNamara, the captain in command of the tactical patrol, urged the crowd to disperse. He was answered by a barrage of rocks and rotten fruit. A RIP partisan with a bullhorn began leading a chant, "WE WANT NIGGER BLOOD. WE WANT NIGGER BLOOD."

They could hear these words over McNamara's walkie-talkie as he reported in a dour voice that the situation looked grim. "We can clear Tipperary Square with gas and clubs, Commissioner," McNamara said, "but there ain't no way you're gonna get them school buses up the Slope. If we spread our guys too thin, they can take us apart. Two or three cops on a corner ain't gonna stop sixty or a hundred or two hundred people with rocks in their hands."

The direct line from City Hall rang. Charlie LoBello reported that CPI Director Ray Grimes and Councilman Adam Turner were outside the Mayor's office. Charlie said they were in a highly emotional state.

"Tell them to get over here. Police headquarters."

The Mayor placed a call to Eddie McKenna. His wife, Marie, said he was still in bed. "At ten-thirty?" the Mayor said. "No wonder he's going broke. Get him up."

"What the hell's going on, Jake?" a groggy McKenna growled.

The Mayor told him. "Eddie," he said, "I want you to go up there to Buchanan with me and talk those people into going home."

"Anybody who tries that is gonna get his teeth down his throat."

"Don't be ridiculous, Eddie. We've got to stop this thing before it spreads to the rest of the city."

"Let it," Eddie said. "Maybe them boogies will finally learn a lesson. Maybe you'll finally learn a lesson, Jake."

"Eddie, this isn't a request. It's an order. You get the hell over to that school or we're through."

"I think we've been through for quite a while, Jake, but neither of us knew it."

The Mayor slammed down the phone. *If only Paula could have seen that performance,* he thought. Her husband just kissed a hundred and fifty thousand votes good-by.

"Take it easy, Jake," Tarentino said. "You're not serious about going up there to talk to those people, are you? You got away with that visit to the ujamaa in Bayshore. You can't be that lucky twice."

"If I can't talk to those people I should get out of politics."

"Jake, they're crazy. They've been driven crazy. You didn't do it. I won't let you risk your life. You're too important to this goddamn city. I can't protect you in a mob."

"I don't want to be protected. I mean what I just said. If I've got to be protected from my own people, the kind of people my father worked with all his life, the kind of people I grew up with, I'm in the wrong job."

The Commissioner's secretary announced over the intercom that Councilman Adam Turner and Ray Grimes had arrived. Grimes was shouting as he came through the door. "What the hell are you doing down here behind a desk when black children are being massacred?"

For a moment the Mayor thought he was yelling at him. But Grimes was glaring at Commissioner Tarentino. "He's doing his job, Ray. This is where he can do the most good," the Mayor said.

"Have you called out the National Guard, Jake?" Adam Turner asked. Compared to Grimes, he was cool.

"No. We've got two hundred tactical patrols around the building. The kids are safe for the time being. The problem is how to get them out of there."

"I say use machine guns, bombs. Show these people you mean business," Grimes said.

"Now, wait a minute, Ray," the Mayor said. "Remember, a black kid stabbed a white kid."

"In self-defense, I'm sure," Grimes raged. "What about the black boy in the Medical Center with the fractured skull?"

"You're gonna need five thousand cops down in the ghetto, Jake, if you don't get those kids out of there in the next hour or two," Adam Turner said. "Every black man and woman in this city is gonna come up that slope to save those kids."

"They won't get there in time."

"I know it. I'm telling everybody in my organization to cool it. I've got all my people on the streets trying to hold them back."

"Maybe you shouldn't hold them back," Ray Grimes said. "Maybe it's time everybody in this city, in this country, found out that black people aren't going to take any more shit. Even if those hundred and twenty-five kids die, a lot more whites will die with them."

For a moment the Mayor thought he was dreaming. Ray Grimes, the voice of racial peace at any price, was calling for civil war.

"Nobody's going to die if I can help it, Ray. I'm going up there in a police helicopter. I want you to come with me. We can land on Buchanan's roof, and go down in the street to talk to these people."

"What the hell are you trying to do, Jake, get rid of me?"

"It would be very dangerous, Jake," Commissioner Tarentino said in his official voice. He obviously did not want to embarrass the Mayor by calling him a damn fool.

"I'll go with you," Adam Turner said. "I put those kids in that school. The least I can do is risk my ass to get them out."

The Mayor thought about it for a moment. "It might help. You might be able to talk turkey to them better than anyone, including me."

"You're both being absurd," Ray Grimes said. "Adam, the black people in this city need your leadership. You can't be a leader if you get your head busted. The same thing applies to you, Jake. You're not exercising any leadership or responsibility going up there to talk to a bunch of mad dogs. If you want to do your job, call the Governor and ask for the National Guard. That would be real responsibility."

"We don't have time to call out the Guard. That takes five or six hours. Adam's people aren't going to wait that long. The mob in front of the school may not wait another ten minutes."

Tarentino picked up the phone. "I want a police helicopter on the City Hall pad in five minutes," he said.

The helicopter was waiting for them. The pilot, Police Sergeant Charlie Morgan was a husky black with a trim mustache. As they buckled themselves into their seats, Adam said, "Brother, I hope you fly this damn thing better than you shoot pool."

Shouting above the motor's roar, Adam explained that he and Charlie were old snooker buddies.

They took off. Adam grabbed his somersaulting stomach. "Jesus," he yelled. "I never thought I'd do a thing like this for a hundred and twenty-five cats who can't even vote."

"Think of the mothers and fathers, uncles and cousins, Adam," the Mayor shouted back.

"It won't do any good. If we pull it off you'll claim it was your idea and I was just your boy."

"Ray Grimes will claim we were both his boys."

"Maybe you're right. Ray doesn't have a hell of a lot of guts, does he?"

"I wish you'd stop hanging around with that asshole. He's strictly little league material."

"Can't hit a curve?"

"Or throw one."

They were high enough to see the whole city now, in all its massive ugliness, gleaming dully in the winter sun. "Jesus, it's old," Adam said.

"Look at that crowd," the Mayor said.

It was awesome. Tipperary Square and the four side streets leading into it were jammed with people. A brown and gray and blue coated mass of humanity in restless motion, churning like they were being stirred by some giant invisible beater. The Mayor ordered Charlie Morgan to approach the school from the rear, where the streets were relatively empty.

Morgan nodded, banked sharply to make a wide swift semicircle, and set them down on the roof with professional precision. Captain McNamara opened the door of a kiosk in the center of the roof and beckoned them inside. As the helicopter soared into the blue sky again, they could hear a rumble of anger from the crowd. They descended to the first floor and McNamara led them to a classroom where he had set up a command post. The windows overlooked the square. MacNamara's tactical policemen lined the seven-foot-high iron fence. They looked like visitors from another planet or some future century, with their dark blue padded jackets, white helmets, and plexiglass visors. On their left arms were round black bamboo shields which Commissioner Tarentino had acquired from the Tokyo police department. In their right hands were extra-length billy clubs. They stood a half dozen feet behind the fence. The mob pressed against the iron bars, shouting questions, insults, comments at them.

"One way or another," Joe McNamara said, "we gotta get them to go home."

"If we use nightsticks and gas, a black man won't be able to show his face up here for the next ten years," the Mayor said.

McNamara nodded. "And you'll need the whole tactical patrol to get them kids to this school each morning."

"I hope you've got bullhorns we can use."

"Sure."

Adam Turner had been studying the crowd while they talked. "They don't seem—like mad, you know what I mean?"

"They're mad, take my word for it," McNamara said. "Wait till you hear a few of their chants."

A half dozen bullhorns began bellowing: "WE WANT NIGGER BLOOD. WE WANT NIGGER BLOOD." The crowd took up the chant, four or five thousand voices shouting this obscene thing. The sound rumbled against the building.

"How's the Finch kid? Have you got a report from the hospital?" McNamara asked.

The Mayor got on the radio to Tarentino, who was back with good news in five minutes. "He's on the operating table right now. They don't think it's too bad. The blade perforated the stomach wall, but it didn't hit anything like the liver or the pancreas."

The Mayor nodded. "Let's go see your—the kids, Adam."

A small slip, but it made him think, sadly, how much he was a part of his divided city. Black kids were his, white kids were ours. It was wrong.

The kids were sitting in the center of the auditorium. The Mayor was struck by how much more neatly they were dressed than the class he had visited in George Washington High School in Bayshore. They did not seem particularly impressed to see the Mayor and Councilman Turner. The Mayor told them he was sure they would be going home soon. He and the councilman were going to talk to the crowd outside, and tell them that the boy who was stabbed was in no danger. Once the crowd dispersed, the buses would arrive to take them downtown.

"What if they don't go 'way, Mister Mayor? We gonna hafta stay here all night?" one older boy asked.

"No," the Mayor said. "I guarantee that you'll be home before dark."

"You just leave it to the Mayor and old Uncle Adam, we'll cool them cats," Adam Turner said.

The Mayor thought they looked dubious. They had been on the receiving end of this business for six weeks now.

Out in the hall, McNamara waited for them with two bullhorns. "Here's the equipment," he said. "I brought along a coupla helmets and some shields, in case you—"

"No," the Mayor said.

"That'd ruin the act," Adam agreed. "We got to look like we expect applause, not rocks and bottles."

They walked down a stairway lined with helmeted shield-bearing cops, their plexiglass visors up. The Mayor said hello to several faces he recognized.

"I'll talk first," he told Adam as McNamara opened the double doors and they walked out on the red-brick landing at the top of the stone steps. The crowd had stopped chanting. A rumble of recognition swept across it, like a gust of wind on a sultry day. The Mayor raised the bullhorn to his lips. "My friends," he said, "I don't have to introduce myself to you. I'm here to ask your help, your trust. A terrible thing happened inside this school today. But it won't make this city a better place to live, if your answer is revenge. The boy that was stabbed—"

A half dozen bullhorns in the crowd destroyed the rest of the news about Jimmy Finch. "O'CONNUH'S GOTTA GO. O'CONNUH'S GOTTA GO," they chanted. "NIGGER LOVERS GOTTA GO. NIGGER LOVERS GOTTA GO." A rock hit the wall of the school about two feet above the Mayor's head and bounced back onto the lawn.

"I'm here for your sakes as well as for the sake of the students inside this school," the Mayor said. "I can't believe you want to be remembered as people who—"

"WE WANT NIGGER BLOOD. WE WANT NIGGER BLOOD," the six bullhorns outside the fence responded. About a third of the crowd took up the chant for a minute or two. As it dwindled, Adam Turner said, "Let me give it a try, Jake."

He raised his bullhorn to his lips. "My fellow Americans," he said, "I'm here to ask you to forgive and forget. I want to accept responsibility for some of the bad feelin's you've got about black—"

"WE WANT NIGGER BLOOD. WE WANT NIGGER BLOOD," the bullhorns began again, obliterating the rest of his sentence.

"This ain't workin', Jake," Adam Turner said.

"We're going to have to do it face to face," the Mayor said. "Maybe if we can get the people up front to leave, the rest will follow them."

Adam hesitated, studying the crowd. "Okay," he said, "if that's what we gotta do."

They put down their bullhorns, walked down the steps, and told the tactical cops at the fence to open the big double gate. The Mayor stepped into the crowd, Adam Turner beside him. The people near them stopped chanting. Farther back the bullhorns continued to bellow. "They won't let me make a speech, but they can't stop me from talking to you," the Mayor said. "You're my people. I can't believe you'd do something that would make me sick, that makes me sick even to think about it. I can't believe you'd hurt innocent kids—"

"Innocent," shouted a big-bellied man directly in front of him. He had a button nose and a round ruddy Irish face. "You call them niggers innocent when they stab defenseless white kids?"

"One kid got stabbed. But he's all right. He isn't in any danger. I just heard from the hospital—"

"Our kids don't carry knives," yelled a woman whose belly was bigger and her face even redder and more Irish than the man's.

"One black kid had a knife."

"They all got knives," shouted somone else farther back in the crowd.

"That isn't true," the Mayor said. He saw a familiar

face. "Joe," he said, "Joe Reilly." He reached into the crowd and dragged a stocky man in a mackinaw toward him. "Joe and I played baseball on the old St. Pat's CYO team."

Joe's eyes were bloodshot and wary. He wore a RIP button on his lapel. There was a two-day beard on his swarthy face. What did he do for a living? The Mayor could not remember.

"You're not here to hurt black kids, are you, Joe? You just want to find out what's going to happen next. We're going to close this school for a week, so everybody can calm down."

Reilly pulled his arm free. "I'm here to help my friends, Jake. Gil Finch is a good friend of mine. Jimmy's father, ya know?"

"Listen," Adam Turner said. "Give me a chance. Give us all a chance to learn a lesson from this thing. Maybe we can work out some kind of deal."

"Fuck you, nigger," screamed the big-bellied woman.

The Mayor saw they were getting nowhere, and looked over his shoulder to check their line of retreat. He and Adam were standing about six feet beyond the fence. They had not been entirely swallowed by the crowd, which had formed a crescent around them. Through the open gates the Mayor saw Joe McNamara standing at the bottom of the school's steps. The sun glinted on his gold captain's epaulets. He was wearing a helmet with the visor up.

The Mayor turned his head back toward Adam Turner, who was still talking. "Let's give the kids a chance. Let's not start them off on the wrong track, hatin' each other the way we—"

There was a thud. Adam's mouth remained open but no more words came out. He had been holding his hands high, his elbows tight against his rib cage, palms facing each other in a style acquired by politicians who spend a lot of time talking in crowds. As his hands dropped, the Mayor knew that someone had kicked Adam in the crotch. It was the big-bellied woman. She was kicking him again with ferocious accuracy as his hands descended in a futile attempt to protect himself, which became an instant later a need to clutch the demoralizing pain. In the same instant, the Mayor saw the red-faced fat man, who had to be the woman's husband, swinging a blackjack. The weapon did not travel more than six inches. There was no room for the man to pull his hand back any farther. But you don't have to swing a blackjack more than six inches to break a skull. It hit Adam on the side of the head above his left eye. He was already falling into a crouch. The blackjack turned the crouch into a crumple. As he fell, the Mayor stepped past him and punched the fat man in the face with an overhand right. The blood spurted from his nose down the front of his green and yellow mackinaw.

"Get him and his nigger," the woman screamed. "Look what they done to my husband."

An animal roar erupted from the crowd. From all sides of the crescent they surged at the Mayor. He could feel Adam Turner's body writhing against his legs. Police whistles were blowing. His old friend Joe Reilly was in the front rank, his face as berserk as the rest of them. White helmets flashed on the extreme left and right of the Mayor's field of vision. McNamara and his tactical cops were pouring through the gate to meet the charge. They disrupted two sides of the crescent, but they could not reach those directly in front of the Mayor. He had to meet them alone. He ducked a wild swing of the blackjack and hooked a left well below the big Irishman's belt. His wife hit him with the full weight of her 300 pounds, her nails reaching for his eyes. He fell backward over Turner's body.

"Get the nigger," Joe Reilly screamed and began kicking Adam Turner. A tactical cop bounded over the Mayor and hit Reilly on the mouth with his club. A big redhead grabbed the cop from behind and pinned his arms. Another cop kicked the fat Irishwoman in the side of the head. She screamed and let the Mayor go. He reeled to his feet and from behind gouged the eyes of the redhead pinning the cop. The man howled with pain and let go. By that time the cop had been kicked low by three or four people and he staggered out of the fight.

There were at least fifty tactical cops outside the gate now. But they could not stop the insane momentum of the crowd. A melee still raged around and over Adam Turner's body. The Mayor charged into it. He bent to lift Adam under the shoulders. Someone kicked him in the chest. He fell to his knees. A fist with brass knuckles on it grazed his cheek. He kept his head down, letting the cops do the fighting. He concentrated on getting Adam back inside that iron fence. Fists punched him in the face, feet kicked him. More feet kicked Adam. The Mayor kept on dragging him. It was only six or eight feet to the gate. Where was it? Someone planted a size twelve shoe in his rib cage. A sixty-yarder, that one. Somehow he hung onto Adam. It was no worse than a football game, he told himself. He tried to remember how much he hated the last five minutes of every football game he ever played, when there was nothing left in the body but pain and weariness and will. Another kick, this one on the other side of his rib cage. The world began to grow confused. Sounds, shouts, thuds, pain, breathing short labored gasps. Where was the goddamn gate?

Two sets of hands jerked him to his feet. His fists came up, ready to fight. He stared into the plexiglass visors of two tactical cops. "We got'm, Yer Honor. We got'm," one of them shouted. Rocks and bottles were flying through the air. A bottle struck him in the shoulder and smashed at his feet. The cops half ran, half carried him up the steps into the school. In the first-floor corridor, they stood him against the wall and asked if he was all right.

"I don't know. How do I look?" the Mayor asked.

"Like you got run over by a garbage truck."

The Mayor looked down at himself. All the buttons had vanished from his shirt. There were two huge rips in his suit coat, the knee of his right pants leg was gone, he was minus a shoe. He looked up and saw Adam Turner being carried down the corridor.

"Where are they taking him?"

"To the nurse's office."

Joe McNamara appeared beside the Mayor. "Jesus Christ," he said, "I thought sure you were gone. Are you all right?"

"I think so. I'll ache for a week. But I don't think anything serious is broken." He tried to take a deep breath and an exquisite pain tingled deep into his right side. "A cracked rib, maybe," he said.

A tactical policeman walked up to them holding the Mayor's other shoe. "Does this belong to somebody? They just threw it at us."

"Thanks," the Mayor said. "Thank everybody for me, will you? You guys were great out there."

The cop did not look particularly pleased by the compliment. He just nodded and disappeared back down the stairs.

"You'd never know they weren't enthusiastic, the way they swung those clubs," the Mayor said.

"They're riot control professionals. But the rest of the force—you won't get the same kind of help from them, Jake," Captain McNamara said.

The Mayor tied the lace of his returned shoe. "Let's go see how Adam's doing."

Adam was not doing very well. A prim gray-haired nurse was gingerly swabbing his forehead and face with an alcohol-soaked cloth. The eye hit by the blackjack was swollen almost shut. His nose drooled blood. His suit and shirt were ripped and smeared with blood and dirt. The fat woman's kicks still hurt. He kept raising and lowering his knees convulsively as the pain hit.

"He should be in a hospital," the nurse said.

The Mayor knelt beside him. "Adam," he said, "I'm sorry."

What did this man think? the Mayor wondered, what did he feel, looking into the face of the white man who had just arranged to get his head smashed, his gut ruptured? He knew what he would think, what he would say, if he was in Adam's place. *Fuck you, Your Honor*.

Adam's knees kept going up and down, his hands

kept reaching for the pain in his belly. "Thanks. Thanks —for getting me out of there, Jake."

"The cops did it."

"You—were there when I really needed it. Did—you get that big Mick who sapped me?"

"A right in the nose and a left in the belly."

"—Makes me feel—a little better."

"We'll call the helicopter back and get you over to the Medical Center."

"No. My belly hurts too much to handle that helicopter, Jake. Besides, I want to—go with the kids, one way or another."

The Mayor nodded. "We'll go together. Take it easy while I try to figure out the next move."

Down the hall in the classroom-command center, Captain McNamara was telling Commissioner Tarentino what had happened to Mayor O'Connor and Councilman Turner. Tarentino said he was not surprised.

"If it wasn't for the Mayor, we never woulda got the councilman outa there. He deserves a goddamn citation, he really does, Commissioner."

"We'll make him our civilian hero of the month," Tarentino said.

The Mayor asked the Commissioner if he had any ideas on how to get the black students out of the school without calling out the National Guard.

"We've got to use the buses, there's no other way," Tarentino said. "We'll just have to do the best we can to protect them."

"There won't be a window left on a single bus by the time they get here," McNamara said.

"Wait a minute, Vic," the Mayor said. "I've got an idea."

In his mind he was in the helicopter again looking down on the city. From a lifetime of driving and walking around it, he knew every intricate turn and twist of its main streets and side streets.

"What if we brought six buses to the front of the school as decoys and brought six buses to the back for the real thing? Can the tactical patrol clear Tipperary Square for the decoy buses?"

"Sure," McNamara said. "We'll just break the crowd into two big wedges."

"Can you stop them from getting around to the back door? It might take five, even ten minutes to load those buses."

"We can do it," McNamara said. "We'll use a hundred out front and hold a hundred in reserve for the back."

"What route would the real buses take?" Tarentino asked.

"Up the South Slope," the Mayor said. "Over the crest along the Parkway to Van Zandt Street."

He proceeded to describe all the left and right turns in the labyrinth of side streets from Van Zandt, at the crest of the North Slope, to Buchanan Place at the rear of the school.

How would the bus drivers turn around in Buchanan Place? It was very narrow. They decided to back the buses up Blaine Street, the only side street that fed into it. That way they would park facing their escape route. They spent the next hour working out other details. The bus drivers were issued riot helmets and plexiglass face masks. They gave the same equipment to the black escorts who would be riding on each bus. Two cops were assigned to each bus in case it was isolated by an attack which punctured a tire or damaged an engine. They were equipped with radios and riot shotguns and had orders to fire on anybody who tried to board the bus or attack it with anything lethal, such as a fire bomb.

Each bus had a reserve driver. The drivers were ordered to keep going, no matter what happened to the buses ahead of them or behind them. Fifty mounted cops would accompany the decoy buses and clear Van Nostrand Avenue, the street which the decoys would use to reach Tipperary Square. At the same time the tactical police would move from behind the iron fence to wedge the crowd against the north and south ends of the square and give the decoy buses room to turn around.

As they finished going over the plan for the fourth or fifth time, Tarentino said: "CPI Director Grimes wants to talk to you."

"Jake," said Ray Grimes. "I just finished a tour of downtown. There are five or six thousand people in the street. You've got to call out the Guard."

"We've got a better idea, Ray."

"Is Adam Turner dead? That's what we hear. The mob tore him to pieces."

"He's hurt, but he isn't dead."

"I don't believe you," Grimes said. "He's dead. But a hundred and twenty-five black kids are not going to die to help you win an election. Either you give me the authority to call the Governor and ask for the Guard, or I'll do it myself."

Taking the walkie-talkie with him, the Mayor dashed down the hall to the nurse's office. Adam Turner was still writhing in pain. "He's got a rupture of the stomach wall, I'm sure of it," the nurse said.

The Mayor explained what was happening downtown. He gave Adam a fast description of the decoy bus plan. "Tell Grimes you're not dead and you go along with getting these kids out of here as soon as possible. The buses are ready to roll."

"You're sure it will work, Jake?"

The Mayor's stomach revolved. For a moment he had a vision of 125 black youngsters being kicked and battered by the mob. Was he sure? Could he trust his own police? He decided not to lie to Adam Turner.

"Nobody's sure of anything, Adam. But it's the best chance we've got to stop a race riot. Your people will come up that slope if we don't get these kids out of here inside another hour."

Adam switched on the walkie-talkie. "Hello, Ray," he said. "This is the late Adam Turner speaking. It's great up here in nigger heaven. Got all kinds of white folks waiting on me."

"This is no time for jokes," Grimes screamed. "Do you support me in calling for the National Guard?"

"You call in the National Guard when you got the wrong Governor, it takes a year and a half to get them out, like in Wilmington, Delaware. I think I'll stick with the Mayor, Ray. He stuck with me a half hour ago, when I was gettin' stomped by about twenty thousand crazy honkies."

Adam handed the walkie-talkie back to the Mayor. He spoke into it. "Now, get off this goddamn radio, Ray, and go back to City Hall and clean out your office. You're fired."

The Mayor rejoined McNamara in the command post. They went over the escape plan with Tarentino one more time. "Cross all your fingers on both hands," the Mayor finally said. "Let's roll them."

McNamara went down the hall to brief his lieutenants and sergeants on the tactics to be used in Tipperary Square. He said nothing to them about decoy buses. He gave the officers in command of the hundred men assigned to the rear doors a separate briefing. The black students were led out of the auditorium and lined up in the corridor near the front door. As far as anyone could see, including them, they would board the buses that were coming to the front of the school as usual.

The Mayor went back to the nurse's office and asked Adam if he could make it to the buses. "With a little help," Adam said.

"Maybe you ought to stay here. Leave later in an ambulance."

"That'd convince everyone downtown I really was dead."

"No TV cameras for these buses. No votes."

"What the hell you ridin' them for then, you Mick honky bastard?"

On the walkie-talkie they could hear Tarentino telling McNamara that the buses were leaving. "In ten minutes start to clear the square."

In exactly ten minutes, McNamara blew a whistle. One hundred tactical patrolmen poured through the school's gates and went to work on the mob. In the nurse's office, the Mayor and Adam listened to the radio reports from both fleets of buses. The lead bus in each column was ordered to state its location every six blocks. At first there was only a droning series of street names from Yellow One, the real buses, and Yellow Two, the decoy buses. Then the voices from the decoy buses underwent a chilling change. First, tense reports of rocks, then the sound of breaking glass, then excited shouts above the mob's roar.

"This is the leader in Yellow Two. Our windshield just went. The driver's on the floor. The reserve driver is takin' over. There goes too more windows."

"This is Yellow One. We're at the top of the South Slope. No problems. Turning onto the Parkway."

Yellow One had twice as far to go, but they were betting it would take them the same time as the decoy buses plowing up the North Slope through the mob.

"Yellow Two. There ain't a window left in this bus or any other I can see. The fresh air feels good."

The Mayor went across the hall to check Tipperary Square. The tacticals had done the job. They had broken the mob into two big wedges and pressed them against the eastern and western sides of the square. The center of the square was open. Through the closed window, above the roar of voices, the Mayor heard a new sound, the straining motors of the buses coming up the Slope, which was at its steepest in the blocks just below Buchanan. "GET READY, GET READY," bellowed the RIP bullhorns. "HERE THEY COME."

"This is Yellow Two," squawked the radio in the Mayor's hand. "We're four blocks below the school. The mounties are clearin' the streets ahead of us."

"Yellow One. We're on Van Zandt Street. Estimate arrival five minutes. No problems."

Adam hobbled to the window beside the Mayor. He was leaning on the nurse's arm. "Are they makin' it?"

"Both ways. Let's get the kids around to the back door."

Adam clutched his shoulder. "I'm going to need that help."

With one arm on the nurse's shoulder and the other on the Mayor's, Adam managed to get down the hall to the black students. He told them what they were going to do.

"That sounds crazy. We'll get killed," said the boy who had asked tough questions in the auditorium.

"I don't think we ought to go anywhere until we see the U. S. Army," a girl said.

The Mayor could not blame them. Neither he nor Adam with their ripped clothes and battered faces, were an advertisement for law and order.

"This man knows what he's doin'," Adam said, pointing to the Mayor. "He's going with us. He just saved my ass out there with that crowd. Now, come on."

At Adam's labored pace, they plodded around the building to the back door. As they reached it, the Mayor's radio squawked. "This is Yellow One. We're backin' up Blaine Street."

The crash of a hundred pairs of boots on the stairs below them signaled the emergence of the tactical reserve. The Mayor and Adam stood at the head of the stairs and watched them race out of the door, visors down, clubs ready. The first bus appeared at the head of Blaine Street and backed swiftly to the curb, followed by the next five. As the last bus reached the curb, the Mayor nodded to Adam. "Let's go."

The nurse stepped back and Adam almost fell on his face. "I'm not going out there," she said.

"Go, go," Adam said to the kids who hesitated, their courage almost collapsing at this glimpse of panic. "The Mayor will take care of me."

The kids stampeded down the stairs into the sunlight. Adam swung his left arm around the Mayor's shoulder, and the Mayor looped his right arm under Adam's left arm. They went down the stairs in a three-legged lockstep after the kids. Outside, at first glance it looked good. The tactical patrolmen formed a blue wall at each end of Buchanan Place. The yellow buses were at the curb, the adult escorts standing at the open doors wearing their white helmets and face visors. The black kids were pouring down the two flights of stone steps to the street. Then the Mayor glimpsed dozens of people running down the side streets toward the lines of tactical patrolmen. From Tipperary Square he heard a roar of rage. The mob had discovered the ruse.

"Run," the Mayor shouted to the kids at the end of the line, then realized it was bad advice. Someone slipped or was pushed and four or five kids went sprawling onto the rough bricks on the landing between the first and second flights of steps. Books, papers, pencils, pens were scattered all around them. One of the fallen, a very pretty tan-skinned girl, tried to pick up her property and simultaneously rub a bleeding knee.

"Leave them," the Mayor said. "There's no time. We'll buy you new ones."

She glared up at him. The Mayor saw terrible hatred in her eyes. "I'm sorry," he said. She shook her head and ran toward the buses.

A fat ugly girl was helping a small thin girl wearing steel-rimmed glasses to her feet. The thin girl was gasping for breath and weeping with fear. "She gotta heart condition. She can't run," the fat girl screamed.

The Mayor leaned Adam Turner against the iron fence, picked up the thin girl and ran down the steps to the lead bus. He handed her to the escort. The door slammed and the bus roared away. "What about me?" screamed the fat girl. The Mayor shoved her down the street toward the next bus. He raced back up the steps and put his arm around Adam again. Slowly, painfully, they descended the last flight of steps.

Two more buses had loaded and were racing down Blaine Street toward safety. On both sides of the school the roar of the mob was reaching an enormous intensity as if all the animals in all the jungles of the world were going berserk. The Mayor could see waves of people smashing against the blue walls of tactical patrolmen, pushing them back foot by foot. At least fifty more tacs erupted from the back door of the school. McNamara had withdrawn them from Tipperary Square, where they were no longer needed.

The Mayor and Adam were on the street now. The fourth and fifth buses pulled away. Adam and the Mayor labored along the sidewalk toward the sixth bus, which was still loading. The Mayor was drenched in sweat, gasping for breath. Pain lanced through his chest with every lockstep he took with this man he had first maimed and then rescued and to whom he now was joined as if they were one animal. Adam was groaning with pain and streaming sweat too. The Mayor could smell him, the way he used to smell black athletes on the football field and basketball court. *Nigger stink,* they called it. *What am I doing, where am I going with this funky nigger bastard on my back?*

Suddenly the Mayor was out of the pandemonium, walking in hospital silence with another man clinging to him, a man who was both a dead weight and a source of strength and power, a man who lived with his roots in another time, a man he called Father. This man he was carrying now in the same way into a city that was driven half mad by the confusion, the terror of history, this man with different roots in the past, different time in his blood, different skin on his face, but who was like him, an American who ignored fear and accepted pain and joked in the middle of a disaster, was this man his brother?

The sixth bus roared toward them, its front door open, a very black fullback-size escort standing on the step. The driver squealed to a stop beside them and the escort lifted Adam onto the step.

"Is there room for one more?" the Mayor asked.

"Shit yes," the escort said. "Come on, man."

The Mayor leaped aboard, the door slammed, and the driver barreled into Blaine Street as if he was at the wheel of a Triumph. In five minutes of similar driving they were on the Parkway. The spacious homes of the city's upper class gazed blindly at them. Sitting beside Adam Turner in the seat behind the driver, the Mayor looked around him at the black faces in the bus and felt a new loneliness, deeper, more pervasive than the anxiety he had felt on the stage at the Malcolm X Ujamaa. He did not belong in this bus. He did not belong on this street, at the center of which sat Bowood like a complacent jewel in an expensive necklace. He did not belong where this bus was going, downtown's littered streets. He no longer belonged on the streets of one- and two-story houses that ran from Tipperary Square down the North Slope to the Thirteenth Ward. What had happened in Tipperary Square today made those streets as foreign to him as the garbage-filled alleys of Bayshore. He did not belong anywhere in his city. Yet somehow he remained stubbornly, despairingly entangled with it. The city still belonged to him. He still belonged to it. He could still say that, because of what he had thought and felt back there with his arm around Adam Turner and Adam Turner's arm around him. He did not understand any more than the fact of that feeling. Before he spoke to Paula again, if he ever got the chance to speak, he had to understand more. Somehow he had to get to the heart of it all, this city, politics, himself.

15

More and more, Paula felt like a ghost in this house. A ghost who passed unseen down halls and across rooms. A ghost whose tenuous hold on life was dwindling away. She tried to tell herself that there was no basis for this feeling. She tried to believe that this house was as much a home to her as Bowood. She tried to insist that this was her family, that she belonged here. But it simply was not true. Too much time had passed since the ramrod man had taught the thin frightened little city girl how to ride her first horse, since the warm gentle woman had gathered her in motherly arms and read her to sleep while pine logs blazed in the huge fireplace. Time passed, flowed, subtracted, leaving the man and woman with diminished strength, subtle griefs, unspoken regrets. She was not part of the inner family where these losses lived. She could only sense them as barriers to the need for refuge, belonging, that she had brought with her when she drove away from Bowood, tears streaming, almost a month ago.

For the first time Paula realized how powerless Maria Stapleton was in this house. She was a spectator of the past and present, revered, even loved. But still a spectator. She spent much of the day in her bedroom, fingering her rosary, praying, she said, for the soul of her dead oldest son—and for his father, who seemed intent on killing himself with overwork. She said this in a leaden, lost voice, that made Paula shiver. When she talked, Maria preferred the past, the happy days when her boys were young, when Paula had been a constant visitor. Her present was a void that only prayer and nostalgia helped her endure.

Her husband still lived grimly in the present. But it was a present with very little room for consoling nieces with troubled marriages. The busing case devoured him. He came home each day at seven or eight o'clock, ate a silent, hurried dinner, and retreated to his room to spend five or six hours studying the petitions and counter-petitions, the motions of attorneys from the Board of Education, the NAACP, RIP, the Italian American Alliance, demanding everything from federal marshals to treble damages for police brutality to court-ordered hiring plans to achieve better racial balance among the city's teachers. He never said a word about any of these things to his wife or Paula or anyone else. She learned about his decisions when she read them in the newspaper. What she felt was more personal—the loss of his advice, his concern. He was too exhausted to do anything but cope with each day's crisis.

Gradually she realized that her emotions were demanding something that she could not expect him to give her. Stapletons did not pry into each other's lives. Personal privacy was a family tradition. Until recently, Paula had been grateful for it. Now she yearned to talk to someone. She was appalled by her own ignorance. She did not know if other marriages survived such catastrophic breakdowns. She knew nothing about the possibilities of forgiveness between a man and a woman. Did anyone? she wondered. She could not see herself seeking such wisdom from a modern guru, a psychiatrist or a marriage counselor. The real question was too fine for their conventional wisdom. It was harshly, bitterly specific. Could Paula Stapleton, should Paula Stapleton forgive Jake O'Connor for what he had said and done? No, it was even finer: for what he was?

Even if such forgiveness could be achieved, would it be worth anything without a similar effort on his part, an effort which she found hard to believe he would make? She picked up the newspaper and reread for the third or fourth time the story of the Buchanan High

School riot. Beside it was a picture of Mayor O'Connor getting off one of the school buses in Bayshore, his clothes ripped, his face covered with dirt and bruises. He did not look as if he was ready to forgive his wife and her uncle for getting him into such a mess.

She picked up the next day's paper and reread Dennis Mulligan's column.

ECLIPSE OF A STAR

Some people feel a little sorry for Mayor O'Connor, but that is a passing emotion. Beneath the sympathy there is a growing contempt for his ineptitude. By any standard, the Mayor's performance in front of Buchanan High School was inept. Public officials do not allow themselves to get trapped by mobs. They are supposed to have better judgment. Above all they are supposed to have the ability to calm, not arouse, already excited people. The Mayor once demonstrated some ability in this department. No more. No one believes in a leader who doesn't lead —this is the heart of Mayor O'Connor's failure. Once he got 95 per cent of the votes on the North Slope. Now they kick him in the face. He would get the same treatment from a black mob in Bayshore. Perhaps the best thing he could do for the city at this point is resign. He is the featured speaker at tomorrow's St. Patrick's Day Dinner. What better place to confess his futility and end his political career?

Beside the newspaper was Mayor Mortimer Kemble's journal. It had arrived in an envelope from the Mayor's office about a week after she had left Bowood. At first she had flung it aside. She had seen it as a snide attempt to continue the argument. Here was the proof, he was saying, here was the proof of your ancestral greed and prejudice which justified my ancestral corruption and my own moral indifference. But as silence consumed the next week and the following week, as the days and nights revolved and there was not another word from him, only strained calls from Mahoney or Mackey arranging to have the children brought out to the farm for the weekend, as time absorbed their mutual rage and transmuted it into a failure which neither could confess, she had begun to see the journal in a new way. It became a message from him, preferable to silence, no matter how unpleasant.

Last week she had started to read it, first with revulsion, then with mounting fascination. The man was a monster, that was her first thought. But he was part of her blood and bones. The Kembles and the Stapletons had been intermarrying since the eighteenth century. Her mother had been a Kemble. Then she had begun to see and hear other things. The man's incredible self-confidence, so different from Jake's inner doubt, his hesitations, his bouts of discouragement. Mortimer never doubted that he had the answer to everything, from the evils of industrialism to dealing with the immigrant hordes. He had steamed grandly along, like a brash engineer of one of those gaudy triumphant locomotives. Jake was more like a man at the throttle of a tired train moving by night along a route menaced by guerrillas.

Was she the reason for Jake's caution, was her querulous voice reminding him of ethical standards, moral goals, what entangled and enraged him? Or was it the residue of that old American confidence, personified by her perpetual faith that God would be on their side, as long as they were in the right? Jake simply did not believe this. In the deepest, most fundamental sense, he was a man without faith. She suddenly saw that Ben O'Connor and his friends had been the same way. The ruthless political machine they had created was their answer to a brutal meaningless world, their attempt to impose some certainty, some control on a city that had betrayed them from birth. Could she blame them, or Jake, after reading Mortimer Kemble's visit to the downtown slums? Wasn't it even possible to forgive Jake's rage, now that she had seen its roots?

More than once, she had been tempted to reach for the telephone and say: *Jake, I'd like to come home.* But an image paralyzed her hand, the old Model T Ford in the frozen pond in the north pasture, half in and half out of the ice. The image of this long forgotten thing, broken and abandoned in the winter cold, stopped her.

The phone rang. Maria answered it and a moment later called, "Paula, for you. A Mr. Grimes."

"Hello," Paula said cautiously.

"Jake told me where you were. I asked him point-blank if there was something wrong. He told me enough—can I see you?"

"Really, Ray—what for?"

"Look, this is more than a personal quarrel. The life of this city—its future—is involved. I want to talk to you about it. If you want the blunt truth, I've just about had it down here. I think we've got to do something drastic. Let's have dinner—tonight."

"Where?" Paula said dazedly. Amazing how someone with energy can take command of your soul, when you are in despair.

"There's a restaurant in the Wagon Wheel Motel. On Route Thirteen. I'll meet you there in an hour."

"All right. But—"

He had hung up.

She told Maria Stapleton not to expect her for dinner. In the car she wondered why that voice on the phone had belonged to Ray Grimes. Why not her husband, saying quietly, earnestly, *Look, let's talk.* . . .

The Triumph was an icebox on wheels. She was shivering violently by the time she reached the farm gate. It took another five minutes for the heater to begin working. The country road was utterly black, not a car on it. The March wind sighed angrily through the bare trees. For a moment pure panic assailed Paula. She was utterly, absolutely alone, driving down this tunnel of darkness into more darkness, always more darkness. In the distance, the city glowed against the night sky. It was a relief to reach Route 13, a much more traveled highway, and in another mile or two the motel, with its garish wagon wheel turning on the roof above the drive-in entrance. The restaurant had a separate parking lot in the rear. Walking to the door, Paula got a glimpse of a dim interior, with small flickering lanterns on each table. It struck her that the place was made to order for clandestine meetings.

Ray was waiting for her beside the cashier's counter. He looked very intense. "I didn't want to leave my name, or yours," he said as he escorted her to a booth. Muzak murmured softly in the background. They were the only diners in this section of the room.

"Would you like a drink?" Ray asked.

"Sherry?"

Ray ordered Dubonnet. While they waited, he looked at her critically. "What have you been doing with yourself?"

"Riding, mostly. Reading, helping with the housework. Worrying about Uncle Paul."

"I saw him the other day. He looks terrible."

"He's driving himself eighteen hours a day."

"Have you talked to him about—?"

"No."

"He'd be on your side."

"I know that. I'm not sure whose side I'm on."

Ray looked disconcerted. Paula decided to alter the meaning of that last line to make it sound less contrite. "I've almost reached the point where I could use some good advice."

The drinks arrived. Ray fingered his glass and said, "That's all I'm here to do, Paula, offer you some advice. On behalf of another man."

"Another man?"

"You've heard the story of John Alden and Priscilla. But I don't expect you to say, speak for yourself, Ray. I might dream about it, but I have enough humility to realize that it's nothing but a dream."

"Who is this other man?" Paula said. With preternatural foreboding she knew the answer before his lips formed the words.

"Dwight Slocum. He'll be here in a few minutes. You've known him in the past, Paula. In—what he calls a previous incarnation. I've had several long talks with him. He's changed, Paula, changed tremendously. He has a sense of responsibility about his wealth that—equals yours. But he wants guidance, Paula, he wants help from people like you—and me. He's—open to advice. Not like —other politicians we know."

Paula shook her head. She could not believe it. Ray Grimes with his chubby idealist's face, his earnest voice saying these things about Dwight Slocum. That was enough to make the scene unreal. But the words were driving her back to another place, another memory twenty years old now, the memory of Paula Stapleton sitting on the couch in her apartment listening to Jake O'Connor tell her in a dogged choked voice what it had meant to love and lose Dolores Talbot. The pain-filled words had released the memory of her own pain. For the first time she had been able to admit it, to him and to herself. *I loved someone like that once, too,* she had said. But there was a difference, a difference that perhaps she as well as Jake had never faced. Dolores Talbot was dead. Dwight Slocum was alive.

"Here he is," Ray Grimes said.

She heard his footsteps come down the empty room. She felt his presence looming above the booth, but she did not look up. She let Ray Grimes spring to his feet, hold out his hand. She saw it enveloped by the bigger, stronger hand, heard Ray's hushed ecstatic greeting, then his hasty explanation to her. "I'm superfluous around here now. Let me know if there's anything else I can do, Paula."

He was gone and Dwight appeared on the opposite side of the booth, sliding into the seat with that effortless grace that characterized all his movements. He wore a dark blue blazer and a scarf carelessly tied at his throat. On his lips was a small tight smile.

"Forgive the melodrama," he said. "But I knew you wouldn't see me if I called you directly."

"What is this about?" Paula said, disliking the quavering ghostly sound of her own voice.

"About a lot of things. About you and me and Jake and politics and the past and the future."

"We may be here a long time."

"Maybe. Basically I thought it was time we had a talk. The Judge told me about your departure—from Bowood."

Paula nodded. She felt trapped and profoundly wary. Once before this man had played with her emotions. She was sure the wounds had healed. Now new wounds had awakened at least a memory of that earlier pain. She was not going to let it happen again.

"I gather Jake is coming apart. He blames the debacle on you."

"I haven't seen Jake for three weeks. I don't know what he's thinking."

"It was never right, was it, Paula? You must have found that out a long time ago."

"Dwight. I haven't the faintest desire to discuss my —marriage with you."

"I'm bringing it up because it's part of the bigger picture. I'm on my way to the Senate, Paula. I'm already talking with Bernie Bannon and the other party leaders. They know Jake is finished. They're just hoping he'll bow out gracefully. I've got them all convinced that I'm the most reasonable guy in the world. I've got jerks like Ray Grimes thinking they're part of my conversion experience. After forty-seven years of irresponsibility, Dwight Slocum has discovered a social conscience. It's ridiculously easy. They want to believe it. Above all, they want to win that election."

"I still don't see why this should interest me."

Dwight's face lost its ironic smile. "I'm not going to hand you that line, Paula. I'm hoping by now you've learned how ridiculous it is to treat these people as equals. You do it when you're with them, of course. But you don't get involved in their squalid ethnic and racial disputes and obsessions. You go where the real power is alive and well, where the big decisions about this country's future are being made—Washington. I—I want you to come with me, Paula."

She said nothing. She was silenced by the vulnerability on his face. She knew what it cost Dwight Slocum to confess this vulnerability, to admit that there might be a need that Dwight Slocum could not effortlessly satisfy.

"I've had a lot of women, Paula. I took a long time to grow up. I think it was partly the Old Man, always there looking over my shoulder like God. He's dying, Paula. He's had a stroke. He's a hulk in a wheelchair. I'm a grown man now. I think of you the same way. Someone who had to work through a lot of adolescent needs. Now we both know the score. There's never been any other woman who meant as much to me, Paula. When we were young, you scared me because I didn't have a meaning of my own. Now I've got one. I'm not afraid of you anymore. Paula, I want you. I need you."

Was any of it true? Paula wondered. Or was it the ultimate deception, brutal honesty precisely calculated to get Dwight a wife named Paula Stapleton, one of the few things that life had denied him? If he had said these words twenty years ago, would it have made all the difference? Or would she be a sullen divorcée in her New York apartment, brooding on the mystery of Dwight's compulsive infidelity?

"The truth, Paula, nothing but the truth. I'm telling you things I wouldn't say to another living human being. Things that could ruin me politically."

The truth, the truth, what was this truth he was telling her? Beyond or beneath the rhetoric of hope and faith that all the politicians use, there was a harsh ugly reality, a cruel necessity, a secret circle of old money, old power to which she naturally belonged. Even if it was true, did she want to join it? Did she want to pay the price of admission—casual contempt for everyone outside it? Even as she said no to this question, Dwight was anticipating it.

"I appreciate the genuine sympathy you have for the hewers of wood and drawers of water. I want to do what I can, within reason, to make this sympathy into something real, something practical, to make their lives a little better. But we have to know where to draw the line. We have to say no when they start talking about electing people to the board of directors of General Motors, chartering corporations every five years, wrecking our overseas operations with idiotic investigations, crippling our intelligence services, destroying the defense budget. Those are the real problems, Paula, problems that require finesse, judgment. Compared to them, shuffling kids from one ghetto to another is a sideshow. I'm almost inclined to think we should encourage more of it. It keeps a lot of people distracted enough to let us make the important decisions without too much harassment."

Paula listened to that arrogance and asked herself, could it ever speak for her? No, her heart was still in the grip of the hope that saw Jake O'Connor speaking for a new city, made whole with a new promise, a city healed of its old hatreds. For the first time she saw her wish to escape the city as cowardice, her distaste for the city's ugliness and mediocrity as the ancient primary sin, pride. For a moment she toyed with trying to explain this to Dwight. She even toyed with the awesome challenge of trying to transform his pride or at least to warn him about it, to tell him that a personal and perhaps national fall was inevitable if he tried to make the cynical half truths of his new view of reality come true.

But she saw this was impossible. She also saw that even if the hope with which she and Jake had begun their marriage was in ruins, she was not ready to replace it with a vision that was closer to a waking nightmare.

"You may be right, Dwight. But I don't want to be part of—making it happen."

"Why not?"

"I'm a woman—who doesn't change her feelings about a person, about her husband—easily."

"I can't believe it," Dwight said. He was so annoyed he took a hasty swallow of Ray Grimes's Dubonnet and put it down with an exclamation of disgust. "I thought he did everything but punch you in the mouth—told you—"

"I know what he told me, Dwight."

"Look, I'm not suggesting anything immediate. Nothing in bad taste. I'm willing to wait a year after you get the divorce."

"I don't know whether I'm going to get a divorce. I haven't talked to Jake since—it happened."

"Paula, let me give you a little advice from someone who's been through it. You don't forgive humiliation. You don't forgive a takeover attempt. In every marriage that I know, once the balance of power shifts—or someone tries to shift it—divorce is the only answer. Otherwise the one who loses the power play is the other person's creature. With us it would be different because we instinctively regard each other as equals. I tried it the other way, Paula, just like you. I tried to be a man of the people with my first wife. Everything was great for a year. Then she handed me a list of demands. She had a contract drawn up that I was supposed to sign, promising I'd fulfill every one of them. It was like a coup d'état."

"I don't know whether I can go back to him, Dwight. But whether I do or not, take my word for it, the comparison is not valid."

"Okay," Dwight said. "Okay. I thought you'd overcome it. But I guess it goes too deep."

"What?"

"Your martyr complex. You're not happy unless you're suffering, losing. I'm offering you a chance to come home, Paula. Come back where you belong. They're all losers, Paula, even when they win they're losers."

"Maybe—maybe we made them that way, Dwight. Maybe we've got to go on trying to change it."

Slowly, almost imperceptibly, Dwight withdrew. He leaned back against the wall of the booth and the feeble light of the lantern on the table caught only flickering glimpses of his face. It made him look amazingly like the Adonis she had known twenty-five years ago, surly, troubled—a dangerous combination of promise and threat.

"I'd better go," she said.

"I guess you'd better."

"I'm sorry, Dwight. I—"

Sorry was the wrong word. Resentment froze Dwight's face. "Get going," he said.

It was several minutes after nine o'clock when she

reached the Stapleton farm. She had to walk through the living room to reach her first-floor bedroom. To her surprise, Paul Stapleton was sitting in one of the huge Spanish chairs in the center of the room. He was dozing until he heard her footsteps. His head came up and those gray penetrating eyes studied her as she walked toward him.

"Not working tonight?" she asked.

"Taking a break," he said. "Did you have a nice dinner?"

"I skipped it. I'll get something in the kitchen for myself."

"I'll join you. I wasn't hungry at dinner time. We had ham. You can fix me a sandwich."

He took a seat at the scarred oak kitchen table while Paula found the ham in the refrigerator.

"Did you have dinner with Jake?"

"No," Paula said, concentrating on slicing the ham.

"Oh. I wondered who else—"

"Mustard?" Paula asked as she put the ham on a piece of rye bread.

"A little."

She found the dark spicy mustard that he liked in the cupboard above the stainless steel sink and put a generous smear of it on the meat.

"I'd love a beer, but I'll settle for water. I've got two hours of reading ahead of me," he said.

She gave him a glass of water and went back to slicing the ham for herself.

"Daughter," he said, "I hate to be a prying old man. But it's time we had a talk."

"Did you know Dwight was meeting me?"

"No. He called here and asked me if I thought it was a good idea. I didn't think it could do any harm. But I didn't give him any advice about the time and place. You're a grown woman, daughter. I try not to interfere in the lives of my grown children."

Paula felt bewildered. For the first time in her life she was *opposed* to this man. For the first time, she was not eagerly listening to his advice. Why? Nothing had changed. She knew he only wanted to help her, it was

312

all he had ever wanted. She felt guilty. But she could not prevent her resistance—even her resentment—from speaking again.

"I—I didn't like it."

"Maybe that's not so important," he said. "Let me be blunt, Paula. My blood pressure gives the doctor hives every time he sees it. My heart seems to have developed three or four different rhythms. I'm not a very healthy man. I could go almost any time. I'd like to see you settled before it happens."

"Settled?" Paula said. Grief confused her resentment. The love she felt for this man clashed violently with what he was saying. "You've never really—approved of my marriage to Jake, have you?"

He looked embarrassed. His wish to avoid involvement in her personal life was obviously genuine. "Let's say—I had fears from the start. Now they seem to be coming true."

Paula laid aside the carving knife and sat down in a chair at one end of the long table. At the opposite end of it, Paul Stapleton looked incredibly frail. His skull was even more visible beneath the wasted flesh of his face. But the eyes still retained their controlled intensity.

"I was happy. Quite happy until recently," she said.

"I'm glad to hear that. For your sake. But now I gather it's—is over too strong a word?"

"I don't know."

"Can I tell you what I think?"

"Of course. I've always wanted to know what you think—about everything."

"I think perhaps—you've confused sympathy and love. You wanted to help the unfortunates of this world. We Stapletons have always tried to do that. I felt the same thing when I was—young. But a man can control his—situation. He can give the children his name—his heritage. A woman—"

Paula found herself wondering what expression was on her face. Astonishment? Disbelief? Dismay? These guarded words told her more about Paul Stapleton's marriage, his life, than she wanted to know. She saw the chilling dimensions of his Stapleton pride. His wife,

313

Maria, and Jake were among these unfortunates; in Maria's case treated with compassion, even love, because she accepted, however mournfully, Stapleton control; in Jake's case to be treated with condescension and finally with contempt for failing to meet Stapleton standards. Was she hearing her own voice, the voice Jake heard?

"And you'd rather see me—married to Dwight?"

"Not necessarily. I would hope you'd approach something like that very cautiously. I know Dwight's no prize as a husband. But he does seem to be changing. Finally growing up. He could—use some help from a woman like you, Paula. He is—well—your own kind."

Those last words flung her back to the study at Bowood. She saw Jake's enraged face, she heard the vicious bludgeoning words. Not her own kind, she thought numbly. But now she had glimpsed the world that had spawned that primitive rage. She had looked into the chasm she had tried to ignore. She could never again deny the existence of that world with phrases like our own kind. But now she was incapable of crossing the chasm. She who thought she was a master at such high-wire acts.

"I don't know what to do," she said.

"If it's as bad as—the pain I see on your face every time I look at you, daughter," the Judge said, "maybe you should consider a divorce. When two people start quarreling, it's not a good idea to let them have equal access to the money involved—especially when one of them isn't very adept at handling it. Resentment does funny things to a person's judgment. And Jake is going to need a lot of money to make this Senate run against Dwight."

Paula nodded. She was acquiescing to the way, the wisdom of her world. But her tears were for what else she saw on the hard old face of this man she had loved so long. A judgment of her as a woman and Jake as a man. It filled her with desolation. But even as the ashes seared her, she struggled against their meaning. His hopes, his expectations were not her hopes, her expectations. His victories were not her victories, his defeats not her defeats. She was bound to him by love, but love did not require unconditional submission. That was the iron law of pride.

She could not tell Paul Stapleton any of this. She could not look at him. She put her head down on the table, and felt the cold wood against her burning cheek. Her hot helpless tears wet the wood around her. She heard him get up and walk down to her with his heavy old man's tread. His hand pressed her shoulder. "It's hard. I know it's hard. It's hard to be a woman. It's hard to be a man, too. But you'll come through it. You've got the stuff, daughter. You're a Stapleton."

There was a farewell in those words. Paul Stapleton could not hear it. But Paula heard it, saw it in the slump of his proud old shoulders as he left her there in the kitchen, surrounded by the gleaming machinery of domesticity. Slowly, the desolation became bearable. Then an extraordinary thing began to happen. Although the cold March wind howled menacingly outside, her image of refusal, the wounded memory that had paralyzed her will, the old car frozen in the ice of the north pasture pond, inexplicably loosened. The ice shuddered, shook, and began to crumple beneath a warm mysterious wind that flowed magically north from that island where dark Negro laughter mingled with calypso music. With a sigh, the old car sank beneath the living water.

What was happening? Where, why was she getting this floating sense of freedom? Was this what happened to the dead? Or to the living—those who were living their own lives for the first time? She did not know. She did not know or understand anything that was happening to her. She was only five minutes old. But she did know this. She had to leave this house as soon as possible. She had to escape it, this house of birth and death and rebirth, finally and forever.

16

On the day after the riot, the Mayor was up at 6 A.M. He had had trouble sleeping. The doctors at the Medical Center had diagnosed the cracked rib that he had suspected, and had taped him up. Pain still knifed across his chest every time he took a deep breath, or made a wrong move in the bed.

Toward dawn he had had a curious dream. He and Paula were alone on a tiny atoll in the center of the ocean. They were both naked. She had drawn a line down the center of the spit of sand and forbidden him to cross it. He crossed it anyway. With an angry cry she sprang into the sea and began swimming toward the horizon. He shouted warnings about sharks, barracudas. She kept on swimming. With a curse he started swimming after her.

It reminded the Mayor of a dream that he had had several times during World War II in the Pacific. The ship was hit by a Kamikaze and blew up. He was the only survivor. Treading water, he turned slowly, until he had made a full circle of the immense horizon. He was alone. But for some reason, he was not afraid. He seemed relieved to be alone, even if the loneliness meant death.

At nine o'clock he called the Medical Center and was told that Adam Turner had had a peaceful, sedated night. X-rays showed no rupture of the stomach wall. There did not seem to be any serious damage to the optic nerve of his left eye. A day or two of bed rest and he would be able to go home. The Mayor called

Charlie LoBello at City Hall and told him that he would not make an appearance today. "Tell the newshawks I'm recuperating from my injuries," he said. "Maybe it will get the sympathy vote."

Charlie scuttled that idea by telling him what Dennis Mulligan had written about the riot. Charlie added that he and press secretary Dave O'Brien had the St. Patrick's Day speech almost finished. They would send it up to Bowood around noon. The Mayor switched his call to Helen Ganey and told her to take the folder marked "Turner—Confidential" from his private file and send it along with the speech.

Helen said Commissioner Tarentino was looking for him as usual. The Mayor told her to route him to Bowood. "Tell him to bring along the McKenna file," he said.

Tarentino arrived with a deeper than usual scowl on his handsome face. He handed over a bulging file on Eddie McKenna and began warning the Mayor against using it. "Eddie is bad-mouthing you all over town. A push like this and you'd lose him. You'd lose the whole regular organization vote."

"I just want to read it, Vic."

Tarentino began spouting worries about one of the downtown high schools to which white pupils were being bused. An informant had predicted that the blacks were going to do a Buchanan in reverse. His tactical patrol was exhausted from yesterday's exertions. They were 80 per cent white. They could not hope to be as effective fighting downtown in a sea of blacks. Maybe the National Guard should be alerted.

"Let's live one riot at a time, Vic," the Mayor said. "I talked to Adam Turner about this possibility last night. He guaranteed me that it wouldn't happen."

"I don't think much of his guarantees."

"Have you got any copies of that confidential dirt on Adam?"

"Only one, in my personal file."

"Shred it."

"What the hell? Did somebody kick you in the head harder than—?"

"Shred it, Vic. That's an order."

"Did you make a deal with the guy?"

"Maybe. But the file has nothing to do with it."

"How about Eddie McKenna's file. Shred that too?"

"There's a difference between dirty rumors and breaking the law. Between chasing a little tail and double-crossing your friends."

"Politically speaking—"

"Vic—it's about time we got something straight. I think you're a hell of a cop. Maybe the best in the country. But you're not a politician. That's my job. And I'm going to do it my way."

Tarentino walked out, stiff-jawed, glowering. The Mayor wondered if he meant a word of what he had just said, or worse, if he could deliver on it. He read Eddie McKenna's file. It filled him with disgust and sadness. It was all so familiar. The mob money to bankroll the setup. The tapped calls full of greasy confidence. The deposition by the cop who agrees to testify for the prosecution and finger everyone in return for immunity. In the middle of it was Eddie McKenna, his man. He thought about Eddie's wife, Marie, her loyalty to Jake O'Connor, bred in her bones by her father's loyalty to Ben O'Connor. He thought about Eddie's four boys. Could he do it? Could he turn him in? Everything in the Mayor's blood, his nerves, said no. Especially now, when there was no one upstairs to talk to about it, no uncompromising Protestant voice transcending doubts, ambiguities, sentiment.

Around noon, Dave O'Brien's speech arrived. It was a good workmanlike job that kicked hell out of the Republicans as the party of privilege and incompetence, and called for a "metropolitan crusade" to restore the nation's cities. It also included some clever jabs at candidates who thought they could buy elections instead of earn the voters' respect with a record of genuine service and accomplishment. The boys were practically tying on his gloves for the primary brawl with Dwight Slocum. The Mayor took Adam Turner's folder and threw it into the fireplace beneath the portrait of Charles Stapleton surveying the slaves at work on the manor. He threw the speech on top of the folder and put a match to them. A few feet away on the library desk was the folder on Eddie McKenna. He did not put it in the fire. He sat and watched the mounting flames and wondered what he was going to say to his fellow sons of St. Patrick tomorrow night.

On the big desk beside Eddie's folder were his father's papers. Was the answer to the question he was asking there, in the random debris of the life of a man who was careful to do most of his business with a handshake and a promise? The Mayor only knew that he still had an immense reluctance to go near them. He spent the rest of the day avoiding them. He took Dolores for a walk in Washington Park. He tossed a football with Kemble when he came home from school. He read Dolores to sleep with Winnie-the-Pooh. He talked with Kemble about the Buchanan riot and was pleased to see that he had no fears of being trapped downtown by a countermob of blacks.

He watched the eleven o'clock television news and learned that Ray Grimes had joined Congressman Dwight Slocum's staff as a special advisor on urban problems. The Mayor turned off the set in the middle of a preview of tomorrow's St. Patrick's Day celebrations. It was time. He had to go through those papers before he could decide what to say tomorrow night. He knew why he had avoided looking at them for the last three weeks, ignoring Simon Burke's repeated pleas. He was afraid of what he would find—and what he would not find—in those folders. He was afraid they might reduce to his true dimensions the man who had been the source of strength, equilibrium in his life. He was afraid that he would find documentary proof of his original blunder—following a man who was not going anywhere, who was only part of history's blind fatality, fleeing the memory of degradation in Ireland and in the city's slums, a man who was ready to do anything, from stealing to shooting, to make sure he and his children were not sucked back into that whirlpool of poverty and humiliation.

The first folder was a jumble of letters, each of them a tiny glimpse of ward politics.

December 30th, 1934

Dear Mr. O'Connor:

Many thanks for your kindness in putting Patrick Boyle in the Alms House for me. I assure you that it will always be remembered, especially for you on Election Day.

       Sincerely,
       Lillian McKee

Dear Mr. O'Connor:

I thought you would like to know that Joseph J. Keller has in his possession affidavits from several persons stating that they had received their jobs on the WPA through your office by means of falsified relief numbers. Keller is one of the newspapermen who gathered most of the information for the Seabury probe in New York City. This fellow is a slick article. You might expect me to call on you sometime for a favor in return for this information.

       A friend.

Dear Mr. O'Connor:

I am in a very poor condicticon. I have a blader ailment or kidney. So I thought I would write to you I am one of the old stock about fifty come from Germantown and landed in Bayshore with Doc Heffernan, Lord mercy on his sole, and I am with Jim Doolan on the election board for the past twenty-five years and was one of the first call on the McCallister probe in '28. So all I ask from you is can you fix it so that I can get in the famous Medical Center for a month or so.

       I remain yours
       A real Democrat,
       Charles Wittenburg

Dear Mr. O'Connor:

I have four children they are in need of clothing i have a boy ten years old and he is away from school a month for the want of shoes. The schoolteacher reported it & that was the last I heard of it. I am a WPA worker and i injured my leg November 1 but i didn't hurt it on the job i was not able to work—there is nothing to eat. . . .

The next folder was a set of bookkeeping records of the cash disbursements in the ward on each election day. It was not big money. The final figure seldom passed ten thousand dollars. But this was very important grease, these dozens of five- and ten-dollar bills, guaranteeing the machine's championship performance. The Mayor noted without much surprise that the largest amounts were always debited to the Tenth District, on the outer fringe of Bayshore—the only black district in Ben O'Connor's ward. How many times had he heard his father's committeemen claim that it was wasted money, that "the goddamn boogies" took the cash and did not bother to vote, or voted the wrong way? Maybe that was where his fundamental distrust, his secret contempt for blacks began.

Next came a collection of pictures. He and Paul at the beach, their arms draped over each other's shoulders. His mother posing with her sons when they were in grammar school. Formal, cheerful, proud, him in a Buster Brown collar, Paul in a suit and tie. Tintypes of his paternal grandfather and grandmother. She had died in 1916. He remembered his grandfather, a hunking old man on a bench in the park, with a brogue so thick everything he said was incomprehensible. He was good for a nickel every time they met him. He carried a gnarled cane, not quite a shillelagh, but a formidable weapon. Once Ben O'Connor told him how the old man had knocked an insurance salesman down two flights of stairs with it. He had found out that the man was cheating him and almost everyone else in the neighborhood by collecting double the price of the premiums. Dadda, they had called him, because he did not like Grandpa. There was a frown on his face, a mixture of bafflement and anger.

That was the end of the picture file. The end of the O'Connor lineage. Thereafter they blurred into Ireland and her sorrows. The Mayor thought gloomily of the generations of Stapletons on Bowood's walls. He looked up at the founder of the line, above the fireplace behind him. In the history department, it was no contest.

Next came a folder marked PERSONAL LETTERS FROM THE MAYOR. These were of two kinds. One exhorted Ben O'Connor to rally the troops and produce every available voter living or dead in the Thirteenth Ward. The second congratulated him on "the fine showing made by the Thirteenth Ward in last month's great election victory." There was not a single personal reference in any of the letters. They were obviously mass-produced by the maximum leader to stiffen the spines and raise the spirits of his colonels. It also reminded them that the Big Man was watching them very closely. The pressure was always on the ward leaders. He remembered how tense Ben O'Connor had always been the night before an election. One wrong word and he took your head off. He was like a fighter so eager for action, he was ready to punch his best friend—or his wife—in the mouth.

According to the newspaper, the Big Man was worth eight million dollars when he died. Ben O'Connor was worth forty-six hundred. The price of loyalty came high. Ben O'Connor was not a stupid man. He knew what was happening. Maybe all the talk about loyalty, all the apostrophes to the organization and its great leader, maybe these were part of his act. Maybe he didn't even mean, or at least mean all the way, those words to the citizens of the Thirteenth Ward: "You are my people." What was it he said to Paul once, when the newly ordained priest was gassing about the "potential nobility" of politics? *You have to listen to an awful lot of bullshit.*

The Mayor picked up another folder, marked SPEECHES: He expected these to be painful reading. His father never pretended to have any talent as a speaker. His power as a leader came not from stem-winding oratory but from persistent attention to detail on a person-by-person basis. When he was standing at a bar, or sitting at a table with an individual or with a small group, Ben O'Connor was irresistible. A mysterious blend of physical and psychological strength emanated from the man.

The first several speeches began: "I HAVE NEITHER THE TALENT NOR THE DESIRE TO OCCUPY MORE THAN A BRIEF PORTION OF THIS PROGRAM." How many times he had heard these words from the platform, Ben O'Connor humbly—and wisely—dismissing himself as an orator and earnestly assuring the audience that they had come to hear their great leader, His Honor the Mayor. But as he turned the pages different sets of words leaped out at him.

> SOME MAY ARGUE THAT I HAVE SPENT TOO MANY YEARS IN THE SERVICE OF THE GOVERNMENT: AGAINST THEM I CAN ONLY SAY THAT AS A YOUNGER MAN THE OPPORTUNITY FOR A PROFESSIONAL EDUCATION WAS NOT MY LOT. AS A MEMBER OF THE DEMOCRATIC ORGANIZATION, AND HAVING BEEN A COUNTY COMMITTEEMAN TWENTY-NINE YEARS, LONG BEFORE I EVER SOUGHT A POLITICAL POSITION, I LEARNED POLITICS THE HARD WAY AND I AM NOT ASHAMED OF IT.
>
> I CANVASSED THE ELECTORATE IN MY DISTRICT, I RANG DOORBELLS, I WALKED DOWN INTO BASEMENTS AND UPSTAIRS TO TOP FLOORS PREACHING THE DOCTRINE OF DEMOCRACY. I ATTENDED PUNCTUALLY WARD CLUB MEETINGS AND IN LATER YEARS ORGANIZED SUCH MEETINGS AND RALLIES. I'VE ALWAYS GIVEN ONE HUNDRED PER CENT SERVICE TO ALL THE CITIZENS OF THIS CITY, NOT ALONE THOSE WHO VOTED FOR ME, BUT THOSE WHO VOTED AGAINST ME IF THEY SOUGHT MY HELP.

As a younger man the opportunity for a professional education was not my lot. A new image of his father began to coalesce in the Mayor's mind. The strength was still there, but it was a contorted, trapped strength. What had Ben O'Connor said to him once, while he was loafing through college and law school? *You work at it, and if I'm still around, I guarantee you'll be worth a million bucks by the time you're thirty.* That was the freedom, the power Ben never achieved, the only kind he understood: money. But he had refused to take a cut from the impressive amounts of cash the organization framed from the ward's numbers wheels, card games, and horse parlors. He had promised to deliver it untouched, when the Big Man made him a ward leader in 1926. Ben kept the promise. For thirty years he had delivered a half million dollars annually to City Hall and never touched a cent of it.

Why didn't you? the Mayor found himself asking bitterly. Maybe if you'd banked two or three million, I would never have heard those words that tore the skin off my body: *you can't tolerate integrity*. I might never have blundered into this game of buying and selling with a woman whose mouth said words that destroyed me while tears of regret ran down her cheeks.

In the next folder the Mayor discovered a scrapbook. It was a homemade affair, news stories pasted in a black marbled school composition book. On the inside cover was an astonishingly youthful picture of his father, one the Mayor had never seen, beneath a headline describing how the Thirteenth Ward had just given him his first testimonial dinner. Beside the story, in his mother's elaborate handwriting was a small paragraph surrounded by a large outline of a heart.

COMPILED WITH MANY LOVING THOUGHTS AND
MUCH PRIDE IN MY HUSBAND'S PROGRESS
KATHERINE O'CONNOR

On the opposite page was a clipping of a poem entitled *A Maiden's Ideal of a Husband*.

> Genteel in personage,
>   Conduct, and equipage
> Noble by heritage
>   Generous and free;
> Brave and romantic;
>   Learned not pedantic;
> Frolic, not frantic;
>   This must be he.
>
> Honor maintaining
>   Meanness disdaining

      Still entertaining,
          Engaging and new.
    Neat, but not finical;
      Sage, but not cynical;
    Never tyrannical
        But ever true.

    The Mayor felt his flesh crawl with revulsion. Here in sixteen saccharine lines was the story of his parents' ruined marriage. Another idealistic woman. His mother wanted to make a Galahad out of an Irish mug. Women were incredible creatures. They wanted, wanted, wanted, and it was impossible to satisfy them. Above all, the Mayor thought mordantly, they wanted power. Because they were essentially powerless, they had to win it by subterfuge. Worst of all, they saw themselves as reformers, capable, indeed predestined to change the inner selves of the people around them. When they asked for equality, they were really asking for the right to assert their presumed moral superiority. Jesus! He thrust the scrapbook back in its folder as if he was trying to confine an evil spirit.

    The Mayor opened the next folder in the pile. It was almost empty. Only a half dozen letters in his mother's handwriting. The first one had no date, only the words *Saturday late afternoon* in the corner. It began,

Dearest Honeyboy.
    My watch reposes in the drawer so I know not the time. I wore your picture to bed last night around my neck. I wanted to dream of you. But didn't exactly—only in a vague way. I dreamt of a baby in a white dress whom I took to see the Mayor. I seemed to have your raise in mind but didn't want to mention it and acted rather sheepish. Hope the white dress signifies good luck and the baby does not mean any sickness.

    I'm so proud of the way you have worked hard to improve your grammar and I am so glad that I have been able to help you in something so important to your career. Someday you may be running for the highest office in this state, and by then you won't have to be ashamed of any speech you make. It makes me mad, the way so many Irish politicians murder the language—and that includes our great leader.

Did you make inquiries about a Sunday night train? I hope there is one so you can come down Sunday night late. I have had a lot of time to think about you and me, and I have decided we are nicer than we ever were before—more companionable and better chums and everything nicer. That's because we are *one* now and not two really separate beings. I'm more in love than ever before because I can realize your goodness to me in so many different ways.

I hope your sunburn is better. Mine is peeling. I want lots of loving and rough treatment. So please be minus the sunburn. Love from your baby who misses your arms always at night. This morning I couldn't get back to sleep like I do when I feel your presence. It took me a long time. It makes a big difference, dearest. Always.

The Mayor read the letter again and again and again. They had been in love, this man and woman who had never seemed to have a civil, much less a tender word for each other in his boyhood. Once that tough, angry man had done his utmost to please the dreamy romantic woman he had married. The fact that he had *tried*. That was the overwhelming discovery. And, of course, failed. Why, why, why? Because women were impossible to satisfy?

The Mayor wandered through Bowood, gazing at portraits of previous Stapletons. It was the first time he had ever paid much attention to the women. Kate Stapleton Rawdon, a dazzling redhead with a striking resemblance to Allyn Stapleton, gazed haughtily at him across the ballroom. The rest lined the walls of the upper hall. Anne Randolph Stapleton, Paula's imperious grandmother, Caroline, Paula's mournful-eyed mother. A half dozen others whose names he did not know. He wandered into his bedroom and stared at his Irish Corner. There was not a single woman in any of those pictures. Nor did it occur to him to include a picture of his mother when he had originally hung the gallery. There were no women allowed in the O'Connor world. With good reason, he had thought at the time. Now he was not so sure. He went back to the library and found the folder marked *Pictures*. He sat there for a long time studying the picture of himself and his mother and his brother Paul.

He began thinking about the last time he had visited Paul at the hospital. They had had one of those maddening conversations, in which Paul had insisted he was dead and the voice you heard was Father Paul's ghost. The doctor had asked him to pretend he was existing, and talk to his brother as if he was alive. Paul had shaken his head. "His brother helped kill him," he said.

The Mayor had felt his body harden, as if he was suddenly encased in armor. A tremendous rage had flared in his chest, beneath his contemptuous calm. *All right,* he had wanted to shout. *All right I got more of his love if that's what you want to call it and he turned out to be more important in the long run he was the one who knew how to live and how to die and she didn't even know how to boil water but we didn't know that when I was eight and you were eleven. Most of the time he was never there. He spent his life down in that goddamn ward chasing votes. You had her cheering you on to the spiritual heights all day every day while all I ever got were put-downs.*

The Mayor searched the folder and found his mother's wedding picture. She was beautiful. He pondered the thick dark hair coiled on her slender neck, the ripe figure, the smiling oval face. Not one of the lumpy ones, as Paula once admitted she called the white ethnics. More important, there was intelligence, hope, happiness, on her face. Were these what his father had married? Did she fail to deliver on these promises, for reasons that were part of her heritage—the spoiled daughter of an overprotective mother, with sentimental ideas about religion and gentility? Was that the reason for the rage that erupted from Ben O'Connor so often? Or was the rage roused by his discovery that she was not the magic answer to his huge somewhat childish ambitions? She could correct his slum grammar but she could not teach him how to conquer the claustrophobic political system that trapped him all his life in the paralyzing trivialities of the Thirteenth Ward, settling quarrels between drunks, getting jobs for an endless succession of losers, struggling with their greed, their stupidity, their perverse helplessness. What was it the old Irish pastor had told him? *Jesus Christ couldn't keep these people happy.*

What did he see on his wife's face? He went back upstairs to the Newport lowboy in his bedroom, where a miniature of Paula in her wedding dress stood between larger framed pictures of his daughter and his son. She gazed directly into the camera, her face composed, unsmiling. There was a subtle pride in the lips, a serene confidence in the unlined brow, and intelligence, obvious intelligence in those striking eyes. What words came to mind? Masterful, competent, yes, there was even a kind of power in that face, the power of old blood, old money, old certainties.

If that is what he saw, what did he discover? A woman who seemed certain of nothing, who preferred to question, always question, the morality of this decision or that policy. A woman who had no real interest in money, much less a mastery of it. A woman whose old blood meant a family of snobs and dogmatists, which she persisted in admiring for reasons that either escaped or irked him. A woman whose sense of mission was more attuned to the nobility of defeat in a good cause than to the satisfaction of victory in the neither good nor bad one. A woman at odds with reality as he knew and understood it. A woman impossible to dismiss as a fool or a charlatan. A woman he had finally to face as a human being, his wife, not as a problem to solve or a situation to manipulate.

The Mayor stared at the photograph of his mother in his hand. All his life he had told himself he would love someone totally unlike her. But Dolores Talbot had been catastrophically like her in many ways. His drunken year of mourning for dead Dolores, wasn't it partly relief, an emotion that easily blended with guilt? He had never wanted more than his hands on those ripe breasts, his body enveloping that downy skin. Hadn't the thought of a lifetime with her appalled him?

That was probably unfair to Dolores. In the long run, the mind cannot sum up a person. He could sit here and think for the rest of his life and he would never be able to find all the reasons why he once said I love you, any more than he could understand why he now said I didn't really love you. Any more than he could understand why he now said to his mother, this woman in his hand, I loved you and I wish you'd loved me. Any more than he understood why he said to that miniature woman in the wedding dress on the lowboy, I loved you, or, saddest of all, I still love you. He could think and think from now until the end of the world without explaining any of those words. They had to be said and then lived. At the very least the admission had to be made that he had loved them and could now face the truth about them. The truth which is also the truth about himself. He looked in the Queen Anne mirror above the lowboy and saw himself, his mother's picture in his hand. Tomorrow he would tell Mahoney to get a frame for it, and hang it in his Irish Corner.

Feeling funereal, the Mayor went back downstairs to his father's folders. All empty now. His heritage stood there in pathetic piles on the huge mahogany desk. Bit and pieces of a life. What did they tell him to do, besides call his wife and confess his sins? He had come here looking for political guidance and he had found a personal revelation. He picked up the last folder and shook it. Something rattled inside it. He turned it upside down and a card fell out. It was crumpled and faded. On it was typed a poem.

THE GUY IN THE GLASS
When you get what you want in your struggle for pelf,

*And the world makes you king for a day,
Then go to a mirror and look at yourself,
And see what that guy has to say.*

*For it isn't your Father, or Mother, or Wife,
Who judgment upon you must pass,
The feller whose verdict counts most in your life,
Is the guy staring back from the glass.*

*He's the feller to please, never mind all the
   rest,
For he's with you clear up to the end,
And you've passed your most dangerous, difficult
   test,
If the guy in the glass is your friend.*

Fifth-rate poetry. But it stirred the Mayor enormously. For a trembling moment his father, the new or at least different father he was seeing for the first time in these pieces of paper, seemed to be speaking directly to him. What was he saying? He was telling him that the man he had seen in the shattered mirror was not going to disappear. He would have to keep talking to him for the rest of his life. No one, not his wife with her checkbook and her hunger for power and her political principles nor Victor Tarentino with his policeman's prudence could help. Nor was there any point in searching for even a small cheering section. He would have to do his talking with this man alone.

Alone. But that was no longer the unnerving thought that it might have been six months ago. Alone was a destination he had already reached. Alone was where he had been living since that mob had kicked the last vestige of Irish solidarity out of him in Tipperary Square.

For the first time the Mayor was able to think about the commitment he had made to that limping man in the hospital corridor twenty-five years ago, think about it in isolation from the city, from being Irish, from being a son. Slowly it became more than an act of personal allegiance, which time had confused to the point where he wondered if it had not been extorted unfairly. His commitment was not only to that contorted crippled raging man who had made him both proud and sad, afraid and grateful. It was to a heritage, it was to the one good thing he had represented, the caring. Even if the son did not possess it, he could seek it, he could imitate it. A heritage was something that lived in both the heart and the head. Maybe, eventually it would reach the heart, now that he had gotten it straight in his head.

It was time to stop playing the self-pity game, time to stop secretly yearning for the mythical solidarity of the old organization. Face it. They were well rid of the old order. The handout and the handshake. How are ya, Judge? How much, Sheriff? Ireland invoked like an incantation that forgave everything and explained nothing. The organization or the Church devouring the souls of bright young men. The world where all the answers were written in advance in the Baltimore Catechism and the okay from City Hall. Well rid of it, Your Honor. It was time to scour from his soul the last iota of regret for its passing.

He picked up the telephone and dialed Eddie McKenna's number. One of the boys answered. "This is the Mayor. Let me speak to your mother."

A cautious Marie McKenna came on the line. "Marie," the Mayor said. "I've got bad news." He told her what Eddie was doing, what they had on him.

"O Jesus," she said, and began to cry. "He just needed the money, Jake. He needed it for the boys. We had to borrow ten thousand dollars for their tuition this year. Give him a break, please, Jake."

"I'm going to do everything I can for him, Marie," the Mayor said. "But I've got to put it on the record. I want you to handle him, so he doesn't do something crazy, like trying to slug it out with me. I want him to step down as party chairman, tonight. I want his resignation in my hand tomorrow morning. I'll handle the plea bargaining. He can probably get off with a fine and a suspended sentence. But it means he'll never do business with the city again."

"I know, Jake. I'll handle him. Just keep him out of jail. For the boys' sake."

"I'll do my best, Marie."

The Mayor hung up and poured himself a drink. He was ready to write his speech. He put everything back in the folders, took a yellow legal size pad out of the desk drawer, and went to work. He had scratched out two opening sentences when the telephone rang.

"Jake. This is Paula. I'm coming—home tomorrow morning. I don't know what will happen. But I'm coming—"

"I was going to call you—tomorrow morning. I wanted—I want you to come to the dinner tomorrow night. To hear my speech. That's the most I can ask you to do for the time being."

17

He was so wary. That was the only explanation Paula could find for his behavior. Incredibly wary. He had not even kissed her when she walked into the library. He said he wanted to talk, he wanted to talk very much. But he had to finish his speech. "Maybe it would be better if we talked after the speech."

What could she do but nod? She wanted to tell him what she had discovered about herself, her family, Ray Grimes, Dwight Slocum. But his wariness made her wary too. She wondered if the speech was going to be an attack on her, the blacks, Judge Stapleton. Then he would confront her, defiant, even arrogant with the pride of a man who had made his choice, and say: *Take me or leave me.*

As she had driven down the cold windy road from the farm, two voices had argued in her mind. One warned her against appearing at Bowood as a supplicant, begging Jake O'Connor's pardon. That was fleeing from power to power, that was only another perhaps more certain self-destruction. A long time ago she thought she had escaped the power of the world into which she had been born. Now she knew, perhaps too late, that she had been duping herself. Perhaps it was better to run from both powers, admit her essential futility, retreat to Florida, California, Arizona, or follow her father into New York's special loneliness.

Another voice argued against this despair. Did not love, the biblical love that had once stirred her soul, did not that love include humiliation, abasement, being a fool for Christ's sake? Was not that how she had defended herself from the simpleminded criticisms of the family, when she first tried to practice the social gospel? She no longer trusted that kind of love. It devoured the self, that not quite definable but profoundly knowable person named Paula Stapleton. A love that destroyed Paula Stapleton was not an emotion or an ideal she could accept. That kind of love belonged to the dreaming vagaries of youth, inexperience. Now the word love was defined by her life. She wanted—and the wanting brought tears to her eyes—the kind of love she had known in the first years of her marriage. Love that shared power and respect and affection. Love that asked and gave in return without invoking absolutes, demanding extremes. Love that tolerated failings, but not failure, that forgave hurts without fear of abasement. Love, in a word, that kept its promise.

"Incidentally," Jake said as she retreated from the library, "I wouldn't take any calls. They're probably from reporters. If you take one, I'd stick to no comment."

"Why?"

"Haven't you seen the morning paper? I thought at least you'd have heard the news on the car radio."

"I was thinking—about other things," Paula said.

The Mayor handed her the paper. Beneath six-inch headlines was the story of her $20,000 gift to the Malcolm X Ujamaa, by-lined by Dennis Mulligan.

"Oh," Paula said. "Oh, Jake. What—what can I say?"

"Nothing. I'm not surprised. I figured it was coming, as soon as I heard Grimes had gone to work for Slocum. Dwight's moving in for the kill. He figures he's got me on the ropes."

"No matter what happens between us—I want you to know that I'm ready to spend every cent I've got to help you beat that—that bastard."

"Thanks," Jake said.

Paula fumbled her way into the center hall, devastated. Everything she had said was wrong, above all, that last grandiose offer. That was the old Paula, buying him up again, doing the same thing that had ruined their love. It was compulsive. She was hopeless. He had every right to keep her at arm's length, room's length. She was a disease, a Typhoid Mary whose virus was guaranteed to destroy affection, respect.

Upstairs, after greeting a delighted Kemble and Dolores, she retreated to her bedroom and read Mulligan's story. It was crammed with slanted phrases and vicious innuendos. After stating the facts, from his "highly placed, unauthorized source," Mulligan suggested that the gift proved that Mayor O'Connor was his wife's creature, and his supposedly evenhanded approach to busing was a fraud. More dismaying was a statement from the anti-busing spokesman Kevin McGuire, condemning the Mayor as "two-faced." McGuire said he thought the public was tired of both O'Connor faces. He had reason to believe that the political leaders of the city, including Party Chairman Eddie McKenna, thought the same way. He himself was not a candidate, but he was ready to support any "responsible" leader in a recall election to get the Mayor and his fascist police commissioner, Victor Tarentino, out of politics.

The phone rang. Mahoney informed her that it was Adam Turner. "Paula? I've been calling you all over the state. Listen. We can't let Mulligan get away with that story, no matter how things stand between you and Jake. I'm prepared to make a statement saying Jake didn't know a damn thing about that gift."

"I don't think it will do any good, Adam. Let me ask him."

She went downstairs and asked Jake. He shook his head. "Tell him when he gets to be Mayor of this city, he'll need all the credibility he can find. No point in losing it five years ahead of schedule."

She repeated this to Adam.

"What is the man talkin' about?"

"I don't know," Paula said.

Outside on the Parkway, a blare of bugles and a clatter of drums announced the beginning of the St. Patrick's Day parade. After lunch, Jake emerged from the library and asked her if she would like to join him on the reviewing stand. She was tempted to make some feeble joke about political masochism, but he was so polite, so distant, that she could only match his tone and say, "Of course."

The reviewing stand was crowded with politicians, as usual. The Republican Governor was there and the incumbent Republican Senator, both looking bored. Congressman Dwight Slocum was having an intense conversation with Democratic State Chairman Bernie Bannon. City Council President Dominick Montefiore was talking guardedly with Kevin McGuire. Paula noted that Montefiore broke off the conversration when he saw the Mayor. Obviously the demand for a recall election was not mere phrase making. A lot of people felt that the city's balance of power was about to shift. And who was responsible? Who else but Paula Stapleton O'Connor, the ultimate political mess maker.

It was a beautiful day, full of rich sunlight. The breeze had a hint of spring in it. Paula remembered other St. Patrick's Days when they had stood on the reviewing stand enduring an icy downpour, or a cruel north wind. Was this warmth and sunshine a good omen? For what? She did not know.

She needed faith in something to withstand the stares as Mayor O'Connor took his accustomed place in the center of the first row. He shook hands with a half dozen people within reach, and forced Paula to do the same thing. "Paula, you know Senator Fuller. Paula, there's Commissioner Corbin. Paula, there's Dominick Montefiore. I don't know what the hell he's doing here but say hello to him. What's the trouble, Dom? Your calendar running fast? Did you hear the music and think it was Columbus Day?"

Only when she was forced to smile and nod greetings did Paula realize that she had walked to the front row with her head down and was standing there like a guilty prisoner waiting for the judge to pronounce sentence. Numbly, she listened to Montefiore tell Jake that it was a shame the way Eddie McKenna had come down with the flu and was unable to lead the parade. For months

Eddie had been looking forward to being grand marshal. He would probably miss the dinner tonight too. "A real shame," the Mayor agreed.

"MRS. O'CONNOR, ABOUT THAT GIFT—DID YOU DISCUSS IT WITH YOUR HUSBAND?"

"MRS. O'CONNOR—WHAT DID YOU HOPE TO ACCOMPLISH—?"

On the street below them were a dozen reporters shouting questions. Jake leaned on the railing of the reviewing stand and greeted several of them by name. "Mrs. O'Connor has nothing to say. No comment. Later in the week she may be willing to discuss the story with you."

The reporters retreated. Bernie Bannon sidled up to Jake as a brass band went past, blaring "It's a Great Day for the Irish." Bannon said something Paula had no hope of hearing.

"I don't see why it should make any difference, Bernie."

Bernie looked pained. "Jake, be reasonable, for God's sake."

"Who does your thinking for you, Bernie? Denny Mulligan?"

A band of bagpipers shrilling "The Minstrel Boy" to a marching beat drowned Bernie's reply. Irritation began to mingle with Paula's bewilderment. What was Jake doing? One moment he seemed to be humiliating her. The next he was protecting her. Then he was ignoring her. She was not sure she liked his strange serenity. His calm seemed artificial, as if he had taken a drug or performed some feat of self-hypnosis.

Going back to Bowood in the limousine, she asked somewhat testily: "Is it permissible for me to find out what's happening?"

"It would take too long to explain. I haven't finished that goddamn speech yet." For a moment he looked gloomy. "I may not finish it. I may just stand up there and wing it. It probably won't make much difference."

At six o'clock, as they came downstairs to depart to the St. Patrick's Day dinner, the Mayor asked Paula if she would mind stopping at the bicentennial exhibit that

Simon Burke and Allyn Stapleton had created in the armory. "It opened today. I'd like to get some idea of the crowd's reaction. I'd like you to see it too."

"Of course," Paula said, and wondered how much longer she was going to keep saying that, before she exploded. She let Jake take her hand and lead her to the open back door of CITY-1. Jesse Owens smiled warmly at her. "Sure nice to see you back and lookin' so healthy, Mrs. O'Connor."

"It's nice to be back, Jesse."

Was she back? Or was she being treated like an important, respected but not particularly loved visitor? Was there something she was going to find out at this bicentennial exhibit, besides the history of the city? Something about her husband and Allyn Stapleton?

"Simon and Allyn worked like hell on this exhibit," Jake was saying. "Incidentally, Simon's in love with her. It's the most pathetic thing you've ever seen. Beauty and the Beast."

"It sounds bizarre."

"Everything about Allyn is bizarre. She's been wrestling Charlie LoBello for the sexual championship of the state. When he told her that he loved her, she stopped seeing him. She said he wasn't mature enough. She's turned poor Charlie into a lovesick zombie."

Allyn was another Stapleton neurosis? Was that what he was trying to tell her? Or was he telling her that it did not matter what Allyn did or what Judge Stapleton did with their lives? Each individual lived a single life. The trouble began when a person began living someone else's life—the life of a father or a mother or a family or a clan or a tribe or a race. If that was what he was saying, agreement was on her lips.

But she could not stop suspecting his cool distant manner. It went beyond wariness. Was he telling her that she had to pay a price for her absence? She had had the temerity to walk out on the great O'Connor. Was a little groveling necessary to obtain his permission to return?

"By the way," Jake said, "did you ever read Mortimer Kemble's diary?"

"Yes."

"What did you think of it?"

Now, now was a chance to tell him. But it was the wrong place, with the chauffeur listening. The way he asked the question was wrong. It was too casual. She avoided a genuine answer.

"I thought he was a—monster."

"I kind of got to like the old bastard. He made it all the way, you know. I had Simon check him out. He ran the state for about fifteen years in the eighties and nineties. They called him Czar Mortimer. His Irish entourage finally got caught stealing everything but the bathroom fixtures out of the state capitol. But by then Mortimer was a nice repectable judge."

"Here's the armory, Your Honor," Jesse Owens said.

Jake pushed a big brass bell that clattered dully behind the huge steel doors. Simon Burke opened a door in the wall a few feet away and they walked into the outer lobby, full of flags and trophies from the regiments and divisions the city had sent to the nation's wars. Allyn Stapleton greeted her cheerfully. She was looking spectacularly beautiful in an aqua off-the-shoulder gown. Simon was wearing a tuxedo that bulged in all directions, making him look like he might self-destruct at any moment. They explained that they were going to the St. Patrick's Day dinner.

"I've never been to one," Allyn said. "Simon says it's a basic part of my political education."

"He's right. If you can put up with these drunks and stay in politics you're ready to graduate," Jake said. "How did people react to the exhibit?"

"The kids loved it," Allyn said defiantly. "Most of the adults too."

"But we've gotten hell from the president of the Friendly Sons of St. Patrick, ditto for the Ancient Order of Hibernians and the Knights of Columbus," Simon Burke said. "Some character who claimed he was head of the County Association of Holy Name Societies and controlled 40,000 votes denounced it. Tony Perotta was outraged and Dominick Montefiore wasn't too enthused by the Italian section and Kitty Kosciusko said she was going to sue you for slandering the Poles. I hope we haven't endangered your candidacy, Your Honor."

"We'll cool them off," the Mayor said. "Paula would like to see it. Can you turn on the lights?"

Simon disappeared into the shadows at the end of the lobby. They stood in front of the cavernous doorway to the darkened interior while Paula tried to find hidden meanings in the conversation she had just heard.

"Don't stop in any one place too long," Allyn said. "Walk through it at a steady pace so it all hits you."

"Stand by," bellowed Simon from the dark end of the hall.

The interior of the armory suddenly blazed with light. Confronting Paula was a twenty-foot-high blowup of Irish immigrants coming off a ferryboat. More beaten, battered, despairing people she had never seen in her life. There was not a glimpse of hope in those sullen eyes. On the pinched faces of the children there was an occasional flash of animal cunning. But on the faces of the adults, men and women, defeat was stamped with all the cruelty and ugliness of a massive bruise. At the top of the picture was a title: THEY CAME.

Once past that vision, Paula faced a forty-foot-high blowup of a Fourth of July parade. Soldiers in blue uniforms came at her, twelve feet tall. Red white and blue bunting dangled from Bowood. On a platform in front of the house Mayor Mortimer Kemble in a frock coat and stovepipe hat saluted the colors. Around the central image of the parade there were panoramic glimpses of the city's factories belching huge clouds of black smoke, massive locomotives doing more of the same, interspersed by pictures of services in the Grace Episcopal Church, the First Presbyterian Church, and other houses of worship. The title of this one was: THEY SAW.

Next came an even bigger blowup of about fifty Irish standing in front of a tenement that looked in imminent danger of falling down. In front of it lay a dead horse with a bloated belly. On top of the horse's belly stood an urchin with a face that emanated pure evil. He could not have been more than ten years old. He had a glass, undoubtedly of whiskey, in his hand. He raised it defiantly. Behind him everyone else was raising glasses too. The title of this one: THEY CONGREGATED.

"It was Allyn's idea to do it here, in the armory. It had to come from someone her age," Simon Burke said.

"Oh, bullshit, Simon," Allyn said.

"No, it's true. This huge inner space was a void until we filled it with these pictures. A void. The perfect image of the past for most of the city."

"I agree," Jake said.

"I was going to cover the walls with a couple of thousand pictures and posters and texts. It was her idea to select a few dozen and blow them up to this size."

Simon explained how they had pasted the pictures on huge pieces of wallboard and hoisted them erect on triangles and squares and hexagons, dangled them from girders on ropes, laid them flat on the floor and built platforms around them. They did the same thing with newspapers, political posters, pages from letters and diaries. Everywhere the effect was the same. Instead of the visitor standing in the omnipotent present selectively surveying the past, history broke over him like an engulfing wave.

On one side of an immense triangle loomed a page from the Garden Square *Journal* in 1880. Beneath a cartoon of an apelike creature with a shamrock in his lapel and a pipe between his grinning teeth was an editorial.

TEDDY O'FLAHERTY VOTES. HE HAS NOT BEEN IN THE COUNTRY SIX MONTHS. HE HAS HAIR ON HIS TEETH. HE NEVER KNEW AN HOUR IN CIVILIZED SOCIETY. HE IS A SAVAGE—AS BRUTAL A RUFFIAN AS AN UNTAMED INDIAN, THE BORN CRIMINAL AND PAUPER OF THE CIVILIZED WORLD. TO COMPARE HIM WITH AN INTELLIGENT NEGRO WOULD BE AN INSULT TO THE LATTER. THE IRISH FILL OUR PRISONS AND OUR POORHOUSES. SCRATCH A CON-

VICT OR A PAUPER AND YOU ARE CERTAIN TO TICKLE THE SKIN OF AN IRISH CATHOLIC.

The second side of the triangle was covered with stories of people with Irish names being arrested for every crime from robbery to rape to murder. There were lists of Irish being admitted to the poorhouse. There were pictures of Irish gangsters, Irish gangs, an Irish hanging. On the third side in gigantic letters was a newspaper ad: WOMAN WANTED TO DO GENERAL HOUSEWORK. ENGLISH, SCOTCH, WELSH, GERMAN, OR ANY COUNTRY OR COLOR EXCEPT IRISH.

Next came a hexagon of pictures of Irishmen and Irishwomen working. On one side was a twenty-five-foot-high picture of a burly jut-jawed hod carrier with a torn coat and incredibly dirty face and hands. On the other sides of the hexagon the Irish laid railroad tracks, scrubbed floors, dug ditches, drove wagons, tended factory machines. Another hexagon told the story of the titanic battle to get equal religious education in the public schools—a battle the Irish lost. A triangle dramatized the first inauguration of an Irish mayor in City Hall.

Then came another huge single picture—again a horde of immigrants pouring off a ferryboat. The same mélange of defeat and deprivation. But these were Italians. More triangles and squares of pictures and texts told the story of their struggle against prejudice and distrust, their work, their success. The motif was repeated for each of the city's immigrant groups. Finally, there was an identical swarm of newcomers pouring off an identical ferryboat. But their faces were black. Again the title: THEY CAME.

There was no more. The exhibit was over.

"I told them it would stir up the animals. They didn't believe me," Jake said.

"I still don't see how anyone can possibly object to it," Simon said. "It's beautiful. It's true. I will defend it to the death."

Simon was looking at Allyn as he said these melodramatic words. Paula saw the pain of hopeless desire in his eyes. It was pathetic.

"Simon should have been born in the ninth century," Allyn said. "By instinct he's a Galahad."

Paula had thought the cool animosity in Allyn's green eyes was directed at her, the spokesperson for the older generation's conformity. Now she sensed it was a self-consuming fire. She saw bitterness in the tiny droop at the corners of that proud mouth. Perhaps for Allyn love had become impossible. Paula did not know why. She could only know that for her the opposite was true. She knew how ready she was to renew her love. But she was not sure, she was more and more unsure, if her husband cared.

Jake was telling Simon not to worry about the critics of the exhibit. "I told you I'd take the heat," he said.

"Why don't they like it?" Paula said.

"They don't want to remember how bad it was."

"It makes me ashamed of being a Stapleton," Allyn said. "We did this to the Irish, the Italians, to all of them."

"That kind of thinking is a waste of time, Allyn," Jake said.

Allyn was startled and not at all pleased by this reproof. "Why did we put all this together?" she said.

"For the wrong reason, maybe," Jake said.

"You learn something new around here every day," Allyn said. "If it keeps up this place may get so interesting I'll never go back to New York."

"I seem to be missing something in this conversation," Paula said.

"No," Allyn said. "I think I'm the one who did the missing."

Paula was tempted to persist in confessing her ignorance. But Jake interrupted them. "Let's go to the party. I need a drink if I'm going to make this speech."

They strolled across the street into the crowded lobby of the Garden Square Hotel. A squad of reporters launched a guerrilla attack on them, with Paula their main target. Jake steadily repeated what he had told them from the reviewing stand. A sweating Charlie LoBello rushed up to them as they waited for the elevator. He hastily greeted Paula, looked longingly at Allyn, and asked the Mayor if he had a copy of his speech. The reporters simply refused to believe one did not exist, and were threatening to torture press secretary Dave O'Brien until he produced one.

"They're going to have to do the unprecedented. Listen to it. I hope they don't crack under the strain," Jake said.

He took a sheaf of yellow pages out of his inner coat pocket. "You couldn't read my writing, Charlie, even if you had time to copy it."

"Could you give me a synopsis? The major points?" Charlie asked.

Jake shook his head. "This is basically an outline. There are things I may—or may not—say. Depending on how certain things go upstairs."

They got off the elevator at the third floor and strolled down a corridor lined with mirrors. The hotel had pasted green shamrocks on them. Through double doors at the end of the corridor came a rumble of voices from The Emerald Room. Inside, cardboard shamrocks dangled from the ceiling, barely visible in the cigarette smoke. In a distant corner a six-man band was playing "Has Anybody Here Seen Kelly?" Most of the six hundred guests were already enjoying their cocktails. Not many of these sons of St. Patrick were young. Nor were they all Irish. Dominick Montefiore and Victor Tarentino were as at home beneath the dangling shamrocks as drinkers named Kelly or Walsh. Over the years, the dinner had been transmuted into a political conclave at which favored candidates, usually Democrats, were invited to speak to a wealthy, influential audience. Enough Irish remained to constitute a narrow majority. But none of them bore much resemblance to the gaunt, beaten, ragged people Paula had seen in the bicentennial exhibit. These Irish sported the latest styles in evening clothes. Their wives' hair had delicate contemporary touches and they wore their expensive gowns with assurance. Money created a mixture of complacency and arrogance in their attitudes that Paula always found discouraging. If only their thinking matched their status, that had been her reaction in other years. The women talked about golf scores and trips to Europe more than they talked about politics, national or local. The men retained an ancestral interest in the subject, although few of them were active politicians.

Dozens of old friends came over to shake Jake's hand and ask His Honor if he planned to take on any more rioters. Jake answered them with jokes that made Paula uneasy. She found it hard to laugh about what had happened at Buchanan High School. Then she realized that they were probably trying to avoid the topic that was foremost in their minds—how much damage the Mayor's wife had done to his Senate campaign with her compulsive checkbook. Maybe that was why Jake had wanted her with him tonight—to disarm such questions. She suddenly remembered one of his political aphorisms: when you make a mistake, flaunt it. Perhaps tonight he was translating it into: if you're married to a liability, display her.

They followed Simon and Allyn through the crowd to the bar where a circle had formed around Joe Mullen, a Dublin policeman. Each St. Patrick's Day the Ancient Order of Hibernians flew an Irish cop to the city to testify to their sense of identity with the Ould Sod. The Mayor and his wife were introduced to Mullen, who raised a dark brown glass. "Here's tew Yorr Grace. From what I hear, you've got more trouble than the Shan Van Vocht."

Jake obviously did not know what he was talking about. Paula was surprised to see that everyone else around the bar was equally mystified.

Simon handed the Mayor and Paula two dark brown scotches and glared at the rest of the drinkers. "Don't any of you know what the Shan Van Vocht means? Your grandfathers did. It's the traditional name for Ireland. It means The Poor Old Woman. Sing it for them, Joe."

Mullen grinned at the discomfited Irish-American faces, and sang:

"And will Ireland then be free?
Says the Shan Van Vocht.

> Will Ireland then be free?
> > Says the Shan Van Vocht.
>
> "Yes! Ireland *shall* be free
> > From the centre to the sea;
> Then hurrah for liberty,
> > Says the Shan Van Vocht."

"Greatest little country in the world," said a big jut-jawed man who had a remarkable resemblance to the twenty-five-foot-high hod carrier Allyn had created in the armory. "You gotta come visit me some time at my place in County Cork, Jake. Twenty rooms. I picked it up for thirty grand. You and Paula oughta buy a place. There's some real bargains available."

"I'll keep it in mind, Tom. What can I run for over there?"

A hand seized Jake's arm. It was connected to Bernie Bannon. "Jake," he said, "maybe we ought to have that little talk. I've got a room down the hall."

"Sure," Jake said. "Excuse me for five minutes."

He drew Simon to one side. "Listen," Paula heard him say. "Get to a phone and call Adam Turner at the Medical Center. Tell him I'd like him to sneak out and come over here to catch my speech. My car can pick him up in front of the main building about nine-fifteen. He won't be out of bed for more than an hour. But if he doesn't feel up to it, forget it."

Jake vanished into the crowd, leaving Paula with Allyn. She smiled. "I'm glad you liked the exhibit."

"Like is an inadequate word. I was awed."

"I worked damn hard on it. Jake was right when he said I did it for the wrong reason. But it wasn't simpleminded Stapleton hatred. It was to impress him. When I heard you'd left him and retreated to the farm, I thought sure you'd get divorced, and let the all-knowing Judge and the rest of them take charge of your life. How did you get away from them? It's given me new respect for you."

Paula was tempted to treat Allyn like a reporter and say "no comment." Simon Burke appeared to rescue her.

"Councilman Turner says he'll make the scene. But he'd like to know what's going on."

He is not alone, Paula thought gloomily.

"Do you think the Mayor—Jake—can beat Slocum?" Simon asked.

"I don't know," Paula said.

"It's pretty common knowledge that the Congressman's entering the primary," Simon said. "That's what Bannon is probably telling Jake now."

"Yes," Paula said.

At the bar, the Dublin policeman began singing more verses of the Shan Van Vocht. For a moment Paula had another spasm of dislocation. *Wrong,* a voice whispered. *Wrong. You do not belong here among these alien faces and voices, these big hands clutching dark brown drinks.* But she fought it. She did belong here. She had married these hands and faces and voices.

Suddenly Jake was standing next to her. At first glance, he looked solemn. But his eyes were extraordinarily cheerful. Something close to rage stirred in her. What right had he to look cheerful when they had not exchanged one personal word? When all the wounds they had inflicted on each other were unhealed by so much as an apology.

"I just saw the shadow of a gunman, Benny O'Farrell, the local agent for the IRA. He says he's going to have me shot for our bicentennial exhibit. I told him his boys will have to get in line. A couple of other assassins are ahead of him."

"You haven't had any more calls from that nut?" Paula asked.

"He faded away. All talk and no action, that's the story of Frank Donahue's life."

Bells began chiming. It was time for dinner. They drank a quick toast to St. Patrick and followed the crowd into the hotel's main ballroom. More green cardboard shamrocks hung on wires from the lofty ceiling. There were quarts of scotch, gin, bourbon, and Irish whiskey on every table. Red-haired Gerry Mulvaney, toastmaster for the past ten years, rushed up to babble apologies. They did not have a seat for Paula on the dais. They had not been expecting her. There were no other ladies on the dais anyway. It was reserved for the panjandrums of the Irish societies and distinguished guests. The Mayor said he would sit with his wife and let someone else have his seat on the dais. Gerry conferred with a few graying oldsters and led Paula and the Mayor to a table directly in front of the dais.

On Paula's left sat Archbishop George Petrie. Paula did not like him as much as his genial predecessor, Cardinal Matthew Mahan. Petrie was a smaller, less charming man. He had the false smile and other mannerisms of a salesman, compromised by a querulous tone of voice. He was always complaining about something. In the past, he had filled Paula's ears with his disappointment at the Mayor's refusal to co-operate politically with the Church on issues such as abortion and aid for parochial schools. Petrie always claimed he "understood" and shifted his lamentations to the financial woes of the archdiocese, a problem he obviously felt she could alleviate. This time, Paula listened politely to the travails of the city's parochial schools. They were being swamped with applications from parents trying to avoid the busing order.

She could not resist inserting a ladylike needle into the Archbishop.

"I'm surprised you haven't banned that sort of thing. Didn't the Church do that in Boston?"

"Yes," the Archbishop admitted somewhat uncomfortably. "But their school system was solvent. Our schools are in desperate straits. To put it bluntly, we need the business."

"Oh," Paula said, and was not displeased to see the Archbishop squirm, and change the subject to the parlous state of the city's Catholic hospitals.

On the dais, Gerry Mulvaney began spewing Irish jokes and introducing distinguished guests. Judges, bank presidents, corporation executives, politicians, monsignors. Then came an introduction that was somewhat more elaborate. "One of the city's upcoming politicians, Kevin McGuire."

The room exploded with clapping, cheering, whistling for the anti-busing spokesman. Paula saw Dominick Montefiore on his feet a few tables away. When Montefiore was introduced, McGuire leaped to his feet to lead the applause. It was hard to believe that Jake would take calmly a McGuire-Montefiore coalition. What was wrong with him? He usually saw these things coming and stopped them before the acrimony became public. Maybe behind the calm there was some kind of brain damage, a mental or psychological collapse from the beating the Buchanan mob had given him.

They drank some consommé and ate some roast beef. Simon Burke got drunk and began reciting Irish poetry to Allyn. The Archbishop droned in Paula's other ear. She twitched when Simon cried: "What shall I do for pretty girls now that my old bawd is dead?" Simon got drunker and abandoned poetry for philosophy. "Dialectic of history. Survival and return. Irish fate," he muttered. The Archbishop told Paula how much he wanted to build a home for the aged.

Gerry Mulvaney returned to the lectern with more jokes about Pat and Mike, and began the program for the evening. There were three Irish folk singers playing guitars, straight from a stupendous success at Carnegie Hall, and there was the city's own Patrick McCarty, with his slightly fading tenor, to sing some traditional airs. Then Mulvaney began introducing the Mayor—"our feature attraction," he called him. "I've been celebrating St. Patrick's Day with him since the first grade in old St. Patrick's School. He didn't hold his liquor as well as he does now, but he was a broth of a boy even then and you could see that he was on his way to the top. I have a feeling he may have some political news to tell us tonight about a new phase in his career. Isn't that right, Senator—er—I mean, Mayor? Well, it doesn't matter what hat he's wearin', he's still our darlin' lad, and here he is to speak to us—Graham—Everything's Jake—O'Connor."

The applause was encouraging. Jake mounted the dais and adjusted the microphone.

"Thanks, Gerry," he said. "It's certainly flattering to get promoted before you win an election—in fact, before you even say you're a candidate. Much as I hate to disappoint you and the rest of my friends who are gathered here tonight, I'm not a candidate for any other office but the one I hold, and I do not intend to become one. I could say the obvious thing—that I can't walk out on this city at a time when it needs leadership—but that would only be true in part. I haven't given it much leadership lately. The real reason goes deeper. There are certain things in life that you are born to do—you feel it in your bones. Other things come your way if you get lucky. Bigger things, in the opinion of some people. But they're not bigger to you, compared to that thing you were born to do. For me it's leading this city. It's what I thought about doing as long as I can remember thinking about anything. I intend to stay in the job, as long as the voters tolerate my idiosyncrasies, and agree with my goals for the future."

Those calm self-deprecating words crashed against Paula's ears like gunfire. He was turning his back on her ambition for him, flouting, without so much as a consultation with her, a hope that they had shared and struggled for so many years to realize. She glared at the dais, her head tilted back, rigid with anger. Then she felt his eyes on her, and saw on his face that familiar mixture of strength and vulnerability, that wordless plea for both understanding and help. *Listen,* Paula told herself.

She listened while he talked about why he loved the city. The Irish camaraderie of the North Slope saloons, the Italian food in the South Slope's Little Italy, Polish weddings on the North Slope, and St. Patrick's Day in Tipperary Square. He talked about the athletic fields where he had played as a teen-ager, the memorable teams, the championship games. And the politics. The famous rallies and marches, the parks and squares where Presidents and governors had come in search of votes and said great things and silly things. She heard the authentic sound of his caring, his love for this dirty decaying violence-ridden place, a love that was intertwined with father and Irish shame and Irish pride.

"Those words about the future of this city may only

convince some of you that I've lost my marbles. You don't think this city has a future. Especially after what you've been reading in the papers for the last ten weeks.

"A lot of our trouble has been caused by extremists on both sides. I can forgive extremists like the people in RIP. They're not politicians. They're only voicing the anguish of ordinary people caught in a hammerlock by history. I can also understand—though I deplore them—extreme statements by black politicians, speaking from a deeply felt concern for their own people. But there is one man who joined the extremists that I cannot forgive or understand. He is a friend of mine and it isn't easy for me to condemn him here on St. Patrick's Day.

"But I have to do it. Eddie McKenna has dishonored the profession of politician. It is a title—an honorable title—that he no longer has the right to hold. Once a man wears that title, he forfeits the right to think and speak only for himself—or his own group. A politician is a leader who is trying to help men and women live in a community, to live in peace by reconciling their differences. That's why I have asked for—and received—Eddie McKenna's resignation as chairman of the Democratic Party in this city."

Paula saw the pain on her husband's face. She knew better than anyone else in the room that this was no performance. Every word was genuine. She listened while Jake told them what Eddie McKenna had said to him when he asked him to help disperse the mob in front of Buchanan High School. For a moment Jake hesitated and Paula wondered if he might lose control of himself. Now she understood the artificial calm, the strange detachment that had irritated her all day. He was steeling himself to do this thing, to break once and for all with this side of his Irish past, to tear up this deep root of sentiment, to cut away the web of friendship and shared memory that had become entangled with his very flesh.

"I'm sorry to have to say that about Eddie. He was—and is—my friend. I'm even sorrier to say what's coming next. There's another reason why Eddie has forfeited his claim to that title, politician. I have evidence

—hard evidence—that he has betrayed your trust in the style of other Irish politicians who have disgraced this city and state in the past. Tomorrow, I intend to give the evidence to the district attorney and ask him to present it to the grand jury."

There was not a sound in the room. Paula saw a mixture of amazement and anger on Kevin McGuire's face. Dominick Montefiore looked dazed. The Mayor took a swallow of water from a glass on the dais.

"Not very cheerful talk for St. Patrick's Day. But I don't think we've got much to be cheerful about this St. Patrick's Day. I want to use this day to talk seriously to you about this city. I'm going to talk as an Irish American, but I hope what I'm going to say will mean something to those who aren't Irish but share similar American memories. Almost every man and woman in this room was born in this city. A lot of you don't live here anymore. But most of the men visit this city every day. You come here to work. You sit behind desks and make decisions that affect the life of this city. You don't vote here anymore. But you can open your wallet or your checkbook and cast a much bigger vote than the average citizen. You're important.

"Where did you get that importance? A hundred years ago, our grandparents arrived in this city with not much more than the clothes on their backs. Here we are spending as much in one night as they earned in a month—maybe even in a year.

"I'll tell you where most of the money came from. From politics. We bargained votes for jobs, and then we used the jobs to create more jobs. We spread the work around, and did our damndest to make sure, if a street had to be torn up or a sewer laid, there were some Irishmen working on it. Eventually we got around to being in charge of it. Irish contractors were born, and Irish cement makers, construction companies, lumber companies. Always in the teeth of the Wasps' sneers. They kept saying we couldn't do it. That we didn't have brains enough, that we were a bunch of lazy bums who didn't really want to do anything but drink all day. Our grandfathers lived in those downtown slums along the river. Most of our fathers grew up in them. When they talked about it, they made it sound like fun. Rolling dice in the alleys, hooking food from the grocer, pouring the old man into bed when he came home from the saloon, breaking heads on election day. But believe me, while they were living it, it wasn't fun. It was a struggle, a brute struggle for survival.

"Across the street in the armory is a collection of pictures that dramatize the history of this ordeal. They were selected by our city historian, Simon Burke. You won't like some of them. You may not like any of them. They tell the truth about that agony our grandfathers and fathers endured. Here's a few facts and figures to back up those pictures."

The Mayor took a card out of his pocket. Except for the occasional clink of a coffee cup, there was not a sound in the room.

"In 1869, seventy-two per cent of the people arrested in this city were Irish. Eighty-six per cent of the families in the county almshouse were Irish. Sixty-three per cent of the prisoners in the county jail, serving sentences of less than a year, were Irish. In the state, seventy-five per cent of the prisoners serving sentences of more than a year were Irish. Eighty-six per cent of the people on poor relief were Irish. In the Personals of the city's leading paper at the time, I counted twenty-five pleas in a single issue, from women begging a father who had deserted his family to come home.

"They didn't have a good time in those downtown slums, my friends. We're descended from the lucky ones, the strong ones, the ones who had the stamina, or got the kind of help that meant survival. We've forgotten about the ones who didn't make it. But I bet there isn't a man or woman in this room tonight who doesn't have at least one relative who became a casualty of those slums.

"At this very moment, my brother is sitting in a mental hospital about fifty miles from here, staring at the wall. He tore his head apart trying to understand how my father could tolerate the kind of city that we grew up in—a city where one Irishman's word was the law and everyone knew that man was a crook. One of the biggest crooks in the history of this country, in fact. A crook who stole millions and spread damn little of it around. A crook who had the Archbishop and half the monsignors in the city on his side, who made corruption a way of life for himself and all the other people in his organization.

"But I don't condemn that man. I don't like him but I don't condemn him. Why? Because he turned losers into winners. Losers. That's what we Irish were when we arrived in this country. A beaten people. An inferior race. Taught to regard ourselves as scum for three hundred years in conquered Ireland. That kind of psychology is awfully hard to break. It wasn't enough to get us jobs, although the jobs were crucial. It wasn't enough to build playgrounds and gymnasiums and fill the boxing rings and baseball fields with Irish athletes, even though that was also important. The jobs, the achievements in sports were all individual accomplishments. Somehow, somewhere, there had to be a sense of victory as a people, a group, to turn losers into winners. That's what the Democratic organization did for the Irish in this state.

"Let me read you a few lines from a speech that my father made forty years ago in the Thirteenth Ward.

> I can remember the days of my boyhood when a man with an Irish name could not get a decent job in this city. It was even tougher for a man with an Italian or a Polish or a Slovak name. We were all Catholics and there was an unwritten law that Catholics couldn't get jobs in the schools, the courts, the fire and police departments. We changed that. The Democratic organization of this city changed it. We showed those people who were trying to deprive us of our birthright as Americans what it meant to pick a fight with men who knew how to organize and vote to make their voices heard. We did more than that. We took over this city. We organized it so that people with Irish and Italian and Polish names had a real voice in its government. That's

why I'm loyal to the organization. Because I know what the organization did for the people of this city.

"I found that speech only last night, when I was looking through my father's papers, trying to understand what was happening to me and to this city. We are faced with a very strange situation in this bicentennial year, 1976. We have a lot of people living in downtown wards whose ancestors spent about three hundred years living in the worst kind of defeat—living in slavery. It took them another hundred years to escape from the region where they were born, and move to free soil. They now account for a high percentage of the crimes in this city. They fill up our welfare rolls.

"Wait a minute, you say, why can't they make it the way we made it, the hard way? My fellow Americans, think for a moment about what this means. Think of what I have tried to remind you tonight. Is this all we have learned from a hundred years in America? To demand the right to inflict the same misery on others that we suffered? Is our record that good? Were we then— or are we now—such moral paragons? Eddie McKenna's story reminds us that we have a way to go before we get perfect enough to look down on anybody.

"A few days ago I faced a mob of people who were threatening to massacre a hundred and twenty-five black teen-agers at Buchanan High School. When I tried to talk to them, I got kicked in the stomach, in the face. Some of you probably think I got just what I deserved. You may be surprised to hear that I agree with you. If I am the man Gerry Mulvaney introduced to you tonight—your representative in City Hall. But the kicks should have come from the black people, not from people with names like Reilly and Kwaitkowski. We've been running this city for over fifty years. There were black Americans—a lot of them—living here during those years. What did they get from us, the boys in charge at City Hall? Not a hell of a lot, if you want the blunt truth. We spread some cash around their districts on election day. But when it came to jobs, political power, it was wait in line and the night stick in the teeth for anyone who talked back.

"This Irishman—the one you're listening to—your man in City Hall—has yet to be kicked by a single black person in this city. A majority of them still believe that they can get some kind of justice from me. Maybe that's because I've tried to help them, I've moved to give them a fair share of the jobs on any payroll I control.

"But let me remind you of what I just finished saying: jobs aren't enough. You don't change from losers to winners without a sense of having won a struggle as a people. Putting their children on those buses, sending them to white schools, and asking white parents to send their children to black schools—that is their struggle. And from this day I am going to dedicate myself to helping them win it.

"Maybe that sounds crazy to you. Maybe it even sounds crazy to me. Pollsters tell me it won't help me win any votes in future elections. I say, nuts to that numbers game. This is a fight. A fight to change the minds and hearts of the white people of this city. We've only lost the first round. I don't believe that you are going to let me carry on this fight alone. I can't believe that you agree with the hatred on the faces and in the feet of that mob I met outside Buchanan High School. As your spokesman, I repudiate that hatred. I dismiss it as the frenzy of a single day, not the summation of a lifelong heritage.

"Repudiation is only a first step. From there we need to go to work on a program that is designed to *prevent* history from repeating itself. Let me tell you why I feel so strongly about this. I didn't come by this compassion naturally. I was absorbed, like too many sons and grandsons of immigrants, in the bitter memories of our own hard times. But I happen to have the good fortune to be married to a woman who comes from another tradition—an American tradition that I have learned to admire. It is a tradition that believes in this country's ability to change, to escape the past. You read in the paper today about a gift she made to the black people of this city. I am proud of that gift, proud of the courage, the trust with which it was made. Without that kind of courage and trust, we can't hope to prevent history from repeating itself. I ask you to join us in this trust. I ask you in the name of the tradition that the Irish brought to American politics, the tradition of generosity, of caring for those who are suffering, for thse who are hungry and sore in body, who are cold in flesh or in spirit. We cannot afford to let that tradition die. America cannot afford it.

"Forty years ago, my father stood on a platform in the Thirteenth Ward and said: 'You are my people.' My ambition is to say the same thing to this entire city and make those words mean even more than they meant to him. He was talking to people in the slums, telling them that he was there to get them the coal, the food, the coats, and shoes they needed to survive. I want to go beyond survival. I want to speak to people who are united by a common pride, a common trust in their leaders, a common concern for the future of all the people in this city.

"I ask for your support, not in a spirit of reproach, but in a spirit of hope. In a spirit that is both Irish and American. I would only add that the task is immense, and we have no right to expect or seek gratitude. Launching this program, we will be paying a debt we owe America. We will be forging in this city a new kind of community, rooted not in religion or ethnic pride or economic power, but in mutual respect and understanding, a community that has learned from its past and no longer fears its future."

Paula watched, frozen beyond thought, beyond feeling, while Jake gathered the pages of his speech from the lectern and walked slowly along the dais to return to his seat. Not a sound came from the audience. Not a hand clapped. Not a voice cheered. Paula could not believe it. Hurt and anger and accusation had vanished from her mind and body forever. Was it possible for them to hear the same words and feel nothing? Or worse, feel more of the hatred and resentment that was convulsing the city?

Jake's face was drained, dazed, like the face of an

athlete who had just made an enormous effort. Paula was swept by new pain, new dread. She had created this disaster. She had made him destroy himself. Would he be able to bear the memory of this silence? He had done and said these things for her. But he could not have foreseen this abyss of rejection, this void of refusal that was swallowing him.

Things began to happen in the silence. Allyn Stapleton was on her feet, glaring at the audience, then slowly, methodically raising her hands to clap as the Mayor approached them. Simon Burke lurched to his feet and leaned across Paula to hiss in the Archbishop's ear. "Get up, Your Excellency, or I'll drag you up by your sacred collar. If the Church doesn't support that man, they better get out of this city."

A stunned look on his face, the Archbishop slowly rose and began to clap. In the back of the room, another man was on his feet. Police Commissioner Tarentino. He was promptly joined by everyone at his table. Charlie LoBello and Dave O'Brien brought another table to their feet. Dominick Montefiore, his eyes on the Archbishop, joined the standing applauders. Kevin McGuire's table remained unanimously immobile, their arms folded on their chests. But by now half the audience was clapping, slowly, steadily. It was grudging, reluctant. But it was applause.

Jake sat down beside Paula. "We may get out of here alive," he said.

She seized his hand under the table. "I love you," she said.

18

Walking toward Paula through the silence, the Mayor had been filled with an immense revulsion against everything he had just said. *Too far, you went too far. You broke all the rules,* whispered a mocking voice. *She had won. She had made you go too far.*

Of my own free will, he answered.

For her, the first voice mocked.

No, he answered, *no. For her and because it was the right thing.*

He could not keep his grip on this thought. It was an act of faith and he was not a believer. He was like the man in the Bible who cried out, "O Lord, I believe, help thou mine unbelief." His mind told him one thing but the rest of his body, his flesh, blood, nerves, cried out against it in berserk rebellion. Through the chaos he struggled to preserve the promise he had just made. It was a gift he had wrested from the brutal feet and maddened fists of the mob, from the dark and bitter pit of childhood, from the labyrinth of history. A gift for Paula, for the city, for himself. He did not know how much longer he could hold it in his trembling hands. He was afraid it would smash to the floor or, worse, that he would fling it in Paula's face with a curse.

When the grudging applause began, he knew what they were saying. *Maybe you're right, you Irish son of a bitch. We don't have to like you for saying it. But better that we heard it from one of our own.*

Listening, he began to feel almost alive again. It

was new to him, this deliberate choice of an adversary position, this risk of turning friends into enemies. Maybe this was how it worked, when you tried running the ball without the usual fakes and feints. He did not really know. He had never tried to change minds and hearts in this unnerving way.

The sons of St. Patrick quickly deserted the ballroom. The Archbishop congratulated the Mayor and joined the exodus. Simon Burke slobbered drunken praise. Allyn Stapleton said she would make sure he got home safely. Tarentino, Charlie LoBello, Dave O'Brien and a few other loyalists shook hands and left, sensing that the Mayor wanted to be alone with his wife.

A voice called from the balcony. "Hey, Jake. Is three a crowd down there?"

It was Adam Turner. He descended a spiral iron stairs in the corner behind the dais and limped toward them, leaning on a cane. "Usually, when an old pol tells me not to miss a speech, I go into hiding. This is one I'm glad I heard," he said.

"Is that the best you can do?" the Mayor said. "I figure I rate the Nobel Peace Prize at the very least."

Adam laughed. "I'll check with the NAACP to see if they got any awards hangin' around. I think you changed some minds, Jake."

"It doesn't mean I'll be in your corner every time, Adam."

"Don't worry, white boss, I'm not goin' to be in your corner every time either, except maybe to hit you with your stool."

"You've got to teach this guy humility, Paula," the Mayor said.

"Adam, should you be out of bed?" Paula asked, raising her hand toward the ugly bruises on Adam's face.

"If this guy can stand up and make a speech, I got to be able to sit down and listen to it. Those friends of his up in Tipperary Square stomped him as much as they stomped me." Adam shook his head. "These Micks sure have peculiar ways of tryin' to change a man's mind."

"I know," Paula said. "But if you put up with their

idiosyncrasies, you eventually lose your prejudice against them."

"You're sure?" Adam said. "Maybe I'll hang in for another year or two."

"We better get you back to the hospital, Adam. You don't look too steady on that cane," the Mayor said.

"I got some hooch in a dresser drawer. Maybe we can have an antiseptic drink and talk a little more about that school deal you mentioned on the phone."

The Mayor explained to Paula that he had asked Adam to join the Board of Education in a petition to the court asking Judge Stapleton to rescind busing for the city's high schools. "The teen-agers are the flash point," he said. "If we wait a year or two and start again with kids who are used to integration from the lower grades, it might work."

As they stood up, Paula impulsively kissed him.

"What's that for, sympathy or congratulations?"

"What do you think?"

"See how clever these women are?" the Mayor said. "They work it around so you've got to congratulate yourself and the next day they tell you that you've got a swelled head."

"It was a great speech," Paula said. "Does that satisfy you?"

"For the moment."

They strolled across the empty ballroom toward the corridor that led to the elevators. The Mayor began telling them about his conference with Bernie Bannon during the cocktail hour. "I'd already decided not to run but Bernie didn't know it. He thought he was talking me out of a primary fight that would wreck the party. He got on the phone to the majority leader of the assembly and started making offers. By the time we finished I walked out with an extra fifty million in state aid—twice as much as we need to pay our busing costs—and one third of the jobs that open up on the state payroll if we win the governorship and keep control of the legislature. They're going to add two lanes to the turnpike. That's ten thousand jobs right there."

"I've got a candidate for governor," Adam said.

"Thanks, Adam. But a lot of things will have to happen before anyone listens to you. I'm going to pick a young party chairman and work with you on getting out the vote downtown. I want to organize this city to give us maximum clout with the statehouse boys and the feds. Then we'll worry about other things."

They were in the corridor leading to the elevators. A cost cutter on the hotel staff had turned off most of the wall lights. Only dim overhead bulbs were shining through the shadows. The green shamrocks pasted on the mirrors were dull colorless outlines. The Mayor thought about his father and the man in the glass and his inner chaos as he walked toward Paula through the silence. Was it over, that kind of grappling with ghosts and accusing voices? Probably not, he decided, eyeing the multiplied images of himself and Paula and Adam in the facing mirrors.

About a dozen feet down the hall, a door opened and a man stepped out. A black man. It was the teacher, Robert Coleman. He had a gun in his hand. In the doorway was a white man with disheveled hair and a gaunt leering face. Frank Donahue.

"No," Paula cried as Jake's right arm swept her against the mirrored wall and his left arm swept Adam against the other wall. "No," Paula cried again.

The Mayor walked toward the gun, saying: "Wait. Wait, Robert. Don't shoot."

The Mayor knew what had happened. Frank Donahue had stayed a step ahead of Victor Tarentino and his cops all the way. Frank had spotted Coleman for an informer from his first visit and had turned him into the assassin. He had brought him here to destroy Jake O'Connor on the night that he announced that he was running for the Senate—a run that Frank's hate-blinded eyes still saw as a sure thing.

The Mayor walked toward the black hand holding the black gun with the past and the present and future in his heart and head. Every step seemed effortless. He seemed to be gliding like an underwater swimmer down a swift silent river time out of mind, out of body, seeing himself and his assassin not once but three, four, five, six times in the mirrors. All the truths, the new ones and the old ones, the lost ones and the found ones, blended and divided and blended again in the multiplication of himself confronting Robert Coleman's tormented black face, and looming behind him like a ghost from the dead past, Frank Donahue's hollow-cheeked white hatred. In one flashing moment the Mayor saw all the connections from the moment of his birth until this, the moment of his possible death.

The Mayor walked toward the gun with his hand out, palm upraised in an instinctive gesture of peace, asking why me, why my death, now? Choosing it as possibility and nauseated, enraged, horrified by it as reality. He wanted a chance to govern this city as a more open man. He wanted more days—and nights— with this complex woman that he was trying to love. But the Mayor also saw the possible value of his death. He saw himself as an exception, a fluke, a traveler between two worlds, inheritor of too many wrong things. History beat in the Mayor's bloodstream with lethal knowledge. That was another reason why he faced the gun in Robert Coleman's hand so calmly.

"Give it to me, Robert, give me that gun. You don't want to kill me."

Up and down nodded the black head. Yes, I do, he was saying, yes, I do.

"Robert," the Mayor said, "I want the same things for this city that you want. More freedom, more justice, more brotherhood. Give me a chance to prove it."

Back and forth shook Robert Coleman's head. He was saying: You had your chance, Mayor. You had fourteen years. Your father and his friends had thirty. And my kids are still being bitten by rats. Still staring at poems they can't read.

The Mayor was only a foot from the muzzle of the gun now. He felt no fear. Whatever happened, he was all right. He heard the echo of those words that he had just spoken to Robert Coleman's contorted black face. He knew that he meant them, beyond blather, manipulation, performance. He had found his father's caring again. Maybe found something even better than it.

"Don't do it. He's a brother," Adam Turner shouted.

The gun wavered in Robert Coleman's hand. The deadly snout drooped, rose, drooped again. It slipped from his uncertain fingers to thud on the green rug. Coleman fell to his knees, fists raised to streaming eyes. The Mayor looked past him at Frank Donahue and saw hatred convulse his face.

"I told you not to listen to him," Donahue screamed.

The Mayor knew even before Frank Donahue moved what was going to happen. What he did not know was whether he could stop him, whether the Irish past with its imploded guilts and regrets would reach like a dead hand from the grave to paralyze his will.

With a snarl Frank Donahue lunged for the gun on the floor. He landed on top of it like a cat, cradling the deadly thing against his belly, his body between the Mayor and the gun. His eyes rolled up. In another second the hand would rise, finger on the final trigger. Behind the wasted hate-consumed face, the Mayor saw a million other faces. They came at him out of the steerages of a thousand ships, out of the doorways of ten thousand tenements. It was the face of the punk, poverty's face, and the face of the hood, evil's face. The Mayor knew they were all part of him, part of his face, part of what he saw and would see in every mirror for the rest of his life and he wondered by what right, what privilege, he could escape them.

"No, Jake, don't let him!"

For an instant those words flared in the shadows. An instant outside of time. It was all outside of time, they were all frozen in this moment of mirrors and murder that was also in time, in split flickering seconds that shed splinters of light. The Mayor knew that Paula was moving toward him, toward that murderous gun. She had seen it too, seen the meaning of the face and the other faces in the armory but it was her guilt not his guilt that she was offering to the bullet out of time. Guilt and something more. She was joining him there in the cold slimy Irish darkness, joining him with guilt and with love.

All this inside and outside the multiplying mirrors with the shamrocks, all this meant death—or freedom. *No, Jake, don't let him.* Those words filled the split second with the brightness of an exploding sun. The Mayor saw with the clarity of the athlete that he had the chance if he chose to take it, if he chose this woman this city this fate now and forever. It was precisely the same as the split second when the curve started to break, when the runner faked in the broken field. He had Frank Donahue but did he want him, did he want the chance or did he really prefer the dark taste of defeat, was this moment, was that saturnine choice the real meaning of his life? Was it too deep in his blood to escape?

No and yes, yes and no. The Mayor chose not out of this choice but out of the other thing he knew, Paula's movement toward him, the gun, the bullet. The gun crashed and the bullet shattered mirrors mirrors mirrors in the corridor that ran back into history and forward into time. Frank Donahue was lying on his back clutching his ruined face. Paula was clinging to her husband. Robert Coleman whimpered poetry against the smashed mirror. Adam Turner picked up the gun and stared numbly at Frank Donahue.

"Who—who the hell is he?"

"An old enemy," the Mayor said.

Cops came charging down the hall with drawn guns, summoned by terrified guests in nearby rooms. The Mayor ordered Coleman and Donahue taken out a back door and booked at a precinct in the other end of the city. He wanted to keep the story out of the newspapers for at least twenty-four hours. Adam Turner said he no longer felt up to coping with the reporters downstairs and the Mayor sent him out another rear door and back to the hospital in a patrol car.

The Mayor put his arm around Paula's waist. "Let's go home, sweethaht," he said in the old kidding accent.

"You—you betcha, boss," Paula said, fighting tears.

In the lobby reporters swarmed around them. They wanted to know what the Mayor thought of the reaction to his speech. "Hopeful," he said. "No one threw anything."

Why was Mrs. O'Connor crying? "I was moved by what my husband said," Paula said. "I hope the rest of the city will feel the same way."

They went through the swinging doors into the square of light beneath the hotel's marquee. A whistle blew and a chant began on the other side of the street. "O'CONNUH'S GOTTA GO. O'CONNUH'S GOTTA GO." It was Tony Perotta and the Italian American Alliance, protesting the Mayor's public endorsement of St. Patrick's Day. "DOWN WITH IRISH BOSSISM," they screamed.

The Mayor smiled at Paula. "Tony's still working for the don's dollar," he said.

He led Paula toward CITY-1. Jesse Owens stood with his hand on the open door, muttering curses on the protestors. In the back of the car, when the door slammed, Paula clung to him, crying very hard.

"I want to be us again," she whispered. "Us."

"We can try," the Mayor said.

The limousine's engine rumbled. "O'CONNUH'S GOTTA GO," cried the protestors. In a moment the Mayor and his wife had turned the corner and disappeared into the darkness of the city.

OUTSTANDING READING FROM WARNER BOOKS

IN SEARCH OF HISTORY
by Theodore H. White   (97-146, $5.95)

This is a book about the people who, making history, have changed your life—and about a great correspondent who listened to their stories for forty years. Now he has woven all those stories into this splendid tale of his own. "IN SEARCH OF HISTORY is the most fascinating and most useful personal memoir of this generation."
—William Safire

THE CULTURE OF NARCISSISM
by Christopher Lasch   (93-264, $2.95)

Have we fallen in love with ourselves? Have we bargained away our future for self-gratification now? With an unsentimental eye, Christopher Lasch examines our society and our values and discovers that we are in thrall to a new enchantment—self-involvement. We live today in THE CULTURE OF NARCISSISM.

THE NEW TYRANNY: How Nuclear Power Enslaves Us
by Robert Jungk   (91-351, $2.50)

From the inner circles of nuclear scientists... From the mouths of embittered plant workers... From the records of the international Atomic Authority... comes Robert Jungk's inside information about the dangers of the Nuclear Age. A frightening indictment of the nuclear power industry, it predicts—convincingly—that the industry will eventually rob us of our freedoms, if not our lives."
—Benjamin Spock, M.D.

ALEXANDER SOLZHENITSYN
by Steven Allaback   (71-926, $2.50)

In ALEXANDER SOLZHENITSYN, Steven Allaback explores the rich world of Solzhenitsyn's imagination, illuminating for us the craftsmanship and vast creative energy of this 20th Century literary giant. "Allaback's interpretations are lucid and lively, free of academic abstraction, and his final assessment of the Russian's fiction is positive."
—Publishers Weekly

A CAPTIVE OF TIME
by Olga Ivinskaya   (83-968, $2.95)

A CAPTIVE OF TIME is the story behind "Doctor Zhivago"—the extraordinary romance that inspired it—the passion between the genius poet and the woman who shared his life and his work and who went to prison for loving him. It is the story that only Olga Ivinskaya could write, revealing the man she alone knew.

THE BEST OF BESTSELLERS FROM WARNER BOOKS

BLOODLINE
by Sidney Sheldon (85-205, $2.75)
The Number One Bestseller by the author of THE OTHER SIDE OF MIDNIGHT and A STRANGER IN THE MIRROR. "Exotic, confident, knowledgeable, mysterious, romantic . . . a story to be quickly and robustly told and pleasurably consumed."
—Los Angeles Times.

PALOVERDE
by Jacqueline Briskin (83-845, $2.95)
"Briskin lets the reader peek into the lives of three generations of a mighty California family. Hear their conversations . . . learn their secrets . . . as they bring in a gusher, prospect for gold, rub shoulders with the elite of Hollywood. Every page is a new adventure, and the reader is caught up in the excitement. Truly a book that's hard to put down . . . and gutsy enough to appeal to men as well as women." —United Press International.

SCRUPLES
by Judith Krantz (85-641, $2.75)
The most titillating, name-dropping, gossipy, can't-put-it-down #1 bestseller of the decade! The fascinating story of one woman who went after everything she wanted—fame, wealth, power, love —and got it all!

WARNER BOOKS
P.O. Box 690
New York, N.Y. 10019

Please send me the books I have selected. Enclose check or money order only, no cash please. Plus 50¢ per order and 20¢ per copy to cover postage and handling. N.Y. State and California residents add applicable sales tax.

Please allow 4 weeks for delivery.

———— Please send me your free mail order catalog

———— Please send me your free Romance books catalog

Name_____
Address_____
City_____
State_____Zip_____